Lavender and Lightning

Pack Saint Clair Book 2

Thora Woods

Contents

To Taylor Swift.
Without her music, this book wouldn't exist.

Content Warning

The book contains material that is not suitable for all audiences. This is an adult romance, with graphic descriptions of sexual and fetish activities, including BDSM, D/s relationships, degradation, same sex encounters (FF and MM), and polyamory.

This story also contains, but is not limited to, descriptions of: physical, emotional, mental, and sexual abuse; religious trauma, homophobic language and behavior, anxiety and panic disorders, violence and injuries, and stalking.

Reader discretion is advised.

Prologue

LYDIA

MY HEAD SWIMS AS I sit in the darkness of my car. There's a long, droning noise, like someone is laying on their car horn. Voices around me sound muffled, and I try to take a deep breath to clear my head and focus, but my chest explodes with fiery pain. My head feels wet, and something warm is sliding down my face. I try to lift my hand to wipe it away, but I can't feel my left arm, and my right arm only twitches limply in response to my command to move.

Flashing red and blue lights reflect strangely in the cracks of my windshield. Cracks? Why...

My thoughts feel like pudding as I try to sort them into order. Leaving the pack house. The pictures. Driving. The headlights. Crunching metal.

My head flops to the side, and I find my phone sitting on the floor of the passenger seat. I try to lean to get it, to call... my alpha. Rhett. I need Rhett.

"Hold on, ma'am. Please don't move. The paramedics are on their way," a male voice says sharply, cutting through the fog.

I try to turn my head toward the voice, but another hot flash of pain makes me hiss, setting off the agonizing pinch in my ribs. The inhale brings a scent to my nose: coconut, bamboo, nutmeg. Soft, but not threatening. Beta. I whine, trying to hold back my tears. I need graham crackers and fresh towels. Whiskey and old books and dark chocolate. Lemonade and ozone. Mulled wine. My beta. My alphas.

"You've been in an accident. I need you to stay still until the medics get here, okay? Can you do that?" the beta says again, voice deep and calm.

I try to nod, but it only makes me dizzy and nauseous with pain. The beta seems to understand, and the heat of his body radiates near my shoulder. I look out of the corner of my eye, finding a man, maybe in his early thirties, leaning down into my broken window. He's wearing all black, with a heavy vest and utility belt wrapped around his torso. The blue and red lights reflect off his badge. Police.

"What's your name, ma'am?" he asks, tone gentling.

I swallow, throat raw and mouth dry. Something drips off my chin and hits my collarbone. "Lydia Anderson," I croak.

"I'm Officer Nyueng, but you can just call me Lee, okay? Where were you headed tonight, Lydia?" the beta asks.

I look at Lee's face, his dark slanted eyes and close-cropped black hair weirdly distorted in the dark, only illuminated by the lights of his squad car.

"Home. I... I was—" I swallow again, as other vehicles pull up, trying to get my brain to clear enough to focus.

"Where's home? Do you live alone?" Lee prompts, hand coming up to muffle a radio on his shoulder as it squawks.

"I—my pack. I'm supposed to spend the weekend with my pack," I whine, voice cracking with unshed tears.

"You have a bond mate? Someone I can call?" Lee asks urgently.

I try to shake my head but whimper in pain. I twitch my hand toward my phone again. "My phone—Rhett, my alpha, I need—"

"Hey, okay. It's okay. I'll try to get your phone. Do you remember what happened, Lydia?" Lee soothes, shifting a little in his crouch.

"I was—" The photos. Darren's text. "I need my pack. I'm—I need them. Please," I beg, tears flowing down my face and mixing with whatever was oozing from my forehead.

"Shh, you're safe. You're going to be just fine. The medics just pulled up. I'm going to find your phone and let them take over, okay?" Lee asks, throwing a quick look over his shoulder.

"Don't leave, please—I need—Please." My words fade into sobs, my head swimming again as the pain returns.

"I'm not going anywhere, Lydia. We've got you," Lee says softly, his scent edging into clean water and bamboo.

Another scent, cherry pie mixed with orange juice and maple, hits me like a slap. I flinch away. Alpha, bonded. Voices become muffled again, my vision fading in and out as it gets harder to breathe. Hands touch my face, warm and rough. I whine, trying to find Lee with my eyes as the hands hold my neck still and straight. He's on the passenger side, leaning through the broken window to scoop my phone and bag off the floor. My hands are wet, but the red and blue lights make it impossible to tell with what, even as my finger leaves a smear on the screen when I unlock it for Lee.

I close my eyes as more hands touch my arms and legs. I want to lean away, the urge to vomit strong, but I'm held in place. All the noise—running diesel engines, shouting voices, hydraulics—sounds like it's coming from the other end of a tube filled with water. My eyelids are pulled open, a bright light flashing in my eyes. I glimpse a younger man, the cherry pie alpha. His lips are moving, and he looks at me expectantly, but I don't want to open my mouth, too afraid that I'm going to throw up.

"Lydia, we're going to get you out of here. It's going to be quick, but it might hurt. Ready?"

An unfamiliar voice. I open my eyes again. When did I close them? Cherry Pie is still close to my face. His eyes are green, more seafoam than my bottle-green. I try to nod, but my head is still being held in place by those hands on my ears.

"Lee—"

"Still here, Lydia. I'm trying to call your alpha."

The beta's voice soothes something in me, and even that pie and juice scent is making me breathe a little easier. "Okay," I whisper, closing my eyes again and bracing myself.

Cherry Pie counts down from three, and all the hands tighten at once. Suddenly, I'm weightless, even as pain screams up my left arm and through my chest. I bite my lip to hold back a sob as my legs tingle with white-hot pins and needles. I'm laid flat on a hard board, and more burning agony pinballs up my spine and neck. I try to breathe through it, try to use the techniques for endurance I'd mastered so long ago, but it only makes my chest burn with each desperate inhale.

"Hard part's over, sugar. You're doing great," Cherry Pie says, voice fading in and out.

"My chest. My arm—"

"Don't look, sugar. We've got you. Just stay awake. Lee said you've got an alpha? Tell me about him," the alpha prompts.

I try to swallow, but my throat is raw, and my nose is plugged from my tears. When I take a gasping breath, it only makes my chest hurt more. Everything is fading out again as I try to focus. Cherry Pie is asking me more questions, but I can't seem to piece his words together enough to understand. The edges of my vision blur and turn to black, the dizziness returning with a vengeance. Someone calls my name, but I can't keep my eyes open. Everything turns to droning static as I fall into blackness again.

ONE

Lydia

MY EYES FLY OPEN, my chest heaving with a sudden gasp. The water in the bathtub sloshes around me as I scramble upright, wiping away the moisture from my face, and only relaxing when my hand doesn't come back stained with blood. My fingers slip on the edge of the tub as I lean against it to regain my balance. When I unthinkingly put weight on my left arm, sharp pain flares and I suck in a harsh breath. I manage to get upright and steady despite the handicap, and I glare at the plastic covered cast that encases my arm from mid-bicep, holding my elbow at nearly a ninety-degree bend, and past my wrist.

It's been three days since the accident that totaled my car on my birthday, and I'm still achy all over, battered and bruised. It hurts to take deep breaths, and superficial cuts cover my right arm. I try to pull my knees to my chest, but have to stop as my purple-and-black mottled joints protest the movement. Giving up, I let my head hang forward, my hair sticking to my back. The clock on the wall of my studio apartment's kitchenette ticks loud enough for me to hear even through the mostly closed door, but otherwise, it's quiet. I look up to the ceiling, the block of morning light that filters through the narrow, frosted window bright against the chipping white paint. I let out a silent sigh. Time is slipping away from me again.

"Hey, Rhett. I'm done," I shout, trying my best to keep the bland resignation in my chest out of my voice.

Not a moment later, Rhett Cooper pokes his head into my tiny bathroom. His golden blond hair gleams in the morning sun, icy blue eyes alert to my every move. With my broken arm, bruised ribs, and mild concussion, the emergency room doctors told me I shouldn't be alone right away, at least not until I can see my primary for a more thorough evaluation and prognosis. So, a member of Pack St. Clair has been with me every moment for the last seventy-two hours. It's been an adjustment, especially after spending the last four years basically on my own. No matter how much the constant babysitting annoys and chafes, I try to keep my sour mood to myself. They've been nothing but accommodating, and it wouldn't be fair to them if I made this difficult because I didn't want to be coddled.

Rhett reaches down and helps me get to my feet, wrapping me in a big fluffy towel the moment I set my feet on the bathmat. I step out from his reach as he lets out the stopper of the tub, hugging the towel close. Moving to the sink, I look at the reflection in the aged mirror. My toffee brown hair hangs in limp strands around my face, my green eyes vibrant, even with the dark circles under them. There's a bruise across my chest, a wide stripe of black and purple from where the seatbelt had been. Only one end is visible above the towel, but there's still residual soreness all the way across my ribs and hips.

"What can I help with, love?" Rhett asks, sliding up behind me and gently resting his hands on my shoulders.

I bite my lip to stop my knee-jerk denial from escaping. I want to tell him to go back out to the main living area, to let me get ready on my own. But the ticking of the clock reminds me that we don't have time for me to be stubborn today. And Rhett's bright-eyed concern makes me melt. There's something about the way he looks at me like he can't believe I'm real that makes me forget all about being a strong, independent woman.

"I need to dry my hair if we're going to get out of here on time," I say at last.

"No worries, love," he says without missing a beat, grabbing my hair dryer off the edge of the sink and kissing my cheek as he straightens.

Despite myself, I blush. Rhett has been doting and affectionate from the start of our relationship. His natural alpha instincts to care for the people in his life took some getting used to, with my hard-won independence battling my omega urge to melt and let him fuss over me. We're still finding our balance, but the connection between us has become a fundamental part of my being. His whiskey and leather scent soothes something in my soul I've never experienced before. We took our time, not rushing into bed despite the electric attraction on both sides, but it was worth the wait to get to this level of connection.

The last few months have been a whirlwind. Meeting him and his pack mate, Mateo Hutchenson. Getting swept off my feet by these incredible men. Developing friendships, and possibly more, with the other two members of their pack, Rhett's long-term partner and beta, Lucas Klausen, and the prime alpha of the pack, Alexandra St. Clair. My relationships with Lucas and Alexandra are still very new and nebulous, but I can feel that same inexorable draw to them that I felt with Rhett and Mateo. I've fallen so deeply for both alphas, and at times I forget how I could have existed without them. Even them learning that I have more baggage than an airport didn't dissuade them from their pursuits. And my feelings for them weren't diminished at all by learning that they have a past nearly as complicated as my own.

Rhett starts up the hair dryer, and I let him work, my mind drifting. As I have many times these past few days, I wrestle with the ball of nervous snakes in my gut as I remember where I'm going today. Once I'm ready, Rhett is driving me to the courthouse to meet with Mateo and Alexandra. Today is the day we're going before a judge to sign the paperwork and officially make me part of Pack St. Clair.

I'm not nervous at the prospect of joining this pack, not really. If I'm being completely honest with myself, I've known for a long time now that these alphas, and their beta, are my future. There isn't a single daydream of the road ahead of me that didn't have them on it. But the circumstances surrounding my sudden induction are enough to make my stomach twist itself into ever-tightening knots.

Before Rhett and I caught each other's scents across a hotel lobby, I'd been living what could generously be called a decent, if boring, life. I woke up, went to work at Grandmother Wila's Flower Shoppe, and occasionally worked an event. I'd spend my nights alone or with my best friend, Gabby Fitzgerald, my boss's granddaughter and my co-worker. I didn't go out, and certainly didn't put myself out there romantically. Sure, Gabby had tried to set me up with a few of her beta friends, but it had been casual at best. I was safe. I was anonymous. Which was exactly how I liked it.

Because drawing attention could mean my family figuring out where I was. Four Christmases ago, my ex-boyfriend and abuser, Darren McLaughlin, had proposed marriage, and when I rejected him, he attempted to force me into a mating bond. He used his alpha bark to try to force my heat. But my body rejected the order, not yielding to the normally inexorable command that comes with a bark. And because I never went into heat, the mating bond never took hold, despite his best efforts. I ran the next day, and have been trying to stay hidden ever since.

My family—my mother, Diane Anderson, specifically—believed the lie Darren fed them, and have been treating him like a son, while casting me as the crazy, over-sensitive omega who was too defiant for my own good. I found out most recently that my mother has been pretending that I'm a missing person rather than a victim fleeing her abuser. And Darren has been spouting the family line because it makes him look like the wronged party in all of this. How could anyone reject the son of famed televangelist, Pastor Joe McLaughlin, after all.

I've always known it was a matter of time before all of this would catch up to me. I didn't expect it to be because the alphas I decided to open up to romantically had their own batshit ex, hellbent on ruining their lives.

Seth Douglas is an omega like me, but our similarities stop there. He's built like a brick shit house, with muscles in places I didn't even know you could get them. Some people would call him conventionally attractive, but there isn't any amount of polishing and primping that could mask the true ugliness that lurks below his tanned skin. He's manipulative, cruel, petty, and obsessed with Pack St. Clair. He used the natural charms inherent to the omega designation to lure them in, and then trapped Mateo and Alexandra into bonds they didn't want. But when they rejected him, he refused to be silenced and has been a thorn in their sides for the last several years.

And now that I've gained Pack St. Clair's attention, Seth has made it his mission to force me away from them, by any means necessary.

Up to and including leaking my location to my ex.

I know this because on the night of my accident, he texted me several pictures that someone had taken without my knowledge or consent, including one of Mateo and me making love in my own bed. If the photos weren't bad enough, a text followed, promising punishment for my "naughty behavior."

If it were just the photos and the threat, it would be stressful, but nothing I couldn't handle. But if Darren knew my location, it would only take him revealing that information to my father for my entire world to come crashing down. My father, Samuel Anderson Sr., is still considered my prime alpha in the eyes of the law, despite us having next to no contact over the last four years. But because I'm unbonded, I still technically belong to my family pack, and the prime alpha has ultimate authority over all members of their pack. If he wanted, he could use his rank and order me home and there would be nothing I could do to stop it.

Which is why I have to join Pack St. Clair. Once I sign the documents, Alexandra will become my prime alpha. Then the only way Darren can get near me will be in person, and we can take steps to guard against that. It will also grant me protection from Seth and any future harassment that could come from him. Joining this pack is what I want, even if I've only known them for a few months. But I trust them, love Rhett and Mateo, and it is the best possible solution to my current problem. Even if a small, irrational part of my brain is screaming that I don't deserve this, that I'm just a burden and they are only offering me safety out of obligation. But that voice is easy to push aside, especially when Rhett's fingers in my hair feel like magic.

Rhett shuts off the hair dryer, and I hand him my hairbrush. His touch is gentle, and I can't help my little hum of pleasure at the sensation as I let my eyelids fall closed. A wave of whiskey and dark chocolate settles over me, and I smile wider. Someone playing with my hair has always been a weakness of mine. I open my eyes when he stops, and I catch his fond grin in the mirror.

"You ready for today, love?" he asks softly, taking a half step closer and wrapping his arms around my waist.

I shrug with my good shoulder. "As ready as I think I can be. It's not going to be a huge thing, is it?"

"It shouldn't be. If this takes more than twenty minutes, I'll be surprised," Rhett replies with a small smile.

I laugh lightly, wincing as my ribs pulse with dull pain. Rhett tries to hide his frown of concern, but I still catch the expression in the mirror. I give a pleading look, and he sighs, kissing my still bare shoulder, but thankfully doesn't start up again about my pain meds. We'd had a tense discussion after we'd woken up, but I'm not budging on this one. I'll take the aches and pains over the weird, hazy, dull filter that the drugs put over everything. I'm easily startled on a good day; intentionally lowering my overall awareness of my surroundings was not high on my list of priorities.

Rhett straightens, setting the brush on the edge of the sink and backing up a step. He runs his fingers through my hair, ignoring my attempts to catch his eye in the mirror. We lapse into tense silence, and I try not to let the guilt show on my face. I know he just doesn't want to see me in pain, but with everything so chaotic, I need to have just one thing in my control. Rhett soundlessly motions for the dryer again, and I hand it over with a silent sigh. I try to let myself enjoy the warm air and his touch, but the nerve snakes rise again.

A sudden knock at the door, loud enough to be heard over the dryer, makes both Rhett and me jump. We make eye contact through the mirror, and Rhett shuts off the dryer.

"Is Mateo coming by for something?" I whisper.

Rhett shakes his head, setting the dryer down gently. There's another knock at the door, harder this time, with enough force to shake the solid wood slab in its frame. The handle jiggles, but I know it's locked, along with the deadbolt. We both go still, not sure what to do as whoever is at the door pounds again.

"Lydia, Lydia, little omega, are you in there?"

My blood runs cold at the sound of a male voice as he calls his sing-song taunt through the door. I look at Rhett, his mouth set in a vicious snarl. Flinching, I slap a hand over my mouth to stifle a yelp as there's a loud slam from the front door, backing away as my heart kicks in my chest.

"Call the police," Rhett says sharply.

TWO

Rhett

LYDIA STANDS FROZEN FOR a heartbeat before she scrambles to find her phone in the pile of clothes on the floor. I open the bathroom door slightly, hiding the hinges' squeak behind the next series of pounding knocks. As I try to take a step toward the main room, Lydia's hand shoots out and seizes a fistful of my shirt. I whip back around, swallowing the growl that tries to emerge. My protective instincts are flaring hot, and I want to snap and bark and tell her to hide. But the absolute terror etched into every pore of her beautiful face strikes deep enough to let me gain some semblance of control.

"Don't leave me," she hisses, her voice shaking.

"I won't, little one," I reply automatically.

A metallic snapping makes my head whip back around to the front door, and I swallow as the handle rotates freely, the lock destroyed. It was a flimsy handle, but there's still a pulse of fear at the sound. Whoever is out there is determined to get inside, and I can't let that happen. I dash out and grab the first piece of moveable furniture I can find, a metal folding chair. Lydia whispers frantically to the dispatcher, and I push down the urge to shout or rage, to stand up to this intruder on my omega's home and nest. Instead, when they start to pound again, I close and latch the bathroom door. I grunt as I jam the folding chair under the handle before stepping back and inspecting my work. It wouldn't hold for long, but it would at least slow this asshole down.

"The police are almost here," Lydia whimpers, stepping into my space and clinging to my back.

I purr involuntarily, trying to soothe her fear. The bathroom fills with the scent of burning sugar, and my heart kicks in my chest. Her fear sets off my primal urge to fight, to protect what's mine. But she needs me here more than I need to be out there. As I turn and slide my arms around Lydia's shoulders, I realize that the towel she'd had wrapped around her chest has fallen. Leaning over to the door, I find her robe hanging on its hook, getting her to let go of me long enough to work her cast through the oversized sleeve and secure it. She jumps and squeals as a loud slam, followed by splintering wood, comes from the front door, and I swallow the sudden lump in my throat.

There's a heartbeat of absolute silence, and then the front door hinges squeal like injured animals, followed by the thunk of the door hitting the wall.

"Little omega, come out, come out wherever you are," the intruder taunts, the sing-song tone raising hairs on the back of my neck.

Lydia whimpers, and her body shakes uncontrollably as she presses against my back. I don't dare turn or try to put my arm around her. I need my hands free if the worst should happen. Outside the door, the intruder paces, his steps heavy but methodical

"Oh, my, my, my, what a lovely nest you've built, little omega. So soft and warm, just like you."

Lydia sways behind me, and I turn just in time to catch her, gently placing a hand over her mouth to muffle her ragged breathing. Even still, a low, predatory growl from the other side of the door makes my heart hammer. Lydia's tears are hot as they splash over the back of my hand, and I'm supporting most of her weight as she loses strength in her legs. Three more bootsteps, each louder than the last. A series of short, huffing sniffs.

"Even your fear is sweet, little omega. But who—"

His next words are cut off by the sound of sirens. A low, frustrated growl from outside the door comes before heavy running steps, moving away. There's the sound of chair legs scraping on the floor, and the crash of the card table flipping. As much as I try to fight it, my muscles quaver, itching to get out there and stop this bastard from violating any more of my omega's space. The blood rushes in my ears, and my jaw aches from clenching it so hard. Lydia's good hand digs into my forearm, the bite of her nails piercing my skin hardly even registering over the pounding rage and primal urge for violence coursing through me.

"Everton PD! Freeze!"

The shout is loud enough to carry through walls. Lydia whimpers behind my hand, but more shouting covers her. Multiple voices overlap, and it's impossible to tell what's happening. Running steps, multiple sets, moving away from us. Lydia sags, but I don't lower my guard, not ready to declare it safe until the fucker who tried to hurt my omega is in handcuffs. I shift so I can pull her into my side, minding her injuries. My eyes stay fixed on the bathroom door, my ears straining to hear anything. My heart hammers against my ribs, but I try to focus on Lydia. I need to be calm, or at least appear calm, on the outside. Now that the rage is fading, the fear and worry are taking over.

"He knew my name. And my nest... what did he do..." Lydia says, her words cracking with unshed tears.

"I know, love. But you're safe. I've got you," I reply, kissing the top of her head.

And that was the worst of this entire situation. Because this wasn't a random home invasion attempt. It was morning, when people would normally be getting ready for work, still at home. And he called out not only her name, but her designation. He *knew* who lived here and wanted to get to her specifically. That could only mean one thing: Seth or Darren is involved, maybe even both.

A knock at the front door draws my attention back to the moment, and Lydia nearly jumps out of her skin behind me.

"This is Officer Nyueng. Is there anyone home?"

Lee Nyueng. The officer who was the first person on the scene of Lydia's accident, and the first person we spoke with at the hospital. After he stopped accusing Lydia of being drunk or high, I found that I sort of liked the beta. He had a bad case of gallows humor, but was otherwise just a cop trying to protect his city, which I could respect.

"Just a minute, Lee," I call back.

I look down at Lydia, who has her face buried in my shoulder, taking deep inhales of my scent. I whisper soothing words as I extract myself from her embrace, then remove the improvised barricade from under the handle. She sticks close to me as I open the door, and I have to turn back and stop her before exiting.

"Wait here for just a minute, okay? I'm going to go see what's happening," I say, ducking down so I can catch her gaze.

My gaze roves over her pale cheeks, now almost translucent, with tear tracks carved into the creamy skin. I reach up and cup her jaw, using my thumb to wipe some of them away and bringing her attention to my face. Her body still trembles against mine, her breath catching as she tries to keep from falling apart. She nods slightly, though I don't like how her lower lip quakes as she tries to put on a brave face. I lean down and give her a soft kiss before pressing my forehead to hers.

Turning to face the main living area of Lydia's apartment, my stomach rolls as my eyes land on the door. Or rather, what's left of it. The frame is battered, the molding on the inside loose or missing from how hard the intruder was pounding and shaking the door. Its handle is barely hanging on, the knob at an unnatural angle. The bottom corner is cracked, with chunks missing and the entire thing bent in. When I reach the door, my heart skips as my eyes trace the spiderweb of damage in the wood and plaster around the deadbolt. It hangs by one of the three hinges, mostly supported by the wall. I have to close my eyes for a moment to avoid looking at Lydia's bed. I don't know if I could control myself if I see what he may have done. So I force my eyes to the hallway outside the apartment doorway. As I do, I find Officer Nyueng standing on the threshold, hands clutching the neck of his tactical vest as he looks up and down the hallway. There's chatter over his radio, but it's too fast for me to understand.

"Mr. Cooper, lovely morning we're having," he says with a heavy, sarcastic sigh.

I snort derisively, rolling my eyes. "Where's the asshole?"

Lee lets out another sigh, but this one sets my teeth on edge. "Ran. Officers tried to pursue, but he must have had a vehicle nearby."

"So he's still out t'ere?" I snap, red creeping into the edges of my vision.

"We're going to get the forensic team here; see what evidence we can pick up. But for now, I'd like to get y'all's statements, if you don't mind."

I hear the words, but my mind refuses to acknowledge anything except a screeching, wailing inner alarm. Lydia is still in danger. The intruder who turned the solid oak door into kindling in an attempt to reach her, who violated her most sacred space, is still on the loose. I have to get her away from here, to someplace I know she's safe. And I don't have a moment to spare.

"I'm going to have our lawyer set up a time for you to take our statement," I say at last, turning to walk toward Lydia's clothes storage.

But as I try to take a step, Lee's hand snaps out and closes on my wrist with almost bruising force. I look down at where he's holding and then back up to his face, jaw slightly slack and eyes wide. I'm too stunned to speak, which Lee capitalizes on.

"I know that it's not ideal, but I'm afraid I have to insist," he says, tone stern and serious.

It takes me another moment to recover, and I have to push down my first instinct to break his hold and retaliate. While it may satisfy the primal urge in my brain to remove an obstacle standing in my way of getting my omega to safety, punching a cop would do more harm than good. I do shake off his hand and take a step back. He matches, still keeping a respectful distance, but clearly taking my retreat as an invitation. I take a slow breath, clenching and relaxing my fists at my sides.

"Will you at least give me a moment? Lydia was... indisposed when this happened, and she's not decent," I say through my gritted teeth.

Lee stops unabashedly scanning Lydia's apartment and gives me a small nod of permission. He turns around and starts talking into his radio. Moving over to the metal bar and four-cube storage that serves as Lydia's closet, I pick out a pair of sweatpants and a loose t-shirt, as well as a zip-up hoodie that I recognize as one of Mateo's. It should be big enough to close, even with her arm strapped into the sling.

I nudge the bathroom door open with my foot, letting the creaking hinges announce me rather than knocking. She doesn't answer, and I find Lydia sitting on the edge of the bathtub, her arms tucked tight to her stomach. She's staring at the wall with a vacant expression, her face still too pale. I crouch down to squat in her line of sight when she doesn't acknowledge me.

"How much did you hear?" I ask softly, placing my hands on her knees.

"Enough. He's still out there," she replies, voice a dry rasp.

I sigh, but nod all the same. I want to take us to the pack house, where I know we'll be safe to regroup and figure out what to do next, but there's nothing to do while the police have us tied down.

"Lee is here, and we have to give statements," I relay, reaching for the clothes I'd brought in.

"What about court?" she asks breathlessly.

I look back up at her, and the stricken look in her emerald eyes cuts me to my core. I'd nearly forgotten about that, but my stomach sinks like a stone. There was no way we'd be able to make it out of here in time. And even if we could, I don't want Lydia out in public right now, not when that psycho is still on the loose.

"One step at a time, love. Let's get you dressed and see how long it's going to take," I say, deflecting the question for the moment.

Lex is going to kill us.

THREE

Lydia

RHETT IS BESIDE ME on the couch, one arm wrapped around my shoulders. Lee Nyueng is sitting on my coffee table, so close his knees almost touch mine, a tiny notebook in hand. We've talked to three different officers and a detective in the last few hours, telling the story over and over to the point I'm ready to scratch the eyes out of the next person who asks for me to "start at the beginning." Lee and Rhett are chatting, but my brain refuses to take in any of their conversation.

I'd heard every horrifying second the intruder had been in my apartment, but seeing the shifted blankets and clothes, the disturbed furniture, the undeniable proof that a stranger touched my safe space, hit me like a cannonball to the gut. I'd sunk onto my tiny couch and haven't been able to tear my eyes from my bed since. Not too long ago, a swarm of people in white paper jumpsuits arrived. The forensics unit had swabbed and dusted just about every surface on or around the door itself, and then fanned out, looking for missing pieces. Each splinter had to be accounted for, as any of them could have evidence. I've never seen anything this thorough, short of a murder investigation on television. Something in me can't help but wonder if my association with Pack St. Clair has anything to do with this.

I'd hoped that they would leave my nest in peace. But between my fixation on my bed, and Lee pressing us into repeating the exact words the intruder used, my bed, my omega nest, had to be examined. People I don't know, who I can't even look in the face due to their masks and hoods, are systematically pulling apart my nest bit by bit. My stomach roils as they take each blanket and pillow, each article of clothing I'd tucked away, and inspect them. They hold up the smaller pieces like a fresh kill, and spread out the larger ones, handling everything I'd worked to create with so much care yet so little regard. Once something is deemed useless, it's tossed in an empty bin they found somewhere.

My eyes burn when a pair of techs start handling an emerald green blanket, my teeth grinding as I try not to move or speak. I can't feel my body, my entire focus on the way these strangers are manhandling my things.

"I think we're done here."

Rhett's voice draws me out of my tunnel vision, and I take a deep breath. His whiskey and old books smell dulls the edges of my raw nerves, but my hands still shake, and I tuck my good one under my thigh. I don't bother looking up, but I can feel Rhett's gaze on the side of my face.

"We're still waiting on–"

"Lee, I've given you as much of my patience as I can manage today. I'm taking my omega home, so she doesn't have to watch this. She's been through enough," Rhett interjects harshly.

I let Rhett pull me to my feet, his fingers sliding into the places between mine on my good hand. Lee rises too, and I realize how much shorter he truly is than Rhett. He's only maybe an inch taller than me, so he doesn't look nearly as intimidating as he thinks he is as he puffs out his chest. His cool bamboo scent grows stronger for a moment, but Rhett brushes right by him. As we pass the forensic team, I stop short, staring at the green blanket in their hands.

"Can... can I have that? Please?" I ask, words coming out a little choked.

"I'm so sorry, honey, but this is all evidence for the moment. We'll have it back to you in two shakes," a female voice says from behind the blue mask, the brown eyes behind her safety goggles sympathetic.

Biting my trembling lower lip, my shoulders fall as disappointment sinks like a stone in my chest. Rhett puts some clothes into a backpack for me and slings it over his shoulder before taking my hand again. I'm too focused on the unsteady feeling in my stomach and knees that I almost miss it as we pass through the destroyed doorway to my apartment and into the hall beyond. But just on the edge of my senses, something makes the hair on my arms and neck stand on end. A pungent scent, one I both recognize and yet somehow can't place. I know every scent in this building, all of them soft or neutral beta and omega scents. Nothing harsh or stomach churning, nothing that burns the inside of my nostrils for a moment before the scent disappears. And while the cleaning products maintenance uses to mop the floors are noxious, they haven't ever made me want to run for the hills as fast as my legs could carry me.

Rhett leads us silently through the halls, where I can hear other officers knocking on doors and speaking with my neighbors. We're out of the building and into Rhett's car in what feels like no time at all, driving through the streets of Everton. My mind whirs, trying to place that trace of scent. Because whoever it belonged to was the intruder, I'm sure of it. If I could just get my head on straight long enough to focus and think. But moving beyond the tar-thick panic of being in a car again is impossible, despite my best efforts.

"Your landlord was notified, and he's going to be getting a new door installed before the end of the day. Lee said there'll be someone there until it's secure," Rhett says after a moment.

"Thank you," I mutter, taking deep breaths as I try to force away the urge to cry.

"I'm sorry you had to watch them do that to your nest. Absolutely heartless," he goes on, voice getting heated and accent getting stronger.

I shrug with my good shoulder, looking at my hand as it rests in my lap. My vision goes in and out of focus, and I have to close my eyes to avoid getting sick. I know I've encountered that scent before, something savory and toxic. Onions and motor oil? Cheese maybe? But not fresh cheese, something that could only be produced in a lab.

Rhett is about to say something else, but suddenly, his cell phone rings out over the car speakers. Glancing up, I see Alexandra's name on the dash screen. Rhett presses the answer button, and barely manages to get a greeting out before her sharp, transatlantic-accented fury comes pouring through the line.

"Where the *fuck* are you? I've been calling for hours, and you can't even send more than a 'can't talk' text? I can't believe you! Of all the days–"

"Lex, if you'd jus' let me fucking speak, I could tell ya that someone broke into Lydia's fucking apartment!"

I flinch a little at Rhett's shout, but it does the trick of getting Alexandra to stop talking. There are several full seconds of stunned silence. I never thought I'd live to see the day Alexandra St. Clair is struck speechless.

"Holy shit. Oh my God. Is she–are you–is everyone okay?" she stammers at last.

"I'm not hurt," I answer before Rhett can speak for me.

He gives me a look, acknowledging my careful choice of words. Nothing gets by him, I swear.

"Am I on speaker? Lydia, sweetness, I'm so sorry. Have you talked to the police? Did they take anything? Can you tell me what happened?" she goes on, sounding almost frantic.

I let Rhett tell the story again, not wanting to repeat myself for the twentieth time this morning. When he's done, he and Alexandra discuss the next steps, but I hardly listen. I'd given up hope of keeping our court date after the first hour of our detainment.

"We're heading back to the pack house. We'll see you and Matty there," Rhett says before they end the call.

Silence falls again as we make the turn toward Bristol Point, the housing development Pack St. Clair owns and specifically built to keep Seth Douglas out. Their haven from the outside world.

Pack houses are, generally speaking, guarded spaces. I've heard of larger packs having whole office buildings as their pack house, where smaller packs often have one central residence. They function as a place to conduct pack business, or be together and bond. Growing up, the Anderson Contracting office was where my father, as prime alpha, would handle inter-pack disputes or other pack affairs, with my childhood home being more of an intimate gathering space. While pack houses don't have the same quasi-sacred status as omega nests, being invited into the pack space requires trust.

When we pull into the wide driveway of the white farmhouse-style house that Rhett personally designed, I can't help but let out a tense breath. There's something intimate and comforting about this building, even from the outside. After parking in the garage, Rhett takes my hand again as we use the side door and cross the covered porch connecting the garage and the main house. Before he opens the door, he stops and turns back to me. I try to hide it, but I can't help the stiffening of my shoulders as his hand comes up toward my face. His fingers are gentle as they cup my chin, tilting my head up to look into his eyes.

"I'm sorry," he whispers, thumb brushing idly over my cheek.

My first instinct is to tell him that it's okay, and it's only the last four years of practice that allows me to swallow the dismissal. Because today has not been okay. Someone who meant to do me harm broke down my door, and my nest has been destroyed. I merely nod.

"We're going to keep you safe, love. *I* am going to keep you safe. I promise."

Hearing the rawness in his whisper breaks my heart. When he leans in and presses his lips to mine, I return the kiss eagerly. It's a brief meeting, but my stomach dips and dives, my heart beating out of time for a moment. By the time we pull away, I find myself a little calmer, even if my mind still races.

FOUR

Lydia

STEPPING INSIDE THE PACK house is more of a relief than I'd like to admit. My skin still feels too tight, but I'm able to relax now that I'm not out in the open. Rhett leads the way through the mudroom and into the kitchen, and I stop short as I'm assaulted with a riot of color. Balloons of every shade and size litter the floor, with streamers hanging from the ceiling. A banner stretches across the picture window, proclaiming 'Welcome Lydia!'.

"Shit! Lex said you were still a few minutes out!"

A familiar voice draws my attention to the kitchen island, and I look up to find Lucas standing on it, arms full of streamers. The kitchen looks considerably less decorated, as if he'd been in the middle of pulling things down when we'd walked in. I can't help but giggle at the flustered and shocked expression on his handsome face. He shakes some of his dark hair from his steel-blue eyes, pink creeping up his neck.

"Was this all for me?" I ask softly, looking around.

"It was supposed to be a surprise," Lucas grumbles, hopping off the island and emptying his arms onto the marble.

I give Rhett one more look, which he returns with a nod, before sliding my hand from his and crossing to stand in front of Lucas. Of all the pack members, Lucas had been the most upset that I hadn't told them about my birthday until the last minute. He'd scrambled to throw together a cookout, which we'd been unable to enjoy due to my hospital stay. Now it appears that another celebration has been spoiled.

Wrapping my arm around his middle, I press my cheek to his deceptively muscular chest. Without hesitation, Lucas returns the embrace, holding me tight around my shoulders. I inhale his s'more and clean towel scent, the last traces of my fears sliding away. Even before the accident, he never treated me like I was some fragile, wilting flower, and I'm glad that hasn't changed.

"I'm surprised, I promise," I mutter just for him.

"Are you okay? Lex said something about a break-in," he whispers into my hair.

I shrug with my good shoulder. "I'm not hurt."

"You know that's not what I mean," he replies seriously.

I sigh, my heart twisting. I'm not sure I'm ready to look my emotions in the face right now. "I'll be okay. I'm just glad I'm here."

Lucas nods, letting it drop for the moment. Rhett's fingers brush along the back of my shoulders, and I hear the briefest kiss between them as he moves past us and into the kitchen. A year ago, that little act of affection may have made me jealous. But ever since I met Rhett, I've learned that there are more types of love, and I know that Rhett has enough for the both of us.

"Is there anything ready to eat? I'm fucking starving," he comments, trying to keep his tone light despite the heaviness in the air.

"Yeah, there's some mac salad in the red dish. You hungry, Lydi?" Lucas says, first to Rhett and then to me.

I look up into his face, smiling slightly at the concern shining in his steel-blue eyes. Shaking my head, I settle back into his embrace. More than anything so far, just being held and breathing in Lucas's calming beta pheromones has done the most for my fragile emotional state. Rhett serves himself, but my focus quickly shifts as Lucas sways gently, one hand running in soothing motions up and down my back. The soft, steady touch helps chase away the last bits of my panic, and I take another inhale. There's something sharp and savory wafting up from Lucas's shirt, and I furrow my brow.

"Were you chopping onions?" I whisper, carefully keeping my voice down so Rhett can't hear.

"No. I was cutting up some cheddar for the charcuterie board," he replies, matching my volume.

I hum, stomach tightening. Cheddar and something toxic. But I'd only caught the faintest trace of the intruder. I'm not sure, and even if I'm right, saying anything right now, when the tension in the air feels thick enough to cut with a knife, would only end badly.

"What's the matter, sweetheart?" Lucas asks, bending down to speak into my ear.

"I... I thought I might have recognized the scent. But I don't know. I don't—"

"What was that, love?" Rhett asks loudly.

Lucas turns and Rhett's standing at the open fridge, a large bowl covered in plastic wrap in one hand.

"It's nothing. I just... yeah, it's nothing," I tell him, stumbling under the intensity of Rhett's stare.

"It doesn't sound like nothing to me," he returns, putting the bowl back and closing the fridge door with a little more force than is strictly necessary.

"If I tell you, can you promise me that you aren't going to storm out of here?" I ask pointedly.

Rhett opens his mouth, but his eyes flick to Lucas, and he stops short. Just like I thought. Rhett doesn't make promises he can't keep.

"Then it is nothing for the time being," I say, trying to put as much finality into my tone as I can manage.

"But—"

"Rhett, just drop it, okay? You're on a hair trigger right now, and we need you here, not out there, taking matters into your own hands," Lucas interrupts heatedly.

Rhett goes quiet, looking at us both for a long time before he sighs and shakes his head. This isn't over, but at least we'd bought time for Rhett to cool off. Because Lucas is right. I'm not going to be responsible for Rhett turning to vigilante justice based entirely on a hunch. The idea of Rhett going to jail and not being here when I need him to anchor me makes my stomach churn all over.

It's not long before I hear the garage door open again, and I look up at Lucas's face. His eyes fix onto the mudroom door, expression neutral but eyes keen. His arms tighten for just a moment before the slamming of the door sounds. I turn as rapid footsteps follow, my chest fully relaxing the moment my nose detects lemonade and fresh cut grass. I'm pulled from Lucas's embrace by gentle, calloused hands, only to be wrapped up again, one hand on the back of my head, holding me with the utmost care.

"Lydia."

The sound of Mateo's relieved exhale warms my chest and fills my soul with light. I use my good arm to clutch to the front of his suit jacket, the expensive material silky smooth under my fingers. Mateo's face finds its way to the junction of my neck and shoulder, his lips pressing a gentle kiss to my skin that makes goosebumps rise on every part of my body.

"I'm safe," I whisper, nuzzling as close as I can.

Mateo only purrs, holding me just a hair tighter. It's not the full, body-melding embraces that I've come to love, but just being close and feeling his warmth is good enough for now.

"Ted is calling EPD and setting up a time to finish your interviews. It was really stupid of you to walk out like that."

At the sound of Alexandra's voice, I look up and find her striding across the room, her red-bottom pumps clacking loudly on the hardwood. Her charcoal gray pencil skirt and emerald green blouse cling to her stunning curves in all the best ways, and I can't help the moisture that forms in my mouth as she slides elegantly onto the stool next to where Mateo and I are standing. A small wave of her scent washes over me, the mulled wine and spice making me shiver slightly. Lucas shimmies out from behind us, brushing a quick kiss to her cheek before rounding the island and hopping up to sit on the counter next to the sink. I turn slightly toward her, my skin prickling with awareness as her hazel eyes slide down my body and then back up again. Her inspection only lasts a moment, but it lingers long after she's nodded ever so slightly to herself, as if satisfied. She reaches up and tucks a loose strand of hair behind my ear, and even that feather-light touch has me leaning in for a moment before I catch myself.

I turn more fully in Mateo's arms, hoping to hide the rising heat in my cheeks. Rhett's icy blue eyes miss nothing, of course, and he gives me a pointed quirk of an eyebrow, only making me blush harder. The corner of his lips twitches up. He stabs his fork pointedly into his macaroni salad as he leans casually against the counter next to the fridge, legs stretched out with his ankles crossed.

"Lee can fucking bite me," Rhett returns through a mouth half full of food.

Oh, right. I'd nearly forgotten that Rhett pissed off a cop. Alexandra simply walking into a room scrambles my brain more than the carnival Tilt-a-Whirl.

"I mean... if it was a big deal, I could have stuck around for a few minutes," I add, trying to keep my voice neutral and force my blush to fade by sheer will.

"It's fine now. Ted smoothed the ruffled feathers, citing alpha priority," she says, turning a placid smile in my direction.

I cock my head to the side, confused. Mateo's hands tighten on my waist, and he brushes a kiss to the top of my head.

"If an omega is in distress, their alpha has authority to limit access to them until such a time when the omega is able to handle the situation. It's usually only applicable for bond mates, but Ted is very persuasive," Alexandra explains, speaking first to me and then very pointedly at Rhett.

He only shrugs and takes another bite of his food. I chew on my lower lip. I knew we should have stayed, if for no other reason than to avoid this sort of mess. A little involuntary shudder runs down my spine as I think about how many people were in my apartment, and how much of my nest has been destroyed by now.

"Just so you know, your landlord was there when Ted arrived. They were installing a new door for you," she goes on.

I nod and let out a little sigh of relief. At least my apartment will be safe for the time being.

"What happened with court?" Lucas asks, redirecting the conversation.

Mateo lets out a huff, and my heart tightens. Well, this can't be good.

"Ted called in his one big favor to get us in this quickly, and the judge didn't take kindly to us blowing him off. So we've been moved down the priority list. To November," Lex says, voice a low monotone.

Rhett snarls, and Lucas lets out a colorful string of curse words. But my stomach drops. My brother is getting married in early September, and I have already committed to going. But if I don't have the protection of being an official member of the pack...

Being an unbonded omega limits my freedoms in a lot of ways, but none has been more of a thorn in my side than the laws regarding prime alphas. When an omega is born to an alpha parent, they become the omega's prime alpha. My father has the authority, in the eyes of the law, to make decisions on my behalf, regardless of my say so. Until I bond and my mate assumes that authority, my father can, at any time, decide that he wants me back under his thumb.

The only thing stopping my father from "pulling rank" before now has been his ignorance to my location. He can't call the cops and have them drag me home kicking and screaming if he didn't know which department to call. Joining Pack St. Clair would have made Alexandra my prime alpha, at least until I decide to bond, which would have removed that particular threat from the chessboard.

But now... I could walk into that wedding and never leave. My father, with a simple command, could force me to my knees and break my will. He could force me to go through with the marriage to Darren, or worse, a bond. He could trap me in my worst nightmare, cut me off from the people who've come to mean more than I can adequately put into words.

My eyes fly around the room, looking but not seeing. My heart jumps and skips, rattling around in my rib cage like a trapped animal.

"Breathe, baby. You're okay," Mateo breathes in my ear, hands sliding around my waist to hold me tighter to his chest.

"Ted is going to try to get it moved up, but he called in a huge favor to convince the judge to agree to cut his vacation short and come back to oversee the proceedings. He's not pleased, so I don't want to push it too hard. If something opens up, then he'll try to get us squeezed in, but we should try to figure out alternatives," Alexandra continues.

The coolness of her fingers on my good forearm makes me jump, and I look down. Her touch is gentle and brief, and my heart lurches for an entirely different reason.

"What about a bond?" Lucas suggests, almost flippantly.

I look up at him, and my momentary flash of panic eases slightly at the true concern pulling his brow down low. I swallow and shake my head.

"It'd still be too late. My next heat isn't until mid-October, and with my implant, there's no guarantee a bond would take. Even taking it out today, one of you would have to..."

I trail off, looking down at the countertop, throat tight. The idea of one of these alphas using their bark to force my body to obey and trigger my heat makes my heart race. Darren tried to do that exact thing on the night I escaped, which is enough for me to reject the idea. And while I know my alphas would take care of me and never do anything to hurt me, the idea of being that vulnerable with them still makes my skin crawl.

"I know it's not ideal, but if we can't get a new court date—"

"She said no, Luc. Drop it."

Rhett's snap makes me jump, but warmth spreads through my chest. I look up again to find Rhett giving his beta a hard, unyielding glare that makes me flinch back, even though it's not directed at me. Luc raises his hands in surrender, his face apologetic.

"Alright, alright. I just wanted to consider all options," he says.

"Option considered. So what's Plan B?" Rhett returns, putting his bowl in the sink.

I give Luc a little smile, and he gives me a little tilt of his head. I'm not mad at him for bringing it up, despite rejecting the idea. His heart is in the right place. Extreme circumstances sometimes require extreme solutions. But reliving my greatest trauma is still a bridge too far.

"We have to just keep our ear to the ground and wait to see if we can get in before the wedding," Alexandra replies with a resigned exhale.

"What are we going to do about this intruder situation?" Mateo adds.

"We let the police do their jobs, and see if they can catch him, I guess. Not much else we can do," I say, leaning back into Mateo.

Rhett snorts, and I shoot him a half-hearted scowl.

"If you've got an opinion, by all means, share with the class," Alexandra says with a wave of her hand.

"Just because we can't go out and hunt the bastard down doesn't mean there isn't anything we can do to protect ourselves," Rhett says darkly.

"What's that supposed to mean?" I ask harshly, eyes narrowing.

Rhett looks me in the face, and there's a flash of that protective anger in his eyes that makes my heart lurch.

"You move into the pack house."

There's a moment of silence, and then a shocked, humorless laugh bubbles up through my lips. Rhett's eyebrows shoot up and he blinks, which only makes me chuckle more.

"You're joking, right? I can't move in," I sputter through my chuckles.

"Why not? You were going to at the end of the year, anyway," he returns, confusion heavy.

I let out a distinctly unattractive scoff of a laugh. "Yeah, because my lease would be up at the end of the year," I retort.

"Right, so what's the difference of a few months?" Rhett asks back.

"An enormous early termination fee is the difference," I sputter, blinking rapidly at him.

He looks back at me blandly, as if expecting me to say more. And there are more words flying through my head, but I can't pin them down long enough to make coherent sentences. Warning bells are blaring in the depths of my mind, but not from my primal instincts. If anything, the primal, purely omega part of my mind wants nothing more than to retreat into a mountain of soft things and let my alphas take care of all the terrifying monsters lurking in the shadows.

These warning bells are the ones that years of trauma and recovery have planted. The ones that are screaming not to let people I've known for less than a year talk me into being reliant on them for my housing and care. I've learned this lesson before, and I can't, *won't*, let myself get caught again.

"No. I can't," I say at last, putting as much resolve into my voice as I can.

"It's just money, love. We have plenty, and it's not—"

"You're not getting it, Rhett," I spit through gritted teeth, cutting him off.

My body feels overly warm, and I try to shake off Mateo's hold. When he doesn't let go, my heart sets off again. My hands shake, and the world seems to spin for a moment. Getting my chest to expand enough to take a full breath is a labor, and I blink back tears.

"I won't ever put a price tag on your safety, Lydia. And with Seth and Darren, and now this stalker knowing where you live, we both know that you'll never feel safe there again. So let me, let us, handle this. Please," Rhett goes on, voice exasperated but rich with a soothing purr.

Even still, the words sound like they're coming from the other end of a wrapping paper tube. Safe is relative. I can get safe on my own. I was safe on my own. The omega part of me craves to melt at the sound, to just agree and stop fighting. But those instincts nearly got me killed. Better to listen to the claxon screaming over and over.

Trapped. Trapped. Trapped.

"What's wrong?" Mateo asks, pulling back to spin me around.

When I look up into his face, all the handsome features heavy with worry, I have to blink and look away. The ceiling above him seems to be getting closer, the walls shifting in. Not again. Never again.

"I just... no, I'm not doing it. I can't. Not again. No," I ramble, shaking my head.

I can sense all of their eyes on me like phantom touches and I can't stand it a moment longer. Turning on my heel, I rush to the door leading down to the basement, ignoring Rhett's call for me to stop as I slam the door behind me.

FIVE

Mateo

As THE SOUND OF the slamming door echoes into the silence, I turn my glare on Rhett. He has the decency to look a little ashamed of himself, but there's still a hard glint in his eyes that I don't like.

"What the hell was that?" I demand, leaning on my fists toward him.

"Don't act like you don't agree with me. If it were up to you, she would have moved in three weeks ago," he returns with a roll of his eyes.

"That's not what I mean, and you fucking know it," I growl, shoulders rising defensively.

He returns the glare, but I don't back down. Just because I love Rhett like a brother, it doesn't mean that I won't teach him a lesson if he needs it. He's right about my feelings toward Lydia's living situation, but he can't make demands like this. Not to mention blatantly ignoring her distress just to push his decision on to her.

"What he's saying is that there's a right and a wrong way to bring up something as big as this," Lex interjects.

"And you think I'm wrong? You think we should let her go back to that apartment?" Rhett questions, voice rising.

"No, but–"

"Because once she's medically clear, you know she's not going to tolerate us being around her like we have. Which means she'll be alone, and that fucker is still out there," he says, voice cracking slightly.

I blink, my anger slipping away. The burning paper scent of his fear hits me a moment later, and I soften more.

"I get that, I really do. But there are better ways to bring that up," Lucas says when Lex and I don't continue.

Rhett runs his hands roughly through his hair, exhaling sharply. "I'm such a fucking asshole. What is wrong with me?"

Lex opens her mouth, but I shoot her a glare that reads "not the fucking time." She smirks and tilts her head in acknowledgement.

"I've never felt like this before. I was ready to start throwing hands with the police if they tried to stop us from getting out of there. And I blew our one real shot to give her true protection," Rhett goes on.

"She knows you mean well, Rhett. And you can apologize after you've had time to cool down. She'll understand," I tell him soothingly.

Rhett nods, not looking at any of us. After a long moment, he pushes off the counter.

"I'll be in the gym if anyone needs me," he grumbles, stalking out of the kitchen.

Lucas, Lex, and I wait until the mudroom door opens and closes before letting out a unified breath. Rhett would beat himself up in the gym for a while, but he'd be okay. But Lydia...

"We're all on the same page with his idea, though, right?" Lex asks, voice barely above a whisper.

I sigh, looking at Lucas. His lips press into a thin line as he considers, head tilting from side to side as he walks through the debate in his head. For my part, the answer is easy. Of course, I think Lydia should move in. Having her here would make keeping her safe from Seth and Darren that much easier. But I won't force that on her, not if it means potentially causing a rift between us and her.

"Why does she have to give it up? What's the harm in letting her keep making payments but leaving it empty while she lives with us?" Lucas asks thoughtfully.

"It wouldn't be right, and she belongs here with her pack, where it's safer," Lex says sternly.

"All the same, it's still a lot to ask. She's not going to take the sudden change well," Lucas goes on, hopping down off the counter and moving closer.

"What do you mean?" I ask, words coming out quicker in my concern.

"Omegas need stability, security. Even in the best circumstances, it's probably going to take weeks for Lydia's instincts to consider this home," he replies, crossing his arms over his chest.

"We can up security for the development, tell people there's been some reports of disturbances. If Lydia stays here, then—"

"That's not what I mean," Lucas interjects, cutting across Lex before her planning gets too far. "Her head will know she's safe. We could walk her through every protocol and patrol, but her omega nature is still going to need time to adjust. If we're going to insist on her moving in, we owe it to her to try to make the transition as smooth as possible."

I nod, looking at the basement door again. Lex and Lucas continue on about ways to help Lydia adjust, but their words fade to background noise. The pull to go to her has been growing steadily, and I've reached the end of my patience. I cross the room, unbuttoning my jacket and loosening my tie as I descend the stairs. I drape both over the back of one of the low couches in the sitting room outside of Lydia's room. The sunlight streams through the patio doors, casting blocks of warm light on the carpet. Lydia's door is cracked slightly, and I nudge it open, letting the creak of the hinge announce my presence.

"May I come in?" I ask, poking my head through the door.

It only takes a moment to find Lydia sprawled on her back in the middle of the massive custom mattress that fits into the expanded window seat platform. Her eyes are closed, but she nods anyway. As I slip through the gap, I close the door quietly, toeing off my dress shoes next to the door.

"I'm sorry I'm an ungrateful, dramatic asshole," she drones, not looking at me.

"No one thinks you're being dramatic, or ungrateful. And you are certainly not the asshole in this situation," I say with an ironic chuckle.

I lower myself onto the edge of her bed, moving slowly enough for her to tell me to stop. When she doesn't, I lean down and lie on my side, facing her.

"Do you want to talk about it?" I offer gently.

Lydia lets out a shaky sigh, her good hand scrubbing her face angrily. She's quiet for a long stretch, but I let her have the space. She doesn't need me to push, or she's liable to shut down, which is the last thing I want right now. At last, she turns her head to look me in the eye. At the edge of her hairline, the faint blue-purple of a bruise still lingers, and the scabs from cuts on her neck. I fight the urge to touch her, to wrap her so tight in my arms it would be impossible to tell where I end and she begins. Even the traces of her injuries make my primal mind want to bury her away where no one could ever find her and hurt her again.

"It's not that I don't want to live here, but I just..." Lydia trails off with a deep sigh, closing her eyes tight.

My heart lurches as she hesitates. I need her to finish that thought, but the longer the silence goes on, the less I want to know. Does she not want us? Want this? Is she rethinking joining the pack?

"The last roommate I had before I moved in with Darren was on the top, bottom, and middle of his shit list. He would tell me that she talked about me behind my back, and secretly hated my guts, and all sorts of other really nasty stuff. I never confronted her about it, but in the back of my head, I was always reading into every interaction, looking for the ulterior motive. The therapist I had for a few months when I first moved to Everton told me it was triangulation. He used the rift he created between us as part of the pitch for us to move in together so quickly. I could get away from my shitty roommate and spend more time with him, a win-win," she drones, voice distant even as her eyes stay closed.

Anger burns in my stomach, and I manage to contain my fury to just gritting my teeth and clenching my fists. The more I hear about the hell Lydia went through, the more I'm considering taking Rhett up on his plan to drive to Louisiana and help Darren find a swamp to get lost in permanently.

"I need my space, Matty. I don't... I can't go back to that place," she whispers.

Unable to resist anymore, I close the distance between us and slide one arm under her neck and wrap the other around her waist, pulling her into my chest. She turns onto her right side, nuzzling her nose into the space between my neck and shoulder on instinct. I run my fingers through her hair, just taking the moment to appreciate the absolutely remarkable woman in my arms.

"What happened today was terrible. I can't imagine how scary it must have been for you, and for Rhett. And when I think of how close you both came to getting hurt..."

I trail off as my throat closes up and I have to swallow hard. My arms flex and I hold her a little tighter, her warmth steadying my racing heart. The hours we'd spent waiting for Rhett and Lydia had been agonizing, not knowing if they were safe or if something horrible had happened. Seeing her standing in the kitchen, shaken up but unharmed, had been the only thing that put my heart at ease. This was the second time I'd almost lost her in less than a week, and I couldn't bear the thought of what could happen if our luck ran out.

"I know it's not what we planned, but having you here, living with us, would mean so much," I finish, words coming out a little hoarse.

"It's not that I don't want to live here, I just don't... it's a lot to ask, and I don't want to put y'all out because of my personal drama," Lydia counters stubbornly.

"This isn't your fault, and we won't think less of you for choosing to do this," I finish, pressing a kiss to the top of her head.

"I need to do something. I won't be a leech. It's not right," Lydia says with a little huff of frustration.

"You're not a leech. Though, if you were, you'd be the sexiest, most adorable, loveable leech there ever was," I counter, trying to ease the tension.

I can practically hear her rolling her eyes, but the small smile I feel pressed against my neck settles me. She relaxes more fully into my embrace, one of her fingers tracing a button on my dress shirt.

"I hate being so... dependent," she mutters.

At that, I frown a little, not sure what to make of it. I don't want to dismiss her feelings, but the alpha in my chest wants to roar in protest. It would be the privilege of a lifetime to care for Lydia, to spoil her rotten and make sure she never wants for anything again. But knowing her like I do, she'd sooner jump off a bridge than be some sort of pampered omega princess in a tower.

"Everyone needs help from time to time. And it's my pleasure to help someone I lo—look up to."

I cut myself off with a hot flush. I've been thinking it for a while, but that was almost too close. Telling Lydia how I feel in this moment seems wrong, too close to manipulation. That's why I can't say it now. It'd be wrong to try to capitalize on those feelings while I'm trying to convince her to move in.

Just keep telling yourself that, Matty. Someday it might actually be true.

I shove aside the voice in my head that sounds uncannily like Rhett as Lydia snorts.

"Look up to?" she repeats skeptically.

"Well, not literally. You are fun-sized, after all," I tease, kissing her forehead again.

"When I have both my arms again, I'll show you how fun-sized I am," she grumbles, and I can't help but laugh.

"I'll make sure to have the step ladder on hand, so we can talk eye-to-eye," I volley back.

She growls the most adorable little rumble and pokes me hard in the ribs, making me laugh harder. I let her tickle me into submission, cuddling her close afterwards while we catch our breaths. I'm happy to let her win, to give her a moment to not have to worry about the darkness lurking just outside of the door.

"After I'm moved in and I get back to work, I'm going to pay back the fee," Lydia says after a long pause.

"We'll just use it as part of the payment on a car for you," I reply neutrally.

"No, you fucking won't. I'm going to buy my own car, and I'm going to pay back the early termination fee, and there's nothing you can do to stop me," she declares with a final nod.

If that's what it takes to get Lydia to live here and be safe, then so be it. I smile and nod, trying not to let my relief show. She settles back into my embrace, and I close my eyes, a prayer of thanks escaping on my next exhale. I'm not a religious person, but whoever or whatever sent such a strong, beautiful fighter into my life has my eternal gratitude.

SIX

Lydia

THE AIR IS WARM *and humid, cicadas a background hum under the slow beat of the classic rock ballad around us. A warm grip, the callouses familiar and comforting, envelopes my right hand. My left arm is free of its cast and draped across a broad shoulder. I can feel the smooth fabric of his expensive suit under my fingers. His whiskey and leather scent fills my head, making my knees weak and head spin.*

Rhett and I sway, my dress brushing against my legs as he leads me through a slow foxtrot. There are other people on the dance floor, Sam and his new bride Ally among the crowd. Rhett spins me in a smooth motion, my elegantly styled hair fanning out around me. I slide back into Rhett's arms, smiling up into his beautiful face. His smile makes his icy eyes dance, the fairy lights reflecting like stars.

"You're so perfect," he breathes, looking at me with that expression of awe and love that I know by heart.

I can only beam in response, stepping closer and closing my eyes as I bask in the warmth of his embrace.

"I can't wait to make you mine."

"I love you," I breathe, words coming out through my happy tears.

"Love isn't enough, though, petal."

My whole body goes cold and hot at the same time. Darren's cruel smirk splits his thin mouth, his muddy brown eyes flashing with anger that freezes my blood and nearly stops my heart. I try to pull away, but his hand fists into my hair, cranking my head back painfully.

"Love isn't enough to save you, my petal. You're mine. Forever."

My shoulder burns and throbs as his teeth sink into the flesh. I scream, trying to shove him away. But his arms are steel bands, wrapping tighter and tighter until I can't breathe. Tobacco and clay and bitter almonds invade my senses, pushing out all other sounds and sensations. The blood runs down my chest, gushing and staining my clothes and skin.

I bolt upright, my skin soaked with sweat. I wipe at my face, wincing as my left arm tries to bend. Looking at the clock, I sigh as I realize that I'm only about an hour from when I'd planned to get up anyway. It's still dark outside, but I'll need all the time I can get.

I'm finally going back to work today. It's been a little over a week since the accident, and there's a big wedding on the schedule. Wila, my boss, had assured me she and her granddaughter Gabby can handle it, but I need to get my life back on track and do something. I've been at the pack house for the last few days, and I've barely had any time alone. If it isn't Rhett hovering or Mateo fussing, it's Lucas trying to distract me. Alexandra has been scarce, with her work schedule keeping her out of the house.

Things calmed down a little once I agreed to move out of my apartment, and Rhett took it upon himself to hire movers to pack things up and bring them here. I didn't like the idea of yet more strangers touching my stuff, but the thought of going back into that building makes me break out in a cold sweat. I'll just add the cost to my tab.

The cease fire ended abruptly last night following a check-up with my doctor, when I'd brought up going back to work. My omega nature has been working hard. Almost all the soreness is gone from my ribs, and only the worst of my bruises are left, and even those are fading to mottled blue-green. My arm needs another few weeks, but on the whole, I feel better every day. Despite this glowing report of my progress, Rhett still wants me to take another week off. Mateo had been no help, acknowledging that he agreed I could go back to work, but wanting to be cautious about what kind of strain I was putting on my body. We avoided an all-out shouting match only because Lucas put dinner on the table, and wisely, didn't offer an opinion one way or the other.

Not fighting at the dinner table was basically beaten into me growing up, so I'd dropped the subject. Rhett, taking my silence as my agreement, also moved on, talking about new restoration contracts that could be on the horizon. Alexandra had come home in time to grab a plate and disappear into her office, not sticking around long enough for me to broach the subject with her. After dinner and dishes, Mateo put a baseball game on in the sitting room, and I curled into his side on the sectional. The boys started up a conversation, but I zoned out quickly, my annoyance reduced to a simmer. Rhett continued under the delusion that he'd won, even as I kissed him goodnight and went to bed.

Joke's on him. I agreed to live with this pack, not be their prisoner.

So, I came up with the plan to just go and face the consequences later. It was better to ask for forgiveness than permission, anyway.

With it being a Saturday and most of the residents not being morning people on their days off, the house is still and quiet. I'm glad for the extra hour, as it is a bit of a struggle to get into my work clothes on my own. I opt for a plain white t-shirt rather than the button-down I usually wear to events, as there is no way I'd be able to fit my cast through the sleeve. But once my pants are on, and I slip into my shoes, I tiptoe up the stairs into the kitchen. As quietly as I can, I snoop through the cabinets until I find a travel coffee mug and the pods for their single-serve machine. I cringe at the noise it makes as it heats up, but I turn my back and go on the hunt again for the proper mix-ins.

"If you're looking for the sugar, it's above the stove."

I yelp and whip around at the sound of Alexandra's voice, breathing hard. She's dressed in eggplant-colored trousers and a cream blouse, hair pulled back in a sleek low bun. Her lips are painted crimson, and one corner of her mouth pulls up in a knowing smirk. I swallow and nod, following her direction and finding the glass jar of sugar.

"You're up early," she comments, voice a little closer.

I look over my shoulder and find her leaning against the counter with the island between us. My face heats, but I try to keep my expression neutral.

"So are you," I return, grateful that my voice is steadier than my hands.

"I've got a few early meetings. What has you up at this hour?" Alexandra asks, a little firmer.

The coffee maker dispenses into the travel mug, and I carefully spoon several scoops of sugar into the steaming cup as I try to think.

"I'm getting ready for work," I say at last, settling on the truth and squaring my shoulders, readying for the fight.

I turn back to Alexandra to find her looking at me curiously. I carry my cup over to the island, stirring the contents before trying to screw on the lid. Alexandra watches me, and I'm even more embarrassed as I struggle. I do it without spilling, but the effort it takes is still frustrating.

"How did you plan on getting there?" Alexandra asks softly, drawing my attention back to her.

"Uber?" My voice lifts in a question.

Alexandra chuckles. "We don't let rideshare drivers past the front gate, just for the record. So what's your back-up plan?"

I clench my jaw, holding back my snarky retort. Of course, they wouldn't let an Uber driver in here. They have a security guard, for fuck's sake.

"Do you have everything you need?" she asks, interrupting my brooding.

I nod with a single jerk of my head, slumping a little. I can feel the lecture coming on.

"Then let's go. If we leave now, we can beat traffic."

My jaw goes slack as I stare at her with wide eyes and raised brows. She's scrolling through something on her phone, not looking at me. When I'm silent for a long pause, she finally glances up expectantly.

"Aren't you going to tell me not to go?" I rasp.

"Do you want me to?" she replies, almost in a monotone.

Shaking my head, I finally get my feet to respond. I round the island and follow behind as she leads the way out into the garage. Then I slide into the passenger's side of her silver sedan, buckling my seatbelt with some difficulty. Alexandra doesn't comment, simply checking her lipstick in the rearview mirror as I finally get the buckle to lock. I wrap my hand around the coffee cup, my knuckles white as Alexandra starts the car and backs out smoothly.

"A little bird told me what happened last night before I got home. Rhett and Mateo may have their opinions on what you should and shouldn't be doing. How you handle them is up to you. But if they are making you feel like you can't say no, I have no qualms about setting the record straight for you."

Alexandra's voice is low in the car's silence as she maneuvers through the winding streets of the development. I study her profile for a moment, unable to stop myself from admiring the smooth slope of her throat, the elegant swoop of her nose, the fullness of her lips. My mouth goes a little bit dry, and I take a large sip of my coffee, shaking myself before I get too distracted, and shrug with my good shoulder.

"They mean well," I reply neutrally.

"There's an old saying about paths and good intentions. But that's not what I meant, and I think you know that," she says coolly, looking over at me with a knowing glint in her eyes as we wait for the gate to open.

"They're not forcing me to do anything, Alexandra. I agreed to move out, and…"

"And you agreed to not go to work today, too," she finishes.

I let out a long exhale, turning to look out of the window. Alexandra drives like a professional, all smooth turns and controlled stops and starts. I want to avoid the question, but the longer the silence stretches, the more I realize that she won't let me.

"I mean, I didn't technically say I wouldn't go. I just stopped fighting with Rhett about it," I tell her cautiously, trying for humor in my tone but failing.

"I know you're smart enough to see how sneaking out of the house while everyone is asleep isn't a great plan," Alexandra returns, and I flush.

Taking another drink of my coffee, I try to think of a response. Hindsight, being what it is, I know that today probably won't end well. But after spending so much time clawing my way out of the pit of fear and paranoia I'd been in after leaving Darren, letting another sociopath like Seth control my life like this makes my skin crawl. And I can't live on Pack St. Clair's good will forever. Joining a pack means contributing to its success. I can't do that if I'm cowering in my room day in and day out.

"I need to do this. I just... I need the normal again. Just to pretend like the world isn't going to shit around me," I whisper after a heavy pause.

"If getting back to normal is going to get you hurt, is that worth it?" she asks, not much louder.

I stay quiet, not wanting to speak the truth on the tip of my tongue and start another fight. "Has your landlord been in touch?" she asks, redirecting when I don't respond.

Sighing, I slump back into my seat. After my initial panic faded, I acknowledged moving into the pack house sooner rather than later is the smart move. And speaking with my landlord had been the last nail in the coffin. The exchange was professional, but his relief was obvious even across the phone line when I said I'd be moving out. I'd picked that apartment based largely on its no-alpha-tenant policy, and while no one had filed a formal complaint, having Rhett and Mateo around a lot was definitely stretching the rules to the limit.

"He's not going to charge me for the damage to the door," I start.

"I would hope not," Alexandra snorts.

I huff out a quick chuckle. "But he's got the paperwork all ready for me to sign, along with the exact early termination fee."

I'd received that email yesterday, and it still makes me sick to think of how much money the pack would be paying.

"I know that this isn't ideal, but we don't mind helping you," Alexandra says kindly.

I sigh, but don't answer. I'd make her accept my repayment check one way or another. But that's a battle for future Lydia to fight. Best not to waste energy on it at this juncture.

"Your independence is so refreshing. Seth... he wasn't like you. He saw my name, what my friends and I were doing, and wanted in. Did Rhett or Mateo tell you we didn't form the pack until after the incident?"

When I turn to look at Alexandra, the distant tone of her words softens my anger. I shake my head, and she smiles ironically to herself.

"I know we've talked about it with Ted, but I'm not sure if it really sunk in. When you join our pack, you're going to have access to all our assets, even the intangible ones. The St. Clair name carries weight, and having it will open doors you didn't even know existed," she continues, not looking at me.

I swallow and look out of the windshield at the buildings, the windows glittering with the rising sun. Ted Calhoun, the lawyer for Pack St. Clair, tried to explain all the benefits of joining this pack, but I mostly tuned them out. I don't want or need their money or their status. I open my mouth to tell her that, but stop short as I think more about what she's not saying.

"Seth wasn't an influencer when he met you. He was a bartender," I say distantly.

"He was aspiring. A few appearances in the gossip magazines alongside Mateo helped to grow his following," Alexandra replies.

"Does the bond not give him access to your assets?" I ask, confused.

"Not the ones that are under the pack's name. Which just so happens to be everything except my personal account, where his stipend comes from," Alexandra answers, with another one of those mysterious chuckles, like she's laughing at a joke only she knows.

The stipend, the money her father pays Seth to keep him quiet, is not an insignificant sum, but with Seth's social media career, it's almost unnecessary. I sit in silence and think about this strange conversation the rest of the way into Everton's Old Town district, where Grandmother Wila's Flower Shoppe is located. I direct Alexandra around to where the delivery truck has backed up to the rear door of the shop.

"I know it may not seem like it, but I'm on your side, sweetness. If Rhett or Mateo become a problem, I have no issue setting them straight," Alexandra says emphatically as she parks a short distance away.

I nod and smile softly at her. She returns the expression, even as her hazel eyes flash with something I can't quite identify. I have to look away before I lose myself in the depths of her gaze, clearing my throat as I suppress the urge to lean across the console and kiss her cheek, or something else equally crazy. I slide out of the car and cross the parking lot, setting my shoulders.

SEVEN

Lydia

I STEP THROUGH THE back door of the shop where I've worked for the last four, almost five years, and my whole body instantly relaxes. The floral scent of the store, along with the familiar aromas of freshly turned earth and caramel-candy-apple, grounds me and helps center me in a way I haven't felt since before the accident. The familiar classic rock radio station plays in the workroom, and my sky-blue apron hangs on its peg in the hall. I slip it over my head, not even bothering to tie it before stepping through the open doorway to the workroom.

"I asked you to keep track of that list, Gabby. We don't have time to print another one!" Wila is saying loudly, bent over at the waist and looking under the main table.

"I had it just a few minutes ago!" Gabby's voice comes from the open door of the walk-in cooler, pitched in a desperate whine.

I smile to myself. "Have you checked your back pocket, babe?" I ask with a little giggle.

Wila straightens at the sound of my voice, mouth agape as she stares with wide eyes. Her already dark skin looks a little darker, a product of spending the holiday weekend in the sun at a family reunion. Her silver hair is pulled back in its usual bun, but there are flyaways giving her a frazzled appearance. A triumphant shout sounds from the cooler, and I watch

Gabby walk back out into the main room, holding a folded piece of paper aloft.

"You'd think I'd remember that, but—HOLY SHIT, babe! What are you doing here?" Gabby shrieks, dashing to close the distance between us.

I suck in a sharp breath as she squeezes me tight, my ribs protesting the most, but I don't tell her to stop. I extricate my good arm and return the embrace just as fiercely. Gabby Fitzgerald has been my friend for nearly as long as I've lived in Everton, and the scent of candy apples that rolls off of her to surround me as I bury my face in her shoulder is like returning home.

"We told you we've got this," Gabby says, her voice muffled by my hair.

"Says the bitch who can't keep track of the order checklist," I say with a watery laugh.

"What did the pack say when you told them you were coming back?" Wila asks, stepping up and putting a hand on my shoulder.

I pull away slightly and give her a sheepish grin. "Um, nothing. Alexandra drove me here, but the rest..."

Wila throws her head back and lets out a full belly laugh. "That's my girl. Well, you've still got one good arm and two legs. Let's get moving before we hit rush hour."

I smile gratefully at the woman who has treated me better than any of my blood relatives ever have. Wila takes no shit from anyone, and while I know she cares, she won't let me wallow or baby me. And it's such a relief.

"I'm so glad you're okay, Lyds. When Rhett called and told us..."

I pull away and look at Gabby, finding her chocolate brown eyes lined with silver. I nod, understandingly. Gabby lost her parents in a car accident, so I can only imagine how awful it must have been to hear about mine.

"Like Gran said, I've still got three working limbs. And it won't be long until I get my other one back," I say with a little teasing shove.

"And it's time to put your collective limbs back to work. Gabby, let Lydia keep track of the list. We don't have time for your scatterbrain self to lose it again."

Gabby and I share another smile before she passes me the list, and we get back to work. The routine of loading the truck and working a wedding works miracles on my nerves. My ribs aren't happy with all the exercise, but I feel more like myself than I have in days.

The first message comes in as we're pulling up to the venue. I slide my phone out of my pocket as I wait for Gabby to clear the passenger door, stomach sinking as I open the notification.

Rhett: Where are you?

I let out a silent, resigned sigh. I should have known it wouldn't take long for Rhett to realize I wasn't in bed. My first instinct is to apologize and submit, but I fight it down. It would only make Rhett think this was acceptable behavior. There's a fine line between protective and possessive, and he's toeing right up to it. Typing is slow with one hand, so I keep it brief.

Me: At work.
Rhett: I thought we talked about this. You're still healing and need rest.
Me: I'm fine. Can't talk right now, need to help with setup.

I slide across the cracked plastic-vinyl seat, grunting slightly as my feet hit the pavement. My phone vibrates again, this time with an incoming call. My thumb hovers over the dismiss button, but I decide to let it ring out before shoving it back in my pocket. I'll text him back once we've unloaded and set up.

Despite my obvious dismissal, Rhett calls me two more times in rapid succession, not bothering to leave voicemails. I eventually set my phone on silent. The buzzing in my pocket has proved too distracting, as I'm trying to focus on doing my job, while also not injuring myself further. Once the bouquets and boutonnieres have all been distributed, and the ceremony has begun, Wila, Gabby, and I find a quiet corner of the reception hall to sit down in and take a quick break before we have to put the final touches on the centerpieces.

"So when you said you didn't tell the pack you were coming in today, do you mean that you didn't let them know you were leaving or..." Gabby starts, trailing off.

I shrug with one shoulder. "Kind of. Rhett thinks he can control when I'm allowed outside of the house."

"Like you're on some sort of lockdown? That's a little fucked up, babe," she replies skeptically.

"Well, no, not like that. I feel fine, but Rhett thinks I need more rest. But I can't lie on my ass anymore, Gabs. I'll go crazy," I continue before taking a swig from a bottle of water.

"Oh, no. You get to lie around and have two hunky alphas waiting on you hand and foot. How tragic a life you lead," Gabby says, words dripping with melodramatic sarcasm.

"If it were my choice, then I wouldn't be bitching. But they're treating me like I'm liable to shatter. Not to mention the paranoia over this stalker," I retort, rolling my eyes.

My phone vibrates again, and I pull it out and watch Rhett's name flash across the screen. When the device goes silent and dark again, Gabby gives me a searching look. I tear my gaze away, face hot.

"Listen, I'd normally say let him stew. You don't owe a man a God damn thing. But, with all the extenuating circumstances, the least you could do is let him know you're not dead or in the back of some creeper's van," she says at last.

I sigh, not willing to say it out loud, but she's right. I swipe the unlock pattern, and sure enough, there are about a dozen texts waiting for me, though I'm surprised to see that not all of them are from Rhett.

Rhett: Lydia, this isn't funny. The doctors said you should still be limiting your physical activity.
Missed Call 10:34AM Rhett
Missed Call 11:02AM Rhett
Rhett: Where are you? One of us can come help out for the day.
Rhett: Seriously, where are you?
Mateo: Hey, what's going on with you and Rhett? He's freaking out. Are you okay?
Rhett: This isn't smart, Lydia. If something happens, we won't know where you are. Please, just answer your phone.

Lucas: If you are trying to torture Rhett, it's working. But maybe put him out of his misery?

I look up at Gabby and show the messages to her with a deadpan stare. She sighs and shakes her head, throwing her hands up in a "do what you want" sort of gesture. I consider for a moment, thumb hovering above my list of message threads. I wouldn't put it past Rhett to drop whatever he's doing and show up here if I told him where I am. And I really don't want to cause a scene while I'm on the clock. I might be able to talk Mateo down from showing up, but he'd probably tell Rhett, and then I'd be back to diffusing the bomb. I take another deep breath before choosing the safest option.

Me: I'm not trying to torture Rhett. Let him know that I'm fine, but I'm working and can't be on my phone constantly. I don't need a babysitter. I'm with Miss Wila and Gabby.
Lucas: Okay. Maybe you should talk to him directly, though?
Me: If he wants to pick me up, I'd appreciate that. We'll be back at the shop around eight, I think.
Lucas: If I promise not to spill, will you at least tell me where you are?
Me: We're at The Grapevine Banquet Hall. And I swear to Christ, if he shows up here, they won't ever find your body.
Lucas: Your secret is safe with me, sweetheart. See you when you get home.

"All right, enough twittering or whatever you kids do these days. Back to work," Wila says with a half-groan.

Gabby and I nod and follow her, getting back to work. I'm hopeful that the fire has been at least temporarily smothered, and when my phone doesn't go off for the rest of the night, I let myself relax. I don't hold any delusions about this being over, but I can at least work in peace for a few hours.

The wedding goes late, and it's almost dark by the time we get back to the shop and unload the remnants. As we're finishing up, I look out of the back window and see a familiar black sedan sitting in my usual parking spot, running but with the lights off. Time to face the music, I guess.

"If you want Gran to chase him off, all you have to do is say the word," Gabby comments, coming up to my shoulder.

I sigh and shake my head. "It's only going to delay the inevitable."

"If he needs help getting with the program, I've been taking some jujitsu classes and I'm pretty sure I could take him," Gabby says, half joking.

I laugh outright. Rhett has trained to fight most of his life, and while I don't think he'd hurt Gabby if she tried to kick his ass, I don't think he would take it lying down, either.

"You can jump him in a dark alley if I can't get him to calm down. Promise," I say, giving her one last hug.

"Don't threaten me with a good time, babe." Gabby laughs before heading up the stairs to the apartment she and Wila occupy above the store.

Turning back to the parking lot, I square my shoulders, bracing myself for impact.

EIGHT

Rhett

"You're going to put a rut in the hardwood if you don't stop," Lucas drones.

I throw a growl over my shoulder but stop my pacing at the picture window overlooking the backyard. I can't see Lucas, but I can smell him. His fresh cotton and sugar scent, something that usually soothes even my worst moods, is thick in the air, but isn't putting a dent in my foul mental state.

It'd started when I went down to Lydia's room this morning, fully intending to spend the day with her in bed, like we'd done on a few lazy weekends before the accident. Hours and hours of just being close, talking, occasionally touching and more. But her bed was cold and empty, and her scent stale in the air. I'd gone into a panic, checking every door and window lock in the house for signs of a break-in. When I'd gotten to the garage and found Lex's car gone, it'd hit me. Lydia had gone to work despite her promising me she wouldn't.

Fear and worry have morphed into frustration and dread, and Lydia's refusal to answer my calls and messages has only stoked the fire in my gut. I'd worked out twice today, even going as far as to spar with Mateo until we both dripped with sweat and were ready to collapse, but nothing has helped.

"She's fine, Rhett. You need to calm down—"

"Easy for you to say. She's answering you," I snarl over Lucas, guilt appearing in my chest for only a moment before it's burned away.

"You're blowing this way out of proportion. It's not like she's been kidnapped," he continues, his even tone grating on my already raw nerves.

"She fucking could 'ave been, t'ough. We shouldn't have given 'er a room so close to an exterior door," I retort, running a hand roughly through my hair.

"It's impossible to remove that risk without locking her in a windowless cell. Which you sure as shit aren't going to," Lucas snaps.

I turn to find him sitting up and glaring at me over the back of the sectional. Even if I hate myself for it, I can't deny that the thought of Lydia hurt or worse has made me consider crazier ideas. But the voice of my mother that lives permanently in my head shrieks in rage, scolding me until I can get that urge under control. Sarah Cooper-Nolan would be ashamed of her son if she could see what I've turned into. I can't stop, though. I don't know how to shut off these instincts that make me want to take Lydia into a bomb-proof bunker and keep her there until we've handled the threats against her.

"I'm going to Wila's. Don't wait up," I mumble, heading toward the mudroom.

"You're still hours early! At least wait—"

I don't hear the end of his protest as I slide on shoes and storm across the porch. I'm out of the garage before I can think better of it, but I don't miss Lucas's disapproving stare out of the front windows as he watches me leave.

Lydia gets one point in her argument for staying at her apartment during the work week. The commute between Bristol Point to the Old Town portion of State Street is at least double that of the distance between her old building and her job. And it puts me on some of the more heavily congested roads in the city, though I purposefully avoid the intersection of Decatur Road and Garrison Boulevard, the place where I almost lost her.

I pull into Lydia's usual parking spot in the large lot behind the row of six buildings that make up this block. The lot is half full of cars belonging to employees of the businesses surrounding the flower shop. Most of the business owners live above their storefronts, like the Fitzgeralds, and I have a friendly relationship with almost all of them. During the restoration project, I'd gotten to know them, and the Foundation owns a fair number of buildings, so we like to keep up with the leaseholders.

Lydia's estimated return time comes and goes, and I get more restless with each passing minute. The sun sets behind the three-story buildings, and darkness settles over the city, the streetlights flickering to life overhead. It's only through sheer force of will that I stop myself from calling Lydia until she picks up and demanding to know where she is. The rational part of my brain knows that there's probably an innocent explanation for her tardiness. But it's drowned out by the rest of my mind and its stream of increasingly dire worst-case-scenarios.

Only a rumbling engine and a pair of headlights turning the corner, making their way toward me, stop the worst of my thoughts. Seeing Lydia in her black pants and white shirt, her arm in its sling and strapped to her chest as she climbs out of the cab, settles me a little more. Though I can't deny the primal surge of annoyance as she looks at my car and then purposefully turns away.

It takes a while for the three women to finish up whatever they're doing, and each second Lydia isn't by my side winds my gut into tighter and tighter coils. By the time she's sliding into my passenger seat, only the wave of her soft lilac and lavender scent keeps me from snapping. She's safe and back where she belongs. That's what matters. I have to remember that, even as the darkest part of my alpha nature wants to lay into her for scaring me like this. And punish her enough to make her second guess ever doing something like this again. But that is a voice I have no issue shoving aside. For now.

"Rhett—"

"Do you 'ave any idea how fucking terrifying it was to go down to your room, expecting you to be there, only to find your bed cold and empty?"

Okay, maybe I couldn't shove the anger away entirely. But after spending a whole day terrified that something awful had happened, I'm owed the right to growl a little. I start the car and pull away, heading toward the lot exit and home.

"That's not fair," she retorts with a huff.

"What's not fair is you going back on your word, Lydia. We agreed you weren't going back—"

"No, *you* decided I wasn't going back to work. I never agreed to that. It's your fault for assuming—"

"The doctor said you need rest, and running around for sixteen hours won't help you get better."

Our voices are rising steadily, but something is loose in my chest and I'm struggling to hold on to it. My hands ache as I grip the steering wheel with white knuckles, and I have to keep reminding myself to take it easy on the brakes and accelerator. I can still scent the shift in the air, burnt sugar tickling the edges of my senses.

"You're acting like I was running a marathon. Wila made sure I didn't lift anything heavier than a corsage all day and made me take plenty of breaks. Despite what you think, I am capable of taking care of myself and knowing when I've hit my limits," Lydia snaps.

I finally look away from the windshield, turning to see her staring out the passenger window with her good arm tucked around her bad, like she's trying to cross her arms over her chest. She's breathing hard and not looking at me, but the tension in her shoulders is visible.

"You know that's not—"

"At this point, Rhett, no, I don't know that's not what you think of me," she interrupts harshly.

I swallow a growl, taking a turn away from my usual route back to the pack house and heading farther downtown. Lydia and I need to figure this out, and I don't want the rest of the pack to interfere.

"I'm trying, Lydia. I really am. But with Seth and Darren and this stalker, I don't know if you're making objective choices," I tell her, trying to keep my voice even.

Lydia lets out a bark of a laugh, the sound cruel and so unlike her that I look out of the corner of my eye in alarm. She's pale, hands clenched into tight fists. The silvery moisture lining her eyes becomes highlighted in the orange flashes of the passing streetlights, and my heart jumps up into my throat.

"Like you've got any room to fucking talk. It's my life we're talking about here, and you're acting like I'm some sort of petulant child acting out, not smart enough to understand the consequences of my own actions. What a load of—God, you sound just like him."

The air in the car feels like it drops ten degrees as her words wash over me. I sound just like... *him.* Everything I've said today, each grim and unreasonable thought that's gone through my head, flashes back, and it's enough to make my vision spin for a moment. Thankfully, we've arrived outside of Wickland House, and I pull into my reserved space in the front of the building. When I kill the engine and silence fills the cavern between us, I can't get my chest to expand enough to take a full breath.

She thinks I sound like her abusive ex, the man who she's still hiding from to this day. And can I really blame her? Have I not been treating her like she's incapable of seeing reason?

Ya bet yer lily-white arse, ya have, Rhett Cooper.

My mother's voice enters my mind again, and I duck my head in shame. Looking at where my hands have fallen into my lap, I suck in a ragged breath. I would never put a hand on a woman in anger, but I've done something just as bad, if not worse, to Lydia. I promised to protect her from men who would treat her like this.

"Rhett... I'm—"

"No, you don't—you don't apologize, love," I whisper hoarsely, cutting off Lydia's shaky words. As I look up at her, I catch the flinch she tries to hide. My heart throbs all over again. "Even now you're... you're waiting for..."

I trail off, not wanting to finish the thought. But I can read the confirmation in her eyes. She's waiting for me to lash out, to scream at her for "talking back," to do all the things I'd been so close to doing. Guilt crashes down over me, crushing my chest and driving the air from my lungs.

I move slowly, keeping my hands where she can see them as I reach over and take her good hand between both of mine. Her skin is cold, and I rub it slightly, trying to warm her on instinct. Her fingers are so delicate compared to mine, skin smooth but not without the callouses that come from hard work.

"I can't pretend I wasn't scared shitless when I saw you gone. With your room being so close to the patio doors... I don't know what I'd do if something happened to you," I start, still keeping my eyes on where my thumbs caress the back of her hand.

"I didn't mean to scare you, but I can't live like this, Rhett. Not after... not after everything," she replies, barely above a whisper.

I look up at her face again, finding her emerald eyes distant, and I know she's back in that place. Back with Darren and the horrors he put her through. She hasn't told me everything, but she has told me enough that I should have known better and seen this coming.

"What do you need, Lydia? Tell me, and if it's in my ability to give, it's yours," I implore, holding her hand a little tighter.

There's a long pause, and her throat bobs as she swallows. She shakes her head a little and seems to come back into her body with a blink before she meets my gaze. I keep my expression open and sincere, trying to tell her without words that I would do anything for her.

"I need you to listen to me, and trust that I know my body and my limits," she says at last, voice the steadiest it has been since I picked her up.

The alpha in my chest roars its protest. It's my job to know what she needs before she does and provide it. The primal urge to protect her, even from herself, is strong, but I have to do better.

"I can't promise I'll be perfect at it, but I will do my best," I reply honestly.

Lydia's little smile lights up my world, and as she leans in, I meet her halfway for a sweet, but intense kiss. When we pull away, she rests her forehead against mine, her eyes closed.

"I hate fighting with you," she breathes.

"And I, you, my love. Can I make it up to you?" I reply, bringing up one hand to brush stray strands of her hair behind her ear.

"What did you have in mind?" she asks, voice dropping to a sultry but playful purr.

I chuckle darkly and feel the shiver run down her spine at the sound. "I can think of a few things. But I don't feel like sharing you tonight."

Lydia tilts her chin, as if she's going in for another kiss. But she stops when our lips are only a hair's breadth apart, and I

can practically taste the vanilla and honey of her arousal on
her exhale.

"Then don't."

How we make it through the lobby of Wickland House
with our clothes still on will forever remain a mystery. I can
barely keep my hands off of Lydia's luscious curves once
we're inside the elevator, my lips crushing hers in bruising
kisses. I'm mindful of her ribs and stomach, but it's hard to
think around the throbbing in my jeans. When the bell rings
and the doors open into the penthouse suite, I growl my
approval as her lithe little fingers start to undo the buttons
of my shirt.

"Safe word?" I pant, hands sliding down to find the Velcro
of her sling.

"No, need you too much," she replies, just as breathless.

A chorus of angels from Heaven wouldn't have sounded as
beautiful as those words coming from the lips of my omega.
I look up for a moment, weighing my options. Bed's too far
away. Couch might be too awkward. Kitchen island. Perfect.

I walk us backward, grinning into Lydia's kiss as she
whimpers with frustration. When her hips meet the
counter-height marble, I lean back slightly and seize the
sides of my shirt in each hand, yanking hard enough for
the buttons to go flying across the room. Lydia gasps, but I
don't give her time to admire it. Reaching down, I grab her
perfectly thick thighs and hoist her up, setting her on the
edge of the counter.

"How bad do you want it, love?" I growl, one hand
squeezing and massaging her right breast with careful
pressure.

Lydia throws her head back and moans loud, and I can't
help myself. I lean down and nip at the skin of her exposed
throat, reveling in the feel of her whines and gasps under
my teeth. I spend a moment longer on the joint between
her shoulder and neck, the place where I've seen my mating
mark in every daydream I've had in the last six months.
I stop short of leaving any sort of mark, respecting her
pre-established limit.

"Rhett, please. I need you inside of me so bad. I've missed
your cock, please," Lydia begs, almost mindlessly.

Well, I've never been one to resist such pretty begging. She lifts her hips as I work her pants down, and I don't even bother to do more than undo the button and zipper of mine. My fingers find her already dripping for me, but slide two fingers inside her tight heat, just because I enjoy the way her eyes roll back when I stroke that perfect spot on her upper wall.

"No teasing, please. It's been too long. I need you," Lydia whines, her hand finding my cock and I nearly collapse at the first stroke.

"You tell me if I'm hurting you, yeah?" I pant, pulling her hand away and stepping closer.

Her thighs part to allow me between them, and we lock eyes for a moment. Her pupils have nearly swallowed the entirety of her irises, and the flush across her nose and cheeks makes her look like the picture of sexual perfection. Desire fills every line of her face, and my heart kicks in my chest. She nods slowly, lips parting slightly while her chest heaves.

We gasp together as the tip of my cock pushes into her channel, the warmth of her, the tight, wet pull of her cunt drawing me in. I rock slowly at first, going deeper with each roll of my hips. But it's not long before I feel her outer lips against the bulge of my knot where it's beginning to swell at the base of my cock.

"I love you," I whisper, reaching up and cupping the back of her head as I bottom out.

"I love you, too," Lydia says, smiling slightly.

I roll my hips, withdrawing slowly so she can feel every inch of my cock. Her sigh as I press deep and slow, the way she melts into my arms nearly undoes me. My other arm bands around her hips, guiding her to rock with me as my pace increases. Her nails dig into the flesh of my bicep, and I purr my approval.

"You feel so good, so wet and tight for me," I gasp, snapping my hips harder, but not moving any faster. I'm determined to savor every moment of this, to give her every drop of pleasure she can possibly handle.

"Oh, God, please. I need more," Lydia moans, throwing her head back.

"So needy, so desperate for me. God, you're incredible."
I purposefully slow down until she's whining and trying to
fuck herself on me.

"More, harder. I need—give it to me." The cutest little growl
of frustration escapes her lips as she yanks on my clothes.

"What's the matter, love? Just enjoy this and let me take
care of you," I purr, nuzzling her hair gently with the tip of
my nose.

"I don't need slow. I need you to fuck me like you're still
mad at me," she snaps.

My spine straightens, my hips coming to an abrupt stop,
and I pull out so I can look at her more fully. My internal
alarms are blaring, and the heated glare she throws at me
does nothing to ease my concern.

"What did you just say?" I ask, hoping like hell I'd misheard
her.

"I don't want you to coddle me. I want you to fuck me like
you mean it, like you would have an hour ago," she tells me,
straightening her spine and lifting her chin defiantly.

"Where is this coming from? I'm not mad—"

"You're holding back, and I don't want you to. If we don't
get this out of our systems now, it'll just fester," she continues,
pawing at my arms weakly.

"Get what out of our systems, Lydia? You're not making any
sense." My concern is now edging forward as I scent a little
hint of burning sugar in the air and her chest starts to rise
and fall a little faster.

Lydia looks away, and I swallow hard as I watch her
disappear somewhere in her mind. Her shoulders lift ever
so slightly, her hands clench and relax, and she shifts almost
restlessly. Honey and vanilla are overpowered by burning
sugar, and I reach out and cup her cheek in my hand and
make her look back at me.

"That's not how we play, love. I'm not going to punish
you with sex when you've done nothing wrong," I say gently,
rubbing her cheek with my thumb.

"But you were so upset, and I thought... don't you need
to get that out of you?" My heart cracks a little at the
vulnerability in her eyes as she looks at me.

"That's my problem to work out, and it would be unfair to
take that out on you. Was I angry? A little, but I was more

worried than anything. And even if I was angry, it's not your job to be my punching bag," I answer, speaking slowly and clearly, so she knows I mean every word.

She nods and takes a shaky breath. There's a pause and I wait, not wanting to push her before she's ready to speak. Eventually, her eyes clear and her shoulders relax. She closes her eyes and leans into my touch, and I kiss her forehead.

"I do want that, though," she whispers.

"Want what, my love?"

"For you to fuck me like you're mad at me. I need to go to that place with you and come back, to know that we're okay and we can fight and make up without it being like... like it was before," she goes on, speaking more to herself than to me.

I bite my lip as I consider. I don't like this, but I have to trust her. She needs that almost as much as she needs this type of play.

"I'm not going to cross any of your limits. And if I think this is doing more harm than good, I'm going to safe word," I say at last.

Lydia opens her eyes and looks at me, and damn it if my heart doesn't melt at the look of surprise and gratitude on her gorgeous face. She nods eagerly, shifting slightly to open her thighs to me again. One whiff of that intoxicating honey-and-vanilla nectar, and my cock is already back to half-hardness.

"Last chance. You say your safe words, and we're going to begin," I say, lowering my hand until I'm lightly resting it along the column of her throat.

"Red to stop, yellow to slow down. Sir."

I growl, tightening my grip on her throat and making her gasp. I bare my teeth, pushing her back until she's flat on the counter, and I'm standing between her thighs. It's almost too easy to let the anger come to the surface, but I keep a tight handle on the leash, ready to pull it back at the first sign of trouble.

"You've been a naughty, naughty omega, little one. Going off on your own and leaving me no word that you were safe," I say, keeping my voice light, but with no lack of disappointment.

I trail my fingers up her inner thigh, and she swallows under my other palm. Her muscles quiver, and I smirk as I feel the wetness pooling in her core. Without warning, I shove two fingers deep into her channel, pumping hard and fast.

"Selfish girls get punished by their alphas, my love. You didn't think at all, and now you're here, at my mercy. Is that what you want? My mercy?"

She shakes her head, and I have to give her points for boldness. I growl, withdrawing my fingers and spreading her cream around her puckered rear entrance. She whines and pushes back as the tip of my finger probes the muscle, not penetrating, just applying pressure. I laugh low in my throat, pushing my thumb into her dripping slit as I continue to tease and taunt her. Her stomach heaves as she struggles to breathe, and I watch her face carefully for signs of pain. But there's only the desperate flush of arousal across her cheeks, and her eyes are shut tight.

"Look at me, little one," I growl, pulling my hand away to spank her inner thigh.

She jumps and tilts her head down as best as she can, cracking her eyes slightly. Her pupils are blown out and hazy with desire. She truly does want this, and that's enough for me.

"You aren't going to come when I fuck you. That's your punishment for today. Do you understand, little one?" I ask gently, massaging the slightly red spot I've just created.

"Yes, sir. Please," she whimpers, lost in the inferno crackling between us.

Hearing that brings my cock to full, throbbing hardness, and I can't hold back anymore. Guiding the tip to her soaked entrance, I don't give her time to adjust before I set a punishing pace. She screams, throwing her head back and arching off the counter as I pound into her, never once complaining as I let out all the lingering anger under my skin. I growl and snarl, releasing her throat so I can seize her hips and fuck into her even harder. My knot swells, but I don't push, just adjusting my angle to avoid any accidental locks while still hitting her pleasure points.

"Sir, please, I can't—it's too much," she pants, her good hand coming up to cling to my forearm.

"I know you can. Take it, and you'll be my good girl again. My sweet, beautiful girl. All will be forgiven, just—fuck!"

I shout as my lower back tightens and I push forward, my legs trembling as I pulse, shooting load after load deep inside of her tightness. Lydia lets out a breath that sounds like half a sob, and when I look up, her good arm drapes over her eyes.

"Lydia? You're okay, it's okay. It's over, we're done," I say hastily, pulling out and gathering her up in my arms and holding her to my chest.

Her breathing is ragged, but she clings to me as I shush and soothe, rocking her gently as I pet her hair and whisper praise. She stops after a moment, swallowing hard before looking up at me.

"Thank you. I... yeah. I needed that," she says, dropping her eyes.

I lift her chin with a finger before slanting my lips over hers. "Always, my love."

Something settles in my chest as we stay locked together in the quiet, just listening to each other's breathing. Lydia smells of flowers and sex, and I wish I could bottle this scent to take with me everywhere.

My purr seems to go on forever, shaking every corner of my body. Her pleasure is my manna from heaven, and I'm addicted. I lean forward, taking her with me until she's on her back. I kiss and suck on her neck as I slide my reawakened cock back into her, relishing the dig of her heels into my lower back as she tries to keep me close.

"I need—Rhett, please, more. I need more," Lydia begs, scratching at my back and lifting her hips to meet my thrusts.

I smirk to myself, unable to help it. Seeing my omega undone and needy for release makes that primal part of my mind turn to mush. And I can't deny her anything. I lean back, taking her hips in my hands in a careful grip, hard enough so she'll enjoy it, but mindful of her injuries. Sweat beads on my back as I fuck her into the counter, the slap of our hips meeting growing louder and more frantic. Her eyes are closed tight, her whole body tense as she hovers right on the edge.

"Come for me. Now," I snarl, adjusting my angle ever so slightly.

Like the good girl she is, it only takes two more thrusts before she's screaming my name and her pussy clenches down on me hard enough that each withdraw is a fight. She shakes as I continue to push her to new heights, circling her clit with my thumb until she's there again, and I can't hold back anymore. Her back bows off the counter for a moment before she collapses, panting hard, and eyes hazy with pleasure, stare unfocused at the ceiling. My lower back tingles and I groan, driving as deep as I can without knotting to spill inside.

My legs shake with the force of my orgasm, and I relax over her, resting my head on her stomach while I catch my breath. She hums, the sound dropping from her throat into her chest for a moment to become a true omega purr before she loses it.

"Have you had supper yet?" I ask into the silence.

Lydia chuckles. "No, but you've sure worked up my appetite."

I smile and laugh lightly, tilting my head to look at her face, grinning wickedly. I lean forward, returning her to her back as I slip a hand between us and slide two fingers into her core. I can feel my release among her slick, and my cock starts to twitch back to life. As I stand and withdraw my hand, I bring my fingers to my lips, moaning at the combined honey, vanilla, and whiskey flavor of us as I lick my hand clean.

I pull out my phone and slide it along the counter toward her before dragging one of the stools around so I can sit in front of her still parted thighs. "Order us something nice from the kitchen. I want to have my dessert before dinner."

NINE

Lydia

"THE MOVERS JUST FINISHED up and are heading out," I say, holding my phone to my ear with my good shoulder as I direct the crew of betas where they should put the last of the boxes.

"Okay. Lock all the doors when they leave," Rhett tells me on the other side of the line.

I roll my eyes, but bite back my sarcastic retort. We've finally gotten to a good place, and I don't want to risk it with a poorly timed snarky comment. I turned in my keys earlier today, along with the check written out in Alexandra's elegant script. My landlord wasn't outwardly sad to see me go, but the booth attendant, Gerald, certainly was. He gave me a big hug when I turned in my parking pass, and I promised him his usual plate of Christmas cookies.

"I'm sorry again that I had to run out. Lucas is getting off soon and he'll be home to keep you company," Rhett says.

"It's okay. I had to entertain myself without roommates or company for four years. A few hours aren't going to kill me." I chuckle.

Rhett doesn't respond, but I can picture the way he purses his lips as he tries to hold back. I know he's worried about my safety, especially since the investigation into the stalker has stalled out. But I feel safe in the pack house, tucked away in the corner of the development, surrounded by open space, behind a fence with a security guard at the only entrance.

"Okay. If anything happens, please call me," Rhett replies.

"Will do. I love you," I say fondly.

"Love you too, little one. Be good."

"Yes, sir."

Rhett's purr makes me giggle as we end the call. The movers bring in the last round of boxes, and I wave as they head back to the truck and drive away. I close the lower patio doors and twist the lock, shoulders relaxing as I let out a long exhale. I turn to the pile of boxes in the lounge, chewing on my lower lip. It's smaller than I thought it'd be, but without my furniture, I guess there wasn't much for me to move after all. Everything is labeled meticulously, which makes sorting through to find my bedding easier.

I drag everything into my room and spend a few minutes ripping the boxes open and dumping the contents onto the floor. I crinkle my nose as I realize everything has a stale, too-clean scent. They washed and covered all my sheets and blankets in scent-blockers. All the comforting scents I'd accumulated in my nest are gone.

I sit down on the floor among the fabric, running my fingers along the emerald green blanket that was Rhett's first gift to me. His first courting gift, if I was being honest with myself. After seeing how much I loved it, he'd gone out and purchased several more of the same blanket in different colors, but this one is my favorite. It's the one he found when visiting his family and bought simply because he wanted to. I'm suddenly aware of how hard my heart is beating in my chest, my head a disorganized swirl of thought fragments as I look around at the pile under me.

A vibration in my pocket pulls me out of my thoughts, and I roll my eyes. It's probably Rhett again, and I'm mentally prepping for talking him down from coming home despite telling him multiple times that I'll be okay. Instead, my brother Jason's name and face pop up on my screen.

"Hey, Jace!" I answer brightly, my lips pulling into a smile.

"Hey, Lydi. I just wanted to check in, see how you're doing," he says, his deep voice warm.

I settle a little farther into the pile of linens, sighing. "I'm okay. Ready for the cast to come off."

Jason chuckles softly, and I can almost picture the way he would roll his eyes. He and I have talked a few times since the accident, and he fusses just about as much as Rhett and Mateo. I'm sure that if it'd been up to him, Jason would have hopped on the first flight to Everton as soon as he'd been told I was in an accident. Thankfully, Rhett was able to talk him out of it.

"How are things with you and Rhett? He taking good care of you?" he asks, tone implying that he's joking, but I catch the edge to his words that makes me think he's not.

"He is. Actually, I um... well, I moved in with him and his pack," I say, speaking quickly to just rip off the band-aid.

There's a long pause. I only know that he hasn't hung up by the sound of passing traffic on his end.

"Lydia, is that... it's a bit soon, isn't it? You've only known him for a few months," Jason starts, voice heavy.

"I guess, but..." I trail off, not sure how to argue with that. I have only known Rhett for just under five months, having met him in mid-March. But I don't know how to explain to my brother that despite that, it feels like I've known Rhett my whole life, or how instant my connection with Mateo had been, or the feelings stirring my chest as I think about Lucas and Alexandra.

"And aren't there other alphas in his pack? How do they feel about you?" Jason continues.

I take a deep breath, bracing myself. This is a conversation that's been a long time coming, but it doesn't make it any less scary. But Jason deserves to know the truth.

"I'm joining their pack, Jason. Would have already if it hadn't been for the accident," I say solemnly, the white lie tasting bitter. Jason already worries enough, and telling him about the break-in attempt would likely send him into cardiac arrest.

"Wow, Lydi... I–I didn't know things were that serious. And the other alphas are okay with that?" Jason replies heavily.

"More than okay, actually," I start, trying to ease into the next bombshell.

"And what does that mean?" he questions, not amused.

"Rhett... Rhett isn't the only one I've been seeing. I've been dating his pack mate Mateo, too. For a while, actually."

The several heartbeats of silence that follow my words stretch on and on, and my chest gets tighter with each exhale.

"And Rhett's okay with that?"

The low rumble of Jason's question makes me jump a little, and my heart twists. The tone is almost impossible to decipher. He doesn't sound outright angry or upset, but there's a tension to the words that sets my teeth on edge.

"Yes. Rhett has a long-term relationship of his own–"

"So he's cheating with you?"

"What? No, that's not what's happening at all. Lucas and I are actually–"

"His relationship is with a *man*?"

My hackles come up at the accusation in Jason's words. "Yes, and that's not a fucking problem, is it, Jason?" I snap.

"I mean, I–no, it–that's not–"

"I can't fucking believe you. It's the twenty-first century, Jason, and you're going to–"

"Don't put words in my mouth, Lydia. This is a lot to take in."

I let out a sharp exhale through my nose. My heart races for an entirely different reason now, my protective instincts kicking in. Rhett and Mateo are my alphas, and Lucas is my friend. I'm not going to let someone get away with judging them.

"With your history, is this really the best situation for you to be in?" Jason asks before I can speak.

"What the actual fuck is that supposed to mean?" I shoot back.

"You don't need alphas who are going to fuck with your heart. And this thing feels like a recipe for disaster," he replies, starting off strong but trailing off toward the end.

"First of all, if you're implying that this is a 'recipe for disaster' because we have agreed, as consenting adults, to be in committed relationships with more than one person, then that's really shitty of you," I reply, shifting my weight and huffing out an irritated sigh.

"It's not shitty to be concerned," he snarls.

"What's there to be concerned about, Jason?"

"Maybe that these alphas are just looking for a sweet, trusting omega to keep locked up and breeding at home while they go out and fuck whoever they want. You've given them the green light on sharing you amongst them, so what's stopping them from finding other people to join the fucking party?"

My jaw falls open and, for a long time, my mind just plays his shouted accusation over and over. *Locked up and breeding. Green light on sharing. Finding other people.* Jason says my name a few times, but I can only manage a choked exhale as I try to process the magnitude of this. I knew Jason wouldn't understand right away, but I didn't expect this... vitriolic judgment.

"That's what you think? That I'd tolerate being treated like I'm some sort of... brood mare while my pack mates disrespect me? Is that the kind of people you think Rhett and Mateo are? You don't even know them, and you're trying to pass judgment like you've–"

"Listen, Lydia, that came out wrong. Please–"

"No, it sounds like you said exactly what you meant, Jason."

He lets out a harsh sigh, and I can almost picture the way he'd be running a hand through his hair, maybe even pacing.

"Lydia, I'm just–with everything going on and your accident, I just don't want you making huge decisions like this without considering all sides," he goes on, a little desperate now.

"That's rich coming from someone who only knows a tiny fraction of the story," I snort.

"Come on, that's not fair."

"I have to go. I'll talk to you soon."

"Wait, Lydi, no–"

"Love you, Jace. Bye."

He's still speaking when I pull the phone away from my face and end the call, but I don't care. My gut is a roiling pit of anger and hurt and anxiety, and I swallow hard against a sudden lump in my throat.

The plastic-y smell of the scent blockers is giving me a headache the longer I sit here, so I stand to drag myself upstairs. My feet feel like they've been encased in cement, and dragging them from one step to the next feels almost impossible. I stumble through the door into the kitchen, swaying on shaking knees. I need to move, do something. I stand in the middle of the empty house, looking around at all the little touches that have made this house a home. The art on the walls, the photos in frames on the kitchen windowsill and mantle. I can scent the mix of them on everything. Alexandra's cloves and mulled wine. Lucas's campfire and s'mores. Mateo's lemonade and fresh cut grass. Rhett's leather and whiskey.

I wander through the house like a ghost, seeing the history of this chosen family. The world seems muffled around me, the central air rushing through the vents sounding more like a whistling mountain gale on the other side of my pounding heartbeat in my ears. There are awards on display in the formal living room, markers of the achievements of the St. Clair Foundation. The light from the windows catches on the gilded display items, striking deep and making my head pound and spin.

Slumping into the foyer, my chest aches as I struggle to draw a full breath. I don't dare open the door to Alexandra's private office, but I lay a hand on the wood of the door and breathe in her scent that lingers there. I close my eyes, fighting the burning behind my lids. My chest feels too full and somehow too empty at the same time. I push off and meander up the stairs until my feet sink into the thick carpet of the hallway. The bedroom doors remain closed, and I stare at them in turns. I'd been inside Mateo's room a few times, having spent those nights in his bed, but the others are still mysteries. They've been giving me space to settle into my room, to adjust things and make them just right before they begin joining me at night. I'd been trying, but without my blankets and pillows, everything has felt wrong. The space might belong to me, but that nest isn't mine.

I wander back downstairs, my palms slick with sweat as I struggle to grip the handrail. I shuffle from room to room, unable to keep still. Eventually, I come to a stop and stand at the kitchen island, staring at the door to the lower level of the house. I want to go back down there, but I can't get my feet to take another step. There's a restlessness in my chest, a need to move and do something, but I can't figure out what. I let out a long exhale of a sigh, closing my eyes and shaking my head.

I turn around and start rummaging through the cabinets as best as I can with one hand, gathering the ingredients for a peanut butter sandwich on the island. Maybe I just need something in my stomach to settle myself for the time being. Then I could try to nest again.

Getting the jar open and bread out of the bag is more frustration than I can take. By the time I'm ready to start assembling, my teeth are clenched, and the flush of anger rises to my face. I maneuver the bread into my left arm, the one still strapped to my chest, and try to wield the knife with my good hand. Gritting my teeth, I struggle to extract some peanut butter, sending the jar tumbling away, knocking into a plate. I watch as the plate slides away, off the counter, and shatters on the floor.

TEN

Lucas

I PULL MY BIKE into a space out in front of Henry's garage. It's been a few weeks since the accident, and the insurance adjuster finally stopped by. Judging by the mechanic's tone during our earlier phone call, it wasn't good news, but he wouldn't give me details.

As I kill the engine and set the kickstand, I pull my helmet off with a shake of my hair. I wave to one of the guys as he walks back from parking a car and take a deep breath before heading inside through the open garage door. The sounds of chatter and tools are like music to my ears. Henry and I became friends when I was working on fixing up my vintage muscle car, and he's the only one my pack trusts to do repairs on their luxury vehicles. It was a no-brainer to tow Lydia's car here the night of the accident.

"Hey, man. How's it hanging?" Henry booms as he spots me from across the garage.

I smile and shrug, slapping palms and bumping fists in the universal bro handshake. "Same old, same old. Never a dull moment."

Henry laughs, his green eyes dancing under a heavy brow. "Well, I've got your girl's car out back. I want to show you something."

My stomach tightens at the serious tone of his words, but I follow him out to the lot behind the shop. In the light of day, Lydia's car looks even worse than I remember. Her entire driver's side is caved in, the windows shattered. The windshield itself is cracked from one side to the other, and it sits almost on the ground on that side, the axel having snapped. And the passenger's side isn't much better, the distinct shape of the utility pole dented into the rear quarter panel. Henry leads me around to the rear passenger wheel well, crouching down and looking at something. I mirror his position, pulling out my phone to shine my flashlight into the shadowy area.

"Did your girl have trouble keeping track of her car?" Henry asks suddenly.

I look at him with raised brows. "Not that I know of," I reply slowly, unease settling in my gut.

"Well, someone wanted to. Cuz the inspector and I found that," Henry says, dropping his voice and pointing up into the wheel well.

I follow his finger, my stomach dropping out from under me. I spot the blinking red light in the darkness before I shine my light on the little black disc. It's about the size of a half-dollar, stuck to the upper inside of the metal frame. The light blinks again, and I sit back on my heels, fingers flying as I type.

Me: You didn't low jack Lydia's car, did you?

I wait for a response, heart hammering. I'm about to send another message when the reply comes through.

Lex: No. Rhett would have my head if I tried something that invasive. Why?
Me: I'm at Henry's and there's a tracker on the car. And I think it's still active.
Lex: That motherfucker.
Lex: Don't touch it. I'm going to call Ted and see what we can do.
Me: If Seth did this, we need to find out when. How much does he know?
Lex: We'll figure it out. Get home. Lydia's there by herself. Rhett had a client emergency he had to deal with.

I shove my phone back into my pocket, getting to my feet. Henry groans as he stands, too, looking at me expectantly.

"What did the insurance say?" I ask with a heavy sigh.

"Oh, it's totaled. But we both knew that. What're y'all gonna do about the..." He trails off, nodding at the wheel again.

"Nothing for right now. I'll let you know more when we have a plan," I explain with a frown.

Henry and I walk back to the garage, parting ways after a few minutes of small talk. My mind races as I consider the implications of the GPS tracker on Lydia's car. Depending on when it was placed there, Seth could know where she's been for work, where she lives. I climb back on my bike and let my thoughts swirl, considering the darker implications of this discovery.

By the time I pull into my lower-level garage and park, I'm full of unease. I'm still lost in my thoughts as I make my way upstairs.

"Fucking bitch!"

The sudden vicious shout makes me jump, my attention going to the kitchen where I find Lydia standing at the island, glaring at the floor.

"You okay?" I ask quickly, crossing to her.

She nearly jumps out of her skin as she whips around to face me, eyes wide. When her eyes meet mine, I feel that little whooshing in my gut that has become so familiar. Her stare is so disarming, emotion written in those green irises as if they were neon signs. And right now, once the fear passes, I only see sadness and frustration.

"Yeah. Just..."

She motions to the floor in front of her and I round the island to inspect. There's a broken plate on the floor, two pieces of toast and a jar of peanut butter completing the crime scene. I bend down and start cleaning without hesitation.

"Sorry. I didn't—yeah, sorry."

Lydia's grumbled apology pulls my attention up to her face. She's leaning back against the counter, fiddling with the strap to her sling. She's not looking at me, but her expression is dark and distant.

"Shit happens, Lydi. Did you yell 'Opa!'? You can't break a plate without doing that," I counter with a little chuckle.

She rolls her eyes, scoffing harshly. "It's just a fucking sandwich. I shouldn't be breaking the china over a sandwich."

I gather the sizeable pieces and toss them in the bin before turning back to her. She looks ready to punch someone or cry, her expression shifting rapidly between the two extremes. Her face is pale, and her hands won't stay still, balling into fists and relaxing over and over again. She still won't look at me, but the way her shoulders slump inward, like she's trying to be as small as she can, sets off a warning bell. I'm silent for a long moment as I weigh my options. Lydia is unlike any other omega I've ever met, and so unlike my sisters that I almost don't know what to do. My instinct is to comfort, to make her the sandwich she clearly wants. But the anger that flashes across her face stops me. There's something else going on here.

Closing the distance between us, I put my hands on the counter on either side of her hips. She tilts her head up to look in my face, and I have to stop myself from leaning in. I've been doing that a lot lately, stopping myself from acting on the more-than-friendly feelings in my chest, but I want our first kiss to be perfect. Certainly not when she looks liable to burst into tears at any moment.

"We can smash more plates if that'll make you feel better. Lex has been trying to find an excuse to replace the set for a while now," I offer with a smirk.

Lydia rolls her eyes again, but doesn't respond. I turn my lips up into a softer smile, tilting my head to the side. She shifts from one foot to the other, huffing out a sigh. Maybe I don't have to say anything. If I just wait long enough—

"If you have something to say, just spit it out. Staring is rude," she snaps after another few heartbeats of silence.

There it is. Lydia and Lex are both like this. Combine silence, direct eye contact, and no means of escape, and they'll both open up under pressure. I don't like how close this feels to manipulation, but I'd rather get to the bottom of what's bothering her so we can fix it. It's my nature to want to help, to smooth ruffled feathers. And Lydia's one puffed-up little sparrow right now.

"Should I have something to say?" I ask neutrally.

"I don't know. It feels like you're going to lecture me or something," Lydia retorts, her voice losing some of its heat.

I take the smallest step forward, so close I can detect traces of scent blocking laundry detergent on her clothes. Where did that come from?

"Why's that?" I press, slowly bringing one of my hands to brush soothing lines up and down her good arm.

"You keep staring and it's an 'I'm not mad, I'm disappointed' look. So just stop stalling and say what you're going to." She wraps her free arm around her stomach, intentionally leaning away from my touch.

She clearly hasn't been on the receiving end of Rhett's 'not mad, only disappointed' stare if she thinks my bland one is bad. I've only gotten it a few times, and I'd be willing to bet Lydia would fold like a cheap suit if it was directed at her.

"I'm curious about what you think I'm not-mad-but-disappointed about and why I'd be about to lecture you," I say, trying to keep my voice even.

"I broke a plate trying to make a sandwich, Lucas! I can't even do that without destruction. I'm so fucking—"

"If you say 'useless,' or anything of the sort, you might get that lecture after all," I growl, anger flaring for a moment in my chest.

Her mouth snaps shut as I cut across her, and her guilty little frown confirms my suspicions. She's lashing out because she's mad, not at me, but at herself.

"Lydia, you know that none of us thinks that about you, right?" I ask, softening my face and voice.

"You should. I can't even piss without someone outside to make sure I don't hurt myself. Y'all shouldn't have to babysit me. I'm an adult, for fuck's sake," Lydia spits, her words starting strong but trailing off until her lip trembles and she sucks in a sharp breath.

I press closer, closing my arms around her and pulling her to my chest. I try to be mindful of her arm, but my desire to hold her close is hard to ignore. She rests her forehead on the middle of my chest, and I feel her taking deep, long breaths.

"This isn't about the sandwich, is it?" I ask gently, hoping she won't shut down on me. My touch is light, rubbing her back in soothing motions.

She hesitates, but then shakes her head. "Jason called. I told him... told him about me and Rhett and Mateo."

My heart clenches, and I hold her a little tighter, pressing my lips and nose into her hair. Her fingers find a hole in my shirt, and she circles it idly, so slowly that I'm not sure she even knows how close to my nipple she's touching. I don't mind, but it's a distraction I could do without right now. So I take her hand and hold it tight between us. While I don't know exactly what she's going through with her brother, I know what it's like to be on the receiving end of family disapproval and disappointment. But with Lydia being an omega, I would have expected her brother to be a little more understanding of Lydia's desire for multiple partners. While it's not the norm, it certainly isn't unheard of.

"And then there's my nest," Lydia starts, breaking off with a sniffle.

"Still haven't gotten it settled, have you?" I ask, voicing my thoughts.

Lydia shakes her head again, but doesn't speak. Knowing that her nest is still incomplete explains so much of her behavior. The restlessness. The irritability. Omegas need the stability of a nest, the comfort and security of a dedicated space, and without it, Lydia's instincts must be going nuts.

"Did your boxes not get delivered today?" I prompt, trying to keep my tone light.

"Yeah. But everything smells... wrong."

I roll my eyes and swallow a frustrated huff. This, at least, explains where the plastic-y scent blocking detergent smell came from. Lex had mentioned that she was going to have Lydia's things washed after she got them back from the forensics lab, but I'd warned her against it. Yes, there would be strange scents on them, but hopefully they would be treated with enough care as to avoid removing the deep scent layers omegas need. I don't understand the science exactly, but the pheromones omegas imbue into their nests are important to maintaining their health, and disrupting that could lead to hormone imbalances, and even serious bouts of anxiety and depression.

It seems that my advice was ignored, and now Lydia is suffering the consequences. I'll have to have a less friendly discussion with Lex later.

"Let's go find some stuff that'll make it right, then."

Lydia pulls away as I speak, looking up at me with furrowed brows. "But my stuff…"

"We'll get the scent blocker off with time, but I'm sure we can find something that you like around here," I say, stepping back and giving her a kind smile.

"Luc, I can't—"

"Can't what? This is your house, too, Lydi," I interrupt, looking back as I pull her into the foyer.

She stops and I wait, studying her face. There's the slightest hint of a blush as she looks at where our fingers weave together. Her eyes follow as I bring the back of her hand up to my lips and brush a kiss over her knuckles. The color spreads out from the bridge of her nose, turning her whole face pink. My stomach does a flip as she steps toward me, finger flexing around mine to squeeze lightly. I hold my breath. Is she going to make the first move? Is she waiting for me to make a move?

My stomach drops back into place as she clears her throat and looks away, breaking the electric tension zipping between us. The back of my neck feels hot as I cough a little and continue leading her upstairs.

She's quiet as we head up the stairs, and as I reach Rhett's door, she pulls to a sudden stop. I turn back to look at her, concern and confusion lining my face.

"It's his room. He hasn't—I've never been in here," she admits, blushing pinker.

I blink at her, but my surge of frustration is directed at Rhett. Of course, she doesn't feel settled. We've been keeping parts of the house from her unintentionally. We're all so used to just floating around each other, going in and out of each other's bedrooms that it never occurred to us to tell Lydia she can do the same. I back off and lead her away from Rhett's door and toward my own.

"We'll ask him for permission when he gets home, okay? But for right now, let's see what we can find in my room," I say, firm but gentle.

Lydia relaxes under my direction, and I feel my heart flip. I have the most experience with omegas, and I try to stay ahead of her instincts as best as I can. I may not have an alpha's drive to protect and care for omegas, but I do enjoy seeing Lydia's face light up when I correctly anticipate her needs. So it's especially rewarding when I lead her through my door and watch her shoulders relax after a long inhale and exhale.

ELEVEN

Lydia

WALKING INTO LUCAS'S ROOM and breathing in the thick layer of not only his scent, but Rhett and Alexandra's scents, relaxes me in a way that I hadn't been prepared for. Tears prick at the corners of my eyes, and I swallow them back as I look around. Lucas's room feels lived in, untidy in a cozy sort of way. His bed is unmade, laundry flows in and around the hamper, papers and books lay strewn haphazardly over a desk. There's an open door leading to a bathroom, and another leading to a walk-in closet.

"This is where the magic happens," Lucas says with a laugh, closing the door and moving around me.

I giggle and watch as he walks over to the bed and throws himself down in the center, making the pillows and blankets bounce around him. A soft smile pulls at the corners of my lips as I take another look around. I step toward his closet, following a pull in my chest, but stop and glance back at Lucas. He nods and motions with one hand for me to continue, his blue-gray eyes sparkling with silent laughter.

"Take what you need, Lydi-bug. I've got more than enough," Lucas calls from the bed.

"Lydi-bug?" I ask in an amused monotone.

Lucas grins bashfully. "Too cutesy?"

My smile softens, heart melting a little. "No. I like it. Just... maybe not in bed," I reply with a laugh.

As our eyes connect for a moment, goosebumps rise up and down my arms, and I take a shuddering breath. The teasing sparkle in his eyes flickers out but is instantly replaced with a molten ember. I stand still, unable to move as his stare slowly drags down my body, and then back up again. It's not quite as predatory as Rhett or Mateo, the phantom touch on my skin feeling more admiring than proprietary.

"And what, pray tell, would you like me to call you in bed?" he asks, and I can't tell if that husky purr to his voice is just a tease, or something else entirely.

I swallow around my suddenly dry mouth, words sticking in my throat. Images I've seen in my dreams, both asleep and awake, flash through my mind. I've only ever slept with one beta since leaving Darren, and it had been... fine. He'd gotten the job done, but it hadn't been a performance worthy of writing home about. But Lucas... he knows how to play. Would he want to submit to me, like he does to Alexandra and Rhett? Or would it be a struggle for dominance, both of us taking and giving, trying to get the other to yield—

"You gonna make it, sweetheart? Or do I need to perform mouth to mouth?"

Lucas's voice pulls me from my spiraling thoughts, and I startle a little, sucking in a breath. His smirk is all teasing humor, and I give him a halfhearted glare that only makes him laugh.

Blushing, I turn away and move to his closet, gathering my wits again. I sigh as I step into the smaller space, graham crackers and chocolate and fresh cotton strong here. My lips pull up in an unconscious smile, and I run my good hand along the row of hanging shirts, enjoying the different textures against my skin. I stop on a particularly soft one, pulling out a concert T-shirt for a band I've never heard of. But the material is thin, almost threadbare, so full of Lucas's scent, and even a hint of Rhett's. I press it to my face, tucking it into my chest.

"That was a shirt I got on one of my first dates with Rhett."

I jump and spin on my heel to find Lucas leaning against the door frame with his hands in the pockets of his jeans. He's shed his leather motorcycle riding jacket, leaving him in a simple short-sleeved Henley. His eyes are distant, but the smile pulling at his mouth is fond.

"Was it weird? Dating the boss?" I ask curiously.

Lucas chuckles. "Technically, he's never been my boss."

"But he owns Alice's," I state, a little confused.

Alice's Kitchen, where Rhett and I went on our first date, is Lucas's primary place of employment, as far as I understand. He's bounced all over the St. Clair properties, but Alice's is his home base.

"Still doesn't make him the boss of me. But we'll just let him keep thinking that he is," Lucas comments with a wink.

I giggle, looking back down at the shirt in my hands. I rub the material between my fingers for another moment.

"But to answer your question, it was hard at first, before we officially became a pack. A lot of accusations of favoritism and sleeping my way to the top. But Rhett and Lex never let me believe the nasty things people said," Lucas continues.

"Alexandra said y'all didn't form the pack until after..."

"After Seth pulled his bullshit, yeah. It might seem a little cold, but Lex wanted to protect us from Seth as much as she could. He can't touch anything we've built now," Lucas finishes as I trail off.

I turn to look at him, my brow furrowed. "I thought bond mates become part of whatever pack their alpha is in."

"They usually do, but it's not an automatic thing. Seth wants in, bad, but that's a line that Lex refuses to let him cross," Lucas says neutrally, his smile dropping.

I nod thoughtfully, turning back to the closet. Nothing else jumps out at me, so I cross to the doorway, but Lucas doesn't move. He's lanky, but somehow manages to take up the entire space, looking down at me with an expression I can't quite name. It's soft, but there's a flash of heat in his eyes. I stare up at him, not backing down as we hold eye contact. Time seems to stretch, each heartbeat feeling like hours.

"If you keep looking at me like that, I'm not going to be able to resist," Lucas whispers, low and raspy.

"Resist what?" I breathe, afraid to break the fragile quiet.

"Kissing you."

My eyes flick to his mouth, then back up to his eyes. The low ember has sparked to life, naked desire dancing in the steel-blue of his irises. I watch as the pupils expand, his nostrils flaring as he breathes deep. My nose detects pine smoke and marshmallows pushing to the front of his scent, and my mouth goes suddenly dry.

"What's stopping you?" I breathe, licking my parched lips.

The corner of Lucas's mouth twitches up in a devilish smirk, and he shifts to stand up straight. I have to take a step back to keep eye contact. He's a full head taller than my five-and-a-half feet, and the powerful set of his shoulders makes my stomach flutter. Lucas takes a slow step forward, as if he expects me to back away or tell him to stop. When I don't move, he moves into my space, so close I can feel the heat radiating off his body. I lose myself in the depths of his eyes, the way they dart around my face, gauging every reaction.

The tips of his fingers brush against my cheekbone with the lightest touch, and I can feel the slight tremble in his hand as he cups the side of my face. All the bravado of moments ago is gone, replaced with trepidation and excitement. I don't move, hardly even breathing as his face inches closer. My eyes slide closed, and I suck in a deep breath, taking the plunge as his lips brush against mine for the first time.

Every inch of my skin comes alive with goosebumps, and I drop the shirt, my hand coming up to cup the back of his neck. I've kissed betas before, but none of them have ever made the primal part of my mind perk up and pay attention quite like this. Lucas's other hand finds my waist, sliding around until I'm wrapped in his embrace. He pulls me closer, fingers flexing against my scalp.

The first brush of his tongue against my lower lip has me whimpering, and I open eagerly for him. He tastes sweet and smokey, like chocolate and gin and fire. He moans into my mouth, his hand sliding back into my hair, pulling slightly at the base of my skull. His kiss doesn't demand my submission like Rhett's, and it doesn't have the edge of feral need like Mateo's. His mouth moves with me, each of us taking the lead in turns.

When we pull away, both of us are breathless and I keep my eyes closed, head spinning.

"Wow," Lucas breathes.

I open my eyes and stare up at him in alarm. His face is bright with a full smile, one that makes him look somehow even more beautiful.

"I... I've wanted to do that for a while," Lucas admits, cheeks and neck turning pink.

My heart skips as my lips pull up in a smile, my face heating. "Really?"

Lucas nods. "Better than I'd hoped," he says with a chuckle.

I giggle, and Lucas leans in, brushing his nose against mine affectionately. "That's my favorite sound."

"What? My laugh?" I ask through my giggles.

Lucas kisses me again, hotter and more insistent this time. His hands tighten on me, and I moan again, molding my body to his as much as I can. My toes curl into the carpet, and I breathe his scent deep into my lungs. The smoke and woody essence of him makes my heart flip and turn, my stomach joining the synchronized swimming routine in my torso. Lucas stays close when he pulls away, forehead resting on mine.

"I changed my mind. That little moan is my favorite sound," he says seriously.

I can only laugh and kiss him again. When we pull away, Lucas laughs, and bends down to gather up the dropped shirt and hand it back. He lets me wander around the room, and I find a cardigan that smells strongly of Alexandra, cloves and orange peels with a hint of smoke. Lucas disappears into the bathroom for a moment, coming back with a towel. I stagger back as I inhale a powerful burst of Rhett's scent.

"We share a bathroom, and that's from this morning. I can get something of Matty's, if you want?" Lucas asks, eyes bright with enthusiasm.

I shake my head with a fond smile. Lucas smiles back, and he takes my hand before dragging me back down two flights of stairs and into my room. I can't help but laugh as he shoots me a grin before gathering up an armful of my discarded blankets. He makes theatrically exaggerated coughing and gagging noises before throwing the blankets on the bed.

"What are you doing?" I ask through my giggles.

"We have to get the blocker off somehow," he says before launching himself onto the pile of linens.

I roll my eyes, holding the dirty laundry tight to my chest and joining him. My breath whooshes from my chest with an 'oof' and Lucas rolls onto his back. My face hurts from smiling as I feel him wriggling like a worm all over the lumpy pile below us before he finally settles with his shoulder pressed to mine. With the clothes in my hand, the scent of the blocking detergent is much more tolerable.

"Jason's your little brother, right?" Lucas asks after a moment of silence.

I nod. "By ten months."

"Your mom's poor vagina," Lucas says with a wince.

I shrug. "When a wife is called upon to do her marital duty, she answers." I'd heard that line more than once after I'd presented as an omega, and it's never gotten any less stomach churning.

"That's... wow, that's fucked up. I'm sorry," Lucas says, letting out a low whistle.

"It's okay. They never said anything, but I think my parents were always disappointed I'm a girl. Being an omega helped, but only because they could trade me like cattle to the highest bidder," I sigh, staring at the ceiling, blinking tears away before they can fall.

"We should have traded. I'm the family disappointment for being a beta male," Lucas says with a dark laugh.

I turn my head and find Lucas staring at the ceiling, his eyes distant. He senses my gaze and turns to look at me. I get lost in the swirling depths for a heartbeat, my stomach clenching as his eyes flick around my face.

"Are you the youngest?" I ask, curiosity overcoming my trance.

"Yep," he starts, popping the P, "and an accident. My dad's an alpha and my mom's an omega, but they never bonded. Even after twenty-plus years of being together. My sisters had already presented by the time I came along."

I roll over to face him more fully, trying to keep the sympathy in my chest off my face.

"Did your parents have a pack?" I ask slowly.

"My dad had one, I guess. But he left with my mom and sisters while she was pregnant with me. They claimed it was because we were being offered military housing at a different base. My oldest sister, Heather, said the rumored real reason was because Mom went into heat out of nowhere and rode it out with another alpha from the pack while my dad was at a training thing," Lucas answers, turning to stare into the space above us without really seeing anything.

I frown at the distant, almost sad look in his eyes. I'm familiar with the expression, having seen it plenty of times on my own face. I sense there's more to the story, but I don't want to push right now.

"It must have been rough, dealing with three omegas and their cycles," I say, trying to lighten the mood with a chuckle.

Lucas laughs with me, but still doesn't look at me. "Yeah, it was the worst when they would sync up. I only remember it happening a few times before my sisters found mates, but it always drove my dad out of the house for days at a time."

"How old were you?" I ask, a little alarm coming through.

Lucas shrugs. "Eight? Ten, maybe? It was before I came into my designation, so it didn't bother me—"

"Who took care of you?" I ask, sitting up suddenly, eyes wide.

Lucas looks at me with confusion pulling his lips into a frown. "I did?" he answers, more of a question than a statement.

I stare at him, seeing a much younger Lucas, with untidy dark hair and chubby cheeks, limbs too long for him yet, alone in a house with three omegas in heat. He may not have been affected by the pheromones, but without his father there to keep other alphas away, it's a miracle he didn't get hurt by another alpha trying to get to the omegas. Not to mention having to take care of himself while they were lost in the breeding haze.

"Don't look like that, Lydi-bug. It's not like they were all the way out of it. It was more like they had bad cases of the flu. And I didn't have to do anything super intensive unless they were all down for the count, and that only happened, like, less than half a dozen times my entire life," Lucas goes on, his casual tone making me sadder.

For all my family's faults, I don't ever remember a time when an omega went into heat without a laundry list of precautions in place. My mother and father went away for the week, leaving my brothers and I in the care of our aunts and uncles. Once I started going through my cycles, I was told about the early warning signs so I could make sure I was brought to a safe location away from the pack—and the world, in all honesty. There was a cabin on Lake Pontchartrain that had been specially built to block pheromones from escaping, with super reinforced doors and windows. And I was never alone, usually accompanied by a trusted female beta from our church. The other omegas who'd mated into the pack always had their children taken care of by someone. Even if Lucas's father and mother weren't bonded, an alpha abandoning his partner and daughters and leaving them vulnerable seems almost impossible. Nothing and no one could have pulled my father away from my mother when she was in heat.

Lucas lets out a heavy sigh. "I think they never thought to shield me from the reality of their heats, because they thought I'd end up like them. I mean, the odds favored it. My dad always tried to nurture the alpha into me, but nature won out in the end, much to my father's and my mother's disappointment."

"I've never heard of a parent wanting an omega for a son," I respond, tracing a stitch in the bedspread under us.

"I think they were hoping for anything but beta. I'm ordinary. No extra special instincts or healing or compulsion powers. Just... garden variety person," Lucas says lowly.

I look over and he's watching my finger, his eyes distant again. I reach out and brush a loose curl away from his forehead, humming lightly at the delightfully soft texture. He looks up, and my breath catches at the vulnerability in his smokey eyes. I trail the tip of my finger along his temple, across his sharp, devilishly handsome cheekbone, and down over the Cupid's bow of his gorgeous mouth. His breathing is short and fast against my hand, and I smile.

"There's nothing ordinary about you, Lucas," I whisper.

He cocks his head as if to deny it, but I press my finger back over his lips.

"Designation doesn't define you. I think it's safe to say Rhett and Alexandra don't care about that. And I certainly don't," I continue.

Lucas looks at me for another moment before he smiles under my finger. My heart skips a beat, and I marvel at how truly beautiful Lucas is, inside and out. He's kind, funny, humble, driven, everything a good man should be. His eyes sparkle with wonder, like he can't believe I'm real, and I find that I'm wondering the same thing about him. He puckers his lips to kiss my finger before reaching up, taking my hand and lacing our fingers together. He sits up on one elbow, supremely at ease, as he just watches me.

"What? Do I have something on my face?" I ask, heat coming to my face.

"No, I'm just wondering if we're too old for a good, old-fashioned make-out session," he says, like he's just pondering what tomorrow's weather will be.

I giggle, face heating more. "We could always try it out, see how we feel?" I offer.

"Excellent idea, Lydi-bug. You're so smart," he gushes, smiling wider.

I laugh harder, only to squeal with delight as he pulls me down by my good hand, pressing his lips to mine.

Turns out, you're never too old for a good, old-fashioned make-out session.

TWELVE

Lydia

"AND HERE YOU GO! You're all set. Have a good rest of your day!"

The words are bright and cheery, but my smile hurts my cheeks as I hand the wrapped bouquet to the alpha on the other side of the counter. He nods absently, listening to the same phone call he's been on since he walked in and hastily picked out a seasonal arrangement. I watch his retreating back, the blast of warm air hitting me in the face as he storms out of the door.

I let my customer service smile drop, the one that never seems to reach my eyes fully but fools enough people into assuming I'm a ray of sunshine. Plopping back down onto the stool behind the checkout counter, I roll my shoulders, relishing the movement of my left one, despite the minor ache remaining. My cast finally came off a few days ago and, while I still have to wear a soft splint around my forearm and wrist, I can finally bend my elbow and raise my arm above my head again.

My head empties as I stare out of the front windows to the deserted patch of State Street, letting my thoughts drift as I watch the rippling waves of heat rising from the pavement. July is just past halfway gone, the time slipping away like so much sand through my fingers. The ancient air conditioning unit is barely able to keep the inside of Wila's cool enough so we don't lose our stock to wilting. If it gets any hotter, the geriatric machine may give up the ghost at long last.

"So what are your plans for your long weekend?"

I jump slightly at the sound of Gabby's voice, looking to find her sitting on the edge of the counter, her back to the door. She recently got her hair done, replacing the tiny box braids with thick silver dreads that bring out the cool undertones to her dark skin. Wila absolutely hates the color, but Gabby has always marched to the beat of her own drum. Gabby's apron is folded in half at her waist, showing off the toned strip of stomach exposed by her crop top.

I shrug. "Probably another weekend of hunkering down at Fort St. Clair," I drone with a sigh.

"You know, you could just stay here, say that I kidnapped you. I have an old magazine we can cut up for a ransom note. It would be legit," she suggests, nudging my knee with the toe of her sneaker.

"That's not funny, Gabs. Rhett would kill you, possibly literally," I retort.

"Murder aside, I still think you need to get out of that house. It's been forever since the last time we had a real sleepover," she whines, kicking her legs slightly.

"We had one before that wedding out in Waynesboro," I remind her pointedly.

Gabby rolls her eyes. "That wasn't a real one. We had to get up for work the next day. I'm talking booze, junk food, staying up till 3am, only waking up before noon so we can hit up a bottomless mimosa brunch—"

"You don't even like mimosas," I interrupt.

"I like anything that's billed as bottomless," she answers without missing a beat.

We share a laugh before falling into comfortable silence. I twist my lips to the side as I consider. I try to remember the last time Gabby and I hung out, just the two of us, with no obligation to do anything the next day. When I have to think back more than four months, I sigh. It has been too long, and I can't blame her for that. She's been there for me as I navigated the beginning of this uncharted romantic territory with Pack St. Clair, and many other crises before that.

"Next weekend. We're hanging out next weekend," I declare with a resolute nod.

"Why not this weekend?" Gabby asks, confused.

"Because I'm trying to be more considerate of my new roommates. Also, I think Rhett would have kittens if I told him I was just... not coming home for three days."

We laugh again, mine less enthusiastic than Gabby's. She finds a certain joy in driving my boyfriends crazy, but I want to make this work. Springing changes in plans on them would be a dumb move right now, with everything happening with Seth and Darren. The investigation into my stalker has not yielded any results, as we'd been informed that there was no hope for any conclusive fingerprint or DNA evidence. There was too much contamination, just from the other tenants, not to mention guests, maintenance people, delivery drivers, and who knows who else. It had been a long shot, and it missed.

Alexandra is doing her own due diligence, discreetly offering rewards in exchange for any security footage or eyewitness accounts that lead to a break in the case. But because of the time of day, the few businesses around my building weren't open, or didn't have cameras pointing in the right directions. And despite the reward being described as (and I quote) "more than enough to get someone to remember seeing something suspicious," not one person has come forward. She's not taking it very well, and has been throwing herself into her work, staying later and going in earlier for no real reason.

Seth has been far too quiet for my liking, and that unsettles me more than anything with the stalker. My gut tells me that everything at the beginning of the month was all designed to get me to miss that court date. Proceedings are public record, so it's not a stretch as to how he could have figured out what was going on. It all feels way too coincidental to me. Now that we missed our window, I'd expected the harassment to continue. But no one has seen spray-tanned hide or greasy hair of the skeezy bastard. It's only a matter of time before he pops up again.

We pass the time hammering out the details of our sleepover. It's fun, inane, and just the type of light-hearted banter I need in my life. If I stop and think for too long, all the craziness starts to sink in, and it spells a one-way ticket to an anxiety spiral. Gabby is in the middle of explaining why we can't use the pack suite at Wickland House–she doesn't want to think about which surfaces the pack has and has not defiled–when my phone buzzes in my pocket. Pulling it out, my shoulders slump as I read the new message.

Jason: Call me when you get the chance. We need to talk about something.

I swipe away the notification, not responding. It's been a few days since our fight, and I've only messaged him once when he threatened to get Rhett involved in our dispute, letting him know I wasn't dead, and I'd let him know when I was ready to talk. I know it's childish to give him the silent treatment, but so is Jason threatening to tattle on me.

"You know, he messaged me last night."

I look up and find Gabby giving me a gentle, concerned stare that catches me off-guard.

"Since when do y'all talk?" I ask harshly.

"For, like, years, babe," she says, like it's the most obvious thing in the world that my best friend and little brother talk to each other when I'm not around.

"What did he have to say for himself?" I ask, deciding to put a mental pin in this revelation and come back to it.

"Mostly, he asked questions about you and your guys. Are they treating you okay, what sort of vibe do I get from them, that sort of thing," she goes on, shrugging one shoulder.

As I consider her words, I frown. I'm not mad that she talked to him, more like surprised that she entertained his round of questions. She'd been justifiably pissed on my behalf when I'd told her about the conversation.

"To answer the question, I know you're dying to ask, yes. I gave him hell for being a bigoted piece of shit," Gabby says, speaking before I can even fully open my mouth.

I give her an appreciative grin, nudging her foot with mine. "Can always count on you to keep the alphas in my life honest."

"How you'd survive without me remains one of the world's greatest mysteries. Anyway, after I gave him the ol' what for, he admitted to acting like a complete tool. He just wants to know how to fix it," she goes on.

I let my head tip back to rest between my shoulder blades, eyes staring unfocused at the ceiling. I want to believe her, but nothing is stopping Jason from putting any of this in a text message and sending it to me.

"I can't say that I'm surprised he had a less than stellar reaction to finding out you're dating not one, but three dudes," Gabby says.

I blush, thinking of the hour I spent with Lucas in my nest, just kissing and talking and kissing some more before everyone came home for the day and we had to go upstairs and be social. He let me help him cook, if helping included handing him ingredients. It could have been patronizing, but it was honestly nice to feel included.

"I'm only officially dating Rhett and Mateo. Me and Lucas haven't really talked about labels," I grumble, looking away to hide the hot flush of my cheeks.

Gabby slaps the counter and shouts triumphantly before pointing at me. "I was only bluffing, but I fucking knew you and Lucas have something going on!"

Gasping, I whip my head around, mouth wide in shock. "What? No, I didn't—there's nothing—What I mean—"

Gabby cackles at my flustered stumbling, and I shove her lightly, my face hot enough to fry an egg. She wipes her eyes and I roll mine, huffing a sigh. Damn her and her overly acute powers of observation.

"So, come on. Spill. How big is his dick? It's always the skinny ones who are packing—"

"Gabby!" I hiss, looking frantically at the door to the back room and hoping like hell Wila didn't overhear.

"For fuck's sake! I'm growing cobwebs over here. The least you can do is give me a ballpark range," she whines, waggling her eyebrows suggestively.

I snort a laugh and roll my eyes again. "I don't know. I haven't seen it yet," I reply neutrally.

"Yet implying that you want to," Gabby presses.

I press my lips together, enduring a few more minutes of her needling as my imagination takes off. It's not strictly true that I've never seen Lucas's cock. A few days ago, I woke up from a mid-afternoon nap and went in search of Rhett and

Lucas to see about dinner plans. I found them in the gym above the garage; Lucas bent over a padded bench with Rhett absolutely destroying him from behind. Lucas caught me in the mirror, but I turned and ran before he told Rhett. I wasn't able to look either of them in the eye for the rest of the day.

So yes, I'd seen what sort of equipment Lucas is working with, and I can't deny thinking about it more than once in the middle of the night, when I'm alone in my nest. And those sorts of thoughts are definitely not the sorts I should be having at work.

I'm about to bring the conversation back to Jason when the front doorbell chimes, much to my relief. My eyebrows shoot up to my hairline as I watch Mateo dart in, closing the door quickly to stop the cold air from escaping. My mouth waters of its own accord at the sight of his broad shoulders stretching the material of his t-shirt in a way that defies physics, especially as it clings to his chiseled chest and stomach, stopping at his tapered waist. He's still wearing his suit pants and loafers, so he must have come straight here from work. I glance up at the clock, my brows bunching in confusion as I see it's still two hours until closing time.

"Don't look so happy to see me," he teases, shoving his hands into his pockets as he crosses the distance from the door to the counter.

"I am, but I thought you had a busy schedule?" I ask, looking back to his face.

Mateo's brown eyes dance with mischief, and my heart skips a beat at the boyish grin pulling at his mouth. He's up to something, and I can't help but wonder what.

"My last meeting got canceled, so I decided to swing by," he says casually, leaning across the counter to give me a quick kiss before settling back onto his heels.

I'm too stunned by his sudden appearance to give Gabby any flack for the stupid eyebrow waggle she throws my way before hopping off the counter and going into the back room. Mateo glances at her briefly before his attention turns back to my face. Once the door swings closed, he leans down onto his forearms, grinning again.

"That look spells trouble, I just know it," I say, only half teasing.

"Am I that obvious?" He laughs under his breath.

I slide off the stool to get closer, leaning down to get to his level. "Only a little. My first clue was you showing up out of the blue. No text first means I can expect the opposite of boring."

Mateo chuckles again, eyes finding mine. Even through the playful sparkle, the warmth simmering just below the surface makes him glow, and my whole body seems to perk up at the sight. His scent is bright and sweet, and just as refreshing as a cool glass of lemonade would be on a day like this.

"What if, hypothetically speaking, someone suggested getting out of town for a few days?" he starts, picking his words with care.

I hum in mock thought, but my stomach is already doing delighted little cartwheels.

"I guess it would depend on where the person asking wants to hypothetically go," I reply, playing along with his game for the moment.

"But where would the hypothetical fun be if the person being hypothetically asked knew the hypothetical destination?" Mateo returns, unable to keep the smile off his face.

"Then I guess if someone hypothetically suggested going on a hypothetical mystery road trip, it would be hard to hypothetically refuse."

Mateo's smile widens, and I can't help myself. I lean in and slant my lips over his in a short but sweet kiss. His hand comes up to cup the back of my neck, and I whimper softly at the first brush of his tongue on my lower lip.

"Ahem, my employee is still on the clock, boy."

I jump back with a gasp, whipping around to find Wila standing in the doorway with her hands on her hips. My face flushes hot, but Mateo only laughs.

"Any chance I could convince you to let her off a little early?" he asks, turning up the charm.

I glance hopefully at Wila's serious expression, but I can see the twinkle in her dark eyes.

"Not like you'd let her get anything done if she stayed," she says at last.

I grin widely before straightening. Wila steps out of the way, but I still throw my arms around her in a quick hug before dashing back to hang up my apron on its hook. Throwing my crossbody bag over my good shoulder, I double check that my cell phone is in my pocket before returning to the front.

"Thanks, Gran. If you want me to make up the hours–"

"Bah, don't even worry about it. I was young once, too, remember?" Wila says affectionately, giving me a sly wink.

"Was that before or after the invention of the wheel?" Mateo adds.

She lets out a bark of a laugh, but still flicks the towel in her hand at him. "Get out of here before I change my mind, boy."

Mateo jumps out of range, giving her an over-exaggerated bow as I round the counter. Sliding my hand into his offered one is as natural as breathing. Mateo parked out front, and I don't miss the small collection of luggage in his backseat. At least he thought that far ahead. Once we've pulled away from Wila's, Mateo turns to me with a fond smile.

"I think we should do something before we get too far out of town," he says, sobering for a moment.

I look at him with a questioning quirk of my eyebrow, and he sighs.

"Let's text the pack and let them know we're going out of town, but then we should put our phones on Do Not Disturb."

I purse my lips as I consider. After Rhett's reaction to me just going to work and not telling him, I'm hesitant to cut off contact completely. I won't be alone, which should help him cope, but I don't want to reignite that argument again. "What if there's an emergency?" I ask.

"I have Rhett's work number set to bypass the block, and you can set someone as the designated contact, just in case. But I want to spend this time with you, and not have to worry about the bullshit of the last few weeks."

And, my God, that sounds like the most heavenly thing. Just a few days where I can be with Mateo and not have to think about anything except enjoying myself. And being somewhere other than the pack house will be just the cherry on top.

"I'm going to let Lucas know to contact Gabby if there's a true emergency. And I'll tell her that if someone isn't dead or dying, then it's not a true emergency."

Mateo laughs as I type out the messages, and then with a resolute press of my thumb, I set my phone to silent and Do Not Disturb, shoving it deep into my bag. Mateo does the same as we stop at a red light. He throws me another one of those stomach-fluttering smiles, and my cheeks heat lightly.

"Let's blow this popsicle stand."

The sound of our laughter accompanies the squeal of his tires as we take off the moment the light turns green.

THIRTEEN

Rhett

I READ MATEO'S MESSAGE as I'm walking out to my car from the St. Clair Foundation offices, and I can't help the little growl that spills out of my throat. It's not the first time Mateo's gone off on his own, but this is not the time for his flighty behavior. I stew all the way home, getting more irritated with each mile.

When I walk into the house, the sizzling and popping of food cooking draws me into the kitchen. Lucas is dressed in just a t-shirt and jeans, minding some pans on the island cooktop. To my surprise, Lex is perched on one of the stools across from him, an open bottle of wine and a half-full glass in front of her.

"Did Mat text either of you?" I ask, the words coming out a little more harshly than I'd intended.

"No, but Lydi did," Lucas replies, not looking up from the pan as he flips the contents with one expert flick of the wrist.

"He's bolted again, hasn't he," Lex drones, the question sounding more like a statement.

"Yep," I say, popping my lips as I take a seat next to her.

"I wish he would stop fucking doing this," she goes on, taking a sharp swig of her wine.

"I don't know why you're surprised. It's not like he hasn't done this before," Lucas mutters, and I catch him rolling his eyes.

I want to argue, but he's right. After Seth used his heat to trick Mateo and Lex into bonds, there were stretches of days when I wouldn't see Mateo at all. He'd show up for client meetings and other work-related things, but beyond that, he disappeared. We were still dealing with getting Seth out of the Valencia suite where we were living at the time, and it wasn't until he moved out that I saw Mateo sleep in his bed there again. He would never say where he went during those months, but it took the public break up announcement, and the completion of Wickland House, for us to start seeing him around more frequently. And, if I were being honest with myself, he's spent more time with the pack since Lydia came into our lives than he ever did when Seth was around.

"I guess I'd just like to know where they went," I say at last.

"Why? So you can intrude on their private, romantic getaway?" Lucas returns with a teasing lilt.

I growl low in my throat, but he just shakes his head, completely unaffected. My nerves are frayed just enough that I consider punishing the attitude out of him right here, but I push that aside. For now.

"We looked into the tracker and it's a bust," Lex says with a heavy sigh.

Another thing to stretch my already paper-thin patience. Finding out that Lydia's car had been bugged was a rather unpleasant surprise. I'd asked the booth attendant from the parking garage near her old apartment if anything suspicious had been happening in the last few weeks, but it was a dead end. No one was seen wandering among the cars, or loitering, or taking weird pictures. And we know someone had eyes on Lydia's apartment, just based on that absolutely disgusting photo she received the night of the accident.

"Have either of you noticed that Seth's been awfully quiet? My team has been keeping an eye on his social media. There's been the usual slew of self-indulgent gym mirror selfies and brand deal posts, but he's not interacting with commenters or anything," she continues, taking a long pull of her wine when she's done.

"Good fucking riddance, I say. It's about time he stops trying to fuck us over and gets on with his life," Lucas replies, flipping the stir-fry again.

"I don't think we'd be that lucky. He's got to be planning something," I say, scratching at my beard in thought.

It is odd that Seth just so happened to fall off the face of the planet right around the time Lydia's stalker tried to break into her apartment. But short of hiring someone to follow him around, all we can do is speculate. And while I would do just about anything to keep Lydia safe, we don't want to sink to his level.

"And there's one more thing," Lex says, swirling what's left of her wine in a slow circle.

"You are just a barrel of sunshine and good news today, aren't you," Lucas says with an exaggerated sigh.

Lex growls at him, and I detect the change in her mulled wine scent, citrus coming forward with spicy arousal following close behind. So she seems just as ready as I am to teach our mouthy sub a lesson in manners.

"Toxicology report came in from the driver who hit Lydia. Originally, the police thought that he'd just been a drunk driver, not paying attention. But the report shows he had nothing in his system. He was stone-cold sober."

Now *that* sends a cold spike through my heart. "What?" I stammer, too stunned for anything more coherent.

"That's what I said. I even called the coroner who did the autopsy, just to make sure I wasn't reading the report wrong. But there were no mind-altering substances in that driver's system," Lex explains.

"Then there was no reason he couldn't have avoided Lydia. Witnesses confirmed her story. She was going ten miles an hour if she was moving at all," Lucas says, voice distant with thought.

There's a heartbeat of silence and then we all look up at the same time, the same stricken expression on each of our faces as we all have the same horrifying thought.

"He would have been able to avoid her, unless he didn't want to."

"That's... there's no way he could... have..."

Lucas trails off and I swallow the hot rush of anger that floods my system. There would have been no way to pick out Lydia's car from any other older model sedan in Everton, especially in the dark. But if someone tagged her car, say with a tracking device, then it would have been all too easy to be at the right place at the right time.

"We would have to prove that Seth is the one who put the tracker on her car, and also find some sort of link between the driver and Seth. If there even is one," Lex says quickly.

But I can already see the wheels turning behind her eyes. If anyone could make that connection, it's Alexandra St. Clair. I look at my phone again, hoping to find a message or call from Lydia, even if it's just to tell me she's safe, but I come up disappointed. Anger flashes through my chest for a moment, but I push it aside. She's safe with Mateo. I trust him to take care of her. She's going to be okay.

I jump slightly as my phone goes off in my hand, but my brow pulls down as I see 'Jason Anderson' appear on the screen. I consider not answering, but he may have heard from Lydia. Getting to my feet, I walk the few paces to stand in front of the picture windows overlooking the backyard.

"Hello, Jason," I answer, shoving the hand not holding my phone into my pocket.

"Listen, I know you've probably heard what happened between me and Lydi–"

"Yes, I have. And I hope this conversation isn't going to end with us on bad terms," I reply slowly and pointedly.

Jason lets out an irritated huff of a sigh. "I sure hope not, too. I do want to apologize for what I said. I don't know what she's told you about how we grew up, but Lydi and me... we weren't exactly brought up by the most progressive parents. I've been working on my own issues, but I know what I said wasn't right. It's not how I really think of y'all, and what you do with your life is your business. As long as Lydia doesn't get hurt, then that's all that matters to me."

I have to admit I'm impressed by his honesty and the sincerity of his words, but I don't let my guard down quite yet.

"I would never intentionally hurt Lydia," I say firmly, and I know he can detect the emotion in my declaration.

"I know that. You seem like the sort of alpha that I'd hoped she'd find. But it's my job to take care of my sister, ya know?" he goes on emphatically.

"I know. I have four sisters of my own to look after," I say with a little chuckle. If they ever heard me talking about "looking after" them, it might be the last thing I ever say. Still wouldn't stop me from trying, though.

Jason lets out a low whistle. "God bless your mother. But, hey, that's not why I'm calling. I can't get a hold of Lydia. Something's happened and I hope she's with you so I can talk to her."

"Unfortunately, she's not. She went out of town for a long weekend trip with one of my pack mates. I don't even know where they went," I tell him, my irritation rising again.

He lets out a colorful curse that makes me blink. I wasn't expecting this much of a reaction.

"If there's something going on, I'd have you tell me. We might be able to find a way—"

"Your pack mate, his name is Mateo Hutchenson, right?"

I swallow, my stomach twisting tighter and tighter. "Did Lydia mention him?"

"No. Not by name. I don't know if you've seen it, but my mother showed me an article about Lydia and Mateo."

I whip around to face Lex and Lucas, finding them both staring at me with confusion and a hint of apprehension in their eyes.

"Where did it come from? How long ago did she see it?" I ask, my voice shaking slightly as my mind kicks into overdrive.

"It was some gossip rag. The Everton something," Jason answers, trailing off in thought.

"The Everton Review?"

"That's it. My mother showed me the piece earlier today, and I've been trying to get in touch with Lydia all day."

Jason goes on, but I'm hardly paying attention. At the mention of the gossip magazine, Lex immediately pulled out her phone and started typing. Now she's staring at the screen with mute horror written across her face. I close the distance between us, and I can't fight the growl that bubbles out of my throat at the sight of the headline and the photos that accompany the article.

MATEO'S MYSTERY MAIDEN UNMASKED
Mateo Hutchenson is officially off the market. After weeks of speculation, we can finally reveal who has stolen the heart of our dear alpha. Lydia Anderson, 27, an omega from Louisiana,

has been spotted out on the town for the last few weeks with
Mateo, and it's clear that it's more than just friendship between
them. It's unclear how the couple met, but with Ms. Anderson's
work with Grandmother Wila's Flower Shoppe on State Street,
the two may have crossed paths professionally before crossing
paths romantically. Pack St. Clair has declined to comment on the
relationship.

Bullshit "Pack St. Clair declined to comment." I can tell by
the shocked expression on Lex's face that this is the first she's
hearing about this article. I watch the slow scroll of the photo
gallery that accompanies the damning piece.

There's another photo from the night they went to
Freddie's, this time in the lobby of Wickland House. Mateo
had Lydia pressed against the wall next to the bank of
elevator doors, his hands on her hips while her hands were
tangled in his hair. The angle isn't the greatest, but I would
be willing to bet a stupid amount of money that they were
kissing when this photo was taken. The second photo has
them seated outside of a café I don't recognize, laughing
and clearly oblivious to anyone watching them. There are
a few other snapshots of Lydia and Mateo over the past
few months, but the photo that makes my stomach turn
is the last. It's the most recent, taken within the last two
weeks. Lydia still has her cast and sling, and there's a hint
of yellowish bruises on her knees. They're walking through
a park, judging by the surroundings, Mateo's arm slung
around her shoulders while she looks up at him with a
familiar expression of love and amazement.

"You still there?"

Jason's voice pulls me back into the present. I shake my
head slightly, taking a step back from Lex while she slides
the phone across the island for Lucas to see.

"Yeah, sorry. You said your mother saw this?" I ask, trying to
get my brain to move past the blaring roar of my protective
instincts so I can actually think coherently.

"Yeah. And I'll give you three guesses to figure out who
showed it to her. First two don't count."

Fuck.

FOURTEEN

Mateo

"SAVANNAH?"

Lydia's confused question as I pull off the highway makes me smile. "Ever been?" I ask with a chuckle.

"No, not for personal reasons. I worked a wedding once, but we didn't exactly get to sightsee," she replies.

I glance over to find her staring out of the window with wide, excited eyes. Her lips are pulled up in a smile that I'm not sure she even realizes is there. She looks the most relaxed I've seen her since before the break-in attempt. The late afternoon sun brings out the red undertones in her hair and plays across her cheeks to make her skin glow. It takes almost all of my willpower to look away and keep my eyes on the road, especially with her floral scent swimming around my head.

"Does the pack have a hotel here?" she asks, turning to look at me.

I shake my head. "Lex wants to expand, but nothing has really jumped out and grabbed her interest. Because of the age of the buildings, restoration contracts are a nightmare to win. And we're not at the new-build stage of our business plan."

Lydia hums, and my heart melts a little. She has no practical knowledge of the ins and outs of real estate and hotel ownership, but she still listens with genuine interest whenever Rhett or I talk about our jobs. She'll try to ask questions and learn, and her interest means so much to me.

I pull off the major streets, heading for the coast. It takes a bit, but I find the driveway that winds its way through the patch of trees, lending privacy to this property. Lydia gasps softly as the house comes into view, and my lips pull up in an unconscious smile. Compared to the pack house or the other pack properties, this little beach house is tiny. It sits up on pylons, with stairs leading up to the full wrap-around porch. As I pull into the parking space below the house and turn off the engine, the sound of waves fills the air.

"This is incredible, Matty," Lydia whispers, looking around.

I chuckle slightly, my chest warm at the peace written on her beautiful face. As we step out into the warm, salty air, a refreshing breeze tosses the loose strands of Lydia's hair around her shoulders in a halo of blonde. I remove the bags from my trunk and lead the way up the stairs to the main level. Lydia follows, and we walk to the railing around the back. I open the sliding glass door and set the bags just inside before making my way to where Lydia stands at the railing. My shoulders relax as I look out over the water, the sky painted with the colors of the setting sun behind us.

"What is this place?" Lydia whispers reverently.

"My beach house," I reply simply, standing behind her.

Her delicate floral scent mixes with the briny air perfectly, and I press my face into the top of her head, my arms sliding around her waist. The warmth of her in my arms makes my heart skip, especially when she leans back into my embrace.

"Does the pack know?"

"No one but me, Lex, and now you know about it. Lex knows I have a house in Savannah, because it's technically a pack asset, but she's never been here."

We're speaking softly, the music of the ocean filling the spaces between our words. There's a distant call of seabirds, and the echo of a boat horn, but the world feels utterly empty and still.

"It's so… quiet," Lydia whispers after a long stretch.

"Like we're the only ones for miles," I agree with a happy sigh.

Lydia's shoulders rise and relax as she takes a deep breath, and we fall into silence again. This isn't my only bolt hole, as Lucas likes to call them, but it's by far my favorite. I bought this place shortly after Seth ruined most of Everton for me, using it as an excuse to be away from home for long stretches of time. Now I rent the place out for vacationers. I'd made sure the schedule was clear for this weekend a few weeks ago, thinking that it would be nice to have some time alone with Lydia after she settled into the pack. But after the insane couple of weeks we've had, this was a blessed relief.

Once Lydia turns back to me, I take her hand and lead her into the house. I flick on the lights of the main living space and feel at ease. The open kitchen, dining, and living room are full of worn, comfortable furniture, the color palette neutral and calming. There's a fireplace in the left corner, across from some stairs leading up to the bedrooms on the second floor.

The kitchen has been stocked with some basics, so Lydia and I work together to assemble a simple supper of pasta and frozen meatballs. We move around each other effortlessly without the need to speak, and I can't help the smile that seems permanently fixed to my face. Everything with Lydia feels so easy. We talk about anything and everything, laughing at each other's silly jokes. It's not hard to picture this five, ten years into the future. We'd come here with the pack, and maybe even kids. Lucas would complain that the kitchen is too small, but he would secretly love the challenge. Lex would curl up by the windows, and Rhett would be playing with the kids on the floor. Lydia and I would be in the thick of things, enjoying the time spent with all of us together.

"Penny for your thoughts?"

I look up from my plate to see Lydia looking at me, curiosity shining in her bright green eyes. I push a meatball around for a minute as I try to collect my thoughts.

"Just thinking about the pack, and us, the future, stuff like that," I say after a minute.

"Oh? Anything specific?" she asks, leaning forward to prop an elbow on the table and rest her chin against her fist.

I shrug, face heating slightly. "I guess I was just thinking about... what it would be like to be a family. To have a family."

She hums slightly, taking another bite of her pasta. It gives me a bit of relief that she's not rejecting the idea outright.

"Rhett would be a great dad," she says after a while.

Chuckling, I nod my agreement. "Have you ever thought about it? Having kids? Being a parent?"

Her face falls slightly and I almost tell her to forget I even asked, but she looks at me with so much emotion in her eyes that I can't find words to speak.

"When I was with Darren, my life was sort of... planned out. There's an old saying that girls like me, omegas like me, don't go to college to get a BA or a BS. We go to get an M-R-S degree. After I ran, I didn't think I'd ever meet anyone that would make me feel... would make me want that sort of life," she says, speaking slowly and picking her words carefully.

I reach across the distance between us, taking her hand and threading my fingers through hers. The sadness and pain in her voice makes my heart ache.

"My parents weren't as obvious with their expectations, but growing up, there was a lot of pressure to be a certain way. My older brother, Gio, he sort of set the mold for what I was supposed to be. Anytime I stepped outside of the footprints he laid, my life was miserable. So when I met Rhett and his family and saw that life could be different, my parents started tightening their chokehold on me."

I trail off as I remember those days, when my eyes finally opened to the abuse I'd been subjected to every time my parents thought I stepped out of line. The guilt trips, the gaslighting, withholding their love as a form of punishment. Having Sarah Cooper-Nolan in my life showed me how a parent is supposed to treat their child: with unconditional love and support. She never once hesitated in treating me like one of her own, and didn't even blink when I showed up on their doorstep with the three duffle bags that held everything I owned, heart in pieces after my family finally gave up on me and kicked me to the curb.

"Family isn't the people who share your blood. It's the people who are there for you when no one else is, who see all of your flaws and still stick by you. That's what this means." I break off, leaning back to tap at the spot on my ribs where the pack motto is tattooed. "Lex, Rhett, Lucas, and I chose each other, and we've chosen you, too. If family means half a dozen kids between us, or just the five of us sticking together until we're old and gray, then that's what I want."

Lydia gives me a watery smile and squeezes my hand once before letting go and turning back to her food. She's quiet for a long time, and I watch her as we finish eating and cleaning up the dishes. Her green eyes are distant, like she's lost in thought. I want to ask what's on her mind, but I can't bring myself to do it. As I'm setting the last plate in the drying rack, Lydia slides up behind me, pressing her face to my spine and holding me tight around the middle.

"Thank you for choosing me, Matty. For what it's worth, I think you'd be a great dad, too."

My heart does a series of back handsprings, my lips pulling upward into a grin. I turn in her embrace, wrapping my arms around her shoulders. She looks up at me with such open vulnerability and I can hardly stand it. I lean down and slant my lips over hers, not pushing for more than just a tender expression of how much her words mean to me. When I pull away, I brush a bit of her hair away from her face with the backs of my fingers.

"If it's something you want, I think you'd make a great mom, Lydia," I reply softly.

She leans into my touch as I cup the side of her face, her eyelids falling closed as she takes a deep, contented breath. She opens her mouth to speak, but then stops suddenly with a yawn. I chuckle and brush my thumb against her cheek.

"Come on, sleepy. Let's go to bed," I say, soft but playful.

She looks like she's going to fight, but thankfully, she relents with a nod. I kiss her hairline tenderly before extracting myself from her arms and taking her hand. I lead Lydia past the kitchen island, down a short hallway into the master suite.

The room is decorated in the same neutral tones as the rest of the house, but it still feels homey and lived in. I set the bags down on the bench at the foot of the massive four-poster bed, then turn to find Lydia looking around in sleepy wonder. She lets me guide her out of her clothes and into a tank top and sleep shorts. I try to keep my mind from wandering, but I feel a jolt run up my arm and straight to my cock every time my fingers brush along her creamy skin. The bruising on her chest is much better now, with only patches of yellow and green left. The bruising on her knees has completely vanished, and the stitches from the surgery to set her broken arm are healed, leaving only faint pink marks.

My stomach still clenches with rage when I see the scars on her stomach and the back of her left shoulder. The places where her ex tried to force a bond mark onto her. The marks on her stomach are no more than puckered lines of scar tissue and the one on her back is an angry red divot where the flesh was torn away, but the sight of them makes me want to join Rhett in his plan to remove that waste of oxygen from the world. He doesn't deserve to breathe the same air as my omega, let alone look at her or touch her ever again.

My omega.

The thought brings a surge of warmth to my soul that helps to quell the murderous intent in my heart. Lydia is mine, and I'm hers. I've known it for a while, but I haven't found the right time to tell her. She deserves so much; roses and candles and chocolate and romance. She didn't need the burden of my feelings when she's dealing with my vengeful ex.

When we settle under the covers, Lydia turns and lays her head on my chest, her injured arm draped over my stomach. I wrap my arm under her neck and behind her shoulders, pulling her close into my side as I lie on my back. She's so small and soft, her hair like strands of honeyed silk as it slides between the gaps in my fingers. Her scent fills every part of me, lilacs and lavender and vanilla invading every nook and cranny of my soul with light and bubbly warmth. The sound of her breathing is a lullaby, and I drift off as her little snores reach my ears.

FIFTEEN

Lydia

MY HEART POUNDS AS the front door of our apartment closes. My head still aches, and my throat is sore and bruised, but I'm alive. I look at the dent in the wall across the living room from me, the shape of my head and shoulders distinct in the plaster. I swallow with some difficulty, hands shaking as I pick up my cell phone and dial the only person I can think to help me now.

"Hey, Lydia, what's going on?"

Jason's deep, upbeat tone in my ear cracks the dam that is holding back the tide of fear and desperation that's been growing for the last week since the fight.

"Jace, I need help," I whisper, speaking still difficult around the damage to my windpipe.

"Whoa, what the fuck happened to your voice?" Jason asks back with a laugh.

"I need somewhere to go, Jace. Please," I beg, my voice cracking.

"Will you at least tell me what happened?" Jason counters with a scoff.

"Darren and I had a fight. A bad one. I don't feel safe anymore," I admit, my shoulders slumping as shame builds in my chest.

"Jesus, Lydi. I knew that guy was bad news. Have you called Mom and Dad?"

"Mom told me it's my fault. That I shouldn't have provoked him."

"Well, did you?"

The question hangs between us, and my heart breaks in my chest. Why would my little brother, my best friend, my closest confidant, even ask something like that?

"Jason, of course I didn't. But he hurt me. I need to get out of here, figure some stuff out. Please, can I crash on your couch? Just for a few days," I press, trying not to let the tears streaming down my swollen face come through in my voice.

"I mean... Allen and I have a party planned for this weekend. You sure you can't work it out until Monday?" Jason asks back, his voice full of hesitation.

I swallow my sob, pulling the phone away from my ear so he can't hear my whimper of pain. "I'm so scared, Jace. I need—"

"Listen, I have to get to practice. I'll call you later, okay? Try calling Sam. He might be able to help," Jason says, speaking quickly over me.

My stomach drops, the weight of his dismissal worse than every bruise and cut on my body. When I need him, my own brother is turning his back on me.

"Sure," I manage to get out.

"Sweet. Talk soon. Love you, Lydi."

Jason hangs up before I can even say it back. I break down into tears, falling to the threadbare carpet and curling into a ball. The world is too loud, full of slamming doors and shouting, fists hitting the wall. My phone rings, but I can't find it in the dark pit of fear and despair I've fallen into. Alone in the dark, waiting for Darren to step through the front door and punish me for trying to escape.

"And you thought you'd finally managed it, didn't you, petal?"

I sit up, the apartment lost in a sea of black, but Darren's slanting Cajun tenor fills every corner of the space. I spin on my knees, my eyes wide and straining to find him.

"But there's no escaping me. You're mine. And I'll teach you the consequences of letting another alpha touch what belongs to me."

I feel a hand in my hair a moment too late, and I let out a shriek when my head gets pulled back, my neck throbbing with the strain. I can smell the tobacco and clay of his anger, taste it on my tongue and in my mouth until I'm coughing. I struggle against the grip on my hair, but I can't shake him free.

Suddenly, I'm pitched forward, my face slamming into the hard ground beneath me. The crunch of my nose vibrates through my face before I feel the pain like a white-hot poker against my skin. I'm pulled up and slammed down again. Each time my skull hits the earth, the world erupts with sound. My vision blurs, my throat raw from screaming, and I try to fight as I'm forced to the ground again and again. Somehow through it all, I can hear him laughing, cackling—

"LYDIA WAKE UP!"

My eyes fly open, a shrill scream tearing free from my throat at the same time as a thunderous crash. I thrash as I feel hands on my shoulders, shaking me.

"You're okay, baby. It was just a dream. I'm here, baby girl. I'm here."

The hands on my shoulders pull me off the mattress and into a warm chest. I breathe deep, my lungs filling with lemonade and fresh grass. I feel the wetness on my cheeks, and I exhale shakily. My arms circle around Mateo's ribs, holding him tight as my entire body shakes. We sit for a long moment, a tangle of limbs and blankets, and the world comes back into focus the longer I let Mateo's scent surround me. The room echoes with the sound of rain hammering on the metal roof, along with the crash of waves in the distance. The room brightens in a flash of lightning, thunder crashing shortly after. I jump at the noise, snuggling closer to Mateo.

"It's okay. You're okay. It's just a storm," Mateo soothes, one hand rubbing up and down my back.

"I'm sorry," I mumble, my face hot.

One of his hands comes up and pushes my hair back from my face, tilting my chin to look at him. In the dim light, I can only see the sharp line of his jaw, the tousled hair falling over his forehead. His eyebrows are pulled down, mouth slanted in a serious frown. I try to look away, but Mateo's fingers under my chin hold me in place.

"You never have to apologize for your fear, Lydia. Not to me. Not to anyone."

My lower lip trembles from the intensity of his words, and another tear slips free from my eyes. Mateo leans in and gently kisses it away. I shudder at the warm brush of his mouth, Mateo purring in response. His fingers slide from my chin to cup the back of my neck, and I let him tilt my head back as his lips fit over mine.

My chest expands, filling with emotion as he kisses me ever so gently. His touch is tender, reverent. My whole body warms and melts under his touch, joy settling in every corner, down to my bones. My heart sings for him, so loud I'm sure he can hear it even over the pounding rain above us. I wind my arms around his neck, shifting until my legs straddle his hips. Mateo groans as I press my body to his, and I can feel the hard length of him through our thin sleep clothes.

Mateo moans my name as I kiss down his jaw, the stubble rough and exciting against my skin. His fingers drag down my back, his short nails scraping lightly. The world shrinks to the size of his embrace, nothing and no one else mattering while Mateo holds me close and secure. Every worry, all the fear of moments ago, is gone, replaced by light and heat and soul-deep want. I nibble at his neck, reaching back and pulling his hand away from my neck until it covers my breast.

"Please touch me, Mateo. I need you," I whisper in his ear, the desperate sound nearly lost in the clap of thunder.

"You have me, baby girl. All of me," he pants, squeezing my breast just how I like it.

I throw my head back as his other hand joins the first, a sigh of pleasure slipping past my slightly upturned lips. Mateo's mouth finds my neck, and the scrape of his teeth makes me shiver. The fingers of my good hand drag down his bare chest, and I feel the muscles twitch under my touch.

"Are you mine?" Mateo asks huskily against my skin.

The vulnerability of his voice shakes something loose in my chest, shredding my last thread of hesitation. I cup his chin with my palm, drawing him up to look into my eyes again. The bald emotion in the depths of his stare catches me off-guard, and I stroke his cheek with my thumb.

"Yes, Mateo. I'm yours. I... I love you."

There's another flash of lightning and a slow roll of thunder, and even the rain seems to pause as I hold my breath and wait for his response. I watch as Mateo's face cycles from shock to disbelief before settling on undimmed joy. His smile lights up his entire face, and my heart soars at the sight.

"You love me?" he breathes, words cracking even as his eyes glisten with silver around the edges.

I nod, afraid to shatter this moment with words. He closes his eyes and swallows before looking at me again.

"I love you, too. Lydia, I... I'm so..."

Mateo trails off as his hands come up and brush my hair away from my face before they cradle my head. His thumbs brush my cheeks, and I can't help but return his dazed smile.

"You are everything I've ever wanted, everything I never thought I could have."

Thunder crashes around us as he tilts his forehead to press against mine. The rain pounds the roof and windows, but I can hear him whisper over all of it.

"I choose you, Lydia Anderson. Yesterday, today, and every day until my heart stops beating. You're mine, and I'm yours."

When our lips meet, I can taste the salt of our tears of joy, mixing with his sharp ozone and tart lemonade flavor. He tastes like teenage summers: invincible and eternal. His hands are hot and insistent as we work to peel away our clothes until it's just skin against skin, the heat of his body penetrating deep to the very core of my being. And when his fingers brush against my slit, I breathe his name like a prayer.

His fingers slide into my aching pussy, filling me and stroking all the right places to make me moan and shake. His other hand finds my good wrist, guiding me to wrap my fingers around his throbbing cock. I work my hand up and down his length to match the thrusting of his fingers inside of me, settling fully in his lap as I rock on the waves of building pleasure.

"When I'm finally free to make you my mate, this is where I'm going to put my mark," Mateo says, words vibrating with his purr.

His hand squeezes my wrist, thumb brushing along the soft skin on the inside of my arm. I whimper as I imagine how his teeth will feel in my skin, and I swallow the urge to beg for it, even if I know he can't.

Seth forced a bond onto Mateo that he never wanted, and because Seth was Mateo's first bond mate, the law gives Seth the right of refusal on any future bonds Mateo may want. Seth would never allow me to bond with "his" alpha, so we have to wait until the courts grant a legal renouncement, which would strip Seth of his bond rights and let Mateo go free.

Mateo's tongue on the skin of my collarbone brings me back into the moment, along with this thumb brushing circles over my swollen clit. I gasp and arch into his touch, sparks flying along my skin. I feel Mateo's grin against my breast before he nips and licks at the flushed flesh.

"I want the world to see my mark on you, to know that a strong, beautiful, sexy fucking omega like you belongs to me."

I feel myself teetering on the edge of release, and I try to get Mateo's hand to move faster, to get his thumb to press harder on my clit. But his low warning growl makes my body go limp, even as I keep stroking his leaking cock, spreading his fluid down to where his knot is swelling at the base and back up again.

"And then I'm going to get your mark, whatever you want that to be, tattooed to match. And I'll wear it proudly, showing everyone that I belong to you."

A twist of his wrist drives his fingers deeper, and my legs shake as he thrusts hard, curling his fingers over my sweet spot over and over. I fall over the edge with a scream, my legs shaking and stars bursting behind my eyes.

"Watching you fall apart is the most beautiful thing I've ever had the pleasure of witnessing," he whispers, words heavy with awe and heat.

I hardly hear him over the pounding of my heart in my ears, the pleasure that seems to go on for ages as he works me down from the high. My whole body goes limp, and I lean my forehead against his shoulder, whimpering when he withdraws at last.

"Make love to me, Mateo. Please," I beg, kissing the juncture of his throat and shoulder.

He pulls my hand away from his cock at last, then lifts me off his lap for a moment, adjusting himself below me so he's kneeling. Then he guides me closer until I feel his tip brushing against my soaked, still fluttering entrance. We sigh in unison as he slips inside of my hot channel, the stretch of him the most exquisite pleasure-pain. When he finally bottoms out, and I feel the swell of his knot against my outer lips, we go still. I lift my head and touch his cheek with my fingertips.

"I love you," he whispers, nuzzling his nose against mine.

"I love you," I reply.

Our bodies move together, our limbs tangled as our hips roll and breaths mingle. Pleasure builds in my belly, liquid heat that spreads to every cell in my body. The air is thick with the scent of citrus and sex, the sound of rain and fading thunder. Lightning illuminates the room for a flash, and I meet Mateo's penetrating stare, locking eyes as we writhe faster and faster. The tips of his fingers bite into my ass, and I feel the flex of his arms as he helps me ride him.

"I'm close, baby. So close," he moans, dissolving into a growl.

"Knot. I want your—"

Before I can finish my plea, Mateo snarls and twists us so my back hits the mattress, my legs locked around his waist as he drives hard and fast. The gentle lover of a moment ago is replaced with the wild, near feral alpha that holds my heart. It only takes moments until the relentless tidal wave of ecstasy crashes over us. My walls flutter and I feel Mateo's knot slip inside and lock in place, swelling and pulsing as he coats my pussy with his cum.

For a long, breathless moment, we remain frozen in time. Then Mateo collapses down, resting his damp forehead against my sternum. I run my fingers through his hair, humming low in my throat. I haven't quite gotten the hang of my omega purr, but Mateo's shoulders still relax under my touch. He slips his arms under my ribs, and I bite my lip to hold back my moan as he maneuvers us around until he's flat on his back with me still locked around his knot. I try to slide to one side, but Mateo's hold keeps me from moving.

"I love feeling you like this, baby," he mutters, sounding half asleep.

"Crushing you?" I answer with an ironic chuckle.

Mateo's laugh bounces me, and we both moan as the motion sets off another wave of pleasure. When it fades, he presses a kiss to my hairline.

"No, safe in my arms."

SIXTEEN

Lydia

I WAKE TO THE feeling of Mateo's lips on my shoulder. The storm passed in the night, letting gray streams of watery sunshine filter in through the gauzy curtains above the bed. We ended up sleeping on our sides, Mateo curled around my back and his arms holding me tight. I hum lightly as he kisses my scar again, the horrible red oval from Darren's last attempt to trap me. I push thoughts of my past aside as I close my eyes again.

"I know you're awake, baby." Mateo's husky sleep voice makes goosebumps rise on my arms, and I have to press my lips together hard to keep from laughing.

"Nope, still fast asleep," I manage to get out.

Mateo growls playfully before digging his fingers into my sides, making me squirm and squeal as he tickles me mercilessly. He only relents when I'm breathless and teary with laughter. As I catch my breath, I turn onto my back and look up into Mateo's face as he leans over me. His hair is somehow perfectly messy, his soft brown eyes twinkling with love and playful affection. His perfect lips are wide with a crooked grin, the expression so natural and beautiful that I can't help but return it.

"There's that smile I love," Mateo coos, kissing the tip of my nose.

He swallows my giggle as he slants his mouth over mine, my head spinning and stomach dipping with familiar butterflies. I feel the brush of his tongue against my lower lip, the growing hardness against my hip, and the wetness gathering between my thighs.

That is, until my phone's ringer cuts through the still air.

We both look up at the sound, and my breath catches. I haven't checked it in almost a day, so I know it's still in Do Not Disturb. Which means that Gabby is calling, and that can't mean anything good. Mateo lets me up and I quickly find my bag and fish out my phone. It's stopped ringing by the time I pull it out, but as I look at the screen, my mouth goes dry. My notifications are a mess of missed calls and messages from Rhett and Jason, all variations on 'call me, we need to talk.' There are several missed calls from an unknown number, but that doesn't surprise me. In the age of robo-calls, it'd be weirder to not have those.

"What's the matter?" Mateo asks.

I look back at him sitting on the edge of the bed, concern pulling his brow down low. I bite my lip and shrug. None of the messages hold any clues, which only makes me all the more nervous. A new message from Gabby comes through as I'm clearing out notifications.

Gabby: Hey. Your brother and your boyfriend have both called me asking where you are.
Me: Did they say why?
Gabby: No, but they sounded seriously worried. Maybe give them a call when you've got a sec?
Me: You'd think if it were something life or death, they'd say something.
Gabby: Yeah, but still. I'd freak out too if you just up and left without any way to reach you. Smooth their feathers and then get back to boning.
Me: Ha ha. I'll see what I can do.

"It's probably just Nanny Rhett having a fit because he doesn't know where we are. Let's at least eat something before we have to sit through a lecture," Mateo says when I relay the information.

Mateo's casual response helps calm me a little, but there's something about this whole situation that nags at the back of my mind. Still, we get dressed and head into the kitchen, moving in sync while we throw together scrambled eggs and toast. It's a simple meal, but being close to Mateo like this, with nothing but the sound of the waves outside and our idle chatter, it's so peaceful and surreal. The tranquility of this moment is enough to push aside my anxieties and just be present, which isn't something I've been able to do for a long time.

After breakfast, I practically beat Mateo back with a broom to have a moment to myself to shower and freshen up. After dressing in a simple sundress, I pad out to the main living room on bare feet. The back door is open, and Mateo is at the railing, looking out over the beach and ocean. I slide up under his arm, which he automatically adjusts so I can snuggle into his chest. My phone buzzes in my hand, and I don't bother looking at the screen before answering, expecting it to be Rhett again.

"Hello?" I answer, trying not to let my voice shake.

"Lydia Marie Anderson, I cannot believe you!"

I flinch at the shrill voice coming out of the speaker, my heart jumping up into my throat. It can't be. There's no way.

"Mom?" I stammer, pulling away from Mateo's embrace.

Diane Anderson doesn't even slow down. "Of all the disrespectful things I've put up with from you over the last few years, this has got to be the worst one of them all. I thought I raised you to be better than this. Don't you have anything to say for yourself?"

Mateo looks down, hearing the shouting through the speaker. My whole body breaks out in a cold sweat, my hands shaking.

"How did you get this number?" I manage to croak through my suddenly bone-dry mouth.

"You don't get to ask any questions until you answer me," she retorts.

"I don't know what you're talking about."

"Don't try to play dumb with me, Lydia. I've seen that... *article*." She hisses the word like it physically pains her to speak the syllables.

"Article? What in God's name are you fucking talking about?" I shout over her, my heart rate rising to frantic levels.

Mateo turns and runs back into the house, and I follow, stumbling slightly on unsteady legs. I find the nearest chair to the door and sink into it, not trusting my knees to keep me upright any longer.

"Don't you dare speak like that to me! Darren showed me that gossip rag piece, the one with you and that Matthew Wilkenson boy being indiscreet in front of the Lord and everybody else. Have you no self-respect? No shame?" Diane continues, voice going from angry to indignant back to angry disappointment fast enough to make my head spin.

I can't get my brain to form words, but I hardly need to. She goes on, screeching about what the neighbors and the church ladies and God knows how many other people she knows are going to think, and how could I do this to her. Mateo comes back from the bedroom and holds out his phone for me to see. Everything seems to fade out, all sound muffling except my heartbeat as I read the headline and article from yesterday afternoon that outed me as Mateo's girlfriend. The photos that accompany the article turn my stomach, threatening to bring my breakfast back for a second appearance. The last one, taken when I asked Mateo to just go for a walk so I could get out of the house for one hour, shakes me to my core. It was after I'd moved into the pack house, and very well could have been taken by the same person who tried to break into my apartment.

"—lucky I haven't told your father about any of this. He's been so stressed with work and now his only daughter is going around, acting like the Whore of Babylon—"

"That's enough," I cut in when she pauses just long enough to take a breath. "I had no idea what you were talking about, but I found it. And you're acting like I was out flashing my tits on Main Street—"

"Lydia! This is exactly what I'm talking about. This attention-seeking, vulgar behavior has gone on long enough," she gasps, and I can almost picture the way she'd press a hand to her chest in righteous indignation.

"I'm not seeking any attention! These pictures were taken without my consent, and this article was written and published without my knowledge. This is literally the first time I'm hearing about it."

"If you weren't out parading yourself, then maybe—"

"Oh, for fuck's sake!" I shout, throwing the hand not holding my phone in the air.

"One more outburst like that and I'll–"

"You'll what, Diane? Kidnap me? Force me back home where you can lock me up and throw away the key?" I throw back, my voice cracking. I can't hold back the fear and panic any longer.

"Your father would have to make that decision. He's already upset with your lack of communication with your pack, so I don't think he'd disagree with me if he found out how disrespectful you've been. It's time for you to end this little tantrum and do the adult thing for once in your life, or have you not done enough damage to our family name?"

I drop my forehead into my hand, shoulders shaking as I try to get control over my emotions again. The disappointment in her voice cuts me straight to my core, and it's like I'm back there again. Back where she's convincing me to return to my abuser. Back when everything wrong with my relationship was my fault. Like this is my fault.

I'm pulled from my spiral of misery as Mateo's hand gently moves the phone away from my face and holds it out in front of him, where I watch him press the speakerphone button.

"I really think it would be for the best if you did some praying over all of this, Lydia. You've clearly lost your way and I'm sure if you came home and–"

"That isn't going to happen, Diane," Mateo interrupts, voice deeper and colder than I've ever heard from him.

"What? Who are you? Where is my daughter?" she squawks frantically.

"I am one of Lydia's alphas, and she doesn't answer to you anymore," Mateo goes on, low and dangerous.

I shiver despite myself as Mateo's claim makes my heart flutter. My world is falling apart, but hearing him stepping up and protecting me still warms my chest and loosens the tight knot in my stomach.

"Her alpha is in my pack, not some—"

"That piece of shit lost his claim on Lydia the moment he touched her without her consent, omega." My mother's protests are cut off in a choking sputter as the rumble of his growl fills the space. And despite the seriousness of this dire situation, seeing Mateo furious in my defense makes my lower belly clench.

"Now you listen very closely, Diane. If you or anyone else comes near Lydia with intent of doing her harm, Pack St. Clair will make your life a living hell. If you try to contact her again, I will personally destroy everything you hold dear. Do you understand me?"

The silence on the other side of the line is deafening, and only her harsh breathing tells me that she hasn't hung up. I look up into Mateo's face, but his eyes stay fixed on my phone, his glare molten enough that my mother could probably feel it four states away.

"We'll just see about that. You just give the phone back to my daughter–"

"Anything you have to say to her, you say to me first. I'm done listening to you abuse her." Mateo's snarl is soft, almost a whisper, but it's sharp enough to cut through my mother's false bravado.

"Fine. I'm going to be praying for her. For both of you."

The line goes dead before either of us gets the chance to respond. Silence descends, thick and heavy with everything that just happened. Mateo's breathing and my own little pants are the only sounds filling the room.

"I called Rhett. Your brother told him last night, and he's told Lex. They're trying to figure out what our next move is," Mateo says in a low monotone.

I nod and reach a shaky hand out for my phone.

"What are you doing?" Mateo asks, confused.

I don't answer, simply pulling up my brother's number and pressing the dial button and setting it to speaker. He picks up on the second ring.

"Lydi, holy hell! Listen, Mom—"

"Mom knows. She just called me," I finish, closing my eyes as tears form again.

"I'm so fucking sorry. I've been careful about not leaving my phone anywhere, but I think she got your new number from the bill," he continues, his frustration leaking through.

"She said Dad is pissed and might force me back home?" I ask, swallowing thickly.

"Jesus, no. He doesn't know what's going on. She's bluffing her ass off. Listen, are you safe? I called your boyfriend–well, *one* of your boyfriends–and he said you were out of town."

I look up at Mateo, who's staring at me with a question in his eyes. Taking a deep breath, I nod once.

"Hello, Jason. My name is Mateo, one of Lydia's boyfriends, and she's safe with me," he says with a little ironic chuckle.

"Oh, um, hello. I guess it's good to meet you. Were you the one in the—"

"Article? Yeah, unfortunately our pack is sort of famous, and the local gossip rag isn't bothered with things like privacy or ethics if it gets clicks and sells papers."

"No kidding," Jason huffs.

"Is that what you've been trying to tell me about? Mom finding out about the article?" I ask, unable to hold it in anymore.

"Sort of. Darren started acting weird a few days ago, and I overheard him talking to Sam about you. He's pissed, Lydi. *Real* pissed," Jason says seriously.

I swallow a whimper and ignore the phantom throb in my left shoulder.

"What exactly did he say?" Mateo pushes, kneeling down to be level with me.

"That some omega named Seth finally came through on his promises. He said this guy has been dragging his feet on his end of their bargain, but he finally came through. And now that he knows where you are, our father should bring you back so he can—"

"I can imagine the rest," I say, cutting him off with a shudder.

"He specifically said that Seth got the article printed as part of a deal?" Mateo pushes, eyes brightening and spine straightening.

"Yeah. Darren's not the brightest crayon in the box, and he admitted that he's been working with Seth to get Lydia away from his alphas. I'm assuming that's y'all?"

"Jason, I know we've just met, but would you be willing to speak with my prime alpha and our lawyer about this?"

I look up at the excited spark in Mateo's voice, head cocked to one side in question. But Mateo isn't looking at me. A smile splits his face, a feral, vicious grin that makes my heart skip.

"That's not Rhett?" Jason asks, confused.

"No, my prime alpha is Alexandra St. Clair. You'd be talking to her about what you've heard," Mateo goes on.

"Now that you mention the name, I think Rhett said something about her. If my statement can help keep Lydia safe, then just name the time and place," Jason says without missing a beat.

"Jace, I'm sorry—"

"No, Lydi, I'm the one who should apologize. I shouldn't have said those things. It wasn't fair and you deserve to be happy. If this pack makes you happy and keeps you safe, then that's all I can ask."

Jason's earnest tone makes my eyes burn again, and a single tear slides down my cheek as I blink. I wipe it away and smile slightly.

"They do, Jace," I say warmly.

I hear a faint beep on his side of the line, and Jason utters a colorful profanity. "It's Mom."

"Don't let her know that you've spoken with us. Lex will be in touch soon," Mateo blurts.

We all agree, and Jason hangs up, leaving Mateo and I in silence again. Mateo whips out his phone and starts typing away.

"Why do you want Jason to talk to Alexandra?" I question when the curiosity in my chest fills me to bursting.

"If Seth is actively working with your ex to intimidate you into leaving us, then he's violating the terms of our latest agreement. In exchange for us not telling the judge that he violated the stay away order, he was to leave you alone. He clearly isn't doing that, so it's time for us to show him the consequences."

Mateo's words come out in a rush, and I feel a hopeful little jolt run through me. Maybe something good will come out of this after all.

SEVENTEEN

Lucas

"Thanks, Matty. We'll see you tomorrow," Rhett finishes before hanging up.

Rhett flops back onto the bed, an arm draped over his eyes. When Mateo woke him up an hour ago and told him that Lydia's mother somehow found her new number, he was about ready to walk to Louisiana to have words with the bitch. I managed to get him to settle a little, but this most recent call seems to have finished the job.

"Mateo has the situation under control for the time being. They're going to come back tomorrow morning," Rhett drones.

"That's good. How's Lydia?" I ask gently.

Rhett turns onto his side to face me, and I frown at the stress that wrinkles his forehead. "As good as can be expected, considering everything. I'm going to try to get her to agree to personal security. I'd feel better if someone was watching her back when we can't."

"Just go easy, okay? Honey over vinegar," I remind him.

We'd talked about his frustrations with Lydia's independent streak, and while I know that he'll never be able to shut down his protective instincts, he'll do better to consider Lydia's feelings from now on. Rhett sighs and nods, and I scoot closer until my head rests against his bicep. I can still feel the tension in his body, smell the leather in his scent.

"Besides, if you don't, then I'll tell her all about those baby photos Sarah showed me on our last visit," I tease, running my fingers over his pecs.

I try not to laugh outright as Rhett growls. Like taking candy from a baby.

"You really want to learn another lesson, my pet?" he purrs in my ear, hand coming down to wrap around my wrist.

I hum like I'm considering his threat carefully. There's only a little soreness left from last night, and I can tell Rhett needs an outlet. He hasn't been able to play with Lydia since the accident, not in the way that they both truly enjoy.

"If you're up for it, old man. Don't want to wear you out," I say with mock thoughtfulness in my voice.

Rhett snarls, and I hide my smirk as best as I can. He isn't that much older than I am, only two years separating us, but it's still an easy way to rile him. Rhett finds my other wrist and yanks them up above my head, holding them down with one of his. I can feel the coarse hair of his leg against mine, the rising length of him against my hip. I stare up into that crystal blue gaze defiantly.

"Safe words?" he demands.

"Red to stop, yellow to slow down, sir."

The words are a reflex, so deeply ingrained in my mind that I can always recall them, even when I'm lost in sub space. Rhett's mouth twists in a little grin, and I try not to shiver. The gleam in his eye should terrify me, but all I feel is warm arousal coiling in my gut.

"Do you have to work today?" he asks, like he doesn't already know.

"Covering for Mackenzie at The Valencia. Couple of hours while she has a doctor's appointment," I reply.

"Good to know. Hope you weren't planning on sitting down."

My mouth goes dry, and I suck in a sharp breath, only to have the air knocked out of my lungs when Rhett's lips slam into mine. I can't hold back the shiver that runs the length of my spine as I taste the heady whiskey flavor of his tongue as it presses forward, dominating and demanding. I try to fight it, but his kiss is a force of nature. By the time he pulls away, I'm dizzy with want, my cock already hard against my stomach. Rhett stands, and I want to chase him, to pull him back down, but as I try to move, I realize he used my momentary distraction to slip a loop of rope around my wrists and bind me to the headboard.

Rhett chuckles as I turn my affronted stare on him. I wriggle a little, mostly for show, as he pulls the covers away, leaving us both bare. He lazily climbs out of bed and stretches, and I admire the way his muscles flex down his back to a truly delicious ass. He strolls away toward the bathroom, and I'm left trussed up and bewildered while Rhett heeds nature's call and freshens himself up.

I look back up at my wrists and pull experimentally. If I really wanted to, I could get free. That's just how Rhett plays. And the notion grows more and more tempting the longer I'm left alone and horny on the bed.

"If I come out there and you're not exactly where I left you, you're getting double," Rhett calls.

"Double what?" I toss back, half considering challenging him just for the fun of it.

"Isn't that the million-dollar question, pet?"

I freeze and consider my options. My eyes dart over to the chest of drawers in the corner that serves as Rhett's toy box, and my mind races through all the various implements I know are inside. He said that I shouldn't expect to sit today, so it could be the flogger, or the crop. Maybe even the cane. I could take double of the flogger, but the crop and cane would be a challenge. But where would we be starting at?

"Seeing your bratty little head turning over all the possibilities is so entertaining."

My head snaps around to find Rhett leaning against the doorframe of the bathroom, still naked. His arms are crossed over his chest, and I run my eyes from his feet, up his sculpted legs, over the Celtic knot tattoo on his right thigh, and finally landing on his cock. It's only half hard, but the size of it still makes my mouth water.

Rhett laughs low and dark. "Greedy little pain slut, aren't you?"

"Yes, sir. But only for you," I return, not even aware of what I'm saying while my mind is still running through the possibilities.

"Just for me? What about your Domina?"

I swallow at the mention of Lex, cock twitching. "Her, too."

Because she could push me to places I didn't even know existed before. Lex and I crossed all my previous lines, discovering new and exciting ways to please each other. I love playing with Rhett, but fucking Lex, or getting fucked by Lex, depending on her mood, is a horse of an entirely different color.

Rhett turns his back on me as he strolls over to his toy box, and I try to glimpse what he could be grabbing, but his body blocks my view. I settle back with a huff, which earns me a warning growl. Good.

"You know, this protective streak of yours isn't something I think I've ever seen from you before, pet."

Rhett's words draw me back into the moment, and I feel the heat rising in my cheeks. I don't answer, not sure where this is going.

"Have you been getting close to my little omega, pet?"

"She's not just your omega, sir."

I snap the words before my brain catches up, and I freeze. Rhett's back stiffens, and he turns slowly to face me, a few bundles of rope in his hands. My heart pounds with each deliberate step he takes toward the bed until he's towering over me. I can't quite read the expression in his eyes, but the hair still rises on the back of my neck.

"Have you fucked her, pet?" he asks, voice almost a whisper.

"No. But it doesn't—"

His hand snaps out and cracks along my thigh, the pain radiating up in sharp waves that make me gasp and my cock twitch and pulse.

"No, *sir.* But it's not your business. If she's willing, then—"

Rhett leans down and fists a hand in my hair, yanking hard enough to make me moan and gasp. He cranks back and exposes the length of my throat. The warm swipe of his tongue makes goosebumps rise over my arms and chest.

"Oh, pet. My omega deserves the best of all things, and if you aren't taking care of her, then it is very much my business," he coos, patronizing.

I can't hold back a bark of laughter. Found another pressure point. "What are you worried about, old man? Afraid that once she has a real—FUCK!"

Rhett's hand comes down on my thigh, harder than before, and I try to buck away from the sensation. I'm still panting when he releases my hair and grabs one of my ankles. I don't fight as he quickly and efficiently binds one leg, then the other up to the headboard, effectively bending me in half and leaving my ass, thighs, and cock completely exposed. I test the bindings and find them perfect. As per fucking usual. He stares down at me, head cocked a little to the side, brow furrowed. I sense the shifting of our game, and I nod.

"Lydia's cunt is as close to a religious experience as I've ever had. Do you really think someone as pathetic as you deserves to feel such bliss, hmm?" Rhett purrs, stroking the backs of his fingers up and down my slightly trembling thighs.

"I'd like to think I could rise to the task," I say, settling back against the pillow.

"Ya talk a big game, but words mean nothing. Can you prove you can please her? Be something other than a greedy, cum-hungry pain slut?"

"Yes, sir."

"We'll see about that."

I hear Rhett's footsteps as he crosses the room again, but I don't look. I breathe deep, closing my eyes as I shift to settle more comfortably in this position. Rhett's body heat radiates into my leg as he leans over me, hands rubbing my ass and thighs in deep, massaging motions. I moan despite myself, and pre-cum oozes steadily from my throbbing cock.

"You're so eager for the strike, for that sting, aren't you, pet?"

I nod, tensing for the strike that comes as expected. Pain blossoms along the curve of my ass, and I revel in the endorphins that surge. Another spank comes when I sigh and moan, refusing to give him the answer he wants.

"If you want to come any time in the next week, you'll answer me when I ask you a question, pet."

Rhett's warning comes from deep in his chest, and I try not to laugh. "Yes, sir. But if this is the best you've got, I might have to find someone else to really put me through my paces."

I don't know what's driving me to push him this hard, but the quick series of harsh spanks that follows is worth it. What I don't expect is the sharp sting and snap of leather across the flesh of my inner thigh. I gasp, my eyes flying open, and I find Rhett holding his favorite riding crop, poised for another blow.

"You're going to earn the right to court her. Prove to me you can please my omega," he says sternly, slapping the crop against his open palm.

That tone, that look, is exactly why I love Rhett. As much as I get on his nerves, he knows exactly how to get me back. I tilt my chin defiantly and take a deep breath.

"Do your worst, sir."

I don't have time to utter another word, only gasp as Rhett brings the crop down onto my inflamed skin over and over, each blow bleeding into the next as my body goes haywire. After half a dozen strikes, Rhett leans down and cups my heavy sack, the pleasure of his gentle touch making me shake and writhe.

"Absolutely pathetic," Rhett spits under his breath.

His disdain is an act, but my overstimulated mind can't tell. "More," I pant, not sure what I'm even begging for.

His fist tightens around my balls, pulling them to their limit. I try to arch, to ease off the pressure, but I can't get the right leverage. Thankfully, right when I don't think I can take anymore, Rhett releases his grip and strokes my neglected cock with featherlight touches. I let out a long, shaky moan, trying to thrust up into his hand.

"Is my needy little cock slut going to blow so soon? Just a few licks got you all ready to come in my hand?"

Rhett's taunting mockery sets my teeth to grinding and I shake my head. He brings the crop down harder and faster, and I feel my heartbeat throbbing in each welt. My stomach is sticky with pre-cum, and I have to focus to keep from crying out as I feel Rhett's broad tongue run along my cock from base to tip.

"Had enough yet? Going to beg for my cock? Beg for me to make you come?"

My breathing is heavy as I tilt my chin up to meet his gaze, mouth twisted in a smirk. I can feel the sweat forming on my face and chest, but the adrenaline zinging through my veins makes me stupid.

"Getting tired, old man?"

Rhett's growl is nearly feral, and it runs right down my spine to my aching cock. I lose myself in the next flurry of blows, only surfacing from the pleasure-pain when Rhett touches my cock, my balls, even probing slicked fingers into my puckered entrance. My skin is burning, but my mind only translates that as pleasure. I approach the edge of release time and again, but I'm always pulled back before I fall. The world falls away and I float, babbling responses to Rhett's degradation, but loving every minute.

I don't know how long I hang suspended in that place of warmth and tension, but the brush of Rhett's lips against mine brings me back down ever so slightly. When I open my eyes, I find him leaning over me, smiling fondly. I can feel his cock pressed against my twitching opening, and I whine.

"You've been so good for me, pet. Do you think you deserve a reward?" he purrs, pushing my damp hair away from my forehead.

I swallow with some difficulty, but nod. "Please, sir."

"Good pet."

One of Rhett's hands cups the back of my neck as he leans down and kisses me tenderly. The other guides the flared head of his cock to press against my hole. There's almost no resistance, but what little stretch there is burns in the best way. His thrusts are shallow at first until he bottoms out, where he pauses and lets me adjust for a moment.

"You feel so fucking good, Luc," Rhett pants, withdrawing slowly so I feel every ridge and vein along his thick length.

"Oh, God. I-I'm not going to last," I whine, words shaking.

Rhett kisses up and down my jaw, his facial hair adding that extra scrape to make me shiver. He shifts his angle, and my vision goes white as his head brushes directly on my prostate. I shout a curse, and he growls, picking up speed. Each slam of his hips into mine pushes me closer to that edge, but release still sits just out of reach. Just when I feel my eyes burning from frustration, Rhett sits up and takes my cock in his hand.

The first brush of his fingers feels like electricity over every inch of my skin. I clench and tense, and Rhett's hips falter from their steady pace as he curses under his breath. It only takes a few firm strokes until I feel my spine tingling and balls drawing up.

"Fuck, sir—please. I'm gonna—"

"Come, then. Come while I fill your greedy ass," he snarls through gritted teeth.

Stars burst behind my eyelids as a scream fights its way from my throat, and I feel the hot splatter of my seed against my chest. Rhett thrusts twice more, and I groan as I feel him swell and explode, his cum painting my insides. We sit for a moment, frozen in the receding waves of pleasure. I shiver and Rhett gasps as my muscles clench and release. When he finally slides free, I feel the trickle of cum as it drips from me. It's filthy, but I revel in it.

"Are you okay for another couple of minutes? I want to make sure—"

"Yeah, I'm good. Can still feel everything," I respond to Rhett's breathless question.

I can feel the burn from the crop returning with a vengeance as the pleasure of my orgasm recedes. Rhett pets my leg, kissing my calf lightly before climbing off the bed and moving away. He returns a few moments later with a damp washcloth and a jar of cream for the welts. As much as I like to think that aftercare isn't my thing, feeling Rhett's hand massaging my aching muscles as he tends to my marks and unties me is undeniably enjoyable.

By the time he's finished, I'm tucked under Rhett's arm as he holds me close, the tips of his fingers tracing nonsense patterns on my back.

"You know I didn't mean what I said, right? About you not being good enough for Lydia?" Rhett asks suddenly, his voice low and hesitant.

I look up at him, frowning at the troubled crease in his brow. "Yeah, of course. It was just part of the game."

"Right. I just wanted to make sure I said it. Because I do think you and Lydia... She isn't the only one who deserves the best," Rhett says, speaking more to himself than to me.

"Well, I'm not worried about that," I state, smirking.

Rhett looks down at me, blue eyes clouded with confusion. I stretch my neck and kiss him lightly, a smile pulling at the corners of my mouth.

"Why's that?" he whispers against my lips.

"We have you."

EIGHTEEN

Lydia

THE REST OF MY weekend with Mateo passes in an anxious blur. Mateo does his best to distract me, but no matter how hard I try, I can't shake the pit of churning fear that settled into my stomach. Knowing that my mother and Darren now have confirmation of not only my location, but my relationship with Pack St. Clair, scares me more than I can adequately put into words. During one of my more intense moments of panic, I called Rhett, and we talked through ways to protect me. When he brought up hiring someone to act as my personal security, I didn't hesitate to agree. It doesn't seem silly or overkill to have a trained professional watching my back when Darren knows where to find me, along with Seth and his groupies, all eager to make our lives difficult in any way they can.

On Monday, I finally got the all-clear from my doctors that my arm is healed enough to remove my splint. I'm still on orders not to do any heavy lifting or strenuous activities for another week or two, but being able to bend my wrist again for the first time in nearly a month feels amazing. Despite my appointment being in the morning, Wila gave me the whole day off, which is how I ended up sitting on the back porch of the pack house, staring out over the backyard. Alexandra is working from home today, shut up in her office, so the house is quiet.

And the quiet leaves room for my mind to spiral out of control. Every breeze through the trees makes me jump, my mind convinced that someone is moving through the underbrush. The sound of traffic is muffled, but now and then, I hear a loud muffler and nearly jump out of my skin. It feels like hours, each heartbeat stretching out and distorting until eventually I can't stand it. When I go back inside, a glance at the oven clock shows I'd only been out there for less than an hour. I sigh as I wander through the ground floor, stopping at the windows to fuss with locks and curtains, even though I know they are locked and drawn. I try to settle on the sectional in the family room, but no matter how I position myself, I can't find a place that feels right. My feet take me through the kitchen, and I'm hardly aware of my hands straightening gadgets and wiping away nonexistent crumbs.

My head is full and empty all at once. My thoughts move so fast that I can't pin down any of the distinct threads, leading to a constant anxious drone in my ears. If I focus on it for too long, my heart kicks in my chest. I don't feel shaky or weepy, just unsettled. I meander through the butler's pantry into the formal dining room, eyes darting to the windows at the slightest hint of movement. I straighten the chairs until everything is even around the massive dark wood table, but the grandfather clock in the next room makes my skin jump with each deep tick.

Keeping my hands and feet busy seems to help, so I move from room to room, straightening pillows and dusting already immaculate surfaces. The chairs in the dining room seem to drift out of alignment and I have to start again. I'm in the middle of adjusting the placement of knickknacks in the formal sitting room when Alexandra's voice rings out through the space.

"Lydia, can you come in here, please?"

My stomach drops and swoops at the soft lilt of her words, even as my spine straightens. I scurry across the foyer to the double doors of her office, one of which is ajar. When I slip inside, I find her sitting behind her massive wood desk, eyes darting back and forth as she reads something on her computer screen. I close the door softly, dread filling my chest with each passing moment. Why does it always feel like I've been called into the principal's office when I talk to her?

She looks up at the sound of the latch, her face calm but otherwise unreadable. She motions to the chair in front of her desk. "Sit and talk with me for a moment, sweetness?"

I blink, unable to do anything except nod and shuffle across the room and lower myself cautiously into the leather chair. It's more comfortable than any office chair I've ever sat in, and I have to fight to keep myself from sinking into the cushions. I pull the sleeves of my hoodie down over my hands, toying with the cuffs as I wait for her to speak.

"I'd like to do something that I think might help with where your head's at right now, but we need to have a discussion first," she starts, leaning back and crossing one trousered leg elegantly over the other.

I look up at her curiously, my face growing warmer. Her hazel eyes are laser focused on my every move, and I'm not sure if I'd even feel this exposed if I was naked. I nod again, not trusting my voice right now.

"When you and Rhett began your dynamic, you discussed limits, and what sorts of things you are into, correct?" she asks.

My spine straightens and my jaw falls open slightly, taken completely aback by not only her casual tone, but nonchalant discussion of kink and sex. The anxious buzzing in my mind disappears, replaced with the pounding of my heart in my ears. Alexandra doesn't move or speak, waiting for me to answer. I clear my throat and look back to the worn edges of my sleeves.

"Yeah—yes, ma'am. We did discuss those things," I manage to force out, eternally grateful that I didn't squeak or stumble over the words.

"Look at me when I'm speaking to you, sweetness," Alexandra commands, voice dropping to a sultry purr.

Before I'm conscious of making the choice to move, my head snaps up and eyes lock onto her hazel orbs. I suck in a sharp inhale through my nose, and my mind spirals as the warm, spicy mulled wine scent of her fills the air. My thighs clench together, and it's a fight to stay still and not squirm to relieve the sudden pressure in my lower belly.

"Good girl. Now, I hope you don't mind, but Rhett has told me of your limits. Degradation is a hard no, as is saliva, and you need to have a means of control if someone has their hands in your hair. Have you found any new limits since that talk?"

My stomach flips under her praise, so much so that I almost look away to hide my blush before remembering myself and maintaining eye contact. My hands tighten and relax in my lap, but I can't get them to stop.

"Not-not that I can think of. Do you use the same safe words?" I ask, picking my words carefully.

Alexandra cocks her head to the side as she considers the question, and I swallow, trying to ease the dryness just a little. But all the excess moisture in my body has migrated to pool between my thighs.

"If it makes you more comfortable, we can use the traffic light system. It's been a moment since I've used them, but I'll make sure to be aware of that for you," she answers resolutely.

I furrow my brow in confusion. "I thought you and Lucas..." I trail off as I catch myself in my curiosity. Their relationship is their business, and I shouldn't pry.

Alexandra chuckles lowly, smirking. "Oh, Lucas and I certainly do play our little games. As part of our negotiations, he surrendered his safe words. But I have absolutely no expectations for you to do such a thing at this point in your journey."

"I... I don't know if I ever could," I mumble, looking down at my hands, my nail beds white from how hard I'm clenching around the material of my hoodie.

"And that's perfectly fine. I don't want you to compare yourself to anyone. Whatever we do, whatever type of dynamic forms between us, is ours, completely unique and beautiful," she soothes.

I nod, the muscles in my arms starting to relax, even as my heart races. I don't speak, trying to keep my imagination from zooming off into outer space. The silence creeps in again, and I have to count my inhales and exhales to stop from fidgeting.

"I do want you to know something about me, Lydia," Alexandra says seriously.

I look up again and find her leaning forward, elbows resting on the edge of her desk as she clasps her hands. I wait, catching myself before I move too far forward.

"Your play with Rhett has been structured and controlled, with plenty of protocols and rules. I can sense that you need that from him; a way to let go and just feel without having to think. With me, you'll get a different sort of escape. I want you to give in to your primal instincts, to have no shame in being what nature made you to be. Is that something you would be interested in exploring with me?"

I gasp aloud, my entire body tingling with awareness as I listen to her voice morph from the sophisticated, polished cadence I know into something entirely more... feral. Her pitch drops, her accent making the words that on their own wouldn't be all that scandalous into something decadent and filthy. There's a subaudible rumble that travels from my core, up my spine, and into the deepest part of my nature. The part that sees the apex predator wrapped in designer silk and wants me to throw myself at her mercy.

"I—I've never done anything like this before," I stutter once I've gained some semblance of control over myself.

"Primal play?" Alexandra asks curiously.

I shake my head. "I've never... been with a girl—a woman before," I admit, voice dying to an embarrassed mumble as I tear my eyes from hers.

I expected more silence, but Alexandra laughs, a light, cheerful sound that makes my stomach flutter. "That's not a problem, sweetness. I'm happy to help you learn and explore."

And why does such a simple sentence set my skin alight, making me both nervous and aroused at the same time?

"For today, what I want you to do is very simple, and won't involve anything sexual," she continues.

The fire in my gut banks with disappointment, though I shove that feeling aside for examination later. I nod, moving to the edge of my seat. I try not to seem too eager, but right now, I'm willing to try anything she asks.

Alexandra's smile is serene, but my primal mind senses something almost dangerous on the edge of it. She motions me forward with a single crook of her finger, and like a puppy on a leash, I obey. I round the desk and stop as I see a padded mat and a foam block on the floor beside her chair.

"You are to sit for me and follow my instructions. Can you do that for me, sweetness?" she prompts, voice almost a coo, but too sharp for something so tender.

"Yes, ma'am," I whisper automatically.

She gives me a moment to find a comfortable position, and I settle on the waiting pose Rhett taught me. I use the block to make sitting back on my heels more comfortable, spreading my knees slightly for balance and letting my spine settle into a natural, but straight position. My head rests at the top of my spine, chin up but eyes lowered, and my hands come to rest palms up on my thighs.

"Rhett has you well trained. And don't you look like the prettiest picture of submission," Alexandra sighs.

I resist the urge to smile or preen under her praise, but when her hand comes down and I feel her fingers in my hair, I breathe deep, leaning into the touch. She indulges me with a few more long strokes, and it's all I can do not to whine at the loss of contact when she pulls away.

"I'm going to ask you some questions, and you're not going to think, just answer. Do you understand?"

Her voice has that low rumble again. Not a bark, but something that reaches the same instinctual part of me like nothing I've ever experienced before. So, it's easy to keep my eyes closed and nod.

"You've been pacing the house today. Why?"

My heart thumps hard against my ribs, all the anxiety I'd forgotten about rushing forward again like a tidal wave. I whimper and duck my chin, acting on that pull in my chest.

"Scared. He could be out there, waiting for me," I whisper, a lump forming in my throat as my eyes burn.

"I'll always protect you, my lovely. You're safe with me, and my pack. No one is going to hurt you again."

That rumble cuts through all other noise, and the world goes quiet. My primal mind instinctively recognizes the truth and honesty in the words, and peace fills the spaces of my thoughts, pushing out all other doubts. My hands come up, searching, pawing at the air. Until I feel soft, expensive linen, and I latch onto it.

"He hurt me; he wants to hurt me again. And now..." The words tumble out, and I don't know if I could stop them if I tried. I'm leaning into where my hands hold tight to the fabric, pathetic whimpers coming from my throat as I sink somewhere deep into my mind. Scents become stronger, and I taste mulled wine on my tongue more than I smell it. Her fingers are back in my hair, brushing stray locks away from my face. Her other hand loosens my grip on the fabric. Warmth surrounds me, and I feel a weight settle over one shoulder.

"I've got you, my lovely little omega. You're here with me, and I'm going to take care of you. Just stay right here, where you belong," she purrs, all softness and gentle touches.

Her hand in my hair guides me to rest my cheek on something warm and soft, smelling strongly of citrus and something more, but she stops me from nuzzling closer to investigate. Instead, I let my head loll back, exposing my throat and letting her move me. Eventually, I settle, sitting on my hip with one hand holding on to her leg, judging by the ankle bone under my thumb. My other arm is tucked against my chest, held in place by whatever is weighing down my shoulder.

I'm floating, feeling more like a passenger in my body as my instincts drive me to let this alpha care for me, to keep me warm and safe. She smells like Christmas Eve, spices and sweetness and anticipation. Her touch trails along my scalp, a single finger tracing from the top of my head, down over my temple, along my throat and back again.

"What are your safe words, sweetness?" the alpha asks.

I whimper, turning my head to seek out more of her, but a short growl freezes me in place. I don't want to leave this place, where everything feels right and I'm safe. Two words float up from below, and I whisper them before they drift away.

"Red. Yellow."

"Very good girl. You're so good for me, doing what I ask. But it's time to come back, my lovely."

I whine, shaking my head. Another correcting growl, and I tuck my chin. She soothes me with more light touches, and I melt.

"Remember this and keep it with you, sweetness: I claim you, Lydia Anderson. You belong to me, and I will always take care of what's mine."

I like it when you take care of me.

The thought floats past me, and I use it to help find my way back into the driver's seat. I keep my eyes closed, but more of my surroundings come into focus. And with no small amount of horror, I become acutely aware that I'm sitting between Alexandra's thighs. My head is positioned in such a way that, if I turned 180 degrees, I'd be diving face-first into the apex. My good hand is under the material of her pants of the leg I'm leaning on, clutching her skin halfway up her shapely calf. Her other leg, to my astonishment, is over my shoulder, holding me in place.

I clear my throat and take a slow, deep breath, my face heating steadily as Alexandra's laugh fills the air above me.

"Now that I have your undivided attention, I did want to talk to you about plans for your safety going forward," she says through her chuckles.

Not really in a position to argue—and also lacking any desire to change positions—I simply nod, trying to ever so subtly move my head away from her incredibly distracting warmth. But now that she's found my weakness, she uses those crafty fingers to scritch at my scalp and lure me back to where she wants me.

"I found a security officer who I think will be a good fit. His name is Caleb Novak, and his resume is impressive. He's an alpha, but he's bonded, so he's got experience with omegas. I explained the situation when I spoke to him earlier, and he knows what he's getting into. What do you think?" she asks, back to that casual tone.

I swallow and consider for a moment. "If you think he'll be the best one for the job, then I believe you. I trust you."

Alexandra is quiet for a moment, fingers idly playing with my hair, twisting a strand around one finger. I'm about to apologize and try to explain, but then I feel her shift above me a moment before her lips brush against my hairline. I'm too stunned to speak or move, but my whole body goes hot.

"Thank you, Lydia. That means more than you realize."

I open my mouth to question that, but the sound of an engine outside and the garage door opening makes us both jump. And it's with more reluctance than I'd ever admit to feeling that I untangle myself from her embrace.

Nineteen

Lydia

THE NEXT DAY, I'M waiting with Rhett in the driveway of the pack house. Everyone else is getting ready for the day inside, but I have to leave early to get to work. I feel a little silly, like a child waiting to be picked up for school, and in some ways, I am. I'd let Wila know that Caleb would be with me for the foreseeable future, but I'm still nervous. Old fears about alphas have been bubbling to the surface, but I do my best to push them aside. If Pack St. Clair has taught me anything, it's that there are good alphas out there. I just have to hope that Caleb is one of them.

"If anything happens today, please let me know. Mr. Novak is going to give reports to Lex, but I want to know if anything about this arrangement makes you uncomfortable," Rhett says, going over the same point he's made probably a dozen times since we woke up this morning.

I nod, biting back my sarcastic remark. My eyes snap to the hedge row down the street as a breeze shifts, my body tensing then relaxing as I realize no one is there. I swallow a yawn, taking a long drag of my coffee. Despite the scent-blocking detergent smell finally dissipating from my room, I'm still not sleeping well. Dreams of old fights and running through the dark wake me up multiple times a night, and I always have trouble sleeping after. The pack is giving me space to sleep on my own, but I'm still not familiar enough with my room to not panic slightly when I wake up from those nightmares.

Thankfully, before I can wander too far down that mental rabbit hole, a big black SUV rounds the corner and slows to pull into the driveway, stopping smoothly in front of Rhett and me. The warmth and weight of Rhett's hand settles on my lower back, and I take a step closer to him. The driver steps out and rounds the front of the SUV, stopping a few feet away. I blink, taking him in from head to toe.

I expected someone built like a bouncer at a nightclub, or even Seth, with muscles on muscles and enough bulk to stop an oncoming car. But the alpha before me is considerably trimmer, more like Mateo or Rhett. Athletic but not bulging. He's tall, with a well-proportioned torso and legs. He's dressed in business casual, and I spot the outline of some sort of harness under his suit jacket. His hair is a dusty brown, close cropped in the standard military cut I've seen on Adam before. His eyes are hidden behind sunglasses, but I can almost feel his assessing gaze on me.

"Are you Caleb Novak?" Rhett asks after clearing his throat.

The alpha, Caleb, turns his attention onto Rhett and simply nods. There's another tense moment of silence, and I take a deep breath. It's then that I finally catch Caleb's scent, and I try not to visibly melt. There's a sharp, woody note, like cedar or fir, mellowed out by the potent mix of snickerdoodle cookies.

"Well, if you're done with your staring contest, I'm going to be late," I say with a little laugh, trying to break the tension.

Rhett looks down at me, his hand tightening on my lower back for a moment before he nods. Before I can stop him, he leans down and kisses me soundly. I can't stop the soft moan that escapes my throat, but I pull away before I forget myself.

"Be good, little one," Rhett purrs against my lips.

"Yes, sir." I giggle and step out of his embrace, heading toward the SUV.

Caleb makes a move to open the back door, but I step around him, climbing up into the front passenger seat. I hear a few chuckles before I close the door. By the time Caleb is back in the driver's seat and we're pulling out of the pack house driveway, Mateo's on the porch, waving.

"So, you're Lydia, then?"

I turn at the sound of Caleb's voice in the silence. There's a hint of an eastern European accent of some kind, but I can't tell exactly where it's from. "And you're Caleb. Is snickerdoodle—"

"Sylvie, my mate, yes. You've got a sharp nose," Caleb says with a deep chuckle.

I smile a little at the praise, already liking him. There's something about the way he speaks, the calm, confident way he holds himself that my primal mind recognizes instinctually as safe.

"I'd prefer if you rode in the backseat, you know," he goes on.

I chew my lower lip. "I-I need to be up front."

Ever since the accident, not being able to see the road properly has become one of my triggers. I've tried riding in the back with Mateo and Lucas before, and it only ended with me in a panic attack. I haven't been able to work myself up to driving, but being able to be in a car at all feels like victory enough for the time being.

Caleb glances at me out of the corner of his eye before turning back to the road. I notice then how smooth his turns are, how vigilant he is to everything going on. He looks in the mirrors nearly as often as I do, constantly on guard.

"Your file said you'd been in an accident, and I saw the newspaper write up about it. Did they ever figure out how the guy didn't see you?" Caleb asks, genuine curiosity shining in his voice.

I swallow and shake my head. "He was DOA, I guess. Alexandra—Ms. St. Clair has her team trying to figure out where he came from. The traffic cam footage is a dead end. Just him sitting parked on a neighborhood street for an hour before taking off and..."

I trail off, feeling sweat slide down my spine. I tuck my hands under my thighs, digging my nails into the backs to help focus on something other than sounds of the engine, and my own heartbeat.

"When I was overseas, my convoy hit an IED, and it flipped my squad's Humvee. I couldn't stand being inside enclosed spaces for months. So if you need to ride up front, then that's fine."

As we come to a smooth stop at a traffic light, I look up at him, finding him smiling down at me. The expression helps me relax, and I sink back into the seat, watching out of the windows in silence for the rest of the ride to Wila's. I direct him to park in the back in my usual spot, finishing the rest of my coffee in one long pull. Caleb climbs out and rounds the car, opening my door before I even get my seat belt unfastened. I smile shyly as I slide to the ground, my shoes crunching on the loose stones of the worn pavement. Up close, his wood and cookie scent is stronger, and I try not to lean in. There's something about that combination that just makes me want to be closer and bask in it, but I have to remind myself that he's bonded and that would be wildly inappropriate. I scurry away before I can give in to my weird impulse, Caleb hot on my heels.

When I open the back door, the usual classic rock radio station fills the air, and I sigh. My life might be in total upheaval, but some things never change. I hang up my bag and slip on my apron before moving into the workroom. Wila is bent over a table, counting out the boxes from our most recent delivery.

"I finally have all of my limbs again, Gran," I announce proudly.

"Good. Just in time for—hello, who is that?"

Wila turns and then stops short, looking over my shoulder. I turn to find Caleb standing within arm's reach, looking around and taking everything in with a serious expression.

"Gran, this is Caleb, my new bodyguard? Is that what I call you?" I say, turning my statement into a question.

Caleb nods. "You can call me your detail, if you prefer."

"Is he going to be with you all the time?" Wila asks, drawing my attention back to her.

I shrug. "I think so. At least until this whole situation with Seth goes away."

"Well, then. We've got work to do. This all needs to be unpacked and put up in the cooler, so get going on that while I get the front of the store opened," Wila orders, straightening her shoulders and starting toward the door. "And don't you go lifting anything crazy. I don't need you out of commission again. So you help her if she needs it, boy."

My jaw drops a little as Wila turns her fierce gaze onto Caleb, who looks just about as taken aback as I feel. Wila's no-nonsense attitude shouldn't be such a shock at this point, but she just met Caleb, and she's already treating him like an employee. Neither Caleb nor I have time to object as Wila storms from the room, rounding the corner to the back stairwell where, moments later, a string of particularly colorful curses and threats are shouted at Gabby. Caleb looks back to me, and I can only shrug before unboxing the deliveries.

About a half hour later, I hear footsteps on the stairs a moment before Caleb. He's been standing close to me, careful not to get in my way as I move between the main worktable and the cooler. The telltale cloud of Gabby's scent floats in and I smile to myself, continuing to work. But Caleb moves to put himself between me and the open doorway to the hall.

"Oh, no. That's not—"

"Babe, if Gran gets any grouchier, I'm going to put her ass in a ho—HOLY SHIT! Who the fuck are you?"

Gabby stops mid-step as she rounds the corner into the workroom, jumping nearly a foot as she catches sight of Caleb. He relaxes slightly as he realizes that there isn't a threat. I swallow a laugh as the two stare at each other, Gabby frozen in shock, Caleb assessing.

"Gabby, this is Caleb. Caleb, Gabby," I say, thankful that my voice is steady.

"Wasn't expecting your muscle to be so..." Gabby trails off as she edges around him toward me. Caleb turns to scan the parking lot through the windows, but I swear I see a hint of color on his cheeks.

"He's not my muscle," I scoff, rolling my eyes.

"Oh, I'm sorry. Your security officer," Gabby replies with over-exaggerated bravado.

We share a laugh before she perches on the workbench along the wall, pulling one of her legs up to rest her cheek against it, catching a few more moments of dozing before we open. We chat a little, gossiping about our regulars, teasing each other, and it's so easy to fall into the routine of my workday that I all but forget that Caleb is even there. Wila, however, doesn't forget that she has another set of hands in the shop, and through sheer force of will, has him helping with restocking. Even though I'm sure that acting as an unpaid employee of Grandmother Wila's is outside of his job description, Caleb still complies and doesn't complain. We don't see any of Seth's groupies all day, and by the time we head home, I can't help the optimistic feeling in my gut. It's nice to know that someone is watching my back, but it's also nice to not need the backup. Maybe I wouldn't need Caleb for much longer.

TWENTY

Rhett

"Ms. St. Clair, Mateo just arrived."

Erica's voice comes through the intercom on Lex's desk, and there's no small bit of surprise in my chest as I check the clock on the wall. He's... on time. Not just on time, but actually a few minutes early. Lex and I share a look, but we don't get a chance to comment on it as the door opens and Mateo strides in. He's dressed in a button-down, the sleeves rolled up to his elbows, but it's tucked into a pair of dark designer jeans.

"I thought you had a client meeting," Lex comments, standing from her chair behind the massive glass-top desk.

"I did. They were a couple of Yankee trust fund babies with more money than they know what to do with, so I was frankly a little overdressed. But I did get them to sign on the dotted line, despite not wearing my Sunday best," Mateo returns, making a beeline for the bar cart and pouring himself a couple of fingers of the expensive bourbon.

"Should that be enough for your project, Rhett?" Lex asks, perching on the arm of an armchair near where I'm lounging.

I nod, accepting the glass Mateo puts in my hand before he throws himself down onto the pristine white leather couch. Lex glares in his direction as he puts his shoes on the cushions, but doesn't say anything to correct him.

"I got a call from Officer Nyueng today. He's running out of leads," she says, letting out a long exhale.

I growl low in my throat, knuckles going white on my glass before I take a sharp swig. Everyone knows that Seth and Darren are working together, but we can't prove it. And we've yet to find any connection between either of them and the bastard who broke into Lydia's apartment. Knowing that she has a bodyguard helps calm my nerves, but the irritated itch in the back of my mind that only appears when Lydia isn't in my line of sight resurfaces.

"Do they have any suspects?" Mateo asks, sitting up and leaning forward to rest his elbows on his knees.

The serious angle of his frown, the way his brow furrows with concern, softens something in my heart. Mateo has been in plenty of relationships before and after Seth, but I've never seen this depth of emotion from him. He worships the ground Lydia walks on, and I can't say I blame him. Lydia doesn't know it, but she has at least two alphas who would do just about anything for her. I look away from his face before I can think too long on the feelings stirring in my chest.

"A few, but the descriptions of witnesses are so vague as to be useless. Male, but no one can agree on height or build. And you didn't recognize the voice at all?" Lex starts, turning her question to me.

I shake my head. "I speak with too many people on a weekly basis that unless someone has something distinctive about them, I wouldn't remember."

"Have we asked Lydia if she recognized anything? The voice, or even a scent? You wouldn't have been able to catch anything out of the ordinary, but she might have," Mateo suggests.

"She's under enough stress. I don't want to ask her to relive her trauma again," Lex snaps before I can even fully open my mouth to reply.

Mateo and I both stare for a moment, taken aback by the heat in her voice. Lex doesn't back down, turning her hard stare to each of us, almost daring us to try to challenge her. Her back is straight, hands in fists. She's... protecting Lydia?

"Did something happen?" I ask gently.

"No, not that it should matter. Lydia has been through enough in her life, and we should not ask her to dredge up those bad memories without reason. It's cruel, and we're better than that," Lex retorts, looking away.

If I didn't know any better, I could swear that there's a hint of color to her cheeks, a softness to her eyes as she speaks about Lydia that I've never seen before. I sit up a little straighter, and I catch a hint of citrus in the air before it drifts away.

"Did something happen between the two of you?" Mateo pushes, a teasing edge to his voice.

"I don't ask you to kiss and tell, Mateo," she volleys, and by her expression, that's not what she'd meant to say.

Mateo's face lights up, a grin replacing the frown. There's no mistaking the blush on Lex's cheeks and neck now, and I resist the urge to needle her for more details. Lydia's relationship with our prime alpha is her business, but I can't deny the burning curiosity to know more. How far have they gone together? What is their dynamic like? Lex can be intense in her play, and while I trust her to make sure Lydia is safe and comfortable, I won't deny the part of me that wants to witness their play firsthand.

"Regardless, unless we don't have another choice, Lydia shouldn't be involved in this. She deserves to have some semblance of normalcy," Lex goes on, brushing her hair over her shoulder.

I nod my agreement, but Mateo sucks his teeth before taking another drink of his bourbon.

"If you have something to say—"

"Oh, I do. We can't expect her to take this situation seriously if she doesn't know the stakes," Mateo says, tone light but eyes hard.

I purse my lips as I consider that point. He's not wrong, even if it does pain me a little to admit it. But the desire to keep Lydia from constantly being on the verge of a panic attack or nervous breakdown wins out.

"She's aware of more than I think you're giving her credit for. We don't need to make it worse," Lex says, voicing my thoughts.

"So, we're not going to tell her about the tracker? Or about the articles your people have been squashing?" Mateo goes on, words taking on an accusatory edge.

I look at Lex in alarm. The tracker wasn't news, despite it coming to a dead end. But I have not heard anything about articles other than the one published last week. Lex has the decency to look slightly abashed for a moment before she regains her composure and returns Mateo's glare with one of her own.

"No, we don't need to tell her about it," she says simply.

"How about you tell me what the hell has been happening, then? How many times has the Review tried to publish stories about her?" I ask, setting my glass down on the coffee table before getting to my feet.

"Only two or three times since she's been outed. And they're hardly stories. It's just been rumors—"

"Lex, that's not okay. Where are these rumors coming from? Who's writing them?" I demand.

"It's nothing as serious as all that. The Review has a place for their readers to submit tips or photos or rumors on the website. Since Mateo and Lydia's relationship became such a hot topic, the submissions have been constant," Lex explains.

"That's not making me feel any better," I growl, pacing away toward the window.

"They've been trashing all the submissions since the editor-in-chief was... gently reminded that she could be held liable if someone got hurt based on the material her magazine publishes," Lex says.

I whip around to find her smirking at her own private joke, and I can only stand in stunned silence.

"How... they could sue over that, try to claim that you're violating their right to free speech, or freedom of the press," I question cautiously.

"Oh, I've been assured the conversation was entirely off the record, and Tonya was quite reasonable," she says, putting her hand to her heart. But the Cheshire cat grin she can't seem to remove undermines the sincerity of the gesture.

"No one working for that rag has a soul, so I find it hard to believe you managed to get her to come around, simply because it's the right thing to do," Mateo says darkly.

"Plausible deniability, Matty. In any case, Tonya's been sending me the submissions for my records. It's just been a bunch of jealous keyboard detectives trying to spin stories that have no basis in reality. Nothing truly nefarious like we've seen from the stalker," Lex continues, standing to pick up my abandoned bourbon and finishing it in one swallow.

"After all the shit we went through with Seth and his cult, this is a rather cavalier attitude you're adopting, Lex," Mateo comments, swirling the amber liquor in the crystal glass.

I sigh, my stomach dropping. I've tried to block out that clusterfuck, but I don't blame Mateo for not being able to do the same. The time between the breakup announcement and the day we'd gotten the restraining order had been when the worst of Seth's behavior occurred. He'd refused to move out of The Valencia at first, but once we'd pried him off the ceiling like an angry cat, he'd taken to showing up at our other businesses without warning and trying to cause a scene. He'd nearly ruined Lucas's Michelin-star opportunity by insisting his food was simultaneously raw and burnt to a crisp, and only leaving once the police showed up. Once we'd gotten the stay away order, Seth mobilized his followers to harass us in his place. They'd camp outside of the doors to our hotels and restaurants, flood our review pages with false one-star ratings, even going as far as calling the health department and claiming we had a bedbug infestation. It took following through on our threats of legal action for it all to stop, but it'd been the worst eight months of my life.

"They know better than to step foot on our property, and we hired her bodyguard for a reason. By cutting off their means of easily spreading rumors, it should stop them from doing that kind of damage again," Lex replies.

"Or it'll make them congregate in a dark corner of the internet where we can't do anything about them," Mateo sighs.

There's a long stretch of silence as we all consider that statement. I understand his concern, having been the primary target of the smear campaign, but I tend to agree with Lex. We've shown we aren't going to let these people make our lives miserable without a fight. If they try to go after Lydia, we'll make sure they regret it.

"I still think we should tell her about the investigation. If she knows something, or remembers something from the break in, then it could be the lead Nyueng needs," Mateo says, leaning back and slinging one arm over the back of the couch.

I hum thoughtfully, looking out over the skyline. I've tried to scrub that day from my mind, just to keep myself from dwelling in that pit of anger and fear any more than I have to. But looking back, a detail jumps out again. When we'd gotten back to the pack house, Lydia said something to Lucas that I hadn't caught, but they'd shut me down when I'd tried to push, claiming it'd only make things worse and send me off on a murder spree. Had Lydia actually picked up on something and never said anything?

"I have my team working on something. If it doesn't pan out, then we can reevaluate our options. Can we all agree to that compromise?" Lex sighs, rubbing the bridge of her nose slightly.

Mateo and I share a look. He's got that spark in his eyes, and I narrow my eyes in warning. He's fought with Lex over far less, but I don't think this is one he could win. She's made up her mind, and we'd only be pushing her to exclude us in her future decision making if we continue on like this. He throws his free hand up in defeat, finishing his drink. Lex looks to me and I nod, even as my gut twists. I don't like lying to Lydia, even lying by omission. But if this is what it takes to keep her safe and not terrified for her life every moment of the day, then so be it.

Lex's cell phone vibrates on the desk, making me jump slightly. She moves to answer it, and I turn to Mateo. We're both done for the day, and I'm looking forward to spending the afternoon just relaxing. Lydia's working an event, and won't be home for a while yet, but time apart is a good thing. Or at least that's what I have to tell myself.

Lex sucks in a harsh breath, and Mateo and I whip our attention to her. She's typing furiously, eyes hard and shoulders tense. She looks up after a moment, and her unreadable expression makes my heart stop.

"It's Caleb. You two need to get home. Now."

TWENTY-ONE

Lydia

"So, do you think I should give Wes another shot?" Gabby asks as we sit at one of the round Formica tables in the employee lounge of the hotel we're working in today.

We're in the slow season for weddings, with it being too hot most days to have outdoor gatherings, and the beginning of hurricane season making people gun shy about planning anything big. So we're working a smaller corporate event, some sort of award ceremony and mixer, but I'm not sure. They paid us for the centerpieces, not to give a damn about much else. After everything was set up, they shuffled us out of sight while the speakers did their thing. Now, the soft bass of the inoffensive classic pop music the DJ plays travels through the space. I'm sure things will liven up once more of the suits indulge in the open bar, but it is boring as hell for the time being.

"Absolutely the fuck not. He cheated on you, Gabs," I reply sternly.

Wes is a beta who works at Carlos's Café next door to Wila's. He and Gabby dated for a few months until she found out he was hooking up with other girls from dating apps. Gabby is a bit of a hopeless romantic, so trying to get her to stay single long enough to figure out what she actually wants from a relationship is a task and a half.

"But he said that he was sorry. And it's not like we were super serious, anyway," Gabby says with a longing sigh.

"Trust me, he's going to do it again."

Both Gabby and I snap our gazes to where Caleb is sitting near the door, tipping his chair back onto two legs as he scrolls through his phone. He looks casual, but I've seen how quickly he can spring into full protective mode.

"What do you know about it?" Gabby snaps.

"I've been around enough assholes to know that if they do something shitty once with no real consequences, they're going to do it again," he returns, completely unruffled.

"You don't know him. He's—"

"He is an asshole, Gabby. You know that just as well as I do," I interrupt.

"I thought you liked him!" Gabby whines.

"I liked him because you liked him, and I wanted to support you. But the minute he fucked around with your heart, he was dead to me," I say with all seriousness.

"So we going to talk about the Maserati in the room, or..." Gabby trails off.

I blink at the rapid change in subject before blushing. I'd hoped Gabby wouldn't notice how I'd gotten to work over the last few days, mostly because she's usually still asleep. But of course, nothing slips by her.

Despite Caleb's presence, Alexandra has been waking up around the same time I do, and she's been the one to drive me to work. We make our travel mugs of coffee together before Caleb follows behind us as we commute into the city. We don't talk that much, at least not about anything we'd done. I want to ask if that was a onetime deal, or if there is a chance of us doing that again... and maybe even more. I haven't been able to get that feeling of peace out of my mind, and I'm almost desperate to feel it again. Rhett hasn't agreed to any intense play since our fight, and I miss it. But I haven't been able to work up the courage to say anything yet.

"There's not much to tell," I mumble at last, picking at a chip in the table.

"Not much to tell? Babe, I've seen the way you look at each other, but you have the lady balls to tell me that there's nothing going on between y'all," she whisper-shouts at me.

"I didn't say that, but it's just... not a lot," I admit, face overly warm.

Gabby scooches her chair closer, the legs loud on the stained linoleum. Once she's thoroughly invaded my personal space, she leans her elbows on the table, resting her chin on her fists as she bats her eyelashes rapidly at me. I roll my eyes with a laugh, nudging her with my shoulder.

"Have you kissed? She seems like she'd be a great kisser," Gabby asks.

"What? No, we haven't—wait, what do you mean you think she'd be a good kisser? You can tell that just by looking at someone?" I ask, cutting across myself as I fully absorb her words.

"Some people you can. Like, take your Siberian shadow here—"

"I'm not from Russia," Caleb interrupts in a monotone.

Gabby plows on, not even acknowledging him. "He's got an okay mouth, lips a little thin for my taste, but he seems like the type to do everything by the letter. So maybe a six out of ten?"

"My mate would disagree," Caleb retorts, shaking his head a little.

"She's biased," Gabby drones, turning back to me. "But Alexandra St. Clair has that look, like she definitely knows what to do with her mouth. You'd enjoy kissing her whether you wanted to or not."

My mind immediately spins into overdrive, and I have to count my inhales and exhales to stop myself from imagining all the things I'm sure Alexandra could make me enjoy. Gabby laughs at my silence, and Caleb lets out a soft, exasperated sigh.

"If something happens, I'll let you know if your theory holds any water," I say after I compose myself.

"I'm holding you to that. Do you think Gran would mind if we took advantage of the open bar?" she asks brightly.

I chuckle and shake my head. "Like she'd have any room to judge us. Remember the Dickerson wedding last year?"

Gabby sits up with a gasp, then throws her head back and cackles. I can't help but join in; my best friend's laugh is always infectious. Wila tried the house wine at the Dickerson wedding last year and ended up liking it so much that she drank two bottles by herself before it was time to pack up and go home. Gabby and I ended up letting her sprawl out in the back of the truck on the ride home.

"Let's go find something to drink. Maybe there's a single billionaire waiting to sweep me off my feet," Gabby says, jumping to stand.

"You need to stop watching so many movies," I say with a sigh, following behind her.

Without missing a beat, Caleb falls into step silently behind me. It still makes me jump to see him move without making a sound, but I think that's a good thing. I would rather be jumpy than oblivious.

As I'd predicted, the mixer is in full swing by this point in the day. The DJ is playing party staples, and there are plenty of people in their business attire getting their groove on. We spot Wila picking over the buffet and chatting with the caterer, an older man I recognize from other events here. Gabby and I order our fruity cocktails, standing along the edge of the room, out of the way while we people watch.

"Oh my God. Are you Lydia Anderson?"

I freeze at the nasally voice, spine curling into a defensive position. Of all the places, how could I possibly be recognized here? I turn around to see a group of three women, all of them attendees by the way they're dressed, moving in closer. They're all beautiful, of course. Lean muscle and shapely curves with similar trendy haircuts and spiked heels. I scent Caleb before I see him, snickerdoodles and cedar growing stronger as he steps within arm's reach of me.

"I'm sorry. Have we met?" I reply pleasantly.

"No, but we saw your picture in the paper. You're Mateo's new thing," the woman in the center remarks, her massive statement necklace catching the colored lights from the DJ booth distractingly.

The way her voice wraps around that last word does not make it sound like a compliment. Even still, my heart does a little skip to have my relationship with him acknowledged. The primal part of my mind preens, and I have to resist the urge to snicker triumphantly, like I'm gloating over a win of some kind. Mateo is a person, not a prize.

"And we follow Seth's fitness blog. His workouts are goals," the woman on the right continues, tossing a few strands of her blonde hair over one shoulder.

"Ladies, I think it'd be for the best if you return to the party," Caleb interrupts, stepping around me to partially shield me from them.

"Oh, who are you?" the third one practically purrs, and I have to hold back a gag. It's not that I thought it was wrong of her to make a move, but subtlety is an art, one she clearly hasn't studied.

"Unavailable. Now, if you don't mind—"

"Seth was totally right. You really don't fight your own battles," the first snipes with a fake giggle.

The other two titter along, and I feel my face go hot as my grip tightens on my glass. It shouldn't bother me, because it's not like she's saying anything that I haven't heard from the man himself. But it just confirms my fear that there are people, strangers, that talk about me and my life without ever having met me.

"Hey, bitch. Keep it up, and we'll see how good you are at fighting your battles," Gabby snarls, advancing a step toward them.

The women gasp in unison, and all start squawking their indignation. I manage to catch Gabby's arm to stop her from following through with her threat, and Caleb squares his shoulders in front of us.

"This is your last warning. If you don't leave, I will be forced to assume you mean to do Ms. Anderson harm, and take appropriate countermeasures," he says, the most serious I've ever seen him.

"We're so posting about this. I can't believe you've got this meathead threatening us like this," the blonde says, voice somehow more shrill.

"Enough. Leave," he commands, taking a step toward them, gently trying to guide them away.

"You're a fat fucking slut and not good enough for Mateo! I hope next time Seth tries, you get what's coming to you!"

The world seems to slow as I watch the girl in black cock her arm back, ready to throw her drink like a baseball. But faster than I thought possible, Caleb is there, grabbing her wrist and twisting her arm until she drops the glass to the floor and shrieks in pain. The other two stumble back unsteadily on their heels, watching as Caleb maneuvers his target to the floor, face down, with her arm twisted behind her back.

"What's going on here?"

I turn to see a woman with a headset approaching, a clipboard clutched tight to her chest. The event coordinator. I feel my hands shaking, the room getting fuzzy. Gabby steps up next to me and pulls me under one arm as Caleb gets up and explains the situation, but the sounds around me are starting to fade. I let Gabby guide me away, but I'm hardly aware of anything. It could be seconds or hours later when she sits me down in a chair and I feel a gentle pressure between my shoulder blades, guiding me to tuck my head between my knees.

"Just breathe, babe. You're okay. I've got you," Gabby coos from nearby.

I feel her hand against my back, rubbing in slow circles. I count my inhales and exhales for several cycles until I scent wood and cookies nearby. Caleb's voice comes into focus as he exchanges clipped, brusque words with someone, though I can't make out the responses.

"Gabs, I'm sorry," I whisper after a few moments.

"Shut the fuck up, babe. Those bitches had no right to bother you, and they got what was coming to them," Gabby says with a scoff.

My lips quirk up in a smile before I take another deep breath. Steps approach, and Caleb's scent grows stronger. I feel a hand on my knee, and I look up to find him crouched down to be at eye level with me. His brow is set in a stern line, but his eyes are soft.

"I just got off the phone with Ms. St. Clair. If it's possible, she wants you to come home. Mr. Cooper and Mr. Hutchenson are at your pack house waiting for you," he says.

I look up at Gabby, who sighs. I hate doing this, especially when we're probably going to have a lot of work at the end of the night. She looks at me with understanding in her dark eyes, and I feel a twist of guilt in my gut.

"You can make it up to me with a girls' night," she says at last.

"I'll even buy the booze," I tease.

"It better be the good shit."

"Done."

We share a soft laugh as I sit up, and Caleb unfolds to stand. Gabby is sitting on a chair beside me, and I can't help but lean over and hug her tightly. Her caramel-candy-apple scent fills my nose as I bury my face in her neck for a moment. I don't know what I ever did to deserve a friend like Gabby.

Twenty-two

Mateo

I HEAR TIRES IN the driveway a moment before Rhett does, my head snapping around to watch the front door. Rhett stops halfway through the circuit he's been pacing for the last half hour, eyes locked on the door as the handle turns. I jump up from the sectional and vault over the back to meet Lydia as she crosses through the open doorway from the foyer to the living room. She's dressed in her ill-fitting event uniform, but there's a weariness to the slump of her shoulders that tugs at my heart.

"Come here, baby girl," I coo softly, pulling her into my arms.

She only whimpers, nuzzling her face into my chest, one of her hands bunching my shirt into her fist. I rub gentle strokes up and down her back, kissing the top of her head softly. Lex didn't provide any specifics of what happened, but it didn't take a genius to guess that it had something to do with Seth.

"What do you need, love?" Rhett asks seriously, stepping close to encircle her between us.

"Just... this. I just need you like this," Lydia says, her voice so small.

I look up and catch Rhett's concerned glance. We share a moment of silent conversation, agreeing without words not to push for details right now. I nod in the direction of the stairs, and he dips his chin in understanding.

"Let's get you somewhere more comfortable, yeah? My bed should be big enough for all of us," he suggests.

Lydia looks up suddenly, turning to face him. "Your room? I thought..."

Rhett shakes his head and gives her a kind smile. "I'm sorry I didn't say anything sooner, love, but you're always welcome in my room. As stupid as this seems, I never thought to tell you because, well... closed doors are more a suggestion than a deterrent in my family."

I snort a laugh, smiling to myself. He's got that right. After I moved in, it'd taken me a while to get used to the Nolan girls and their liberal interpretation of privacy.

"Growing up, if my sisters wanted to come into my room, they just did. I tried to ask them to at least knock, but that only resulted in them knocking on the door as they were opening it, at the same time shouting, "I'm coming in now!" I sort of gave up and just accepted my fate. My door doesn't even have a lock on it, so if you want to go in, regardless of if I'm home, you are always welcome there," Rhett explains.

"Ditto for me, baby. This is your house, too," I add, snuggling a little closer.

Lydia hums contentedly and sighs. "If we're saying things for the record, I um... I wouldn't mind if y'all wanted to sleep in my nest with me. It's... pretty big and empty all by myself," she mumbles, picking her words with care.

Rhett leans in and kisses her forehead. "We can do that for you, love. Let's go have a lie down," he whispers gently.

Lydia nods wearily and lets us guide her down the stairs and into her room. I breathe a deep lungful of her lilac and lavender scent that floods over me as the door swings open, my lips pulling up in a little unconscious smile. I love the way her scent calls to my soul, soothing and exciting me in equal measure. Rhett nudges the door closed with a foot once he and Lydia are inside, and I step back to give them a little bit of space. She silently acquiesces to Rhett's undressing, both of them stripping down until he's in his boxers, and she's only wearing panties, a bra, and the t-shirt Rhett had just removed from himself and slipped right onto her.

Watching them move together is like music in motion for me. There is enough familiarity that they don't need to speak, a push and pull, call and response that's soul deep. His fingers trail over her skin, and she shivers, so acutely aware of his touch. Even when they aren't trying to be, the depth of their sensuality makes my cock twitch in my jeans.

"Are you waiting for a special invitation or something?" Lydia teases with a little giggle.

I blink and shake my head, realizing that they've moved to lie on the massive bed. Rhett smirks at me, his knowing look lost on Lydia as she settles with her back to his front. I scramble to remove my jeans and shirt, leaping into bed when I'm down to just my boxers. I move in close, my face inches from Lydia's. I stretch out my arm, letting both of them use it as a pillow. Rhett's hand splays over Lydia's hip, pulling her back until he can hitch a leg over her calves. We shift until we're all relatively comfortable, though I would sleep on a bed of nails if it meant being close to Lydia.

"What happened tonight?" Rhett asks, barely above a whisper.

Lydia's face falls and she sighs. "Nothing, really. Some of Seth's cult members recognized me and tried to start something. Caleb stepped in when things escalated."

"That's not nothing," I reply seriously, heart sinking.

Once again, Lydia is getting caught in the crossfire of my stupid mistakes. We'd submitted Jason's statement to the court, but they threw it out as hearsay. Ted is fighting the ruling, but it doesn't look like anything will come of it. Every time we think we're close to getting Seth to pay for his behavior, we get dragged back to square one. But in the meantime, Lydia has to endure harassment.

Lydia's hand on my cheek draws my attention back to her. Her emerald eyes are clouded with concern, and for a moment, I forget to breathe. In the soft light filtering through the frosted windows, her hair shines gold, and her skin practically glows. My omega is radiant.

"It's not your fault, Matty. People are just awful sometimes," she whispers, tracing the ridge of my cheekbone.

"I know, but..."

I let out a heavy sigh and look away from her piercing gaze. She's right, and I shouldn't try to take the blame for other people's shitty actions. But it doesn't stop me from feeling bad that she's tangled in this mess to begin with.

"We've talked about this. You have done everything in your power to remove Seth from your life. What he does or says isn't on you," Rhett adds.

I look back up at my best friend, his icy blue eyes staring straight through me. We have gone over this Seth situation countless times since it happened, and he helped me through the worst of the guilt I had weighing down on me back then. All I have control of are my actions and my responses to Seth's actions. He's doing all of this to get a rise out of me, to push me until I break no-contact and confront him. Feeling guilty and letting this stuff eat away at me is exactly what he'd want. I nod, leaning more into Lydia's touch.

"Still doesn't make me want to kick his ass any less," I grumble, smirking to take the edge off my words.

"Oh, trust me. He's got more than just an ass kicking coming his way, if I have anything to say about it," Rhett agrees, his chuckle darker and more dangerous.

Lydia sighs, and I catch the roll of her eyes that belies the fond smile pulling at her lips. Unable to resist a moment longer, I lean in and capture her lips with mine. I'd intended to make it a short, sweet kiss and then go back to cuddling, but then Lydia's hand slides around and fists into the hair at the base of my neck, that little moan slipping free.

I run my tongue along her bottom lip, and she opens with no hesitation, moving forward slightly until her chest brushes mine with each inhale. Rhett hums appreciatively, and I move the arm under Lydia until I find the skin of Rhett's back. He sucks in a sharp breath as I knead my fingers into the lean muscle of his shoulder, and I'm pleasantly surprised when I feel his calloused hand on my outer thigh.

"Do you want this, love? Both of us worshiping you in your nest?" Rhett purrs, a wave of his whiskey scent crashing over me as he leans close, murmuring into Lydia's ear.

She moans again, back arching even as her lips stay with me, her tongue still twining with mine. But that's not enough. I pull away, kissing down her jaw until my bruised lips are brushing the shell of her ear.

"Words, baby girl. Tell us what you want," I croon, running my hand up from her waist, through the valley between her breasts, and back down.

"I want... I need you. Touch me, please," Lydia begs between heaving breaths.

I nibble on her earlobe as I let my hand drift down her leg, making goosebumps rise along her clenching thighs until I find the waistband of her panties. Rhett takes Lydia's weight for a moment, slipping the t-shirt over her head and then her bra, leaving her practically bare between us. My head spins as my cock springs to life at the first sight of her perfect tits, and I lean down, capturing one nipple in my mouth. The air is heavy with the smell of honey and whiskey, and the floral taste of her skin under my tongue makes me moan.

"You are so wet for us, love," Rhett groans, speaking over Lydia's gasping inhales.

"Let me taste her," I say between open-mouthed kisses on the swells of her breasts.

I open my eyes as Lydia lets out a shaky exhale, my gaze drifting to Rhett's hand below the pale gray lace of her panties. He withdraws a moment later, and I catch his wrist, bringing two gleaming fingers to my mouth. They both let out low moans as I lick every drop of her essence from Rhett's skin, the sweetness of it mixing perfectly with the heady musky leather of his flesh.

When I pull away, I'm surprised when Rhett's hand darts out from my grip, clamping down on the back of my neck and dragging me down into a heated kiss. I haven't done this with him in years, but my body still remembers. My skin lights up, my nose filling with more of that honey and vanilla omega arousal as Rhett tries to dominate the kiss. When he pulls away, I'm left a little breathless. Lydia's little whimper draws both of our attention back to her, and I can't help but chuckle at the wide-eyed shock displayed on her face.

"I'd almost forgotten how good of a kisser you are, Coop," I tease, throwing Rhett a sideways look.

"You've definitely improved," Rhett tosses back, not missing a beat.

Lydia's cheeks are bright pink, and it's almost too adorable for words. I lean down and gather her up in my arms, rolling slightly so her upper body is draped over me.

"You taste like a cocktail together," Lydia muses when we pull away for air.

"What sort of cocktail?" I ask with a raised eyebrow.

She hums thoughtfully, but whatever she's about to say next is cut off, her eyes going wide and mouth forming a perfect little 'o'. I glance behind her to see Rhett has shifted, half sitting up as he helps her hitch one leg toward her chest, opening her for him. His eyes are closed, pure bliss coloring his cheeks and neck as he slowly rolls his hips against her.

"Is he filling that pretty little pussy, baby? Stretching out that tight little hole?" I ask, a purr slipping into my words as I brush back a piece of her hair.

"Oh, God. It's so good, so—holy shit, just like that." Lydia's voice is high and desperate, her body rocking over me as Rhett's hips snap up in sharp thrusts. My hands wander up and down her body as I watch her every facial expression, the way her eyes screw tight right when he hits that perfect spot, the deepening pinks and reds as she gets closer and closer to falling apart. It only takes a moment for me to rid myself of my boxers, and then I bring one of her hands down to wrap her fingers around my cock, moving in time with Rhett. I look up at his face, his attention fixed on where they meet.

"He's fucking you so good, isn't he, baby girl? Giving you that thick alpha cock deep, just how you like it?" I growl, tangling a hand in her hair to make sure she can't look anywhere but me.

She whimpers and nods as much as she can, but I tighten my grip ever so slightly in correction. Her hand flexes around my cock, a reflex that makes my hips buck up off the bed. Rhett growls, and I feel his hand on my hip, holding me down.

"I can feel you holding back, my good girl. But you aren't going to come just yet, not until Matty gets his turn," Rhett says, and the dangerous lilt to his words sends a shiver down my spine.

"Do you want my cock, hmm? Want me to fuck you until you come all over me?" I ask, almost innocently.

"Please, I need—I need your cock," Lydia begs mindlessly.

Rhett pulls back, and Lydia falls forward when she loses the support. I sit up slightly, using a pillow to brace my upper back. Lydia throws one leg over my hips and reaches for my cock, but an idea strikes. I seize her hips before she can lower herself down, and she looks up in confusion.

"Let's give Rhett something to admire, baby. Show him how good you take my cock," I say smoothly.

I gently start to twist her hips, and she picks up on my meaning. I adjust beneath her so I'm flat on my back, and she turns around, the delicious globes of her ass presented to me. As she leans back, I help support her weight, guiding my cock to her entrance. We both groan as she impales herself all the way to the base, right where my knot is beginning to swell, and we freeze for a moment. Leaving one hand on her upper back, I wrap my other around her stomach, bending her back even farther until her breasts are fully on display. When I start thrusting up, her hands scramble to find balance, one arm settling on my abs.

"Look at that," Rhett breathes, and the heat in his whisper brings a feral grin to my lips.

"Holy shit, you feel so good. Please–right there," Lydia babbles, her head falling back.

I pick up my pace, and the warm, wet heat of her channel ripples around me every time my cock brushes along that sensitive patch of nerves. It only takes a few strokes, and then Lydia's body locks up, and I feel the squeeze and gush of her release as she screams. I don't stop, but I slow down, working her through the aftershocks. But then I feel a warm, wet slide of a tongue on the base of my cock and balls, and I jump.

"That's right, love. Keep going while I clean you up," Rhett says, voice coming from between our legs.

There's another long, broad stroke of his tongue, and I groan, bucking under the sensation. Lydia takes over, riding me in slow, deep rolls of her hips. Rhett alternates between sucking on Lydia's clit and licking my cock and my knot, sending white-hot flashes of pleasure through my entire body. Moans fall unabashedly from my lips, their names intermingled with sighs and gasps. It's not long before I feel the tightening in my lower back.

"I'm not going to last, baby. Do you want me to–"

"No, I want to taste you," Lydia snaps, sitting up from my hold.

Before I can protest, she's kneeling between my legs, lips locked around the head of my cock. My shout is almost drowned out by her moan, and I look to find Rhett positioned behind her, cock buried inside of her slit once again. But I'm distracted again as Lydia's head bobs up and down, the wet sounds of her mouth the most erotic thing I've ever heard in my life. When she comes up for air, she reaches behind her to grab Rhett's wrist, pulling his hand away from her hip to down between her legs.

"I want to taste my come on your cock, too, sir. Please," she says sweetly, turning to bat her eyelashes at him.

In that moment, I can tell Rhett's questioning whether he's died and gone to heaven. Because I can't help but wonder the same thing. Lydia returns to trying to suck the life out of me, and I do my best to control myself, but each flick of her tongue makes my hips buck. I try to pull back when she chokes a little, but she only follows, taking more of me down until I feel the head of my cock slip down into the tight squeeze of her throat. She swallows around me, and my eyes fly open wide, shouting profanities. Her moans vibrate down the length of my cock, and there are spots at the edges of my vision as I reach the very edge of release. She doesn't stop, screaming around me as she reaches her peak, and I can't hold back. I pull out slightly, as not to be rude and shoot directly down her throat, but that's the best I can manage. Pulse after pulse, feeling like forever, as I release a massive load of cum into the eager mouth of my omega. She suckles and licks me clean, not losing a single drop.

"Fuck, I can't–mouth open, now," Rhett gasps, voice raw with pleasure.

Lydia springs into action, moving to position in front of Rhett's gleaming cock. She takes the head into her parted lips, and despite just coming not five seconds ago, I feel my cock beginning to stir at the sight of her bobbing head, and Rhett's glistening chest and stomach as he strokes what she doesn't take until he, too, is shouting profanities to the ceiling, driving deep into Lydia's waiting mouth.

When he's spent, Rhett collapses back onto his heels, panting. Lydia moves to curl into my side, grinning like the cat that got the cream.

"What's so funny?" I ask with a breathless little chuckle.

"I was right. Y'all taste like a whiskey sour together," she says, falling into a fit of laughter.

I stare for a moment before I catch her case of the giggles, burying my face in the crook of her neck and holding her tight. Rhett's deep chuckles join ours, and I feel his weight and warmth on Lydia's other side. We laugh ourselves breathless, falling into a comfortable silence after.

"I love you," Lydia says into the quiet.

"Love you, too, baby," I reply without having to think.

"I love you, too. Both of you," Rhett says.

He's looking between both of our faces, a fond smile stretching his handsome face. I lean down and give him the slightest peck before doing the same to Lydia. And right now, I can't think of a place I'd rather be than right here, tangled up with the love of my life, and my best friend, basking in pleasure-induced euphoria.

TWENTY-THREE

Lydia

AUGUST BEGINS INNOCUOUSLY, DESPITE the tension that lives in my chest almost constantly. It's been about two weeks since the run-in with Seth's groupies at the event, and we still haven't heard a peep from Seth himself. The silence is worse than the harassment, not knowing when and where the next hammer strike will fall.

My nest is finally coming together now that I've been able to get Rhett and Mateo to join me in it a few times. It still feels like I'm missing something, and I'm stubbornly ignoring the little voice in the back of my head that keeps pining for mulled wine and orange peels.

Caleb hasn't seen any action since the corporate mixer, and despite my jokes about it, he's relieved. He'd rather have boring days than ones spent dodging literal bullets. So when I'm sitting on a stool behind the counter at Wila's, I'm not surprised to see him helping Gran move bags of potting soil just for something to do. I've asked if Alexandra knows that he's doing this side work on her dollar, but never got a straight answer. I'd hate to ruin Gran's fun, so I can keep a secret.

"Yugoslavia?" Gabby asks from her perch on the counter.

Caleb doesn't answer, despite the fact that this game of "Guess Where Caleb is From" has been going on for several minutes. We've gone through almost every country in Eastern Europe, but Caleb has yet to confirm or deny anything.

"You've guessed that one already, babe," I say with a low chuckle.

"Just want to keep him on his toes. Latvia?" she returns, speaking first to me, then to Caleb.

The alpha is silent, grunting slightly as he sets down another bag.

I chuckle slightly, looking down as my phone buzzes on the counter with an incoming text. After unlocking it, I open the message, not recognizing the number right away. I'd changed my number again after my mother's call, and my contacts list was still updating.

Unknown: So, you think you're bringing a guest to the wedding?

I furrow my eyebrows at the strange message. Jason knows Rhett is coming with me, and has known for a while. Maybe it's Sam messaging me?

Me: Yeah. But don't worry about finding a place for us to stay. We've got it covered.
Unknown: Is it that fag from the paper?

"What the fuck?" I whisper under my breath, mind reeling.

"What's going on?" Gabby asks, whipping her head to face me.

"Someone's messaging me about the wedding and just went full homophobe. I don't know who the fuck they think they are—"

My words get cut off as another message comes in and my blood runs cold.

Unknown: It doesn't matter how many of your pity fucks you bring, petal. We're going to be having a good long talk, and we can clear up these misunderstandings.

Fuck.

"Caleb... I—holy shit," I sputter, chest going tight.

My phone disappears from my hand, and I try to take a deep breath but only manage a sharp inhale and a stuttering exhale. Gabby, Wila, and Caleb talk around me, but I can't discern their words. The world seems to tilt, and then there's pain blooming along my hip and leg.

"Breathe, babe. You have to breathe. Do it with me, okay?"

Gabby crouches next to me, her face tense but kind. I inhale as her shoulders lift, matching her exhale. She takes my hands in hers, squeezing and releasing in long pulses that match our breathing. My head starts to clear, and I hear Caleb speaking with someone on his phone. I realize then that I've fallen to the floor behind the counter, and the hip I landed on throbs with pain.

"You people better fucking do something about this fucking bullshit. They can't keep getting away with putting Lydia through the emotional ringer."

I look up and find Wila chest to chest with Caleb, looking down her nose at him even though the top of her silver-haired head only comes up to his chin.

"It's not my—"

"You're her security, boy. You're supposed to be keeping her safe. It seems like you're doing a piss-poor job of it!" she shouts.

"Ma'am, I'm speaking with Ms. St. Clair—"

"And I hope she can hear me, too. If you're going to have my Lydia in your pack, you better get your shit together and take care of this before it's too late."

Wila's voice rises and I swallow at the heat behind her words. Even Caleb looks a little surprised to see how intense Wila's glare is. My stomach swoops a little at her claim over me, and I feel the heat in my cheeks.

"Mrs. Fitzgerald, if you would just—"

"Tell me to calm down, boy. I fucking dare you!"

Gabby shifts until she's sitting shoulder to shoulder with me, watching the drama unfold. She wraps an arm around my shoulders, and I let her tuck me into her side. Her scent is cinnamon tinged, but still surprisingly steady despite how hard I can feel her heart beating.

"Ms. St. Clair is asking for Lydia to come into the office so she can make an official statement to the police. Is it okay with you if I escort her there now?" Caleb asks, speaking slowly and calmly, as if he's facing down an enraged bear.

Wila looks the part of a momma bear ready to eviscerate anyone that tries to come near her cubs. She's breathing hard, hands in fists at her sides, eyes wide and angry. There're several moments of tense silence before she finally rocks back onto her heels. Gabby relaxes next to me, and Caleb looks ready to dance from relief. He looks to me and Gabby on the floor and nods. I swallow and return the gesture, but don't move right away from my spot.

"I'm sorry, Gabs. I keep running out on you," I mumble.

"Don't apologize for other people making your life hard. Remember when you first started? We could hardly keep you from bolting out the door at the sight of anyone even remotely resembling your ex. This too shall pass, babe. And then you're going to treat us to a long weekend getaway at the spa," she returns.

I chuckle, knowing she's only half kidding. But I would do that and more to make up for all the trouble I've been causing her and Wila these last few weeks. I squeeze Gabby tight one last time before climbing to my feet and walking to where Wila and Caleb are still staring each other down. Wila breaks eye contact once I'm within arm's reach, crushing me to her chest before I can protest. I relax into her hold, returning the embrace just as fiercely.

"Your alphas better take care of you, or they'll have me to answer to, you hear me? I will not let you get hurt again."

Wila's whisper makes the back of my eyes burn, and I nuzzle into the crook of her neck, breathing in that fresh-turned earth scent I love so much. Wila will always be my protector, just as Gabby will be my best friend, no matter how much trouble I cause. When she finally releases me, I turn to find Caleb standing near the door to the workroom, Gabby whispering something in his ear. He pulls back and nods seriously, which appears to be the answer Gabby was looking for as she gives him a soft smile. Caleb turns back to me and jerks his head. My phone is in his hand, and I can't deny the grateful ease that takes over the strong pulse in my chest. I don't want that thing anywhere near me anymore. Without speaking, I gather my bag and hang up my apron before following Caleb back out to his SUV.

ele

Caleb pulls up into a reserved space in front of the St. Clair Foundation offices, and I feel my stomach twist nervously. Once again, it feels like I've been called to the principal's office. When would I stop feeling so intimidated by Alexandra and her world? I follow Caleb through the lobby and into the elevator as I ponder, but I can't think past the sinking feeling in my gut. Every time I've talked to the police since this saga began, nothing has come of it. They aren't any closer to finding the person who keeps taking pictures of me, and they haven't been able to make the connection from Seth to Darren yet.

Once the elevator rings for the top floor, I'm fidgeting with the strap of my bag, picking at a loose thread as we cross the open space. The room is decorated with modern, minimalist decor, lots of sleek metal and cool neutrals lending an airy feeling to an otherwise unremarkable space. Erica, Alexandra's beta secretary, rises from her seat as she spots us approaching.

"She's ready for you," Erica chirps, motioning to the double doors that lead into Alexandra's office.

I nod, smiling nervously. Caleb holds the door open for me, allowing me to enter first. Alexandra's office is big, the back wall made almost entirely of windows overlooking the Everton skyline. Her desk is a sleek glass-top expanse with metal legs, her computer off to one side with my latest arrangement sitting proudly on the opposite corner. We're out of lilac season, so they gave me freedom to play. The star-gazer lilies sit in their clear glass vase, intermixed with sprigs of greenery. My eyes sweep from the empty desk to the small sitting area to the right of the door, and I find Alexandra in one of the white armchairs, along with two other people.

My eyes linger on Alexandra for a long moment, not able to look away from her stunning form perched with a dancer's grace, one ankle tucked behind the other and her hands folded carefully in her lap. She's dressed in black today, but there's nothing boring about the way the color makes her pale skin look like polished marble, or the way it darkens her hazel eyes to an almost mossy green in this light.

"Miss Anderson. So glad you could make it."

A deep Texas twang finally breaks my trance, and I find Ted Calhoun, the pack lawyer, lounging on the couch on Alexandra's left. He's squat, with a belly that hangs over the large silver belt buckle holding up his slacks. The dark brown streaks in his salt-and-pepper hair seem to be dwindling every time I see him, but he still wears a wide, toothy grin under his bushy mustache. As the other man twists to look back at me, I see the now-familiar face of Officer Lee Nyueng, dressed in his usual uniform with black tactical vest.

Alexandra gets to her feet and crosses to me, her heels clicking on the shiny tile floor. I duck my chin and look at my shoes, shifting my weight from one foot to the other. Her scent hits me first, heavy with spicy cinnamon and cloves over citrus. Her finger is warm as it hooks under my chin and pulls my eyes up to meet hers.

"Are you okay, lovely?" she whispers, words dripping with concern.

I'm stunned for a moment, but shrug. Her frown deepens and she sighs. There's a weariness around her eyes that tugs at my heart.

"I'm sorry—"

"No, don't. It's not your fault. It's fine," I interrupt, one of my hands darting out to take her free one to comfort her before I think better of it and let my hand drop lamely to my side.

"I have the phone, Ms. St. Clair, if the officer needs to see it," Caleb says suddenly.

I jump at the same time as I feel Alexandra flinch, and her hand drops away from my face when we both turn to look at him. His expression is neutral, but I can decipher the flash of curiosity in his gray eyes. I feel my cheeks heating even more and have to look away as he hands my phone over.

"Very good, Mr. Novak. Would you mind waiting outside while we have this meeting? Erica can assist you with getting some coffee or other refreshments," Alexandra says, voice returning to that cool, distant tone she hides behind when dealing with business matters.

Caleb nods and then turns on his heel and leaves the room. Alexandra's hand on my lower back guides me to sit in the chair she was previously occupying, and she perches on the wide arm next to me. Her hand is warm on the back of my shoulder, and I can feel her fingers tracing slow, soothing circles.

"So your ex contacted you, is that right?" Officer Nyueng starts.

I nod, and then sigh before beginning my explanation of what happened. Alexandra stays quiet for the duration of my short story, though I feel her hand tense slightly as I describe how Darren used that slur.

"How do you know it was your ex, and not some random prank?" Lee asks, tone neutral.

"He called me 'petal.' He's the only one who's ever called me that," I say softly, dropping my eyes to where my fingers are twisting in my lap.

"Why would he call you that?" he pushes.

"My scent. I was his delicate flower petal." My sentence ends as my throat closes with emotion.

I used to think the pet name was beautiful, something unique and creative. But now it feels even more sinister knowing that he thought of me as breakable and biddable from the very beginning.

"How would he have gotten your number? You said it was changed recently," Lee continues, and I'm grateful that he doesn't dwell.

"My brother and I call each other, though I try to be careful about using something to block my number. We think my mother got my number from the phone bill. She may have done it again and then passed the number to Darren," I say with a shrug.

"That's a lot of 'ifs,'" Lee sighs.

"The number in the texts isn't blocked. You could call it yourself to confirm who the person is," Alexandra interrupts sharply.

"Which is what I suggest you do, officer. This investigation into the harassment against Ms. Anderson has gone on for long enough without some sort of result," Ted adds sternly.

There's a brief pulse of affection for the lawyer in my chest. He's one of the few people in this profession that I've ever met that actually seems to care about his clients.

"I know it can be frustrating, but these things take time—"

"Officer Nyueng, it's clear that time is something that we don't have the luxury of anymore. We need some sort of order of protection put into place," Alexandra says.

Her spine straightens beside me, and I can't help but do the same as we both look at Lee. The beta shifts uncomfortably in his seat, not looking at us.

"I can talk to my supervisor, see if we have enough to get an order passed by a judge. We need to have evidence, and it's pretty thin on the ground right now," Lee says hesitantly.

"What do you need? Proof that Darren intends to hurt me? Because I can assure you that this is a threat. This is how he would talk to me when I did something he didn't like. And it always ended with some form of abuse," I insist.

"You and I are going to go down to the station and work something out, officer. I think there's enough evidence," Ted says, sitting up and preparing to get to his feet.

I look at Alexandra, but she just nods. Ted stands with a groan and walks toward the door. Lee looks between his retreating back and me and Alexandra, but I take my cue from her and stay quiet.

"You know how to contact me if there's anything else," he mumbles before getting to his feet and walking with Ted out of Alexandra's office.

TWENTY-FOUR

Lydia

THERE'S A LONG MOMENT of silence before I slump back into the chair. Alexandra sighs and rolls her shoulders.

"I told him you can't go another day without some sort of legal protection from these assholes. Ted will get it done," she drones, not looking at me.

"I know. Just wish I knew how it happened. Jason and I have been so careful," I grumble.

"After speaking with your brother, I can tell he seems genuinely worried about you. If you think your mother and your ex are stealing your phone number from your communication with Jason, I think he'd understand if you needed to go radio silent for a while, at minimum, until after you come home from the wedding," she answers.

I sigh, my heart sinking. I don't want to not speak with Jason for three weeks. Just going the few days after our argument was bad enough. But Alexandra is probably right. It would be stupid to keep putting myself at risk just because I miss him. It's been almost a year since the last time I saw him in person, and I'm feeling it. Jason has been the one constant in my life, and not being able to lean on him when everything seems to be falling apart hurts.

"Lydia, I know this situation isn't ideal, and I'd understand if—"

"If what? If I want to leave?" I say, speaking over her sullen words with my own insecurity.

Alexandra twists so she's looking at me then, and there's something flashing in her eyes that I don't recognize immediately. It's not quite anger, or betrayal, or hurt. Her eyes say so many things, but the emotions flicker too fast for me to pin down and name, even as her expression remains cool. A spark in the depths blazes to life, and citrus fills my nose. I hold her stare, trying to ignore how dry my mouth gets, and how my thighs clench when her hazel eyes roam over my face. I swallow, unable to handle the silence anymore.

"Do you... Do you want me to leave?" I ask, barely above a whisper.

There's a heartbeat when I swear that she's going to say yes. That unidentifiable emotion flares in her eyes, and it almost looks like anger, but with something else running below the surface. But then suddenly, she's off the arm of the couch and straddling my lap, knees on either side of my legs as she leans over me. She holds herself up with one arm on the back of the chair, but her face is within inches of mine.

This is the closest contact we've had since that day in her home office, but my body reacts immediately. The warmth of her skin radiates through the layers of our clothes, and my blood turns molten under her gaze. For a moment, I can't breathe fully, my chest expanding in fits and spurts until I gasp, trying to stop my head from spinning.

I let out a shaky breath, focusing on her eyes. I don't know what to do with my hands, so I just let them fall into my lap, too afraid to touch her and mar an inch of her perfect skin. Alexandra's face is smooth, nearly unreadable except for the inferno in her eyes. This is the predator my instincts detected, and I freeze like a deer caught before a mountain lion. I shiver as she brushes a stray strand of hair from my face, the tip of her nail dragging lightly over my cheek. Her finger continues past my ear until suddenly, she has a fistful of my hair in her hand, and she's pulling hard, exposing my throat.

"Do you *really* think you could leave us, sweetness? That there is anywhere you could go where I wouldn't find you?"

Swallowing hard, my body is suddenly acutely aware of every place her body touches mine. Her eyes pin me in place as effectively as any rope, and I can't move. I fight the urge to give in to my primal mind, determined to stay in control this time. I don't want to be a mewling kitten, someone this beautiful, fierce woman would chew up and spit out. But the overwhelming heat of her, the weight of her on my lap, the scent of her desire makes it hard to focus. Alexandra trails a single finger along the jumping vein in my throat, tracing the neckline of my light cotton shirt. Goosebumps break out everywhere she touches. I gasp lightly as her finger drifts lower, along the swell of my breast, tracing the edge of my bra cup before traveling inward.

"You think the noble move would be to leave. You see yourself as our weakness, our pressure point. If you're gone, then all our troubles would just melt away."

I can hardly think about what she's saying. My mind is acutely focused on the point of her fingernail as it draws slow, ever tightening circles around my rock-hard nipple. I try to swallow again, my tongue coated in the taste of cloves and cinnamon. My palms are slick with sweat, and I can feel my pussy clenching on nothing, the hollow ache filling my lower belly.

"But there's no trouble too great to outweigh the joy you bring to me and my pack. And besides..." Alexandra leans in, her cheek nuzzling mine for a moment as she gets close enough to brush those supple, crimson-painted lips against the shell of my ear. The finger circling my nipple slides across my chest until she flattens her palm over my sternum, pinning me to the chair.

"Running only makes me want you more."

I gasp, back arching as she bites down on my earlobe, the pleasure-pain spiking through my chest and straight down between my thighs. My hands fly to her back, nails digging as I struggle to keep my grip on reality. Her teeth release my ear, moving instead to nip and scrape along my throat. Her hand in my hair pulls tighter, and my back arches until my chest brushes hers. The hand on my chest curls into a claw, and she drags her nails hard across my collarbone.

"Don't make this easy on me, sweetness. If you want to play, then play," she purrs, nibbling on my throat.

The challenge in her words strikes me like a red-hot poker. My own growl is pathetic by alpha standards, and she laughs so seductively that I can't stand it. Planting my feet, I use my hold on her waist to propel us up and out of the chair. I don't have the strength to carry her, but I manage to get on top of her as we crash to the floor. I only savor the look of surprise on Alexandra's face for a moment, and I want to capitalize on the sudden surge of courage. So I lean down and slant my lips over hers.

We both freeze for a heartbeat, but then I melt into the softness of her kiss. Her lips are plumper than any of the boys', but the difference isn't unpleasant. If anything, I find myself craving more. I moan and press forward, emboldened by her responsiveness. Her hand in my hair unclenches, holding the back of my head almost tenderly while her hand on my chest drifts to the curve of my waist. I'm so absorbed in the swipe of her tongue against my lower lip that I don't notice her shifting her weight until it's too late. Faster than I thought possible, Alexandra has us flipped, with me on my back, her straddling me.

Now that I've tasted her, I need more. I try to reach for her face, to bring her lips back to mine, but she catches my wrists and pins them to the floor. Her lips are so close, hovering just above mine as she leans down. I strain my neck, trying to reach her, but she only laughs at my feeble attempts. I try to pull free, but she's much stronger than she looks. Giving up after only a moment, I stare up with pleading eyes. Amusement dances across her features and I whine, tipping my head back in submission.

"Are you so desperate for my touch that you'd give up that easily?" Alexandra chides, clicking her tongue at me.

"Please," I pant, my brain too far gone in this place of desire to think straight.

I don't know how she does this, but I don't think I care. Alexandra breaks me down into this creature of instinct and need with a few touches, like some sort of magic trick. If she were a different sort of person, this power would be dangerous, and I'd be inclined to run for the hills, screaming. But instead, I trust her to not hurt me while I'm completely at her mercy. And that's a heady realization that brings me crashing back down to earth.

Alexandra seems to notice the shift in me, letting go of my wrists and sitting up slightly as I stare at the space under the furniture and try not to cry. I never thought I'd let myself feel this vulnerable again, not after everything Darren did to me. But with Alexandra, it doesn't feel like surrender. It feels like freedom.

"You aren't going to leave me, Lydia Anderson. Not now, not ever. Do you understand me?" she states mildly, with enough of a dangerous edge to her tone to bring my eyes back up to her face.

The heat is gone, replaced with something altogether more startling: fear. She lets me sit up, moving back until we're kneeling so close our knees touch. Her words strike a chord in my soul, the weight of them settling on me. She's trusting me in this moment, showing me where to hurt her the most and hoping like hell I don't. I reach out slowly, brushing my fingers along her cheekbone until I'm cupping the side of her face in my palm. Ever so slightly, I feel her relax into my touch and I smile warmly.

"I won't, Alexandra. I promise," I whisper.

She nods and takes a deep breath before closing her eyes and truly resting her head in my hand.

"Lex," she says into the silence.

"I'm sorry?" I reply, confused.

"I want you to call me Lex," she says, opening her eyes.

When I nod, Alexandra's—Lex's—face lights up with a smile that makes my entire world glow that much brighter. Deep in my soul, I know I would do whatever it takes to keep her happy and smiling. After all the hardships and pain, she deserves that and so much more. And when she kisses me again, there isn't a single shred of doubt in my mind of where I belong. Pack St. Clair is my forever.

When Lex pulls away, she cups my face with her palm, and I bring one of mine up to cover it, leaning into her touch. She looks at me for a long stretch, but I don't mind. At this point, I'd sit here until the building came down around us, as long as she kept looking at me and touching me. But I would never be so lucky. Instead, a soft knock on the door draws both of our attention.

"Just a moment," Lex calls out, glancing away.

I try not to let my disappointment show on my face as I let her help me up from the floor, straightening my hair and clothes. The knock comes again, but instead of answering, Lex takes my hand and pulls me back to face her.

"Have Caleb take you home, okay? Get some rest and I'll see you after I'm done for the day," she instructs kindly.

I nod, squeezing her hand slightly. "Will you be home late?"

Lex's little laugh brings a hot flush to my cheeks, but I can't help my returning smile. She brings my hand to her lips and kisses my knuckles gently as the knock comes again, more insistent this time.

"No, not tonight, sweetness," she replies, promise laced through every syllable.

TWENTY-FIVE

Lydia

A FEW DAYS AFTER my encounter with Lex, I'm sweeping the shop floor as we get ready to close up for the day. I reach for my pocket, panicking for a moment as I don't feel the familiar lump of my phone before I remember I gave it to Caleb this morning. I want to let Rhett and Lucas know I'm on my way home, lest I interrupt them again.

Rhett and I have yet to play since the encounter with Mateo in my nest. It's not that we weren't intimate; but the sex has been fairly vanilla. And as much as it shocks me to admit it, I miss the feeling of surrender that I get when I'm with Rhett. I know he'll never press his advantage, and I have a way out if I ever need it. But not having to worry and think and just letting myself enjoy sex is something I didn't know I needed until Rhett showed me. Maybe we could try to play a game soon.

"You've got that look again."

Gabby's voice comes from my right, and I jump, spinning to face her. Caleb is sitting in his usual place by the front door, looking out the front windows to the sidewalk. Wila is in back, but I still shush Gabby as she laughs in my face.

"What look, exactly?" I snap, shoving her shoulder playfully.

"Your 'I'm thinking about my alphas' dicks' look," she manages through her giggles.

I roll my eyes, face heating even more. She laughs harder when I don't deny it. Thankfully, before she can press me for more details, the clock strikes 5:30, and we move into closing duties. We're a well-oiled machine and get the store shut down for the evening before the clock strikes the hour.

"Hey, Caleb. Can you text Rhett for me? Let him know we're on our way home?" I ask as I'm gathering my bag.

He nods, pulling my phone from his pocket and typing out my message. It still feels weird to have someone using my phone for me. With the gossip running rampant, I agreed with the pack's assessment that it would be in the best interest of my mental health if I didn't have direct access to my phone at all times. Caleb keeps it while I'm at work, and I try to leave it on a counter or in my room while I'm at the pack house. Anything to keep me from constantly checking it. I thought I'd miss it more, but it's not like I have a ton of people trying to get in touch with me. The only people I'd be trying to contact are the pack or Gabby and Wila, and everyone around me has ways to reach them for me.

I shout my goodbyes as Caleb and I leave through the backdoor, making a beeline for his SUV. He sticks close to my side, closer than usual. I can feel the tension radiating off of him as he scans the parking lot, but when I do the same, I don't see anything out of the ordinary. I still scramble up into the passenger side, grateful that Caleb hustles to get in and leave. The cabin is quiet as we pull out of the parking lot and onto the street.

"What's going on?" I ask softly, afraid to break the fragile silence between us.

"Something feels off. Just want to get you home safe," he replies tersely.

I nod and settle back into my seat, clutching the strap of my bag hard enough for my knuckles to turn white. Caleb drives a little faster than usual, though his handling is as smooth and controlled as it's ever been. He glances out of the rearview mirror several times, but I can't see whatever is making him so tense. Suddenly, he turns left at a light instead of right, and I know then that something is truly wrong.

"Don't panic, but I need you to tell me if you recognize that blue Ford behind us," Caleb says, his voice even toned.

I turn to look over my shoulder out of the rear windshield, and my heart sinks. It takes me a minute to find the car he's talking about, eventually spotting an older model sedan three cars back.

"No, but that—"

"It drove down State Street four times during the five o'clock hour, and it's been following us since we left Wila's."

My protest catches in my throat, and I ball my hands into fists as they start to shake. Caleb makes another random turn, and now that I know what I'm looking for, I realize the sedan does, too.

"What do we do?" I whisper, as if the other car might hear me.

"To start, you're going to take three deep, slow breaths for me," Caleb begins.

I nod and allow him to guide me through the inhales and exhales, letting the cedar and cookie scent of him soothe my nerves. I still feel the pang of longing for whiskey or lemonade or mulled wine, but the calming alpha pheromones are still effective.

"Now, I'm trying to keep him on our tail."

I whip my head around and stare, jaw slack. "Fucking why?" I demand.

"I don't want to spook him and scare the bastard off. We need to keep him with us long enough for the police to get here and catch him," Caleb continues.

"What? I don't—"

"Stop panicking and think, Lydia. You've said that someone has been taking pictures of you, and can find you, seemingly at all hours of the day. How do you think they could do that if they aren't following you? This guy tailing us is probably your stalker," he continues, unshaking.

I let his words sink in and try to push aside the rush of embarrassment as I realize he's right. This could be the chance we've been waiting for. If the police catch my stalker and can link them back to Seth, we'll have the evidence we need to possibly be rid of Seth for good. I nod and set my shoulders, looking forward out of the windshield.

"Okay. Should I call 911, or should I try to reach the officer in charge of my case?" I ask, my voice steady despite how much my stomach is roiling.

"911. We need someone to get here fast."

Caleb fishes in his jacket pocket before handing me my phone. There's a reply from Rhett, and my heart twists. He's probably freaking out that I'm not home yet. But I dismiss the message and dial the emergency line before putting the call on speaker.

"911, what's your emergency?"

"My name is Lydia Anderson, and I have someone following me," I start, eyes flicking to the mirror to find the car still there.

"Are you walking or driving?"

"I'm in a car, but my friend is driving. He noticed that the same car has been following us since I left work twenty minutes ago."

"Okay, ma'am, I need your location and direction."

I look around to find some sort of landmark or street sign, rattling off cross streets as Caleb gives me the direction we're heading.

"Okay, ma'am, what I need you to do is head east on Decatur. There's a police station we need you to pass by."

"He's going to bolt if we drive to a police station. I'm heading toward the suburbs. Can your officer intercept there?" Caleb asks loudly.

"Sir, we need you to cooperate and work with us. It would be safer—"

"With all due respect, this tail has been driving with increasing recklessness the longer we go. He's already blown one stop sign, and I don't want to keep this going for much longer," Caleb interrupts, taking a hard turn into a neighborhood.

The blue car breaks off from the line of traffic to make the same sharp turn, nearly causing an oncoming car to hit them. I swallow, flexing my free hand as it shakes.

"We have units heading in your direction. Do your best to not engage, please."

My phone vibrates in my hand with an incoming message, but I swipe it away before I even have time to see who it's from. I glance in the mirror again, and the blue car is directly behind us, not even trying to be subtle. Caleb and the dispatcher are going back and forth so the police can find us, but I can hardly make out what they're saying over the pounding in my ears. We make another sharp left, and then a right, and I'm thoroughly lost in the grid of narrow residential streets.

"Officers are inbound, two minutes out," the dispatcher says at some point.

My phone vibrates again, and I see that it's Rhett trying to call. But I can't answer with my phone in emergency mode. I swallow the lump in my throat. He's probably pacing like a caged animal. I can only hope he'll forgive me for this when I make it home.

"You're in a black Escalade, correct?" the dispatcher asks.

"Affirmative. I think I see your unmarked unit behind us," Caleb answers with clipped efficiency.

"There's a cul-de-sac coming up. The officer wants you to turn down there. Other units are incoming to block off the exits."

Caleb grunts his answer, then makes a hard left before making a quick right. The blue car blows the stop sign before we lose sight of him for a moment, but then he's making the same turn, too, caught up with the chase to notice the No Outlet sign. But just as the dispatcher said, the street ends in a wide circle surrounded by cookie-cutter houses.

The lights from the white car that followed behind come on as we're swinging around to leave. I start to relax, thinking that this is about to be all over. But then, there's squealing of tires moments before we're knocked sideways. I scream as the SUV rocks, arms coming up over my head. Metal screeches, the airbags pop, and blood covers my arms. My chest is on fire—

"We're okay, Lydia. You hear me? Open your eyes."

Caleb's deep rumbling command ripples through me, cold for a moment, before settling into something like rain sliding down my back. Refreshing rather than painful. After I open my eyes and realize we're stopped, the compulsion to obey fades almost immediately. The SUV is still running, but there is a significant tilt toward the back corner on the driver's side. The windshield is still intact, and none of the airbags have gone off.

Swallowing around my suddenly sore throat, I lower my arms. I look at my phone as it vibrates again, this time with a call from Lucas. My phone is still locked in emergency mode, but the call with the dispatcher has ended. When I look around, I find Caleb staring intently at me, scent strong with something salty. His concern fades as I take a deep breath and nod my thanks.

He turns and I follow his gaze as we realize that we're surrounded by police officers. The blue car is nearby, angled in our direction. I twist and realize with a jolt that he rammed into us as we were trying to leave.

"Stay in the car," Caleb instructs without looking at me.

He doesn't have to tell me twice. Caleb opens his door and climbs out, moving fast. But the door doesn't close fast enough behind him for me to not hear the garbled roar of shouting that was previously muffled. One voice stirs something in my mind, but I can't figure out where I've heard it before.

The locks engage with a loud thunk that makes me jump and I settle back into my seat with a sigh. I take several deep, measured breaths, trying to stop my body from shaking. My phone buzzes in my hand again, and I look down to a text message.

Luc: Hey, are you dead?

I can't help but smile a little. Leave it to Lucas to know how to break the tension.

**Me: No. There was an incident on the way home. I'm okay.
Caleb is okay. No one is hurt.
Luc: That's unhelpfully vague.
Me: We noticed someone was following us on the way
home, so we called the police. Caleb thinks it might be my
stalker.
Luc: Wow.
Luc: Okay, that's a lot.
Luc: Rhett is freaking out. Can you call him?**

I'm about to type out a response when there's a heavy slam of something against the driver's side door. My head whips up, and the scream rips from my throat before I can stop it. I'm staring into the wild eyes of a face I haven't thought about in months. His buzz cut has grown out a little, but the feral rage in those coal-black eyes is something I'll never forget. Davis, the worker who was fired from the Old Town awning repair job after he came into Wila's and harassed me, is throwing his fists into the driver's door, screaming wordlessly as he tries to get to me.

I've seen an alpha rage twice before in my life. The first was when I was a child and my father found out that my brothers and I were playing on the railroad tracks that ran near our home and only barely avoided being hit by a passing train. He laid into Sam and Adam, the ones who should have been old enough to know how dangerous that was, while leaving Jason and me out of it, but I'll never forget the way his face transformed into something out of a horror movie.

The second time was the night Darren proposed and then tried to force a bond on me for the last time. When he dug his teeth into my skin and ripped out chunks of flesh that I'm still missing to this day. When I was sure that he would kill me, or make me wish I was dead. There was no reasoning with him, no trying to fight back. I only survived because I didn't try to escape before he passed out.

And now, looking at Davis's nearly purple face as his fists come down on the window over and over, I see that madness in him. It's visceral. The raw, truly feral need to fight and kill and maim until the bloodlust can be satisfied. There are officers shouting at him to stop, some advancing with their guns drawn, but no one seems to be making any moves to stop him. Do they not see that he's not going to listen?

I try to move as far away as I can, scrambling to press my back into the door behind me. I want to run, but leaving this vehicle would get me closer, not farther away. I know I can't outrun him, and I can't win in a fight. So I do the thing my instincts demand: I tuck my chin and loll my head to the side, exposing my neck in submission. I let my arms go limp at my sides, trying to make myself as meek and small as possible. I feel the tears on my face, but I don't make any moves to wipe them away. The first crack of glass makes me flinch.

"GET THE FUCK AWAY FROM HER!"

The roar makes my head jerk up again, and Caleb's wrestling Davis away from the door, arms around his neck in a chokehold. Davis fights back, thrashing until he lands an elbow to Caleb's side. Caleb gasps and loosens his hold enough for Davis to turn and break away, throwing wild punches in rapid succession. I can only watch in horror as Caleb blocks each blow, taking two solid hits to his head before he can get his arms up. The senseless roaring coming out of Davis's throat seems to go on forever, but then suddenly Caleb springs like a cobra. His fist flies out and catches Davis's chin with one solid blow, and it's enough to daze the raging alpha. Caleb punches again, a massive right hook that hits solidly against the side of Davis's head, knocking him out cold.

It's over in seconds, but my heart still races like a rabbit in a trap. The police swarm Davis as he lies face down on the pavement, cuffing him before he can regain consciousness. They drag him over to a squad car, one officer staying back to talk to Caleb. I can't make out the words, but Caleb sways, holding his head with one hand. It's that sign of distress that finally lets me regain control of my body, and I scramble to unlock the door and run around the front of the car.

"Lydia, I told—"

"Are you okay?" I ask frantically, speaking over him.

"Headache, but I'll be fine. You should really—"

"Ma'am, are you Lydia Anderson?"

Caleb and I both turn to the officer, and my shoulders bunch as I wait for the vitriol I've gotten so used to hearing from anyone who asks that question.

"Why? What's your business?" Caleb answers, taking a step to put himself between me and the officer.

"We found a file in the suspect's car, and it has your name all over it," the young man goes on.

I blink, stunned. "A file?"

The officer nods. "We were doing a search right before Mr. Fischer..." The officer trails off, waving a hand vaguely in the air. "We're going to take him down to the station, but we'd like to discuss what sort of charges you'd like to press."

"We need to speak with her prime alpha and her lawyer. We'll be in touch," Caleb says sternly, before I have time to recover.

The officer nods, handing Caleb a business card before going back to speak with the other officers. I turn back to my bodyguard to see that he has a split lip, and a bruise is forming on the side of his head.

"Are you sure you're okay? Do you need to go to the hospital?" I ask softly.

Caleb shakes his head, but then winces. "It'll just be me wasting six hours for the doctors to tell me to go home and rest. So, let's just cut out that step. I know this is going to be a lot, but I'm not sure it's safe for me to drive right now. Do you think you..."

My eyes go wide as I look up into his face. His gray eyes are hazy with pain I know he's fighting not to show. I have no idea where we are, and how long it would take for Rhett or Lucas to find us, and then there would still be the problem of an extra vehicle. I swallow the fear building in my chest. He needs me, and I can do this. I take another deep breath before nodding once. No time like the present to conquer this hurdle.

TWENTY-SIX

Lucas

Lydi: I'm driving Caleb back to his house. Can you or Rhett come pick me up?
Me: Sure thing, sweetheart. See you soon.

"SHE'S TAKING HER BODYGUARD home. I guess there was a bit of a scuffle and he got knocked around a bit," I explain as I feel Rhett's eyes boring into the side of my head.

"Wait, she is driving? What the fuck is that fucker thinking?" Rhett exclaims, each word louder and more Irish than the last.

"She'll be—"

"She hasn't driven since the accident, Luc. And right after a stressful encounter is not the best—"

"According to whom, Rhett. Not the best time, according to whom," I shout over him.

He stops his pacing and looks at me with his jaw slack and eyes wide. He's used to me talking back, but full-on shouting is not my style. But I'm frankly sick of the babying attitude Rhett's adopted in the last few weeks. He's treating Lydia like she's made of spun sugar and one wrong step is going to send her scattering to the four winds. But she's so much more than a doll to be dressed up and kept on a shelf.

"Her doctors told her she's clear to drive again. And if she says she's ready, then we have to believe her," I continue, lowering my voice slightly, but not letting up on the heat.

"She could have a panic attack—"

"And if she does, then we deal with it at that point. But we can't keep doing this to her, Rhett."

"Doing what, exactly?"

"Acting like we know what's best for her. If we don't let her be herself, and think for herself, and make her own fucking decisions, then we're no better than that piece of shit we're trying to protect her from."

Rhett goes silent, staggering back a step. I've hit a nerve and I'm just irritated enough to not care. Rhett needs to see what's happening before it's too late. And if he's going to listen to anyone, it's going to be me. He sinks down onto the sectional, and I watch as he hangs his head in his hands, breathing hard. I move on instinct, sliding up to sit beside him and put a hand on his back, rubbing in soothing circles.

"What the fuck is wrong with me, Luc?" Rhett whispers.

I blink in surprise, but don't let my worry for him show in my body language. I've never seen Rhett this torn up before, and it kills me to see my alpha this way.

"I love her so fucking much, but I feel like I'm just ruining everything. I don't know what's gotten into me, but I can't stop thinking that every time she's out of my sight that it's going to be the last time I see her," he goes on.

The realization hits me like a dump truck. Rhett put her in her car the night of the accident. He was the last person to see her before what very well could have been a fatal accident.

"She's okay now, Rhett. She survived, and she's still here," I say gently.

"But what if..."

Rhett trails off, taking a shuddering breath. I move closer, laying my head on his shoulder as I wrap my arm tightly around his back. He shakes under me, and I have to swallow the lump in my throat. My alpha has so much room in his heart, and there are so many feelings trapped there. His love for us, his anger, his drive and ambition, and his fear.

"It's okay to be scared for her. It's okay to want to keep her safe. There isn't anything wrong with wanting to protect us from harm," I start, trying to keep my voice as even as possible.

"But I don't want to hurt her. I don't want to become someone she fears or resents in the name of protecting her."

I squeeze him before pressing a kiss to his shoulder. "You can see that it's wrong. That already makes you better than them. And it's okay to mess up and forget sometimes. You're only human. The important thing is to try to do better in the future."

Rhett nods and goes quiet for a long time. I keep stroking his back in the silence, letting him feel my love and support without needing to speak. After a while, Rhett leans into me, and I support his weight. His head finds its way to rest on my shoulder, and I kiss his golden hair tenderly.

"I'm sorry I've been acting like a total knothead," he mumbles.

"I wouldn't say that. Maybe just a partial knothead," I tease gently.

He chuckles and I relax slightly. He lifts his head to look up at me with icy eyes full of emotion. The fear still dances there, but I don't expect it'll go away soon. I lean down and press a soft kiss to his lips, and he returns it without hesitation. My stomach does a little swoop, but Rhett has always given me butterflies. When we pull apart, he sits up to his full height before gathering me into his side.

"I love you," he whispers into my hair.

"I love you, too. Now, who's going to go get our girl?"

Rhett pulls away to look at me with a raised brow. "Our girl?"

I roll my eyes. "You didn't think I'd be able to stay away from someone as adorable as Lydia, did you?" I ask, only half joking.

Rhett laughs and shakes his head. "Go get her. I've got work I've got to do on that recent donation."

"Oh, you mean the hoarding stash?" I deadpan with a snort as I stand.

I can practically hear his eyes rolling from across the room. "It's not that bad. And who knows what we're going to find."

I shake my head. An Everton ex-pat recently passed, and he was something of a local history buff. His family heard about the work we've been doing to restore historical landmarks in the city and dumped his "collection" with us. According to Rhett, the pallet of boxes we received the other day is a treasure trove, but it just looks like piles of old newspapers and faded photographs.

"I'll leave you to it, then. Don't wait up," I toss over my shoulder as I descend the stairs.

I shut the door before I can hear whatever overprotective nonsense he tries to throw at me. I turn left at the bottom of the stairs and open the door to my workshop and garage. The air smells like grease and spices, and I sigh. I debate for a moment whether I should take my car, but it's such a nice day. I don't know how many of these we have left, and I've been dying to take Lydia for a ride.

So with that thought, I strap an extra helmet on my bike before throwing on my leather riding jacket and my own helmet. I've been riding motorcycles since before I turned eighteen, but this is by far the nicest set of wheels I've ever owned. Lex gifted it to me for my birthday last year, and that only makes me love it more. The paint is custom, dark green and white running along the gas tank and panels. I throw my leg over the seat and let the first roar of the engine wash over me as I start it up.

I rev the engine as I pretend to not hear Rhett. He's shouting something about recklessness and my bike being too dangerous for Lydia right now, but it's not like I'd start doing wheelies or anything like that with her with me. As I back out of the garage and take off up the hill, out of the driveway, and into the fading afternoon light, I smile to myself, imagining all the fun ways Rhett would make me pay for this later.

TWENTY-SEVEN

Lydia

BY THE TIME I pull into the driveway next to a pale yellow house, my back is covered in sweat. My hands ache from holding onto the wheel with a death grip for the fifteen minutes it took to get from the scene to Caleb's house. I sit for another moment after I put the car in park and shut off the engine, letting the shaking in my limbs slow and fade.

"You did great, Lydia," Caleb says brightly from the passenger seat.

I only nod, not trusting my voice right now. He sat patiently next to me as I inched across the city, only giving gentle encouragement as I spent far too long checking crossroads and driving well below the speed limit.

"It's going to be a minute before your pack gets here. You should come in," Caleb says kindly, opening his door.

I nod again, my ebbing fear being replaced by nervousness in my belly. I've never really interacted with other omegas outside of my family, so I don't know what to expect. Some get territorial when I'm around because I'm unbonded. I don't want Sylvie to hate me because of how much time I spend with her mate, but I can't politely refuse at this point. I slide out of the car, wrapping my arms around my stomach as I approach where Caleb waits for me at the bottom of the front porch stairs.

The house itself is simple, but there's an air of comfort around the place. There's a swing off to the right of the front door, with a faded pillow and slightly rusty chains holding it up. The wood under me creaks as I follow behind Caleb and pass through the screen door and plain wood front door.

"*Kokhanyy*, I'm home!" Caleb calls into the house.

I glance around as I follow his lead and toe off my shoes. The front entryway is a comfortable clutter of shoes and coats, but it doesn't feel overwhelming. The living room beyond is the same sort of lived-in controlled chaos. Everything smells of snickerdoodles and cedar and salt and something musky. I drag in a deep breath and my body relaxes even though my mind is still working overtime.

"About fucking time! Dinner's going to—oh, hello!"

At the sound of a woman's voice, a light, bubbly sound despite the profanity, I turn to an open doorway to find the source standing there staring at me. The first thing that hits me is the bubblegum pink hair that sits in a messy bun on the top of her head, pieces escaping in every direction and giving her a distinctly frazzled air. The next thing I notice is that she's visibly pregnant, her swollen belly giving her a slightly unbalanced look.

Caleb moves to her, and I realize how small she is when he reaches her and gathers her into his arms, kissing her tenderly. She has to rise onto the very tips of her toes, and even then, the top of her head just brushes his chin. Seeing my tough-as-nails bodyguard, the alpha who just took three good punches to the head, melting like ice cream in July as he leans down and rubs her round belly and covers it with kisses is almost too much for my brain to take in.

"Hello, I'm Lydia," I start, feeling supremely out of place.

At the sound of my name, the woman, who I gather to be Sylvie, relaxes and lets out a chuckle. "Oh, right. You're Caleb's baby."

"I'm sorry, what?" I splutter, blinking rapidly.

"*Kokhanyy*, I told you to stop calling them that," Caleb growls, but the fond smile on his face really takes the heat out of the sound. He turns back to me and shoots me an apologetic look. "She thinks my job is just glorified babysitting."

I can't help but chuckle. I'm about to respond, but a beeping from the kitchen makes Sylvie gasp. She turns, swaying dangerously off balance as she waddles back into the kitchen. Caleb looks torn between following her and staying with me, and I giggle softly.

"Please, have a seat. Your pack knows where to find you?" he tells me, motioning to the dining room table.

I nod, taking the offered seat and looking around. The walls are covered in a slightly outdated wallpaper, but the blue floral is barely visible under the collection of framed photos and art projects. There are some of the two of them at what appears to be their wedding day, some of a newborn, and the most recent of Caleb, a pregnant Sylvie, and a little boy, maybe five or six.

"I've got it, you giant mother hen," I hear Sylvie snap from beyond the door to the kitchen.

I can't see them, but Caleb reappears with a bag of frozen peas pressed to his head. He's lost the jacket at some point, the empty gun harness still hanging around his shoulder.

"You were armed that whole time?" I gasp in disbelief.

"I'm armed whenever I'm on duty," Caleb replies, like it's no big deal.

"Why didn't—You could have—"

"It wasn't the right move. I knew I could take him out without my weapon. And with the police, nothing makes them twitchier than someone pulling a gun in a fistfight," Caleb goes on, pulling out the chair at the head of the table and sitting.

I can hear Sylvie bustling around, cupboards opening and closing, dishes clattering, and even her muttering slightly to herself. All the while, Caleb looks between me and the kitchen door, a fond smile on his face. I'm quiet until my curiosity can't take it anymore.

"You and Sylvie have been bonded for three years, right?" I ask, dropping my voice so it doesn't carry.

Caleb nods. "She isn't Leo's birth mother, if that's what you're getting at."

I blush and look away, embarrassed to have been caught so fast. Caleb only chuckles and sets the frozen peas on the table.

"My son's mother lives out of state. After I came back from my tour, we tried to make it work, but we'd both changed. Leo was a surprise, but it was for the best that we went our separate ways. Beth and I are better friends and co-parents for it. We trade Christmases, and Leo spends his spring and summer breaks here. Sylvie loves kids, and he loves having two moms," he explains.

His eyes drift to the largest portrait of the three of them, the most recent one by the size of Sylvie's baby bump. There's a sparkle in Caleb's gray eyes that makes my heart melt.

"What's it like? Being bonded?" I whisper, a little bashfully.

Caleb looks at me, and he tilts his head slightly, curiosity in his eyes. "Has no one ever..."

I shake my head. "My parents are bonded, but they never talk about it. My mom never even taught me how to use my omega purr."

Caleb nods, and a sadness flickers in his eyes for a moment before it vanishes. He looks off to the side, not really seeing anything before he answers.

"It's not like having someone else living in your head. It's more like... never being lonely again."

I hum as I consider that, my brow furrowing. When I don't answer right away, Caleb looks at me, his smile warm.

"Sometimes, when I'm stressed or tired, my mind puts me back in that Humvee, trapped with no way out, no one to hear me yelling for help. Before the bond, I could lose days to episodes like that. But with Sylvie... she can help guide me back home. There's never any guessing if we're just having a bad day, or if there's something else going on. We just... know. You'd think that being connected to someone like that would be invasive or uncomfortable, but it's not."

The warmth to his voice, the complete lack of irony toward any of those feelings, makes a lump form in my throat. All this time, being bonded felt like a trap, a cage for an alpha to keep me in and control me. No one had ever described the peace I see on Caleb's face, or the joy in his eyes when he looks at Sylvie's picture on the wall. But now...

Would it be so bad to share something like that with Rhett? Or Mateo? Or even Lex? There would never be reason for fear again, because they would always know I'm safe, and I would know they're with me, even when we're apart. Would Rhett's temper improve if I were there to soothe him, not only with words, but with the very essence of my being? Would Mateo wander less often, because he'd finally be able to feel peace when he's at home? Would Lex hide from us so much if she knew we all care and support her, no matter what?

"Isn't he just a big sap?" Sylvie sighs fondly.

I jump and whip my head around to find her leaning on the doorframe, one hand idly rubbing circles on her belly. Caleb turns and looks, and his smile changes, gets brighter somehow. She pushes off and comes over to stand next to his chair. He purrs a little as she runs her fingers through his hair, and I can't help but smile. The love between them is a tangible thing, warming the entire room with the scent of cinnamon and sugar.

"Are you staying for supper? I can put a plate together for you," she says, looking up at me with kind eyes.

As if on cue, the familiar sound of a motorcycle engine pulls up out front. "Thank you, but my...boyfriend is here." My chest warms as I say the word out loud. Labels haven't come up, but it feels right to call him my partner. Well, one of them at least.

Caleb wraps an arm around Sylvie's hips and kisses her stomach before getting up. "I'll walk you to the door."

I nod, giving Sylvie another smile before following Caleb out. I slip my shoes on and look up at him again.

"You going to be okay?" I ask cautiously.

"Oh, yeah. Drive home safe," he responds, putting a hand on my shoulder.

I smile and nod before heading out of the door. Lucas is parked behind Caleb's SUV, the bike propped on its kickstand as he inspects the sizeable dent in the rear corner. He looks up as I approach, his lopsided smile making my heart do a jig. When I'm within arm's reach, he grabs the back of my neck and pulls me in for a heated kiss. When we break apart, my stomach is fluttering, and I sway on my feet.

"You got a sweatshirt or something?" Lucas asks, walking back to his bike.

Shaking my head, my mouth waters as he swings one leg over the seat and settles. He unzips his leather jacket, revealing a plain long-sleeved shirt and motions for me to come closer. He takes my bag and secures it inside the saddlebag before pulling me close and slipping his riding jacket around my shoulders. It's a tight squeeze, thanks to my ample bosom, but he manages to get the zipper up all the way. When I step back, I can't help but smirk at the open expression of awe and pure need that flashes across his beautiful face before he shakes his head.

I follow his instructions, mounting up behind him and putting my feet on the pegs. He hands me a helmet, which he double checks before kicking over the engine. I smile a little, excitement and nervousness mixing in my belly. I wrap my arms around his waist, leaning into his back as he reverses out of the driveway and takes off down the street.

TWENTY-EIGHT

Lydia

AT FIRST, WHEN LUCAS pulls away, I have the unsettling drop in my stomach that comes right before falling, off balance and panicky. But as we settle into the drive, I become hyperaware of the way my body feels atop a machine like this. I can feel the heat of the exhaust even through my jeans, and the vibration of the engine between my legs. I follow as Lucas leads, tilting with him as he makes smooth curves and turns. I can feel the way his chest expands and relaxes with each breath, and I find a tiny kernel of longing for his scent that I usually get when I'm this close. But the helmet blocks it out, along with the rush of the wind past us.

[]Breathe, Lydi-bug, or you'll pass out."

I jump as I hear his voice inside my helmet, as if he was speaking into my ear. Sucking in a sharp inhale, I realize that I haven't actually done that since we left Caleb's house. I can feel my face heat, and I'm glad that Lucas can't see me.

[]Want to go faster?" he asks.

[]This isn't fast?" I ask back with a breathless chuckle.

Lucas pulls to a stop at a red light and we both sit up slightly from our bent position. I stretch my back, but I find that I sort of enjoy the way my body feels with the exertion.

[]We're in the city, sweetheart. Thirty is hardly that fast," Lucas teases.

I swallow hard, adjusting my grip. Thirty certainly felt fast, but I can't deny the little tickle in the back of my mind that is curious about how it would feel to say yes. Eventually, as the light changes, I can't deny that curiosity any longer.

[]Yeah, let's do it," I tell him, clinging tighter as we lean down again.

[]Then hold on tight."

His words are the only warning I get before the engine roars, and we take off like a shot through the city streets. The buildings are like gray blurs on either side of us, but I can hardly take anything in. The wind whips at the tendrils of my hair that aren't contained by my helmet, and I feel the bite of the air against the exposed skin on the backs of my hands. But all of those sensations are secondary to the soaring in my heart as we continue to pick up speed. I want to scream and laugh and cry all at the same time, but nothing about the emotions in my chest feels wrong or painful. In fact, a weight seems to fall away as we round a bend and Lucas really lays on the accelerator.

The route Lucas takes is definitely the long way home, but I don't mind at all. My cheeks hurt from smiling by the time we make it to the gate of Bristol Point. We don't speak as we drive much slower through the curving streets, pulling into the driveway and down the hill to the lower garage. Once the noise of the engine fades, I realize how hard my heart is pounding. I dismount clumsily, watching as Lucas moves fluidly, swinging his leg over the bike and turning to me. My hands shake as I pull the helmet off and turn to set it on the worktable behind me.

[]Luc, that was—"

I don't get to finish my sentence because his lips find mine in a crushing kiss, his fingers threading into my windswept hair. My eyes go wide for a moment before I relent with a moan, eyelids sliding down as my tongue meets his. His taste is all pine smoke, a heady rush of lust that instantly sets my stomach quivering and my thighs clenching.

His hands move down to cup my breasts through the tight leather jacket, and I arch into the touch, my own hands fisting in the hair at the nape of his neck. We've kissed and cuddled plenty, but it's always been a dance with us, neither of us wanting to lead without the other's permission. Circling the drain of desire has been driving me crazy, and I'm more than ready to be sucked under. I let him walk us backwards blindly until the backs of my thighs hit the edge of the worktable. I hop up and he presses forward into the cradle of my thighs, and I can feel the bulge of his cock against my core when I wrap my legs around his.

[]Fuck, Lydia. I need you," Lucas pants when he pulls away for air.

The raw desire in his voice threatens to undo me. My hands come down to the hem of his t-shirt, and we pull it up over his head in one smooth motion. I can't help but run my fingers across the expanse of colorful images inked into the skin of his chest and arms, admiring the artistry. Lucas uses a finger to draw my gaze back to his face. There's an intensity to his steel-blue eyes I haven't seen before, and I find I can't look away.

[]We don't have to do this, if you don't want to," he starts, words barely above a whisper.

I blink once in confusion, but something roars to life in my chest as I finally recognize that intense look. He's nervous and insecure, emotions I know all too well. I toss my hair as I unzip the jacket, shucking it and tossing it on the floor, letting my shirt and bra follow behind shortly.

[]I want you, too, Luc," I say simply, looking back up into his face.

Lucas groans as he looks me up and down once before leaning in and tilting his lips over mine again. I lean back, drawing him down with me. Papers and books slide under my hands, but I shove them away, not caring as they scatter across the floor. Lucas does the same until my back is against the smooth wood and the warm skin of his chest is flush against mine.

He breaks the kiss, trailing his mouth down my throat and chest in open-mouthed kisses until his lips finally close over my nipple. I whimper and arch into the sensation, my fingers coming to tangle in his hair again. I give an experimental tug, rewarded with a low moan and the brush of teeth against my skin.

I exhale his name as his mouth moves to my other breast, and his hands massage my aching flesh with tender fingers. My entire body fills with the need for more. I tug again, and his fingers flex and relax, digging with the pressure that I crave.

[]You're not the only one who likes a bit of pain," I manage through breathy chuckles.

Lucas looks up at me through the curtain of his fringe, mouth slanted into a smirk. He returns his mouth to my breasts, this time with much firmer touches that make my skin light up. I can feel my slick soaking through my panties as his hips idly grind against mine, but it's not enough.

[]Give me... I need..." I start, words slipping like water through my fingers as I try to voice the all-consuming need under my skin.

[]I know, sweetheart. I've got you," he mumbles against my skin.

Lucas trails down my stomach, his lips brushing feather light kisses until he reaches the button of my jeans. I gasp as he tugs purposefully with his mouth, deftly popping the button and dragging down the zipper with nothing but his teeth. His short nails drag along my skin as he pulls off my jeans, leaving me in nothing but my soaked panties.

[]Lucas? Lydia?"

Lucas groans at the sound of Rhett's voice echoing down the stairs from the main floor, growling with enough heat to rival any alpha I've ever met. My stomach does a little flip, breath hitching in my throat. I turn to look at the door that leads to the rest of the house, but it stays closed. When I open my mouth to answer, Lucas seizes the side of my panties and yanks violently, effectively shredding them in his grip. I don't manage anything other than a low moan as Lucas's mouth descends on my slit, tongue delving deep.

[]What was that? Are you okay?" Rhett asks, voice getting closer.

I gasp as Lucas flicks my clit with rapid licks, my back arching nearly off the table.

[]Can you answer? I'm a little busy," Lucas mumbles when he surfaces for a breath.

[]We're fine!" I try to shout back, the last word more of a squeak than an intelligible word as two of Lucas's fingers slide into my pussy while his tongue returns to my clit.

[]You sure?"

Lucas growls, and I can't help my deep moan as the vibration pushes me right to the edge. He sits up and leans over me, his fingers still pumping hard and fast.

[]Go on and tell him to fuck off when you come on my fingers, sweetheart," Lucas purrs.

[]Oh, God. I'm—FUCK OFF!" I scream, falling over the edge as I squirm across the smooth wood beneath me.

[]Excuse me?"

I swallow hard, fear creeping in despite the buzzing aftershocks of my climax. Lucas slows his fingers and withdraws, leaving me hollow and aching for more. I look up and find him smirking down at me.

[]Ooo, you've done it now," he whispers in a singsong voice.

[]You told me to!" I protest, smacking him lightly on the shoulder.

One of Lucas's hands comes up to brush some hair from my face, and I can feel the other one between us, undoing his jeans.

[]Let me make it up to you," he says with a little chuckle.

I'm about to complain again, but then I feel the head of his cock against my dripping folds. He works it up and down once, coating himself in my climax before sliding into my channel. Mateo and Rhett have impressive dicks, but the girth of Lucas stretches me wide in the best possible way. My head falls back as my eyes roll into the back of my head. I'm still sensitive from my orgasm, and each slow roll as he works himself deeper and deeper feels like heaven.

[]You like my cock? Like feeling me inside of you?" Lucas whispers against my throat.

I whimper and nod vigorously, my hands coming up to cling to his biceps. He groans and snaps his hips when I dig my nails in, adding that bit of pleasure-pain I know he likes. It takes two more thrusts before I feel him bottom out, but he doesn't slow his pace.

[]So, little one, do you want to try that—"

Lucas and I snap our heads to the door in unison, finding Rhett standing there. He's wearing sweats and his hair is mussed, but the heat in his eyes as he looks at us from under a lowered brow makes my pussy throb and my heart race.

[]Again?" Rhett finishes, his tone a strange mix of confusion and amusement.

Lucas thrusts slowly, and I moan despite myself. Maybe it's the pine smoke essence of Lucas filling me with extra courage, or the way every stroke of Lucas's cock inside of me makes my body sing, but I find I like the way Rhett's eyes flicker with annoyance. I gasp and arch as Lucas fucks into me with long, deep strokes, sighing with pleasure.

[]No, I don't," I purr, looking back at Rhett with a smirk.

His growl makes goosebumps rise on my skin, but I only throw my head back and laugh, gasping as Lucas hits that perfect spot inside of me, sending me reeling over the edge again. I watch Lucas's eyes roll into the back of his head as my pussy tightens down on him, and I stroke his hair back and pull a little, riding the waves of another orgasm.

[]Did you just—"

[]FUCK OFF!"

Lucas and I shout in unison, Lucas slowing for a moment as he looks toward the doorway. I look as well, and a little of my boldness fades at the blazing heat in Rhett's eyes. He crosses to us in four long strides, and I release Lucas's hair when Rhett's fingers take over. Lucas's head wrenches back, and he lets out a gasp that I'm not sure is fully pleasure or pain.

[]You best see to it that my omega is satisfied, pet," Rhett growls, leaning in to speak into Lucas's ear.

Lucas nods as best he can with his head in Rhett's grip, and a patch of warmth blooms in my chest. Rhett's eyes lock with mine, and I expect to see jealousy, but there's only pure need and admiration there. I flush, tucking my chin with a bashful smile. Lucas leans in and whispers something I don't catch into Rhett's ear, but whatever he says, a truly evil grin forms on the alpha's face. Rhett lets go, and Lucas's head falls forward. I jump at the crack of flesh on flesh, but Lucas is the one who flinches, turning to watch Rhett walk away. The door latches closed a moment later, then Rhett's feet thump up the stairs, leaving us to finish what we started.

[]We're going to pay for this later, aren't we?" I ask with a sigh.

"Yeah, probably. But this is worth whatever that knothead can come up with."

I laugh again, only to scream when Lucas's hips snap forward hard enough to shake the table. My nails drag down his arms, leaving red marks, but neither of us care. We breathe hard, faces pressed close as we hold eye contact. Each heartbeat brings me closer to the edge.

[]Do you feel how hard you make me, sweetheart? You wreck me," Lucas whispers.

I whimper, nodding as I wrap my legs around his waist, rocking back as best as I can. He sits back, grasping my calves to bring them up onto his shoulders. The new angle allows him to reach even deeper, and I whine his name as he pounds into me over and over. I teeter right on the edge of release, and Lucas holds me there, dangling on the precipice of ecstasy.

[]I want to come so bad for you, Lydia. Please, please come with me," Lucas begs, his head falling back as his hips lose their steady rhythm.

Hearing how overcome he is, the desperation in his voice does something to my heart. I gasp as the table shakes and let go. I fall over into pure pleasure, my orgasm like molten lava as it spreads through my veins. My toes curl and my back bows, nearly lifting my torso off the surface. Lucas grunts and moans with abandon as my walls milk him to his own release. I feel the hot gush of his spend, and Lucas slows his thrusts to draw out our pleasure. Only when I put a hand on his arm and whimper does he finally stop, his cock still hard for the moment. The only sound in the workshop for a long time is our breathing as we collect ourselves.

[]Wow," I puff out on an exhale.

Lucas chuckles and finally withdraws his softening cock. There's a familiar drip of our combined release as my pussy flutters, and I feel my face heat even as my stomach clenches. Lucas finds a clean rag and wipes me up before helping me sit up on the edge of the table.

[]So shall we go make sure our alpha isn't feeling too left out?" Lucas asks with a fake sigh.

I giggle. "We have to apologize somehow."

Lucas hums in mock thought before nodding. I blink as he quickly sheds the remainder of his clothes before extending a hand toward me. I take it and hop down, letting him lace his fingers through mine before he leads me through the door to find Rhett.

Hopefully, no one can stay mad at their naked partners for long.

TWENTY-NINE

Lydia

LUCAS LEADS ME UP the stairs, and my stomach flutters with sudden nerves. In the moment, talking back had seemed like a good idea, but now that I'm about to face the consequences, I'm not as sure. As we step into the kitchen, I wrap my free arm around my middle, my entire body warm with a blush. I can't take my eyes off my feet, my shoulders hunching forward.

"Hey, you okay?" Lucas whispers, coming to a sudden stop.

I look up at the question, finding Lucas standing with his back to the sitting area, close enough to block everything except his face from my view. His brow is pulled low, and his mouth is a serious frown. The hand not holding mine comes up to cup my jaw.

"I'll deal with Rhett if you want me to. You don't have to do this," he continues, voice low enough not to carry.

I blink, taken aback by the sudden shift in his mood from playful to dead serious. "We don't even know what's going to happen," I mutter, not sure what else to say.

"You just look really nervous, sweetheart. If this is too much—"

Smiling softly, I shake my head. His concern for me softens my heart, and I lean into his touch. "Just... we're walking around naked. I don't usually do stuff like this," I admit, wrapping my arm a little tighter around my stomach pooch, fingers digging into the stretch marks on my sides.

Lucas glances down and smirks as his eyes slowly come back up to meet mine. "Feel free to do it more, if you're so inclined. I won't complain," he purrs.

I blush hotter, not able to meet his eye for an entirely different reason. I'm about to respond when Rhett clears his throat loudly and pointedly from the sitting room. Lucas rolls his eyes and gives me a last smirk before turning around and continuing into the sitting room.

"Do you need a lozenge?" Lucas drawls, taking two long strides before vaulting over the back of the sectional.

I look over and find Rhett's icy gaze locked on me as he lounges on the part of the sectional nearest to the picture window. He's changed out of sweats and into black slacks and a gunmetal gray button-down with the sleeves rolled up to the elbow. One of his arms is stretched over the back of the sectional, his legs spread wide. He looks like a golden Viking warrior, dangerous even while at rest. He's holding a crystal glass of amber liquor, and he takes a slow sip as he brazenly rakes his eyes up and down my body.

"So, what's it going to be? The thumb biter? The rack? Are you going to have us drawn and quartered?" Lucas starts, getting increasingly more dramatic as he speaks.

Rhett spares him a glance, but looks back to me before crooking a single finger, beckoning me forward silently. I scurry to obey, moving to stand in front of him with my head bowed.

"Are you going to apologize now, or do I have to pull it out of you?" he asks calmly.

"What for? We didn't break any of your rules," Lucas replies before I can answer.

I look over to find him stretched out, practically begging for someone to paint him like one of their French girls. My stomach clenches as I notice his cock is back to half-hardness, the size impressive even at this stage.

"Your Domina disagrees, pet," Rhett says slowly, taking a sip of his drink.

Lucas sits up with a gasp, and I shiver. It doesn't take a genius to tell he's talking about Lex. I swallow, trying to keep my hands still. If I was nervous before, I'm positively terrified now. Rhett's eyes are bland, and my lower lip trembles at the slight downturn of his lips as he looks at me.

I feel about three inches tall, and I can't stand the silence a moment longer.

"I'm sorry, sir. I didn't—Lucas had me all worked up, and I didn't know what I was saying—"

"Wow, you really *do* fold like a cheap suit," Lucas scoffs.

Rhett smirks and pats the couch beside him. I practically fall over myself to curl into his side, nuzzling his chest as he wraps the arm that had been over the back of the couch around my shoulders.

"Lex is on her way home. She wants you to go into my room and select a ring and a strap for this," Rhett instructs sternly.

Lucas lets out another irritated sigh, but he gets up and walks toward the stairs, muttering something that sounds like "making me pick my own switch from the willow tree." He makes no small amount of noise as he stomps up the stairs and out of earshot.

"I'm really sorry. I didn't—"

"You're fine, love. I'm not upset. You and Lucas have every right to do what you want with whomever you want," Rhett purrs, rubbing my back soothingly.

I look up and find him smiling down at me. Relief floods my chest, and I smile a little. "Then why is Lucas—"

"Picking his own switch, as he so eloquently put it?" Rhett finishes for me with a laugh. I nod and he leans down to kiss my forehead. "Because he wants to. Before I left, he told me not to hold back when I punished him for what happened."

"So, I'm off the hook?" I ask hesitantly.

Rhett shrugs with one shoulder. "If you want to be. I can get you a blanket, or some clothes if you'd prefer, and we can go up to my room while Lex plays with her food. Or..." Rhett trails off, tracing a line up my arm with a single finger. Goosebumps trail in its wake and I shiver, my breath catching. "I can teach you a lesson for mouthing off, but only if you promise not to enjoy it too much. I don't know if I can handle more than one brat in my life."

I look up into the warmth of his eyes, and I lose myself for a moment in the crystal depths. The fire there is more of a smolder than an inferno, and the honesty in his face is enough to settle my roiling nerves. I trust Rhett, and I've missed the dangerously playful side of him.

"Will Lex... will she be... punishing me, too?" I ask, as the concern flares to life in my chest.

While I've thought about what it would be like to surrender to her, now that the opportunity is presenting itself, I find that I'm not sure I'm ready for that sort of... intensity. Rhett must observe my worry in my face, because he shakes his head and holds me a little tighter.

"No, my love. Not today. But this would be a good opportunity for you to see what it's like. And if you feel uncomfortable for any reason, we can leave, no questions asked," he replies.

I look away, taking a deep breath. I don't know what to expect, but my curiosity is nearly overwhelming. I trust Rhett to keep things from going too far, and I always have my safe words. So I look back to Rhett's face and nod purposefully, setting my shoulders.

"I'm ready to accept punishment for what I've done, sir," I tell him confidently.

Rhett blinks, and the softness disappears. His pupils grow wide, leaving only a faint circle of blue visible. His smile sharpens, and I have to fight to keep still. When he leans down and presses his lips to mine, I let my head fall back, melting in his arms and submitting to his will automatically. It's as easy as breathing, and I moan at the taste of his tongue against mine. When he pulls away, I'm left breathless and lightheaded, my pulse throbbing between my legs.

"Up on your knees facing the back of the couch, little one. Hands behind your back," Rhett commands.

I move into his requested position, spreading my knees wide to balance on the relatively narrow seat. Rhett stands and sets his glass on the mantle before moving off somewhere out of my line of sight. I don't dare turn to follow him, knowing better than to move from a position like this. A moment later, I hum with delight as his fingers brush my hair back, gathering it at the nape of my neck before braiding it in a single plait down my back. Once secured, he reaches for something, and I shiver at the first familiar brush of silk rope against my skin.

"I'd like to bind you for the duration of this session, but if anything starts to ache or go numb, you say so immediately. Understand, little one?"

"Yes, sir."

"Good girl."

I smile to myself at the praise, closing my eyes as Rhett begins. It takes less time than I'd have thought, but by the time he's done, my forearms are bound parallel to each other across my midback, the tension of the rope forcing my back to arch, presenting my breasts. More rope crisscrosses over my chest and stomach, creating a harness that digs deliciously into my skin. It's surprisingly comfortable and almost feels like an embrace. I'm starting to feel the beginnings of the floating peace I've come to enjoy as Rhett runs his fingers over the lines before stepping away and sitting back in his spot.

"At my feet, little one," Rhett orders.

I nod and wobble slightly as I rise, my balance off without the use of my arms. Rhett helps to guide me to my wait pose, settling me close enough for him to stroke my hair idly. I close my eyes and let my mind drift, aware of the warmth of his leg as it radiates into my skin. I don't know how long I'm adrift before footsteps sound on the stairs again.

"We really need to do a purge of your dildo collection. It's getting out of h—h-hello, there," Lucas says, words going faint as he cuts himself off.

"I hope you didn't take all that time getting off without your Domina's permission," Rhett replies coolly, not acknowledging the change in Lucas's tone.

"I may have spent a moment getting prepared. You're letting Lydia play this game?" Lucas says, voice growing closer and slightly edged with protective concern.

"She chose this, same as you, pet. But I'll be taking care of her while Lex takes care of you. Speaking of which..."

Rhett trails off, and in the distance, the garage door opens. When I open my eyes, Lucas is turned toward the kitchen, his eyes wide and mouth shut tight. He's holding a bundle of leather strips and buckles, with something red in the middle of it, the shape unmistakable but big enough to make me blush. A quick glance down his chest reveals a black ring around the base of Lucas's mostly soft cock, and I have to swallow. I stop myself from imagining what Lex is going to do with such an accessory, because I won't have to wait long to find out. From my position on the floor, I can only hear the mudroom door opening, then the sound of high heels on the hardwood floor growing closer.

"I'm not sure what you've heard, but I can explain—"

"But you won't. And if you speak without permission again, they're going to need to think up a new name to call the shade of red I'll turn your ass," Lex growls.

I drop my eyes on instinct, shifting closer to Rhett's leg. His hand settles on my hair, a weight that helps to center me. The clicking of her heels and the padding of Lucas's bare feet as he takes a few steps backward come into my periphery.

"I see you're at least capable of following some directions without someone needing to hold your hand," she purrs, and I almost feel her voice like a touch along my back. I breathe through the urge to turn away, to shift to hide my nudity against Rhett's leg. But he hasn't given me permission to move, and if her tone is anything to go by, I'm not sure Lex would tolerate my disobedience even if I'm not part of her game.

The sudden loud thwap of the strap hitting the ground makes me jump, and I look up in time to watch Lex grab Lucas by the neck and shove him onto the ottoman. He lands with a hard thump on his back, and he coughs as the wind gets knocked out of him. Rhett shifts, and I watch a bundle of rope, the same emerald green silk rope he used on me, sail through the air, and Lex catches it deftly. Before Lucas can recover, Lex has kicked off her shoes and moves around the ottoman, catching Lucas's arms and pinning them to the ottoman above his head with her hips. Her hands are a confident blur, but I can't take my eyes off her face. Her lips are turned up in a blood-colored snarl of triumph, her eyes dancing with feral delight as she secures Lucas to a previously unseen hook on the underside of the ottoman. It's not the elegant bindings Rhett favors, more of a quick but secure series of knots that, despite his thrashing, hold Lucas firmly in place. Once she's satisfied and Lucas stops fighting, she stands, looking down at him for a moment before her attention suddenly snaps to me.

"We're going to talk later about what happened today, sweetness," she says, the predator receding for a moment.

"I'm sorry. I didn't mean to—"

"I meant what happened on your way home, Lydia," she interrupts with a little chuckle.

I flush and look away. I'd nearly forgotten about the car chase in the excitement of the last hour. A slim finger lifts my chin, and I look up to find Lex kneeling in front of me. Her smile is kind, and I can't help but return the expression.

"You look as pretty as a present all done up like this, my lovely little omega. Do I get to unwrap you?" she coos, brushing her knuckles along my cheek.

I try to form words, but the connection between my mouth and my brain short circuits as her finger continues down my throat to my chest, brushing feather light over my stiff, aching nipple. My eyes flutter closed, the world shrinking to the size of her fingertip and the trail of molten fire it leaves in its wake as she moves lower and lower. Over my stomach, the seam of my hip, the edge of my swollen, dripping, slit.

"Did you let him fill your greedy little pussy, my lovely? Is his cum dripping from you right now, hmm?" Lex murmurs, so low I can barely hear her over the pounding of my heart.

I whimper as her fingers part my folds, my walls clenching on nothing as I inhale a sharp, shuddering breath.

"Do you think about my boys filling you up? Giving you so much cum that it drips from all your pretty little holes?" Her words float by my ear in a whisper, but I hardly care as her finger finds my clit, circling with the lightest pressure. "Because I do, my sweet. I think about them fucking you until you're spent, and their seed takes root in your belly, and then I'll—"

"You've got your own toy to play with," Rhett interjects, the chuckle in his voice undermined slightly by the heated growl.

My eyes pop open again when Lex sighs in mock disappointment, her hand dropping away. "Another time, then," she laments with a wink.

And why does that feel like a threat as much as it does a promise?

Lex leans in, brushing my lips with hers so fast I don't get the chance to kiss her back before she's straightening and turning her attention back to Lucas. She paces slowly, circling him like a lioness with her latest kill. He's fully erect now, judging by the flushed tip I can just barely see from my position on the floor. I squeak as Rhett lifts me with little effort, settling me up against his side again for a better angle. Lucas's chest rises and falls rapidly, his breathing loud. The muscles in his arms strain against his bonds.

"Didn't your parents ever teach you that staring is rude?" Lucas snarks, not taking his eyes off Lex.

I suck in a breath, wincing as her hand flies out and smacks him hard across the cheek, sending his head whipping away.

"You've enjoyed too much freedom with your mouth today, I think," Lex muses.

Her movements are silky smooth as she drags the zipper of her dress down, letting it fall in a puddle on the floor. My jaw drops as I take in the expanse of creamy white skin of her toned stomach, the swell of her breasts in the nearly see-through black lace bra, the garter belt holding up thigh-high black stockings. The room is full of the scent of arousal: pine smoke, whiskey, leather, and now a flood of citrus and cinnamon invades my senses. My pussy clenches on nothing even as I feel my slick dripping onto my legs that I have tucked under me, and I swallow a whine. Her perfectly manicured nails slide below the band of her panties, pulling them down and off in one smooth movement.

Lex steps forward and straddles Lucas's chest directly over his sternum, making him gasp. She laughs as she takes his chin in one hand and shoves her panties deep into his mouth with the other. Lucas gags and tries to fight, but when Lex covers his open mouth with her hand, he goes still.

"Aw, does the mouthy little cum slut not like the taste of my pussy anymore? I made sure to get them nice and wet for you on the way home. Do you not appreciate all the work I did for you, hm?"

Lucas shakes his head, trying to speak, but the sound is unintelligible around the gag. Lex only laughs and taunts him more, her hips rolling against his chest. I want to lean forward, but the touch of Rhett's fingers along my outer thigh diverts my attention.

"He loves this, you know. Letting us do whatever we want to him, treating him like our little fuck toy," Rhett purrs in my ear, leaning close enough for me to feel his breath on the side of my face.

My next exhale comes out in a shudder, acutely aware of the path Rhett's fingers are taking toward the apex of my thighs. All the while, I can't take my eyes off of Lex, her face bright with delight as she pulls Lucas's hair. She's moved down slightly, and I watch as she moves her hips in a slow roll, just barely brushing her core against Lucas's lower belly. His cock is nearly purple, and his hips buck each time she gets close to it, but never close enough.

"You're so hard for me, aren't you? You want me to come all over your pathetic little cock? Didn't you get enough from our lovely omega? Was she not good enough for you?" Lex sneers.

Lucas shakes his head violently, eyes leaving her face for the first time to look at me. I can read his desperation loud and clear, the denial of her taunt, the pleading for me not to believe her, and I give him the slightest nod. Lex catches the exchange, and she grins. Her nails dig into his chin, and she uses her grip to wrench his head around so he can fully look at me and nowhere else.

"Tell her that you want me, that you need me to make you feel like a man," Lex purrs, a clear challenge.

There's a heartbeat of silence, and Lucas blinks once at me. He won't say it. I almost ask him to do it anyway, just to please his Domina. But then he shakes his head, defiant to the end. Lex lets out a wicked laugh, my skin breaking out in goosebumps.

"Well, if you don't need my pussy, then maybe you need my cock," she says through her laughter.

She stands and moves to where the strap fell, but I'm pulled away from watching her by Rhett's hand on my chin.

"I've thought of your punishment, little one," he says lowly.

I drop my eyes and nod, my stomach a mixture of excitement and nerves.

"You're going to sit on my cock for the rest of Lucas's punishment," Rhett says at last.

I look up again, brow pulled down in confusion at his choice of words. He smirks and drops his hand to his zipper, freeing his cock in a few quick moves.

"You're going to take this in your dripping cunt and keep it there. You're not to move, or come until I've decided if you deserve it," Rhett continues.

Lex laughs and I look between them, not sure what to do. It hardly seems like a punishment, but that's what has me on edge. There has to be a trick to this, but I don't have time to puzzle it out before I feel a hand in my hair.

"Your sir gave you an order, sweetness. Are you going to disobey him?" Lex asks in my ear.

"No, ma'am," I answer shakily.

"Such a good girl," she whispers, kissing the side of my neck lightly before releasing me.

I swallow and take one last deep breath before moving. It takes a moment before I settle with my back against Rhett's chest, legs on either side of his thighs as he helps guide me down onto his waiting cock. I sigh at the stretch, letting my head fall back for a moment as he bottoms out. And almost immediately, I've figured out why this is a punishment. I can feel him pressing against all of my inner nerves, and I want nothing more than to rock my hips, to feel him brushing over my pleasure spots until I can't see straight.

"Don't move, little one. Just watch and feel how hard I am inside of you," Rhett whispers in my ear.

It's a struggle to open my eyes and lift my head, but I manage it. Lex is standing over Lucas again, this time with the harness around her shapely hips, a thick red dildo jutting out toward him.

"Look at how well our omega takes alpha dick, slut. She was made for that, not for you," Lex taunts, leaning down and grabbing one of Lucas's legs in each of her hands and pushing them toward his chest.

My eyes flick to Lucas's face, and I try to shake my head to tell him that's not true, but Rhett's hands trail up the inside of my thigh, making me moan before I can catch myself. His fingers dance up and down my leg. First one, then the other, until I'm shaking with the effort to keep still. I want to grab his wrists and tug his hands away, but the ropes dig into my skin, and I have to stop before I move too much. I can hear Lex's words, but my mind is a fog of warring sensations. The pleasure of Rhett's hands on my skin. The throbbing fullness that is so much and yet not enough. The thick layer of scents in the air that makes me clench and drip. Lucas groans and I echo the sound as Rhett's hand brushes where my entrance is stretched around him.

"You could come like this, couldn't you? Just listening to our pet being tortured by his Domina, with my voice in your ear, my fingers so close to your swollen clit. You're so warm around me, my sweet girl."

Rhett's voice is almost distant as my soul detaches from my body, but that only makes the feeling of his fingers gathering up the slick from around my entrance that much more powerful. My hands clutch the smooth fabric of his shirt in a desperate attempt to ground myself in reality, even as my wrists chafe against my bindings. I can't get a full breath, the harness pressing into my chest with each attempt. Rhett chuckles as the pain of it makes me throb around him, more slick soaking into his pants.

"She's so wet, stretched out on my cock like this. Taste her, Lex," Rhett says, raising his voice slightly.

I don't know when I closed my eyes, but I crack them open just in time to see Lex's red lips close around Rhett's fingers. Her moan goes straight to my core, and I nearly sob in desperation. I've never been so aroused in my life with no way to relieve it. Rhett's unshaking calm cracks for a moment as my pussy clenches hard when her hazel eyes lock onto mine. Lex moans low in her throat, spending more time than is probably needed with her tongue around his digits. She takes her time pulling back, her pink tongue licking her lips slowly after she releases him.

"So sweet, just like I thought. I'll have to taste directly from the source next time," she says, dark and sultry.

When she starts to move away, I lurch forward, forgetting myself as I try to chase her, to taste myself on her perfect lips. But Rhett grabs my braid, hand coming down on the top of my thigh in a sharp strike. I gasp and moan, trying to move away from the pain, but only getting another correcting blow. I sag, boneless, letting Rhett pull me back into position against his chest.

Lex has returned her attention to Lucas, whose eyes haven't left my face. I stare back, even as he groans long and low.

"That's right. Take my cock, desperate little slut," Lex snarls.

I watch her hips slamming hard and fast against his, her face flushed with wild delight. She moans and leans forward, pinning Lucas's legs up with her shoulders.

"She's using a special toy, you know. There's a part in her pussy right now, pressing right against her sweet spot as she fucks his ass," Rhett says in my ear.

I nearly scream as his finger brushes ever so gently over my swollen clit, and it's a miracle I don't jump three feet in the air. My legs shake uncontrollably as he continues his slow, feather light touches over my pleasure center. But I don't dare move again.

"Female alphas lock onto omega cock, and that toy she's using turns that lock into a knot at the base of the shaft. Should we make Lucas take it? I've seen it before," Rhett goes on, fingers speeding up.

"If he takes my knot, she takes yours. I want our little cock slut to see what a true coupling looks like, just so he knows what it's like to truly please an omega. Then he can live with the knowledge he'll never be able—"

"No."

My voice is strong for the first time, and Lex freezes, her head snapping up as she looks at me with wide eyes. But my gaze is fixed on Lucas, and the silvery moisture forming around his beautiful eyes.

"What did you just say?" Lex rasps, true surprise in her voice.

I swallow and try to form words, but I can't get past the look in Lucas's eyes. They're hazy, but something in them is calling out to my instinct to soothe. That's not what I want him to think. He's perfect just the way he is. I don't want another alpha. I want Lucas, my sweet, funny, protective beta. He doesn't need to be anything other than what he is, and I won't let myself be used like this.

"No. I don't want to," I whisper, hoping Lucas can read what I can't say in my eyes.

"That's not—"

"She said no, Lex," Rhett snaps, arms coming around to hold me tight against his chest. "This isn't up for debate."

I look back to Lex, ready to apologize, but her eyes are full of understanding. Time stops for a heartbeat, and each emotion flashes through her eyes. Fear, worry, understanding, contrition, warmth. She tilts her chin in the tiniest of nods, just the briefest acknowledgement of what happened, and a promise to resolve this, before she's back in her playing headspace. Lucas blinks slowly, his lips moving, but I can't tell what he's trying to say through the fabric gag. My name, maybe? Something more?

"You okay, love?" Rhett whispers.

Nodding, I settle back against him. Though my arousal had banked for a moment, it flares back to life with that slight adjustment, and I whimper, closing my eyes to breathe through it.

"You're such a good girl, so perfect. I love you so much," Rhett coos under his breath.

I smile at his praise, whispering my love back before opening my eyes to watch Lex as she drives into Lucas, his face twisted with pleasure as he lets out a long, almost continuous string of moans. My eyes drink in the flex of Lex's body, and as she shifts, my eyebrows fly up when I catch the black ink on her left side. I recognize the pack motto immediately, but there are three more lines of letters below it that I don't understand.

"Do you want to come with us, sweetness?" Lex pants, interrupting my thoughts.

Rhett's hand returns to my clit as I nod desperately, groaning as he sets a fast pace; nothing light or teasing about his touch now. Lex growls and snarls, biting at Lucas's calves as she starts to lose her steady rhythm. She leans down and finally removes her panties from Lucas's mouth, and he lets out a string of curses that would make a sailor blush.

"Please, Domina, can I come on your cock? Please?" Lucas rambles through his ragged breathing.

Lex lets out another bark of feral laughter, taking his cock in her fist. It's slick and shiny with precum, and he screams wordlessly at the first stroke. Rhett's lips kiss along the back of my shoulder, teeth digging gently as he circles my clit. I'm right there, shaking with anticipation, holding back for just the right moment.

"Come for me. Now."

Lex's command makes both Lucas and me shatter, our screams of pure bliss mixing in the sweetest harmony. Rhett purrs and growls, rocking up into me to draw out the waves.

It only takes a few strokes until I feel him fill my channel with his cum, the sensation setting off another flood of warmth. Lex follows right after, her beautiful face twisted with ecstasy as she pushes deep and goes still.

We're all quiet for a long time, the only sound our combined labored breathing. Rhett's the first to move, fingers already starting to undo my bindings. My body still hums with pleasure, and I'm hardly aware of my surroundings as I let myself be moved by more than one set of hands. A cool cloth wipes me clean at some point, thin fingers massaging the feeling back into my arms. A solid chest against my cheek, one smelling of clean towels and chocolate.

"You're so amazing, Lydi-bug. You did so good," Lucas breathes in my ear.

"So are you, Luc. I don't think you're—"

"Shh, I know. It's only part of the game. I know you don't think that," Lucas soothes.

"And I don't either, sweetness. You're both perfect, just as you are."

Lex's voice comes from behind me, and I nuzzle into her hand as she strokes the side of my face. I extract one of my arms to grab her wrist as she tries to move away, pulling her back toward me. She chuckles and lets me, settling in to hold me from behind, the scrape of her lingerie on my overly sensitive skin grounding somehow. I feel the couch sink on Lucas's other side a moment before I feel the familiar, calloused touch of Rhett's hand on my shoulder. I let myself relax, warm and sated among their arms.

"Your tattoo. It's different," I whisper into the quiet, my curiosity unable to be contained.

Lex chuckles in my ear before she kisses my temple. I can feel the smile pulling at the corners of her lips.

"Those are the three most important dates for me and this pack. The day I met Rhett and Mateo." She pauses and I open my eyes in time to catch him kissing her knuckles, his face split with a warm, contented smile.

"The day I told Lucas I loved him for the first time," Lex goes on, and Lucas ducks his chin, though not fast enough to hide the pink flush of his cheeks from me.

"And the day you agreed to join our family," she finishes.

With the way we're positioned, I can't turn to face her, but the warmth in her voice catches me entirely off guard. My heart flutters in my chest, and my face is suddenly very hot. She doesn't elaborate any further, curling more fully around my back. Lucas and I catch each other's gaze, and I see the same question in his eyes that I know is in mine.

How did we get so lucky?

Thirty

Lydia

The rain pelts the store windows, filling Wila's with the soothing pitter-patter sound. The classic rock radio station fills the spaces between the drops, and I lean heavily on one fist, trying not to fall asleep. As August winds down, hurricane season is starting up. This isn't a full storm, just the leftovers from a system that blew through the Gulf Coast a few days ago. It's been miserable for a while, but it wasn't enough for the Waffle Houses to close or anything.

I reach toward my pocket, but stop short. The instinct to text Jason when I'm bored hasn't gone away even after almost two weeks of silence. I still get to send him the occasional check-in message through Rhett, but it's not the same. The longer this goes on, the grouchier I'm getting over it, even if it is working. I haven't received a single message from my mother or Darren since making the choice to go no-contact with Jason. And that stings the worst of all. It's confirmation that they're using my little brother to get to me.

"You okay?" Caleb asks, interrupting my one-person pity party.

I sigh heavily and shrug, not willing to commit to more than that. He chuckles and stands from his stool by the door, stretching slightly. It's been a slow day, hardly a customer willing to brave the storm for the sake of flowers. So when I notice the blurry shape of a car pulling into street parking outside, I sit up. The driver exits and rushes across the sidewalk, ducking inside. It takes me a minute, but when the newcomer turns, the dark hair and casual smile belongs to Lee. He's out of uniform, which is why I didn't recognize him right away.

"Does anyone know where I can find an ark?" he jokes, running a hand through his hair to shake out some of the water.

I chuckle, my shoulders relaxing. "We're fresh out, but I heard there might be one or two left at Rosa's."

Lee laughs back, shoving his hands into the pockets of his gray zip-up hoodie as he approaches the counter. Caleb shadows him, moving so casually that Lee doesn't even notice.

"Is there something I can help you with?" I ask, hopping off my stool to stand at the counter.

"Actually, I just wanted to drop by and give you an update on your case," Lee replies, his smile slipping slightly.

A shiver runs up my back and I swallow hard.

"The good news is that Mr. Fischer is being more than cooperative. I guess it didn't take much for the DA to flip him to be a witness," Lee starts, angling his body to look between me and Caleb as he leans against the counter.

"Witness?" Caleb asks sharply.

Lee nods. "When we started going through the evidence, we found records that show Mr. Fischer wasn't acting on his own. He was hired."

My heart stops for a moment, and I cough. It's not that I hadn't thought Davis was working for Seth, but hearing this confirmation strikes deeper than I thought it would.

"Who was it?" Caleb asks when I don't.

Lee sucks his teeth and sighs. "I really can't get too deep into specifics, unfortunately. The DA is putting his case together."

But the significant look he gives us makes it pretty easy to read between the lines. They have proof that Seth hired Davis to stalk me. I'd expected to feel relief, knowing that Seth might finally see some consequences for all the shit he's been putting me through. But all I feel is sick to my stomach. Before now, I'd felt almost detached from the events of the last two months, like they were happening to someone else.

But this news, that Davis is willing to turn state's witness against Seth and there's proof of the connection between them makes everything feel real. I stumble back a step and find my stool, sitting down as my mind drifts, the sound of the rain feeling like it's coming from the other end of a tube.

"Have you found any proof of the connection between her ex and this whole situation? Something we can use to get a restraining order put in place?" Caleb asks Lee, even though his gunmetal-colored eyes are fixed on me.

"There were some group chats to a blocked number, photos being sent, but I don't know if we have enough to prove it's the ex," Lee says solemnly.

"Photos? What kind of photos?" I ask, voice a dry rasp.

"I'm not sure I'm allowed—"

"They were photos like that one from the night of the accident, weren't they? Of me during intimate moments with my pack?" The question comes out more like a statement, and it only takes one look at Lee's face to know I'm right.

Cold fear washes over me. Knowing Darren has pictures of me, *explicit* photos of me in his possession, and has been stewing on them for weeks strikes me in a place I'd thought I'd long since buried. Memories flood forward, of nights spent trying to endure baseless accusations of cheating, of dodging fists and anything not nailed down, all the while trying to prove my loyalty to an alpha who never deserved it. In Darren's mind, I've proven all those accusations correct.

"Caleb, please give me my phone," I say suddenly, holding my hand out.

"What's going on? What do you need?" he responds, posture straightening as his guard comes up and he goes on high alert.

"I need you to give me my phone, please," I insist, shaking my hand for emphasis.

"I think that's my cue to bow out. I just wanted to give y'all the heads up. The DA will probably be reaching out soon," Lee says, taking steps toward the door.

Neither Caleb nor I speak for a long time, just staring at each other, assessing. The rain hammers the windows, and I can hear Gabby and Wila bickering in the back, but it all feels secondary to the pounding fear in my heart. My head swims, vision blurring.

"*Thinking about his cock, aren't you, slut?*" *Darren sneers under his breath.*

I flinch away, keeping my eyes on the table. We've had this fight before, but never in public. And certainly not in front of my family. Jason is on my other side, my brothers and parents across the table. My dress is loose, hanging off my frame in strange places. I'd sworn it fit only a few months ago.

"*The waiter? Really? Can't keep it together for one fucking meal,*" *Darren snarls in my ear, leaning so close that I can smell the tequila on his breath, strong enough to drown out his clay and tobacco scent.*

"*I don't even know what you're talking about,*" *I hiss under my breath, glancing around nervously.*

No one has noticed how volatile Darren is right now, which works to my advantage. If a scene starts, it would be nearly impossible to stop. But if I could stop one from starting...

"*Do you think I'm stupid? I saw you makin' eyes at that fairy who brought our drinks. Is that what you want? Some skinny little beta bitch who wouldn't even be able to make you—*"

"*Hey, Dar. You think you and Lydi are going to be able to make it for Christmas this year?*"

Jason's voice makes me jump, and Darren's hand clamps down on the back of my neck, fingers painfully tight to keep me in place.

"*Oh, for sure. Mother is going to be with the pastor on the west coast for the holidays. Thanks again for inviting us, Mrs. Anderson. It means a lot to be surrounded by loved ones during such a special time of year,*" *Darren says, his switch flipping.*

All traces of menace and threat are gone, leaving only the charismatic alpha who could smooth talk the bark off a tree. My mother titters and coos, completely under his spell. I glance at Jason out of the corner of my eye. His emerald eyes, nearly identical to mine, are locked on my face, drifting only slightly to take note of the extra layer of foundation and concealer I had to cake on my cheekbone.

What do you need? His eyes seem to ask.

I blink twice, the backs of my eyes burning. I need out.

His only acknowledgement of my silent plea is the slight flare of his nostrils and the tiniest dip of his chin. Jason blinks once, slowly. We'll figure this out. Just hang in there for a little longer.

My heart sinks, my breath catching as I feel the all-too-familiar heat of Darren's stare on the side of my face. I slump back in my chair, trying to make myself as small as possible, keeping my eyes on the table for the rest of the meal.

Later that night, after Darren and I are back in our bed in our shitty apartment, I stare at the wall, counting the cracks in the plaster. Darren is shouting at me, but it's just noise. Jason will help me find a way out of this. He has to.

I blink and shake my head, chasing away the memory. Caleb's eyes are softer, and I feel suddenly very exposed under his gaze.

"Please. I just... please," I mutter, hardly loud enough to be heard over the rain.

I don't know how to tell him about my fears without launching into an hour-long explanation of everything I've been through, but the softening around the corners of his eyes as he considers me is reassuring. We'd talked about how risky going to the wedding could be, even doing a little bit of scouting on the internet to see if we could try to come up with a plan to keep me safe. But this new information changes everything. Darren is a shark who's scented blood in the water. Allowing myself to be anywhere near him would only be asking for someone to get hurt.

And Lord only knows how much of this my mother has heard about. Judging by the phone call from a few weeks ago, she's probably aware of my new relationships, even if Darren doesn't share the details. I would have thought she would be happy that I'd found a pack even more influential than Darren McLaughlin and his grifter father. Something isn't adding up with their behavior, beyond what I already suspect. But with no way to prove any of my theories, I have to try to solve the problems in front of me. And Darren's desire for punishment and retribution can be avoided by simply not getting near enough for him to do anything.

We're still and silent for another long heartbeat, but then Caleb sighs and his shoulders drop. Reaching into the inner pocket of his jacket, he slowly extracts my phone, passing it to me like he's expecting me to change my mind. I snatch it away, pulling up my dormant text thread with Jason.

Me: I'm sorry, but things have changed. It's too much to explain in a text, but the long and short of it is I'm not going to be coming down for Sam's wedding.

Hitting send on that message feels like a lead blanket falling off my shoulders. There will be fallout, but this is the smart move. Going to that wedding would be like dangling a juicy steak in front of a starving wolf. Lex and I can figure some other way to get my trust taken care of.

"What was that about?" Caleb asks, stepping around the counter to stand beside me.

"Before I tell you, can I ask you something?" I dodge his question for the moment and look up into his face.

He simply nods and waits for me to go on.

"Choosing to not put yourself in danger doesn't make you a coward, does it?" I ask, picking my words carefully.

"Quite the opposite. Running headfirst into a situation that you know is dangerous doesn't make you brave. It makes you stupid, and more often than not, it makes you dead. Picking your battles, engaging only when the time is right, that makes you smart. And you're very smart, Lydia," he replies confidently.

I nod and smile a little to myself. "Thanks, Caleb. I'll have to let the pack know that they can cancel our flight plans, then."

Caleb chuckles and nods, leaning in to nudge my shoulder with his. "And hey, just think. If your scumbag ex decides to show up here in Everton, I could always give him an acute case of lead poisoning."

I gasp and stare at him with eyes wide and mouth agape as he lifts one side of his jacket to reveal the butt of a handgun. My eyes bounce between Caleb's serious face and the gun, unable to form words. After a few moments, Caleb lets out a belly laugh at his own joke.

"That's not fucking funny—"

The vibration of my phone on the counter cuts off the rest of my scolding. The number is blocked, but I swipe the answer button anyway, hoping it's Jason. Before I can even get out a greeting, the woman on the other line is already shrieking, familiar Southern squawk rattling my bones and piercing my mind with a cold lance of terror.

"What do you mean you're not going to the wedding?!"

THIRTY-ONE

Lydia

I'M OUTSIDE ON THE back deck of the pack house that evening, lost in my head. The rain has passed, leaving only oppressive humidity behind. Even now, when the sun has already set, and the sky is dark, there's enough lingering heat to make it intolerable to most people. But to me, this sort of muggy weather feels like home.

I snort a little to myself. Could I even call Louisiana home anymore? It's where I was born, where I grew up, but I'd never felt comfortable there. Leaving it behind was tough at first, but the longer I've been gone, the less I've missed it. The only part of home I've ever regretted leaving behind is Jason.

Jason.

My brother, who's done everything in his power to keep me safe ever since he came to realize how serious of a threat Darren is to my life. In the beginning, his support hadn't been unconditional, but that changed the day he helped me escape. He's put his neck out for me time and again, covered for me when my father or mother started asking too many questions. And what have I ever done to repay him?

It's been this way since we were children. I'm his older sister, and by all rights, I should be the one protecting the baby of the family, and Sam and Adam should have protected the both of us. But it was almost like we were children from two different families. Sam and Adam were attached at the hip, already close before I ever came along, just after Adam turned six. And then there was me and Jason. We hardly went anywhere without each other. I know him almost better than I know myself. I know where his secret escape spot is on our family's property, every girl he ever had a crush on, his favorite foods, his irrational fear of roaming black holes, everything.

"Jacey, wait up!" I shout, pumping my legs as fast as I can to catch up with my brother.

Just to taunt me, he turns and runs backwards for a few paces, laughing. Even though I'm older, he's already taller than me at ten years old. Sammy says he's going to be tall like PawPaw Anderson, but I only hope he's wrong.

Jason rounds the corner of the path, disappearing through the trees for a moment before I catch sight of his nearly white-blond hair between the leaves. Grinning to myself, I jump off the well-trod walking trail, taking a shortcut I'd found. I clamber over fallen logs, breathing in the musty, damp air of the forest at the edge of the bayou. I jump over shallow streams, careful of my footing as I hop from stone to stone. At last, I break through the brush, coming back out onto the path just as Jason takes another bend behind me.

"Cheater! You're such a cheater, Lydi!" he yells, but the laughter in his voice undermines the accusation.

"It's only cheating because you didn't think of it first!" I throw back over my shoulder, taking off toward our finish line.

We've run this trail over and over, trying to beat Adam's record. Jason is closest, but I'm not far behind. If I can just push a little farther—

"Lydi, watch out!"

I turn at the shout, my foot slipping on a damp stone, sending me sideways. As I hit the ground, I cough and wheeze, arm and leg stinging. But as I look up, I freeze in place. Not three feet in front of me is a brown coil of scales, a low hiss in the air. Before I can think better of it, I scream and try to crawl backward. Time seems to slow, the cottonmouth's head rearing back and then lurching forward, glistening fangs in a wide jaw getting closer and closer.

And then a stick comes down on the snake's back, stopping it inches from my ankle. Jason brings the heavy branch down, over and over, until the snake stops moving and the forest is quiet. Our heavy breathing eases after a long pause, and we can only stare at each other. And then a chuckle bubbles up my throat and escapes before I can stop it. Then another. And soon we're both laughing, unable to control ourselves. He helps me up off the ground, my clothes a mess of mud and sweat, but I hardly care. We walk back to the house, Jason's arm draped over my shoulder.

Later, when we're at dinner, Sammy talks about the dead cottonmouth he found on the path, and Mom reads him the riot act for messing with something so dangerous. He tries to defend himself, saying he found it like that, but she doesn't believe him. Jason and I share a smile and spend the rest of the meal staring at our plates, so we don't burst out in giggles and give ourselves away. Another secret between us, not the first thing we've kept from our parents. We'd pray for forgiveness later and beg Jesus to have mercy on us for lying and disobeying. But for now, getting away with breaking the rules feels too good.

The sound of the garage door opening breaks through my thoughts, and I sigh. We'd promised to never hide anything from each other. But because of my stupid choices, I have to go back on my word. All in the name of protecting my brother. Jason has jumped in front of too many loaded guns for me over the course of our lives. It's my turn to take the bullet for him.

I groan as I get to my feet, stretching before heading through the sliding door into the house. Rhett and Mateo are just coming in through the mudroom. Mateo's face lights up when he sees me, and he makes a beeline to my side, sweeping me into an embrace. His kiss is brief, but the feeling behind it still makes me a little dizzy. When he pulls away, I look to find Rhett staring at me with a furrowed brow. I give him a sad half-smile and lift one of my shoulders.

"What's for dinner, Luc?" Lex asks, coming in from the hall.

Instead of pots and pans, there's an array of white Chinese takeout boxes. Everyone starts serving themselves, and I listen to the casual banter as I scoop some fried rice and orange chicken onto a plate. Despite the anxiety churning in my stomach, there's a certain comfort in the way we move together, shifting positions without needing to speak. By the time we're all seated, I almost have myself talked out of not saying anything about what happened today and just letting us have one normal night for a change. But, of course, Rhett can't leave anything well enough alone.

"So I got the strangest text from Jason today. He said you messaged him out of nowhere that you are no longer attending your brother's wedding," he says, trying to sound casual but failing spectacularly.

I shoot Rhett a heated look, but he doesn't shift from his bland, curious expression.

"Lee came into Wila's this afternoon and gave me an update on the case. Based on what he said, going to the wedding seemed like a bad idea," I start, pushing some of my food around my plate.

"I was going to suggest we reconsider, but I'm glad you made the decision on your own terms. It really is the smart move," Lex says warmly.

I look up at her, my heart twisting at the sight of her smile. This is going to hurt.

"Well, that was before my mother called."

There is a long pause where I swear I could have heard a pin drop. And then the world explodes with noise, three alphas growling threats, fists slamming onto the table, even the clatter of a piece of cutlery hitting the floor. My arms come up over my head, my eyes squeezing tight. Then suddenly, there's a sharp whistle above all of it. I crack open one eye, and Lucas is on his feet, fingers in his mouth, his glare moving between Rhett, Mateo, and Lex in turns.

"You three need to chill for one fucking second. You don't even know what happened," Lucas snaps as he sits again.

"I don't need to. I told that..." Mateo swallows whatever creative curse he's about to spit, with a glance in my direction, "*woman*, if she tried to contact Lydia again, I would ruin her."

"Count me in on that plan," Lex snarls, more heated than I've seen her in a while.

"What did I just say?" Lucas cuts in angrily.

Mateo looks at me with a trace of an apology, but it's only there for a moment. At least he doesn't start up again. Lex's face has smoothed into something far colder, which is somehow more disturbing than Rhett's clenched teeth and the straight glare of murder in his eyes. I clear my throat and bring my hands down, twisting my fingers together in my lap. Lucas sits back down next to me, intentionally moving his chair closer to put a protective arm around my shoulders.

"Yeah, so, um... after I texted Jason, she called me. I don't know how, because we changed my number again. But it was almost instant. And... well, she somehow learned that I'd decided not to go to the wedding," I tell them, not looking up from my lap.

"Did Jason even respond before your mother called?" Lucas prompts.

I shake my head. "She wouldn't tell me how she knew. Honestly, she hardly let me talk at all. But after she got through telling me how awful I am for trying to ruin this for her, she... she made it clear that I'm going to be at that wedding."

"What is she going to do? Come here and drag you down there by your hair?" Mateo asks with a derisive snort.

My eyes burn, and I blink rapidly to try to hold back the tears. "No. But she made it quite clear what would happen if I didn't go. And I'm not willing to call the bluff," I say, trailing off as my throat constricts.

"Lydia, if she threatened to hurt you–"

"No, it's not–" I say, cutting off the beginning of Rhett's growled oath. "She knows she can't hurt me. Not personally. But she can..."

"It's Jason, isn't it, sweetness?"

Everyone looks to Lex as she speaks, and at the sight of her hazel eyes full of empathy and understanding, my tears finally break through. I nod, pursing my lips together.

"She's going to have him kicked from the pack and disown him. Everything he's done to keep me safe is proof of his disloyalty, and my father... if he knows how much we've lied over the years..."

My words die in a sob, and I press my hand over my mouth, trying to take deep breaths to keep it together. All of my mother's hateful threats echo in my mind, and my whole body feels cold.

Our family is all he has, and you want to take that away because you can't be an adult for one evening?

An alpha without a pack is hardly an alpha at all.

"Have you told him?" Lucas asks softly.

I shake my head. "He'll tell me not to believe her, but I know she'd do it, just to spite me. And I can't–I can't do that to him."

"But if it means keeping you safe, I think Jason would do it willingly," Mateo says, words soft but insistent.

I shake my head. "I was already halfway out of the door mentally when I ran. If Darren had never come along, I would have gone my own way after I graduated college. But Jason... he never had to go through what I did, the expectations, the shaming, the gaslighting. He's seen what they did to me, so he's not ignorant of their evil, but he has a place, a role in the pack. Taking that away... it wouldn't be right."

"We can figure out a way to protect him, love. Just like we've protected you," Rhett insists.

I look at him through my tears, and my heart sinks. His eyes are hard, his jaw set. They aren't listening to me, and I don't know how to make them understand.

"Rhett, look at me," Lucas cuts in.

Both of our heads whip around, and I suck in a breath. Lucas's stormy blue-gray eyes are dark, his brow a dangerous line above them. He's angry, angrier than I've ever seen before. He stares Rhett down, a silent battle of wills.

"Our omega is begging us to listen, and you, all of you, are refusing to do so. We don't know these people like she does, and if she's saying that it's too risky to try to call the bluff, we have to trust her," he says, each word sharp and pointed.

I swallow, my lips trembling even as they pull up into a grateful smile. Lucas looks at me, almost through me, and I shiver.

Lex lets out a long, heavy exhale. Lucas and I both look at her, and I'm caught off-guard by the conflict in her eyes.

"If your mother is intercepting our communications with Jason, we'll have no way to warn him, to come up with a plan," she starts, shaking her head.

My heart soars as my mind fully comprehends the meaning of her words.

"We can use that to our advantage. Lay a false trail, toss in red herrings," Mateo adds, bobbing his head as his eyes swirl with thought.

I look back to Rhett, and my heart flips. The violence is still in his eyes, undimmed by everyone else's shift to my side.

"I know it'll be risky–"

"Risky? That's a wee bit of an understatement, love," Rhett returns harshly, his accent making his words nearly unintelligible.

I flinch back before I can contain the reaction, tucking my chin and closing my eyes.

"If you don't agree, you don't have to go. I can take Mateo–"

"If you think I'm going to let you go near that cunt without me, you've lost your bleeding mind!"

Rhett's shout makes my eyes go wide, and my jaw falls open. There's a wildness to his face, a near feral gleam to his eyes that sends up instinctual alarms. I push back from the table, starting toward the basement door.

"Lydia–"

I stop and look back at the sound of Lex's voice. I simply shake my head and continue down to my nest. The whiskey and leather scent that lingers there brings a fresh wave of tears to my eyes. I pick up a velvet soft, threadbare t-shirt, taking it with me as I burrow under several layers of blankets. The ticking of the clock on the wall fills the air, and I sync my breathing to it, letting my mind drift away from my body, using the scent of campfires and graham crackers to calm me.

A sudden knock at my door drags me out of my trance, and I'm not sure if two minutes or two hours have passed.

"Lydia, please open the door. It's urgent," Lex calls through the wood.

My brow furrows, and I rise on shaky legs. When I open the door, the colorless expression of horror is the last thing I expect to see.

"Lydia, I-I'm so sorry. Wila's... someone set fire to Wila's."

THIRTY-TWO

Lydia

SOMEONE SET FIRE TO *Wila's.*

The words echo in my head over and over as I sit in the passenger seat of Lex's car. She's tearing through the streets of Everton with Mateo, Rhett, and Lucas behind us, all of us dropping everything to head to Old Town. Everything since that moment has felt muffled, like I'm under a thick wool blanket, trying to listen to a conversation happening underwater. It's like I blink and we're suddenly turning the corner onto State Street, where the world erupts in lights and sirens and noise.

My heart slams against my ribs as the red and blue lights flash across my vision, and I have to shake my hands out as the sweat forms on my palms, too close to the feeling of blood as I'm thrown back to the night of my accident. But the orange glow that fills the air, along with the smell of ash and smoke, helps to chase away the memories.

We're forced to a stop several blocks away from Wila's, as police cars and firetrucks, and wooden barricades block the road. We pull off to park haphazardly in a spot, and I'm out of the car before Lex even has it fully in park. A small crowd of people has gathered along a wood barricade, but I push through until I'm at the front, looking down at the blocks of chaos in front of me. I try to sort through all the scents hitting me, but I can't get past the smoke in the air to find caramel candy apple or freshly turned earth.

"Gran! Gabby!" I scream, straining onto my tiptoes to try to find them.

"Ma'am, please stay back—"

"My best friend and grandmother live in one of those buildings. Where are they?" I demand, turning on a firefighter that has stepped up to try to keep me back.

"I don't know. But it's not safe—"

"I'm Alexandra St. Clair, and I own the leases on several of these buildings. I need to know what's going on." I feel the warmth of her arm press against mine, but I'm still scanning the crowd, looking for anyone that I know. My heart clenches as I spot a familiar dark-haired police officer standing near a cruiser.

"Lee! It's Lydia!" I shout over to him, waving.

Officer Nyueng does a double take before striding over to the barrier. He looks tired, but he still has a small, polite grin pulling up at the corner of his lips.

"What are you doing here? Did the detective call you already?" he asks when he's close enough.

"Detective? No, I don't—Gabby Fitzgerald. Her and her grandmother live above Wila's. Have you seen them?" I ask, feeling almost frantic.

Lee shifts his weight from one foot to the other, looking behind him. He nods to the firefighter, who just shrugs and moves off a little way down the line.

"Come with me. You, too, Ms. St. Clair. You're going to want to see this," Lee says, dropping his voice to barely louder than a whisper.

I look at Lex, and her face is drawn, her mouth pulled down in a frown. Unease settles into my gut as Lee helps Lex and me around the barrier and leads the way farther down the block. We weave around EMS and firefighters, trying to keep up and out of the way as they rush back and forth. The air gets hotter as we approach Wila's and I dare to glance up at the row of buildings on the block. There are ladder trucks parked nearest to the building with their baskets extended, several figures silhouetted against the flames from below. Many of the windows are broken, and figures move on the roofs, appearing and disappearing between plumes of smoke.

Nothing could have prepared me for what I would see as we reach the stretch of sidewalk across the street from Grandmother Wila's Flower Shoppe. The retail area is bright orange with fire, the front window displays consumed. The second-floor windows glow from within, but not as much as the ground floor. But what strikes me the most is the paint still visible on the plate-glass windows.

OMEGA WHORE

My next exhale comes out as a sob, and my vision blurs with tears for a moment before they slide down my cheeks. Guilt drops on me like a piano, discordant and crushing and splintering. This is my fault. This is all my fault. I don't know how. I don't know why. But someone did this awful thing because of me.

"Lydia!"

I turn at the sound of my name, just in time to catch a flash of dark braids before a body crashes into me. I breathe in my best friend's scent, clutching her tightly as she sobs into my shoulder. My legs feel like they're about to give out at any moment, but I manage to stay upright.

"I'm so fucking sorry, babe. I'm sorry. I'm so sorry," I babble through my sobs.

"No, don't do that. It's not your fault—"

"Yes, it is. This is my fault, all my fault—I'm so sorry," I gasp out, dissolving into tears again.

"Mrs. Fitzgerald, I'm so sorry," Lex says from beside me.

I glance up to find Wila standing just behind Gabby, her face an unreadable mask as she stares at the building that has been her home and livelihood for decades. There's a sadness in the depths of her dark brown eyes that I pray I'll never have to experience. She nods in response to Lex's sympathy, but doesn't speak. And then a single tear slides down her wrinkled cheek, and what little strength I had left in me gives way. Gabby and I sink into a heap on the sidewalk, sobbing and shaking as we watch the fire burn.

Even with the soaking rain from earlier, it takes several hours for the fire to be declared under control. My back aches, and my ass is numb from sitting on the concrete for so long without moving, but I've lost all connection between my mind and body. Gabby's limbs are intertwined with mine, and I can feel her slow, even breathing. My eyes have been fixed on the front window of Wila's, the painted accusation somehow still there.

Lex has been in full business mode, making calls and speaking with emergency services. Mateo has been moving among the crowd, and I've seen him put a few groups into taxis. I don't know where Rhett and Lucas are, but I haven't seen them around. Which, right now, isn't such a bad thing after that disaster at dinner.

I snuggle into Gabby a little, trying to chase away the acrid burning building scent in my nose with her caramel candy apple essence. Something, anything, familiar and safe. But we're both covered in ash, and I only manage to make myself cough. I let my head hang, trying to breathe through the weight crushing down on me.

My mind has been working in fits and spurts, trying to find the logic or reasoning to this senseless act. But I can't find the missing link. What did I do for someone to get angry enough to commit arson? I try to replay the last few weeks, going over every moment to find some transgression that would be bad enough for someone to destroy a stranger's home and livelihood.

Movement on my free side pulls me out of my thoughts, and I turn to Lex settling on the curb beside me. Her hair is frazzled, with flecks of white and gray throughout. There's a smudge of something across her forehead, and her normally placid features are tight. The last of the flames reflect strangely in her eyes, the color dull and gaze a thousand miles away.

"I just got a call from my public relations team. The Review got a submission a few minutes ago," she starts in a hoarse monotone.

I swallow, the smoke coating my mouth turning my stomach.

"It's a video, some nutjob in a ski mask rambling for forty minutes about how Seth is the most victimized omega to ever walk the planet. They would have trashed it as just another crazy trying to get their fifteen minutes of fame, but he kept talking about some blog post. The editor looked into it, and, well..."

Lex scrolls for a moment before angling her screen for me to see. My heart drops as I read the bold headline and photo. I only skim the text, but phrases like 'unworthy slut,' 'faithless, lying disgrace,' and 'omega whore' jump out the most. The author goes on and on, painting me as this homewrecking liar hell-bent on destroying the lives of Pack St. Clair. And apparently, my plan involves conspiring with Lucas to drive Lex and Mateo away from Seth.

They paint Lucas as this mastermind, as Pack Enemy Number One, and I'm his agent of destruction, and anyone who supports us is against all things good and pure, or some other bullshit. All of this is accompanied by a pair of photos, one of me and Mateo outside of Wila's, loading flowers into the back of his SUV, and another with me in the same outfit, this time kissing Lucas outside of Wila's. I know those photos were taken several weeks apart, but the editing is deceptive enough to imply I went right from making eyes at Mateo to being intimate with Lucas.

I look away when I feel my stomach clenching, and the back of my throat burns.

"The video doesn't show the fire, but you can see Wila's window displays in the background near the end," Lex drones, putting her phone away.

"That blog... is it−"

"Seth? I think it is, just based on my knowledge of his writing quirks," she finishes for me.

I close my eyes, the edges burning, but I have no tears left to cry. Misery sinks deep into my bones. There isn't any denying it now; this is all my fault. I wasn't careful enough, cautious enough. I let myself get wrapped up in my feelings for this pack, and innocent people have paid the price. Pure luck kept anyone from getting hurt or killed tonight.

"I should have gone to Atlanta when you gave me the chance, never should have let things get this far," I whisper, voice cracking as my heart throbs in my chest.

"Lydia, that's not−I thought we talked about this," Lex counters, voice breathy with disbelief.

Shaking my head, the words die in my throat as the weight of everything that's happened over the last few weeks crushes my soul. I should have trusted my instincts and run. Staying hidden kept me safe, and staying with this pack only served to paint a massive target on my back, and the backs of everyone I love.

"I can't be responsible for more pain, more destruction," I mumble, trying to keep it together as best as I can.

"This isn't your fault—"

"Then whose fault is it? Seth's? Because this never would have happened if I'd just left," I interrupt, my body managing to find the moisture for another tear to slide down my soot-covered face.

"You can't know that. And Seth isn't your responsibility," Lex growls, not looking at me.

"It doesn't matter," I say, moving closer to Gabby and closing my eyes.

I can feel Lex staring at me, but I don't move. Eventually, she stands and walks away, which is fine. It's better this way.

THIRTY-THREE

Mateo

AFTER HOURS OF DIESEL engines and radio chatter, the silence that settles when the last police cruiser leaves State Street rings in my ears, almost like I'd been knocked silly by a sucker punch to the side of my head. Exhaustion weighs on me, but I know it's almost over.

I've been coordinating with Rhett and Lucas at Wickland House to get rooms for the families that the fire has displaced, making sure everyone could leave when they were ready and had somewhere to go until we could sort out other arrangements if they wanted. The sky is a dull gray, the sun only an hour or two from rising. I pat the roof of the taxi twice before stepping back, sending off the last couple. The only ones left on the sidewalk are my pack and the Fitzgeralds.

My heart twists as I look at where Lydia and Gabby sit on the edge of the curb. They have been in and out of consciousness, all the while holding each other as if letting go would cause the other to disappear. Wila had moved to the bench behind them, but she's still staring at the hollow shell that was once her beloved flower shop.

I sigh silently, glancing around. Lex has been on her phone nearly constantly, filing claims, talking with lawyers, and just generally doing anything to distract herself from the emotions of tonight. I want to take the device away and chuck it down a sewer drain, but that's not a fight worth starting right now. I can't think of anything more important than the people around us, any phone call that couldn't possibly wait until we've had a moment to process this fully. Then again, I've never understood how Lex can compartmentalize all the trauma Seth's put us through over the last three years and not let it drag her down into a pit of despair. My eyes catch on the flaking paint that somehow survived the blaze, and I have to look away.

OMEGA WHORE

Seth has gone too far this time. I don't care anymore what it will take, but we have to get rid of him once and for all. Even if he didn't personally set this fire, he is still the one responsible for the damage.

"Sit with me for a minute, boy."

I turn at the gravelly whisper to find Wila looking at me, her wise face heavy. I nod and mutter a 'yes, ma'am' before taking a seat beside her on the cold bench. We're quiet for a while, but I don't want to disturb the stillness in this pre-dawn moment.

"I don't care what it takes, what you have to do, but you're going to protect my girl, you understand?" she whispers.

"Yes, ma'am," I respond, not hesitating for a moment.

"When I first met her, Lydia couldn't work the counter, too afraid of any alpha that came in. We can't let her go back to that place," Wila goes on.

I nod silently, realizing that she's speaking more to herself than to me. But I feel the depth of her words in my chest, and I don't even hesitate before swearing to do just that. I'd do anything for Lydia.

"I moved all the important things to a safe deposit box a few years back after someone tossed the place while me and the girls were out of town. There are some pictures, old keepsakes that are lost, but that's just life, isn't it?"

I look at her curiously, not sure how to respond. Wila looks at me, her little smile holding so much wisdom and sadness that it nearly knocks the wind out of me.

"We do our best to remember, but in the end, it's all just a blip in time. We have to do the best we can in the here and now. Love the people in our lives while they're here," Wila explains softly.

We both look back to where Lydia and Gabby are curled up in a tight embrace, their limbs entwined tightly. Their breathing is even and slow, and I can't help but smile fondly at them.

"When Gabby was ten, her father, my son, and his mate were coming home from a Christmas party. There was black ice, and they went off the road. They didn't suffer, but I've raised her ever since," Wila whispers.

"How long have you lived in Everton?" I ask, my curiosity getting the better of me.

"I was born here, as was my late husband, Ernie. We bought that store right after we got married. We didn't know what we would do with it, but it just... spoke to us, you know?"

I nod, looking back up at the building. The frame still stands, as it was mostly made of brick and stone, but the blackened interior of the upper floors is noticeable through the broken windows.

"Ernie was an alpha, like Danny. We had trouble conceiving, but Danny was enough of a handful that we were never bored. We tried all sorts of businesses, but the one that stuck was the florist. Right around the time Gabby was born, we had our grand opening. Danny and Angela helped us run the business and practically lived with us after Ernie lost his battle with lung cancer. But after they were gone, it was just Gabby and me. Until Lydia."

"Did Ernie not have a pack?" I ask.

"Oh, sure. But everyone sort of drifted apart after Danny left us. I still get cards and whatnot, but they weren't like you and yours," Wila sighs, shifting slightly.

She goes quiet, and I'm not sure how to respond to that. My pack is special; I've known that for a long time. We're a family, bound by our choices and love. Lydia is part of that now, and the things that matter to her matter to me.

"I know you're going to fight me, but we're going to help you and Gabby get through this," I promise softly.

"You're damn right. I'll fight you. I'm not taking your charity," Wila snorts, lifting her chin.

I chuckle and shake my head. "It's never going to be charity, Miss Wila. Family helps family. Lydia's part of my family, and so are you."

Wila looks at me for a long time, and I watch her eyes soften. She reaches out and takes one of my hands, squeezing slightly.

"You're a good egg, Mateo," she says at last.

"I try to be. So let this good egg get you put up for the night," I tease gently.

She laughs lightly and shakes her head, but I know she's not going to resist. We spend another moment sitting together before we move in unison, and I kneel beside Lydia and Gabby, shaking her shoulder lightly.

"Come on, baby. Let's get Gabby and Wila settled and then go home," I whisper with a smile.

She inhales sharply, looking at me with bleary eyes. She blinks, the clarity returning to her. Gabby moans and tries to snuggle down into Lydia's arms, and I chuckle.

"I know, but you'll be more comfortable in a bed. Let's get you up," I insist, poking at her side playfully.

"What time is it?" Lydia rasps, extracting a hand to rub at her eyes.

"Not quite sunup. We're the last ones here," I reply.

Lydia nods and shoves at Gabby with her shoulder. It takes a bit, but we finally manage to get Gabby awake enough to load her into the back of Lex's car, along with Wila. Lydia turns to me as I close the door behind the matriarch, her eyes bright.

"Matty, I..." she whispers, voice cracking with unshed tears.

I reach for her, pushing her hair back from her face before cupping her chin with my palms. She steps closer and angles her head to keep looking up at me. My brow pulls down, heart kicking a little harder at hurt in her eyes.

"All of this with Seth... I don't know how much longer I can do this. It keeps getting worse, and it just seems like we're spinning our wheels," Lydia goes on, not looking away.

"We're going to figure it out, I promise," I start, but Lydia just shakes her head.

"I don't want people to keep getting hurt because of me," she whispers.

I swear I feel my heart stop dead in my chest before it suddenly kicks into overdrive. I wrap my arms around her shoulders and clutch her to my chest. She gasps, and I can feel her tears as they splash on my shirt, but I only hold her tighter.

"This isn't on you. None of this is your fault. We love you, and we want you here," I ramble.

There are more feelings in my chest, but they're too big for me to put adequately into words. Since Seth destroyed my life, I've only let myself have the shallowest of connections. Finding people to keep me warm for a few weeks before I have to push them away with my party boy persona. I've had to become someone I hate, because I couldn't give my heart away again. But then Lydia came screaming into my life, full of passion and fight and so much love for everyone she lets into her heart. I'd never expected to fall for her like this, but from the first time I met her, she saw through all of my pretending and sarcasm, straight to the core of my lonely soul.

How could I not want to spend the rest of my life with someone like Lydia, beautiful, inside and out, so perfect for me and my pack? She's saved us, saved me from falling apart. I can't imagine a future without her in it. I don't care what it takes, if I have to beg, steal, cheat, or kill, but I'm going to get my heart back from Seth and give it to Lydia. I belong to her as completely as any person can belong to another. There isn't anywhere she could go and I wouldn't follow. She's a part of me now, and I'd sooner cut off a limb than let her walk away. But if she doesn't feel the same...

"Baby, are you... do you want to leave?" I ask hesitantly, afraid of the answer.

"No, but what if... what if I should?"

Lydia's voice is small, so quiet I almost don't catch the end of her question. I hug her tighter and press a kiss to the top of her head. I can feel my heart cracking in my chest. But then a flame sparks to life in my gut. No. Seth will not ruin the best thing that has ever happened to me.

"If you leave, I'm going with you," I growl, fingers digging as I try to hold her even closer.

Lydia whimpers and her arms come up to wrap just as fiercely around my waist. We stand there for another long moment, and I look up as footsteps approach. Lex is looking down at her phone, and I watch her run her hand through her hair before shoving the device in her pocket. When she looks up and sees Lydia and me, I could almost swear that a flush of color comes across her cheeks, but it has to be a trick of the light.

"Let's go home," she sighs, continuing on until she rounds to the driver's side of her car.

"I'm taking Lydia back to the pack house," I mutter.

Lex nods, not looking me in the eye. Something twists in my gut, but I don't have the energy to read into it.

I lead Lydia back to my SUV as Lex drives away to drop off Gabby and Wila. The city is just waking up, and I have to use all of my willpower to stay awake long enough to get us back into the pack house garage. We're silent as we make our way into the house, flopping down onto the sectional in a tangle of limbs. Her head is on my chest as I lie back, and let the weight of her, the knowledge she's safe at my side, comfort me for the moment. I'm asleep before my head even hits the cushion.

THIRTY-FOUR

Lydia

I DON'T KNOW HOW long I've been asleep, but the sound of the mudroom door opening and closing jerks me awake. I bolt upright, head whipping around as I try to get my bearings. The sky outside of the picture window is iron-gray, still pre-dawn with clouds hanging low above the trees. Rhett, Lucas, and Lex are shuffling through the kitchen, looking half-asleep on their feet. From the depths of the house, the grandfather clock strikes six.

Lucas makes it as far as the kitchen island, throwing himself onto one of the stools before slumping over on his crossed arms. Rhett trails a hand over the back of his beta's shoulders before looking up at the sitting room. He locks eyes with me for a moment, asking without words if I'm okay. I shake my head once from side to side, but don't elaborate. I don't know if I could talk about what's going on in my head and heart right now if I tried. Rhett dips his chin in acknowledgment before moving to the dining table and sitting down.

Lex, however, hasn't stopped moving since she walked in. She sets the coffee machine to heating, before moving from cupboard to cupboard, passing the coffee cups twice before she finally pulls one out and sets about adding cream and sugar.

"What are you doing, Lex?" Lucas groans, voice muffled by his arms.

"Playing Chutes and Ladders," she snaps sarcastically over a shoulder.

"You don't need coffee; you need sleep," he retorts, finally lifting his head to look at her.

I watch her shoulders lift and lower as she takes a deep breath, but the tension in them doesn't diminish. The coffee machine dispenses into the cup, and it feels like no one even breathes until after the last drop falls.

"I'm fine," she grits out at last, her back to the room.

"And I'm a duck," Lucas snorts.

Lex growls a low warning, but Lucas doesn't flinch. My eyes dart between them, not sure what to do. Mateo has woken up, and I shift to let him sit up beside me as we kneel on the seat, facing the back of the sectional and the rooms beyond. His hand finds mine automatically, our fingers laced together as they rest on his thigh. The touch is grounding, and I have to blink away tears. I can feel Rhett's eyes on me, but I'm still staring at the back of Lex's head. She won't turn around. She hasn't even acknowledged me, or anyone else in her pack.

"The sky isn't going to fall if you take one day off," Rhett adds gently into the silence.

Lex sighs and shakes her head, picking up a spoon and noisily stirring her coffee. "The sooner we get the claims in, the sooner we can get working on reconstruction. And then there are calls to make to contractors, and—"

"If you're going to tell me you don't give a shit about me, the least you could do is look me in the face," Lucas nearly shouts, slamming a hand on the counter.

I jump and squeak at the sudden sound, and Mateo's hand tightens around mine. Rhett's eyes snap to me for a moment, assessing at the speed of light before turning back to Lucas. Lex has gone completely still, hand frozen in midair as she was leaning to put the dirty spoon into the sink. Slowly, she sets the spoon on the counter and turns on her heel. I flinch back at the snarl pulling at her mouth, the fiery anger burning in her hazel eyes.

"What did you just say?" she hisses, so low I would have missed it if I didn't see her lips moving.

"We've been through the emotional ringer tonight, Lex. And you just want to fuck off to work like it's any old

Thursday? The Foundation doesn't need you right now. Your pack does," Lucas continues, getting to his feet as he motions wildly in his passion.

"We can figure out what comes next after I get home—"

"Why do you want to leave us so bad?" I ask, unable to hold the question back a moment longer.

Every head in the room snaps to me, but I only have eyes for Lex. She's staring with wide eyes, rimmed with red from lack of sleep. Yesterday's mascara is smudged along her lower lash line, and there's a streak of ash on her forehead where she must have wiped away sweat at some point. Her hair is dusted with light gray flecks, and my heart throbs. Are those the remains of Wila's photo albums? Or maybe another family's treasures, now gone up in smoke.

"Why don't you want to stay?" I ask, voice cracking and fresh tears sliding down my face.

Lex's face goes slack, all of the anger disappearing, but it somehow doesn't matter. She still hasn't answered, and that speaks volumes. She wants to leave, but we need her. Do we not matter to her? Are we not important enough for her?

"I—I can't. If I don't do this, then—"

"Then what, Lex? We're asking you, begging you, to stay and be here with us, and you can't turn off for one God damn day to just mourn with us," Lucas says, stepping toward Lex.

She shakes her head and looks at the floor for a moment. Her hands smooth over the thighs of her pants—the same slacks she's been wearing since she kissed me goodbye at work yesterday morning. She turns around and grabs her coffee off the counter.

"I'm sorry. I'll be back as soon as I can, but—"

"No!" Lucas screams, advancing on her.

His hand is on her wrist, stopping her in her tracks, but she loses her grip on the handle of the mug. It continues another few feet before it shatters on the hardwood, dark liquid spreading like blood on the floor. I yelp and Mateo's arm pulls me into his chest, his protective growl vibrating my teeth as I press my face into his shirt. Rhett's chair scrapes on the floor, and he moves halfway toward where Lucas and Lex are having their standoff. She looks ready to start throwing punches, but Lucas doesn't seem afraid. If anything, his face is sad, and maybe a little disappointed.

That expression drags something out of the depths of my mind that I haven't felt in a long time. Watching as Lex stares up into Lucas's face, his hope that she's going to change her mind crumbling and dying with each passing heartbeat makes me clench my fists tight. She's hurting him, telling him he doesn't matter when he does. He's so important to this pack, and to me, and my control breaks as a single tear slides down his face.

"Let her go if she wants to leave so bad," I call out, voice sharp.

Lex, Lucas, and Rhett all turn to me, but I make sure I'm looking Lex in the eyes. Her mouth falls open a little, but I don't want to hear her right now. My mind is a war of emotions, but I can't focus on any of them except anger. Anger is easy right now. Anger doesn't make me think, or hurt.

"If she's so determined to put us at the bottom of her priority list, then let her go. We can take care of each other if she won't," I continue, looking at Lucas as I finish.

"You're not understanding, Lydia. I need to do these things to protect us. If I don't—"

"I'm understanding you just fine, Alexandra. What we're going through isn't as important as whatever the fuck you need to do at the office," I spit, holding Mateo a little tighter.

"What is that supposed to mean?" she retorts, focus shifting to me as she takes a step in my direction.

"I just had to watch your ex and his stupid cult burn down my best friend's house and livelihood, the one place that's truly felt like home since I walked away from my family. Months and months of Rhett's hard work is gone, the people you claim to want to help, looking to him and Mateo and Lucas in their darkest hour. All because the sociopath you refuse to deal with has it out for me! And you can't spare one day, even a few hours of your precious time, to be here for us when we need you? Some prime alpha that makes you," I snarl, turning my back to her, dismissing her.

There's a heartbeat where no one moves. Even the clock in the other room seems to freeze and inhale. And then Alexandra's snarl slices through the silence like a claymore. I look up in time to watch her lunge for me, and my blood goes cold. Her eyes are wild, almost unhinged, tears slipping freely down her cheeks. She makes it two steps before Rhett is there, catching her wrists as she raises a hand.

"Absolutely the fuck not, Lex," he says, voice a low, dangerous growl.

Mateo's lips brush against my hair for a moment before he's gone, jumping over the back of the sectional and closing the distance between us and Rhett in three long strides. The three alphas stand nearly chest to chest, looking between themselves with narrowed angry eyes. I can smell the burning paper, baking grass, and smoky cloves billowing off of them and filling the room. Alexandra moves first, ripping her hand out of Rhett's grip and stepping back.

"I'm going—"

"No, you're not. Not without talking first. You never answered Lydia's question," Rhett says firmly, stepping around to block her from going out of the mudroom door.

"What question? It seems like she's been making more accusations than—"

"Finish that sentence, Lex. I fucking dare you," Mateo snaps, stepping up to stare down at her.

I never realized how small Alexandra truly is until now. She's always wearing heels, and her aura alone is enough to make most people feel three inches tall. But now, seeing her blinking up at Mateo, I realize the top of her head only comes up to his nose. She swallows and breaks eye contact first, turning back to Rhett.

"Remind me, if you please," she deadpans.

I manage to contain my wince, heart thumping painfully at her dismissal.

"What is so fucking important that the needs of your pack, the needs of your omega and your beta, have to be put on hold?" Rhett asks, slowly and clearly.

Alexandra has the decency to look at least mildly ashamed as she flicks a glance at Lucas and then at me before returning to look Rhett in the eye. I can almost see the walls rising in her eyes, shutting us out.

"Seth. He's clearly behind this, so I need to find the connection," she says with a heavy sigh.

"Even if you find it, will you actually do anything about him?" Mateo sneers, stepping back and turning halfway away, his eyes finding mine for a moment before returning to Alexandra's face.

"I'm trying, Mateo. There's only so much I can do," she replies, words almost sounding a little desperate.

"I'm going to have to call bullshit on that one, I'm afraid," Lucas drawls, sticking his hands in his pockets as he strolls from the kitchen to the sitting room, positioning himself to lean against the back of the section just to my left.

"And I'll second that. You have no problem pulling rank on any of us, so what the fuck is stopping you from doing the same to him?" Mateo adds, turning and putting his back to her.

"It's complicated," Alexandra replies simply, crossing her arms over her chest and rocking her weight onto her back foot.

"Is it, though?" I ask, trying to keep my tone neutral. "I mean, you're his alpha. If anyone can bring him to heel, it would be you."

She scoffs and tries to turn away from me, only to be met with Rhett's chest, his feet planted and eyes stern. For a moment, she seems to consider going around him, but some silent conversation passes between them, and she turns toward the picture window instead. We all wait in the silence, but the longer it stretches on, the lower my heart sinks. She's shut down, shut us out completely.

"If you don't want to be here for me when I need you, if you can't or won't protect me from the monster you created, then there's no point in me joining this pack," I rasp.

Four heads turn to watch me stand from where I've been kneeling on the couch, tracking me as I move toward the basement door, each step heavier than the last. My broken heart pounds in my ears, my chest hollow and aching.

"I'm going with you."

I freeze mid-step at the sound of Mateo's voice, whipping back around to face him. But he's already moving, stepping up to my side and lacing his fingers with mine. His skin is warm and solid and I cling to it like driftwood in a stormy sea. He kisses my hairline before turning to look back at Alexandra. She's staring open-mouthed, truly shocked for the first time I've ever seen.

"I choose this; choose her. I'll figure out how to get rid of Seth on my own, since you can't or won't," he continues, words drenched in finality.

"What? No, you... Matty—"

"I've been trapped in this mistake for nearly four years, unable to move on because you keep dragging your feet and putting your secrets ahead of our family. Seth ran us out of our home, forced us to live behind bars for our own safety. There isn't a month that's gone by when someone isn't slandering Lucas's name on social media. I can't even be the partner our omega deserves because you refuse to do anything to get Seth under control. But I'm done, done with the waiting, and the lies, and the secrets," Mateo says, hand tight in mine as he stares down Alexandra, daring her to challenge him.

She blinks and tries to speak for several moments, but no sound comes out. Then she turns to look at Lucas. I follow her line of sight and breathe in sharply at the intensity in his eyes. He's staring back at Alexandra, head cocked ever so slightly to the side, like he's seeing something for the first time.

"Does she know about the tracker?" he asks after a moment.

"What tracker?" I demand, unable to stop myself.

Lucas doesn't shift his attention away from Alexandra, but my heart races. What is he talking about? But by the looks on everyone's faces, it seems I'm the only one left out of the loop here.

"That's all I need to know," Lucas sighs, pushing off from his leaning position and moving to my side.

"Rhett..." Alexandra whispers, voice cracking and dying before she can say more than his name.

I look to the alpha who showed me that there are good people, good men left in this world. The alpha who, despite all of my flaws and bad days, stood by me and swore to protect me from anything this world could throw at us. His crystal blue eyes meet mine, and the world falls away for a moment. The doubts swirl in the depths of his gaze, but he's waiting for something.

"You would give up on us, on this family, after everything we've been through? Just like that?" Alexandra demands, voice bordering on hysterical.

Everyone turns to look at her, and the last of my anger fades away, leaving only sadness. Tears stain her cheeks, drops flowing freely as she stands frozen in place. Her hazel eyes move from face to face, searching, pleading. When they land on mine, I can only give her a sad smile.

"Give us a reason to stay," I whisper.

The only sound for several agonizing seconds is the deep tick-tock of the grandfather clock in the formal living room. No one moves or breathes too deeply as we watch and wait for Alexandra to make her choice. I can almost see the wheels turning, and at long last, the wall between us crumbles. Her entire posture changes, shifting from defensive to defeated as she collapses into a chair, face in her hands. I take an involuntary step forward, the instinct to soothe and comfort her overpowering me before I catch myself. She's still for a moment before she wipes her face and sits up, setting her shoulders as she faces us.

"If it's the truth you want, it's the truth you'll get."

THIRTY-FIVE

Lydia

IT TAKES A FEW minutes for the air in the room to come down from the charged, ready to explode state it reached, but when it finally does, the pack and I scatter throughout the living space. After cleaning up the broken glass and spilled coffee, Lucas has taken up a perch on the kitchen island, sitting on the counter with a cup of coffee in hand, one leg pulled up to his chest. Rhett is leaning against the wall between the mudroom door and the basement door, arms crossed over his chest. If it weren't for the heat of his stare I can feel on the back of my head, I would have thought he'd fallen asleep standing up. Lex is looking out the picture window, her new mug of coffee clutched tight between her hands. Mateo is sitting on the back of the sectional behind me, his feet planted on the cushion on either side of my hips. His leg occasionally brushes my shoulder, and that little reminder of his presence comforts me more than I can put into words.

"I won't pretend that I didn't grow up in a very privileged household, but money doesn't make someone a better person. If the soul is rotten, money only makes it easier for them to get away with cruelty. Witnesses can be bought, paid off to be complicit in the abuse. And my father is very good at purchasing loyalty," Lex begins, not looking at anyone.

"The few times we met him proved that," Rhett snorts darkly.

Lex nods. "My parents had trouble conceiving, and my birth was hard on my mother. They were warned to never have another child. So, to his eternal shame, I was to be the heir to the St. Clair fortune. I was pushed to be the best in all things, to be smarter, more ruthless than my classmates. Other children were competition, and there was no room for friendship when I was constantly being taught how to analyze them, pick out their weaknesses and exploit them to my own advantage."

"Birthday parties must have been a bloodbath," Lucas huffs with an ironic chuckle.

"Bold of you to assume I was allowed to celebrate simply surviving another circuit around the sun," Lex retorts before taking a long sip of her coffee.

"At least my parents tried to use religion as an excuse. Birthdays were too secular, too indulgent of worldly pursuits," I grumble, rubbing my palms on my jeans.

"I learned very early not to share anything with my parents, good or bad, because even things I thought were said in confidence would get thrown back in my face. My successes were critiqued and dismissed, my failures tallied. To this day, I swear my father has a ledger book with each mistake documented."

Lex breaks off with a low, humorless chuckle, shaking her head as she drifts off in thought. The sadness in her eyes reflects off the glass window, and my heart twists in my chest. Rhett shifts behind me, taking a few steps closer but not speaking.

"I knew I didn't want to get sucked into the soulless world of corporate real estate, of just trying to climb to the top of the pile by any means necessary. After convincing my father to let me do something on my own, I founded the St. Clair Foundation. I traveled as much as I could until I stumbled upon Everton, a town so close to desolation but with so much potential. I knew I could make a difference here, but I couldn't do it alone.

"Meeting Rhett and Mateo at that conference felt like fate. Two dreamers, crazy enough to see the same potential I did in a city on the brink of ruin. We had that same drive to prove the world wrong, to show everyone that nothing is impossible."

"Still do, Lex," Mateo adds, with a small, private smile.

"We brought Bright Hills back to life and rode that high through the Valencia restoration. But then..."

"Then we met Seth," Lucas finishes, spitting the name like it would poison him to keep it in his mouth too long.

"Being with Seth was... indescribable at first. He was one of the first people to treat me like a person, not a means to an end. Don't get me wrong, I've never felt that any of you treated me that way, but with Seth... it was different. He worshipped me, treated me like I was the center of his entire existence. He told me things he swore he'd never told anyone else, and in turn, I told him my secrets. How my father would pay off my girlfriends to break up with me. How I was tricked into taking birth control that was too strong for me so my father could keep me 'focused' and not chasing after omegas. Seth seemed to care, to truly understand me in a way I'd never experienced up to that point. For the first time, I felt like someone loved me for me."

Lex's hand brushes a loose lock of her dark hair back, but I catch the glimmer on her face before she subtly wipes it away. I shift in my seat, wanting to go to her, but not wanting her to shut down either. Mateo's hand falls on my shoulder, thumb brushing gently, acknowledging my struggle without condemnation. I know what's coming next in the story, but only because I've lived it. First, it's love-bombing, when the abuser showers their supply with affection and love, making them feel like they're on top of the world. Once the victim is hooked...

"Do you remember when we first heard rumors that the city was taking bids for Wickland House? I've loved that building since I first saw it, and I knew that I had to win the contract. But at the time, we didn't have the capital to fund the project, and we were still too new to the game for any bank to take that big of a risk. I remember all the nights we spent trying to figure out how we could do it, and when I found the Federal Urban Historical Conservation grant, I thought I'd found our golden ticket," Lex goes on.

"What do you mean? We got the grant, so–"

Lex shakes her head, looking through the reflection at Mateo behind me, her smile sad. He stops mid-sentence, as confused by that look as I am.

"In order to qualify, construction on the building being restored had to have been completed prior to 1930. Originally, Wickland House would have been completed in 1929, but with the stock market crash, the project was delayed, and the official completion date was May 1932."

It takes a moment for my brain to wrap itself around that information, but Rhett gets there faster. He takes several steps forward, leaning with straight arms on the back of one of the dining room chairs as he stares in shock at the back of Lex's head.

"Lex, you didn't–"

"Oh, I did. I lied, claiming that all the records were lost, and the best evidence we had showed 1929. And we got the grant, so it was worth it, right? What did a couple of years matter, as long as I got what I wanted?" Lex asks rhetorically.

"That's not you talking, that's Leopold," Lucas interjects.

He gets to his feet and sets his mug down on the counter, but I can't look away from Lex's reflection in the window. The shame, the guilt, the resignation. Leopold St. Clair, her father, is famous for his ruthless business dealings, his take-no-prisoners style. The Lex I know couldn't be more different, but I know what it's like to have the voices of my parents in my head, criticizing my every move. In my weaker moments, I've listened and fallen back into those bad habits. Could we blame Lex for doing what she was taught, what she was raised to believe was the right thing?

"What happens if someone finds out about it?" I ask gently.

"I'd be forced to pay back the grant money, on top of whatever fines and jail time the judge would deem appropriate. We might be able to recover from the financial hit, but it would mean selling all of our assets and basically starting over from scratch. And even then, the blow to the foundation's reputation may not be something we could come back from," Lex drones, not looking at us.

"Why didn't you tell us about this before you took that risk? We could have found another way," Rhett presses, his words not angry but still heavy with emotion.

"Because I knew you'd talk me out of it. You are so good, and I didn't want you to think less of me for wanting to get my hands dirty to get ahead. I could take the guilt, the burden of that choice. But if I saw you or Matty look at me with the same... disgust I saw in your eyes when you looked at my father, I–I couldn't bear that," she replies, voice cracking.

I can't stand it another moment, so I spring to my feet and cross to the window. When I wrap my arms around Lex's shoulders and pull her to my chest, she goes stiff. I hum, trying to swallow the sound and push the vibrations deeper into my throat and chest. Lex's sadness calls to the primal part of my mind, the instinct to comfort and soothe an alpha in distress too loud to ignore. I can only manage the omega purr for a few moments, but I feel Lex relax into me, resting her forehead on my shoulder. She's a few inches taller than me, but I still try to gather as much of her in my arms as I can.

"That's not the end of the story, though, is it?" I ask carefully, rubbing slow strokes up and down her back.

She shakes her head. "For a while, I let the guilt eat at me, but then I couldn't take it. I had to tell someone, so I turned to the person I thought I could trust."

"You told Seth," Lucas says, more of a statement than a question.

Lex nods solemnly. "He was understanding at first, but it didn't take long for the manipulation to start. He had something to hold over me, so the entire power dynamic of our relationship changed. It came to a head right around the time we were discussing plans to open Alice's Kitchen. Seth wanted the Foundation to back his project, too, but it was a poor investment. With the restaurant, I knew that you, Lucas, had the experience and knowledge of what it actually takes to run a business, and having Rhett as the owner was just a precaution. Seth wanted to open a gym with no business plan, no experience as a trainer or client base. When I told him no, he started threatening to expose me."

"And he's been using this against you ever since?" Mateo asks incredulously, getting to his feet.

Lex sighs and looks up from my shoulder at last. She gives a small smile, cupping my cheek lightly for a moment before stepping back. She wipes her face and throws her hair back, straightening her spine.

"Yes, and no. When he threw down the ultimatum, I knew I had to do something. What we'd built was too important to be ruined by one petty omega who can't take no for an answer." She turns to look at Rhett, who's moved to stand a few paces away, the end of the sectional between him and us. "When you approached me about the possibility of making Lucas a more permanent member of this family, I jumped on the opportunity. I could shelter the foundation and all of the work we've done behind the protection of a pack. Then it would just be a matter of buying Seth's silence."

"So what? You only let me into this pack because–"

"No," Lex growls, whipping her head around to face Lucas. "Do not think for one microsecond that you aren't loved, Lucas Klausen. That you aren't an invaluable part of my life and this family. Rhett can attest to this, but our decision to form a pack, to consider bonding options with you, came long before Wickland House or Alice's. Everything that happened with Seth was just the push I needed to stop overthinking it, and actually make your place with us official."

His teeth click as his jaw snaps shut, and the flush of pink that splashes across Lucas's nose and cheeks is almost too adorable for words. He looks at Rhett with the question in his wide eyes, and Rhett only nods.

"So that's why he decided to pull that bullshit with his heat, then. He was throwing a fit because he couldn't get what he wanted," Mateo says, words twisting with cruel irony.

"Has he been trying to force his way into the pack ever since?" I ask tentatively.

Lex shrugs with one shoulder. "It comes up occasionally, but he's stopped asking outright. Mostly, I think he just enjoys the power games. If I try to make a move to distance us from him, he brings up what he knows. If he tries to get more out of us, I remind him blackmail is still a crime. We're at an impasse."

"What was your end goal? Surely you weren't going to let this go on forever," Rhett asks, a little exasperated but mostly earnest.

"No, it wouldn't. The statute of limitations of my crime is seven years. I was going to try to hold him off until his leverage over me lost its weight, and then I would take all of the evidence I've been collecting, every nasty message and email, every transcript of our mediations, all of the diatribe he's posted on the internet, and use it to get us free of him, once and for all," she replies, voice firm and steady for the first time since this started.

My heart twists at her phrasing. All past tense, and I don't have to think very hard at all to figure out what, or rather who, has changed those plans.

"That's all well and good, but it's clear that things have gotten out of control. People are burning down buildings in his name. It's a fucking miracle no one got hurt tonight, and if we just let this go on, we might not be so lucky next time," Mateo interjects.

Lex nods, but doesn't speak. I go to step away, to try to put some distance between her and me so I can think, but she grabs my hand, holding it tight. Even still, I can't force myself to look at her. My mind is swirling faster and faster, each passing moment bringing a fresh wave of guilt. Things hadn't been like this before I met Pack St. Clair, for them or for me. It wasn't the best life, but we'd been safe from the demons lurking just outside of our doors. Being together has upset the balance, and for what?

"I don't disagree, but I think we need to take a step back. It's clear that this situation is getting out of hand, and we need to do something. But in all honesty, I think the best thing we can do right now is try to deescalate. We lie low, try to get the lawyers involved, maybe..."

She continues on, but her words fade into the growing hum of panic in my mind. I try to pull my hand free again, but Lex refuses to let me go. But wouldn't it be best if I stepped away from this? The only thing I've done for these people is stir up trouble and reopen old wounds. I'm a college dropout, was living paycheck to paycheck with no future and a past I was trying my best to forget. I'm not smart and beautiful like Alexandra, charismatic and charming like Mateo, driven and talented like Lucas, or even grounded and compassionate like Rhett. I don't bring anything to this pack except problems. Wouldn't it be easier for me to leave, to let them go before it's too late?

"...if we're out of public view for a few weeks, they'll get bored and move on. And once we've gone to court and Lydia has pack protection—"

"Wait, what? That's in November," I stammer, speaking over Lex.

She turns and meets my eye, and I'm unsettled by how quickly she's returned to her calm, unshakable center. But I've never felt more off-kilter, my knees liable to give out at any moment. She wants us to hide for that long?

"I can't do that. I have to go to the wedding," I continue, my words sounding pathetic even to my own ears.

"Love, you can't think that's still a good idea after what happened tonight," Rhett sighs.

I jump slightly as I realize how close he's gotten without my noticing, standing just out of arm's reach of Lex and me. Mateo is closer now, too, leaning against the back of the sectional a few feet to my right. Lucas is still in the kitchen, but there's a tension to him, like a coiled spring ready to burst at any moment. Returning my focus to Rhett, I look up into his eyes, and my guard goes up instantly at the look of exhausted exasperation.

"It doesn't matter if it's a good idea or not. I have to go," I say, straightening to my full height and setting my shoulders.

"No, you don't. We can figure out another solution that doesn't involve you getting within fifty miles of the man hell-bent on killing you," Rhett retorts.

"If it were one of your sisters in trouble, you wouldn't let any of us stop you from doing whatever it took to save them," I throw back. I know it's a low blow, but my mind is beyond caring. I need him to understand, no matter what.

"That's not the same—"

"I mean, it kind of is. And besides, if we can figure out how to protect her here, there's no reason why we can't figure out how to protect her there," Lucas says, stepping a little closer.

"As much as I hate to say it, I think Rhett and Lex have a point. Going to that wedding is asking for trouble. Someone could get hurt, and it's just not worth the risk," Mateo says softly.

Mateo's words bounce around my head. Not worth the risk. Asking for trouble. I'm asking for trouble by trying to protect my brother. I rip my hand from Lex's grip at last, shaking my head as I fight back the tears burning the back of my eyes. She moves to catch me, but I dodge her hold. I stumble across the room, away from the arms trying to grab me, to trap me.

"Jason is perfectly capable of handling himself, sweetness. If you tell him what your mother said—"

"No!" I shout, my shoulders heaving up around my ears as I breathe harder.

I'm trouble for this pack. What I need isn't worth the risk. I'm not worth the risk.

"Lydia..." Rhett whispers, his voice trailing off.

"I'm... done. If what I need isn't worth it to you, then that's fine. I can handle it myself," I drone, staring at a knot in one of the planks on the floor.

When I turn and walk down the stairs to my room, I expect one of them, any of them, to follow me. I'm prepared to fight my way past someone standing outside of my door after I hastily pack some clothes in my backpack. But no one is on the other side when I emerge. And no one stops me as I take the keys to Lucas's muscle car, start the engine, and drive away.

THIRTY-SIX

Mateo

FOR A LONG TIME, no one speaks. No one moves. No one breathes. The grandfather clock in the other room runs out of power, its ticking fading into silence. And the roar of an engine, the scrape of tires on gravel, pierces through my head. I move in jerking steps, making it to the front door in time to watch the rear end of Lucas's car disappearing around the bend in the road. She's gone. She left. She...

"GET THE FUCK OUT OF MY WAY, LUCAS!"

I spin at Rhett's roar, slamming the front door closed as I head back to the sitting room. Lex is still at the window, staring at her coffee like she's waiting for a message to suddenly appear, not even blinking as tears pool along the edges of her lashes. Rhett and Lucas are chest to chest in the kitchen, Rhett's face twisted in rage and something else. It takes a moment for the burning newsprint scented fear to hit me, and I cough at the chemical taste coating the back of my throat.

"After the bullshit you just pulled, I think the fuck not, Rhett Cooper," Lucas is shouting back.

Lucas doesn't train with Rhett and me on any sort of regular basis, so when he raises his hands and pushes Rhett hard enough to send him stumbling backwards, I blink in surprise at the display of strength. Rhett tries to advance again, but stops, clutching his chest and pulling at the fabric of his shirt. He sways precariously, his next inhale more of a wheeze.

"She's—we can't let her—she'll get hurt. I can't—"

Rhett's words come out around labored breathing, and I watch as he moves this way and that, stumbling more than walking until he collapses on the floor, pulling at his hair, wiping his face, all the while looking around, searching but not finding what he needs.

"She's going to die. I can't let her. She's—not again. Not again. Not again."

My mind switches into overdrive, and I drop down next to my best friend, gathering him against my chest. I start to purr on instinct, trying to soothe his panic like I would try to soothe Lydia's, but it doesn't seem to help. He's shaking hard enough to rattle my teeth, but I only hold him tighter.

"It's okay, Rhett. You're okay. No one's going to die," I mutter, rubbing his back.

"She's tired. She's upset. She's—I have to—I can't let her—"

"You can, and you will," Lucas says, dropping down beside us.

Rhett looks up, and the conflict is clear in his eyes, the shift from panic to violence, to fear. All of my usual techniques for helping Lydia are failing me, because I can't identify the source of this fear in him. I can't talk it away, explain how it's not true, that there's nothing to fear or worry about. I look at Lucas in question, but the beta only has eyes for his alpha right now.

"If I were a betting man, I'd put every penny in my savings account on her going to Wickland House. We can call in a few minutes, see if she got there safe," Lucas tells him calmly.

"She can't go there. She'll go through Decatur and Garrison if she goes to Wickland House. She can't—what if..."

It hits me like a sucker punch to the jaw as he names *that* intersection. The night before Lydia's birthday, I'd tried to convince her to stay. We all had. But she wanted to go back to her apartment, because she still had to work a half day before she would spend that weekend with us. I'd gone to bed, knowing I had to get up early, so I could get to the store and pick up the last-minute details Lucas and I needed for her surprise party. But shortly after midnight, I was dragged out of bed so we could go to the hospital and wait to find out if Lydia was alive or dead.

It never occurred to me to think about the details of that night, at least not after we got the all-clear on Lydia's condition. But Rhett and Lucas had been up with her. Rhett had been the one to get the call from Everton PD. Had he also been the last one to see her before she left?

"You put her in the car that night," I rasp, not caring that I cut across whatever Lucas had been saying.

Rhett and Lucas both look at me, confused, but I can only shake my head. So much of the last few weeks makes sense. Rhett's obsession with keeping Lydia safe, on making sure someone has eyes on her at all times. His insistence that she never get behind the wheel, even though the doctor cleared her to drive a while ago. The pain in Rhett's eyes confirms it. He's blamed himself for Lydia's accident, and watching her walk out today, when she's tired and upset, and knowing she's going to be driving on those same streets has broken something in him.

"Luc is right. We can't go after her," Lex says faintly.

All of us turn to look at her, still not getting up from where we're kneeling on the floor. She's at least stopped looking at her coffee, but now she's staring out the picture window into the middle distance. I try to find what she's looking at, but there's nothing remarkable out there.

"You're just going to let her go? Just like that?" Rhett snaps, and I'm more than a little relieved to hear the fight back in his voice.

"We have to. Every step we've taken to try to protect her has only served to push her away. If she wants to go, then so be it. We can't force her to be with us," Lex goes on.

And somehow, those flat, emotionless words strike deeper than anything before. Because she's right. And I hate her for it.

I make it twelve hours before my will breaks. Lucas and Rhett had retreated to their rooms, Rhett still shaken up from his panic attack. Lex didn't go to the office, but she's cloistered herself into her study, closing the rest of us out. And that's left me alone to do... what?

I settle on the couch of the basement lounge, positioning myself with a direct line of sight down the hallway to Lucas's workshop/garage and Lydia's bedroom door. It's open, the lights still on and the clock on her wall ticking away mercilessly. Time stretches and warps, one minute feeling like twenty as I stare, and wait, and hope to hear tires, the rumble of an engine pulling in. But minutes turn into hours, and there's still nothing.

All I can do is think. I can't escape my thoughts, the swirl and eddy of blame and guilt and regret. What if I'd never gone up to the bar that night at The Valencia? What if I'd never texted him back? What if I'd decided to leave, to drive away from Everton and never look back? What if I'd never taken that leap of faith and asked Lydia to go to the drag show with me? What if I'd never kissed her, never touched her, never fell in love with her?

That last possibility stops my train of thought short. Could I have avoided all of this by never letting myself be vulnerable with her? Never letting her see how lonely I've been? Was there ever a chance I could have stopped myself from loving Lydia Anderson?

No. I answer myself. *There's not a single version of reality where I meet Lydia and don't fall madly in love with her.*

And that conclusion, that absolute truth, burns like a righteous flame in my belly. I love Lydia more than breathing, and I'll be damned if I stand aside and let her walk away without me.

I'm out in my car and on the road before my mind catches up, slowing my speed to something far less reckless. I still set a new record for the time it takes to get to Wickland House. I park and dash through the lobby, slapping my wallet impatiently against the scanner of the private elevator, bouncing on the balls of my toes as I wait.

"She's not up there, boy."

I turn at the cold, age-worn voice, finding Wila Fitzgerald standing beside me, arms crossed over her chest. Those deep, timeless brown eyes are stony, mouth pulled into a thin, disapproving frown.

"What do you mean? I thought—"

"Gabby and I aren't staying in y'all's pack suite, despite Mr. Cooper's persistent offers," Wila continues, words clipped.

"Where are you staying, then? I need—"

"No, you do not 'need' anything, boy. Not involving my girl," Wila snaps.

I stare open-mouthed, the elevator behind me ringing as the doors open. But my feet are stuck to the floor, unable to move away from the harsh glare this bear of a woman is leveling at me.

"Can... can you at least tell me that she's here? That she's safe?" I breathe, heart hammering in my chest.

Wila's eyes soften a fraction, but her posture doesn't change. "She is. I suspect she's sleeping, but that bodyguard of hers is watching over her."

I slump a little, nodding. At least she's not alone. I sigh, closing my eyes for a moment before deciding. I dig in my wallet for a moment, finding the white plastic card wedged in the back and yanking it free. I extend it toward Wila, who just stares at it.

"I'm going to be up there. When... if she wants to see me, I'll be there," I say, fading off hesitantly.

"How are you going to get back up if you leave?" she asks, looking at my face inquisitively.

I smirk, unable to help myself. "I'm not leaving. Not without her."

It takes a moment, but Wila reaches out and takes the card, and I have to hold back the urge to hug her in relief. It's a longshot, but I'm willing to take it. I'll do anything to see her, even if it's just one last time. I step back into the still open elevator door, letting them slide closed and carry me up to where I'm going to stay until Lydia is back in my arms.

I throw myself on the couch, ready to sit and wait until she walks through those doors. But the nearly two days without a full night's sleep finally catch up to me, because the next thing I know, a hand is shaking me out of a deep, dreamless sleep. I nearly jump out of my skin, but all my fear dissipates when I look up into Lydia's bottle-green eyes. Words fail me, and all I can do is throw myself at her feet, wrapping my arms around her hips and pressing my face to her stomach as tears overwhelm me.

"Mateo..." she starts, the end of my name lifting in a question.

"I'm so sorry, baby. So, so sorry," I mumble against her shirt, repeating the phrase over and over.

She doesn't move for a while, but then her hand comes up and I nearly sob in relief at the first brush of her fingers through my hair. I hold her tighter, too afraid to let go and watch her walk away again.

"What are you apologizing for?" she asks slowly, picking her words with care.

I take a deep breath, trying to get a hold of myself long enough to put a sentence together. She doesn't speak or pull away, her fingers still idly twisting a lock around one finger.

"I'm sorry that I pushed you away. I'm sorry that I didn't try to understand what you were asking of me, but just assumed I knew better. I'm sorry... I'm sorry that my actions and words made you think you're anything less than perfect. I..."

I trail off, not sure what else I can say. Because everything else that comes to mind just feels... wrong. She had every right to think we believed her incapable of making her own decisions. I can't take back the things I said, the things that clearly hurt her, but any promises to do better just feel empty. Why should she believe me?

"I'm sorry I broke your trust in me. You mean so much to me, and I've been terrible at showing you that. I... I'm so sorry," I say, trailing off into a whisper again as I squeeze her one last time and then let go to sit back on my heels.

I feel another tear slide down my face, but I don't move. Then suddenly, my skin comes alive as delicate fingers whisper across my cheekbone, brushing the drop away. I lean into her touch, closing my eyes to bask in the warmth.

"You've broken nothing, Mateo Hutchenson. I still trust you, and I love you, so, so much."

My eyes fly open at the catch in her voice, finding her kneeling on the ground in front of me. Her eyes shine with unshed tears, and I can't stand the sight. Without taking the time to think, I lean forward, cupping her face and bringing my lips to hers.

The kiss is soft at first, our touches hesitant, like we're learning each other for the first time all over again. But then the heat between us rises, hands wandering in search of more skin to touch, to re-memorize. Clothes are abandoned, neither of us stopping until we're chest to chest, arms entwined as we fall to the soft rug, her landing beneath me. I pull back with a gasp as her fingers close around my cock, guiding it to her warm, inviting slit. She's already soaked, and it only takes two slow rolls of my hips to bottom out.

"I love you, Mateo," she gasps, eyes fluttering closed and head tipping back as I set a steady pace.

I lean in, nipping at her newly exposed throat before soothing the tiny hurts away with my tongue. "I love you, Lydia."

We say the words back and forth, over and over, reaffirming the connection that's been undeniable since we first laid eyes on each other. Our bodies move together, each sigh and moan passing between us in concert. She's warm and tight around me, and nothing has ever felt more right than being inside of her, of joining our physical beings as close as our souls. I don't believe in destiny, or that everything happens for a reason. But someone, something, bigger than any one person, stepped in that day, giving me the impulse to check in on the work site. If I'd ignored that whim, I never would have met this incredible woman, my perfect match.

"I want your knot, please. I'm so close," Lydia whimpers, her nails digging into the skin of my biceps.

A primal growl rumbles through my chest, and I snap my hips harder, faster, driving deep until Lydia is screaming, her body shaking as she crests that peak. Her channel pulses, drawing me into her body, and I can't fight it for long. My knot swells, my balls tighten, and with one last grunt, I push deep, locking in as I fill her to the brim with my cum.

I hang my head as I try to catch my breath, purring when her fingers play with the sweat-damp hair at the nape of my neck. I take her free hand and bring her wrist to my mouth, kissing the place where I'm going to leave my mating mark before holding our clasped fingers to my chest tenderly.

"I know what I want you to get," she says into the quiet.

I look up at her, asking for her to continue with my eyes. Her smile is serene, and it warms my heart to see it again after everything we've been through in the last forty-eight hours.

"I want you to get a little lightning bolt, nothing big, nothing fancy. Just a simple design here," she continues, pulling our joined hands back so she can trace the zig-zag shape in the empty space I'd shown her.

"Why that?" I ask, unable to hold back the question.

"You came into my life like a bolt from the blue. You shocked me awake and changed everything I had planned. Electricity is what makes the heart beat, and that's what you are to me, Mateo. The pulse in my blood, the light in the darkness, the jolt I needed to stop being so afraid."

She trails off, eyes on the place her finger touches my skin. I lower our hands and lean up, resting my forehead on hers. Her breathing is shaky, her body shivering slightly. I kiss her gently, reverently. I didn't think I could love her more, but she always finds a way to surprise me.

THIRTY-SEVEN

Lydia

LEAVING MATEO IN THE suite is harder than I'd care to admit. But I need the distance to think, to figure out what I want, and being around him makes it hard to remember all of the very good reasons I had for walking out in the first place. He tried to make me take his access card, but I refused. The temptation to come back would be too hard to ignore. Even knowing he's in the building makes it hard to return to the room Gabby and Wila are staying in for the time being.

While it's not as spacious as the pack suite, their three-room suite is still nicer than some apartments I've been in. Two bedrooms flank an open plan living room, dining room, and kitchen, all decorated to match the glamorous art deco architecture of the building. When I open the main door, I look to find Gabby and Caleb at the dining table, playing cards, of all things. I don't know what sort of game they're playing, or who's winning, but they are both so invested that neither spares me a passing glance as I close the door behind me.

Caleb had arrived hours after I stumbled into Gabby's arms, sobbing too hard to explain why I was even there. He didn't give me a straight answer when I'd asked how he found me, but it wasn't a stretch to guess that Lex had sent him. He didn't ask about the fire, or the fight, or anything. He's been a silent, comforting presence; exactly what I need right now.

"How's Mat?" Gabby asks, laying down a card onto the pile next to the deck.

"Apologetic," I sigh, shuffling to the couch and curling up against one arm.

"He fucking better be," she grumbles, so low I'm not sure she intended for me to hear.

I close my eyes, letting my head fall to one side. I can still see Mateo on his knees, soft brown eyes broken and full of tears, and my heart breaks all over again. Hearing Mateo own up to his mistakes was exactly what I needed, even if I didn't know it. It reminded me that he's not Darren, that he doesn't think I'm worthless or any of the other nasty things that had gone through my head on the drive here.

"You'll never guess who showed up while you were gone," Gabby says, pulling me from my thoughts.

"Santa Claus?" I ask in a sarcastic monotone.

"Rhett," she replies curtly.

I sit up, suddenly wide awake and alert. I turn to look at her, but she's staring hard at her hand, brow lowered in concentration. Caleb, on the other hand, is completely unreadable.

"What did he want?" I ask.

"What else? To see you. But the Eastern Block-Head sent him home with his tail between his legs," Gabby says with a snort.

I look at Caleb, but he doesn't lift his eyes from the cards in his hands. He picks one out and plays it, making Gabby groan in frustration. The corner of his mouth twitches as he draws another card, but there's no other tell in his poker face.

"Why, though?" I ask insistently.

"He doesn't know why he needs you yet, *voyin*. It'll do him some good to sit with this for a few days," Caleb answers simply.

I blink at him, waiting for him to elaborate, but the card game continues in silence. I settle back into my seat on the couch, trying to puzzle out his meaning. But the lack of sleep and emotional exhaustion of the last few days clouds my head, and I give up, slumping down into a more comfortable position. It doesn't take long before I drift off to sleep.

———— *ele* ————

Almost a week later, Gabby and I return to the hotel room after spending the morning down on State Street. With no shop, our days are long and boring without something to do, so we've volunteered to help with the clean-up from the fire. It's hard, heartbreaking work, but there's something soothing about it, like burying an old friend. There isn't much left, but every now and then we find a soot-blackened or water-logged treasure and it makes it all worth it.

Wila has been off trying to find a temporary space to rent so we can get back to work. I know it's her way of dealing with the loss, but only seeing her in passing for the last few days has been difficult. I want to apologize, or try to explain, but she's gone before Gabby and I get up in the morning, and she goes right to bed when she comes home well after dark. Gabby brushes off my worries about Wila eating or sleeping enough, but I can tell she's worried about her grandmother, too.

Gabby goes off to shower, and I head into the kitchen to find the room service menu. We'd ordered takeout the last few nights, but I miss Lucas's cooking. No one from the pack has tried to contact me since Mateo came to live in the pack suite, and it's been nice to have my space. But I've caught myself looking for them more than once, searching for traces of their scents in the air. And each time I don't find them, the aching in my chest grows.

"I've been looking at plane tickets. There's a flight out of Atlanta that leaves early enough on Friday for us to get to Louisiana and then drive to Chauvert before the bank closes," Caleb says, leaning on the counter next to me.

I jump a little at his sudden closeness but nod. He and I have been operating under the assumption that the pack is not going to help me at Sam's wedding. Caleb didn't ask questions or make me defend myself when I explained my insistence. He just started planning. We have the floor plan memorized, all possible exit routes planned, and we're just finalizing details of the time surrounding the event. I want to tie up the loose end of my trust fund, remove another piece off the board, but we have to time our arrival just right.

With no way to contact Jason, we can't guarantee that my parents won't happen to stumble across us, but it's a risk I'm willing to take. This blood money has hung over my head long enough.

"I don't know how I'll pay you back for them," I mutter, thumbing through the menu to avoid looking at him.

"I'll send the invoice to the Foundation," Caleb says, and I look up in time to catch his wink.

We share a little chuckle before I call in a dinner order for the three of us. I manage to catch a quick shower and get dressed in comfortable clothes before the knock comes on the door. Gabby is answering the door as I exit the bedroom, squeezing some water out of my hair with a towel.

"Seriously?" Gabby drones.

"Always a delight seeing you, too, Gabby," a familiar sarcastic voice drawls back.

I rush to the door, shoulder checking Gabby out of the way to throw my arms around Lucas's throat. His arms wind around my waist without hesitation, nearly crushing my ribs with the strength of his embrace. I breathe his clean towel and marshmallow scent deep, eyes burning.

"Missed you, Lydi-bug," he mutters into my hair.

The nickname nearly breaks my resolve not to cry, but I force myself to let go and step back. "What are you doing here?" I ask, a little breathless.

"Well, I *do* work here, remember?" He chuckles with a smirk, tossing his fringe from his sparkling blue-gray eyes.

I notice then that he's dressed in a white coat with the sleeves pushed up. I blush hot and look away, shuffling my weight a little.

"Plus, someone had to check on Matty," he adds.

I look up in confusion. "What do you mean?"

Lucas sighs and runs a hand through his hair. "We didn't know he left until the other day. We thought... but when we called the front desk, they told us he's been here the whole time, so..." He trails off, picking at a stain on the hem of his jacket for a moment. "It's been... well, there's no way to sugarcoat this. It's been hell without you at the pack house, Lydi-bug," he says heavily.

I shift my weight back onto my heels, twisting my fingers around themselves nervously. He looks at me again, and the flash of sadness in the depths of his eyes makes my heart clench. I look down at the cart of covered plates and then back behind me, meeting Gabby's expectant stare. Caleb is just behind her, and to my surprise, his gray eyes are soft and encouraging. He gives me a little nod, and my shoulders relax slightly as I turn back to Lucas.

"Let's take a walk, yeah?" I ask hopefully.

His beautiful face lights up with a smile, and he nods enthusiastically. We push the food cart into the room, and I slip on a pair of shoes before following Lucas down the hall toward the elevators. We're silent until we reach the lobby, where he takes my hand and leads me away from the front doors, toward a set of plain doors marked employees only. It's easy to let him lead, to not ask questions as we wander down a twisting path of hallways, eventually reaching a small office just off the bustling kitchen. There isn't much inside, a desk with a computer, some duct-tape patched chairs, piles of cardboard boxes, a corkboard with layers of papers tacked to it. Despite the cacophony of smells coming from the other side of the door, Lucas's scent covers every surface.

"It's not much, but it's better than trying to do inventory at a prep table," Lucas jokes, motioning for me to sit.

I smile and curl up in the offered chair, tucking one foot under my hips as I hug my other knee to my chest. Lucas leans on the edge of the desk near me, running a hand through his hair as he sighs heavily.

"Is it that bad?" I ask softly, not sure I even want to know the answer, but unable to stop myself from speaking.

"In a word, yeah. It's a tight race for who's handling this the worst. Mateo won't answer his phone, and only spoke to me because I was physically in the room with him this morning and he couldn't pretend I didn't exist. He's canceled or rescheduled all of his meetings and appointments for the next month, and Lex is having a hard time explaining it away to clients, which is only making her more upset with him.

"Rhett, on the other hand, won't leave the pack house. Any work he can do from home, he's had delivered, and he's taken over the formal dining room with it. He's trying to hide it, but I know he's been drinking and working out a lot, and he's barely sleeping or eating. I'll make him a plate before I leave for work, and it'll still be where I left it when I get back.

"And Lex... I have no idea where she's gone. Erica says she's shown up for work, acting like nothing is out of the ordinary, but she doesn't come home to the pack house. She's not answering my calls, and her texts are unhelpful in the extreme. If anyone's seen her, they aren't telling, and..."

Lucas stops, looking at the ground, but his eyes are distant. I grip my leg tighter, my heart galloping in my chest. I'd expected the reaction to be bad, but this is so much worse than anything I could have imagined. My leaving should have helped them, not destroyed them. All of their problems stemmed from my involvement in their lives, or at least that's what I thought.

"I'm not telling you this to try to guilt you into coming home, Lydia," Lucas starts, his tone low.

I meet his eye as he looks up, and there's something hard about his expression that I don't like.

"You were right to leave, right about what you said. I've done everything I could think of to get through to those stubborn fucking alphas and make them realize their heads were too far up their own asses to see they were hurting you, not helping you. You deserve better than what we've been giving you," Lucas goes on, voice deadly serious.

"And you don't think Pack St. Clair can be better?" I ask, barely above a whisper.

Lucas sighs and rubs his eyes. "Honestly, Rhett, Lex, and Mateo are some of the best people I've ever met, and I know they can do better. But we fucked up, bad. It's on them to apologize for what they've done, but after everything you've been through, I can't say I would blame you for not wanting to come back."

I blink at him, eyebrows nearly to my hairline. Of all the things I expected him to say, this wasn't one of them. But Lucas has always been like this, willing to say the hard thing even if it hurts. And maybe that's why my heart aches so badly. Because he's right. I've seen so much goodness from this pack, so much kindness and selflessness, but fear has run this pack ragged. They've resorted to merely surviving, not living, and that is a struggle I understand more than they could ever realize. When you're living in constant fear for your safety, things that would otherwise seem outlandish suddenly become perfectly reasonable. How often did I lie to Jason in those first few months, telling him I was going out and making friends, when in reality, I was spending my days behind locked doors and drawn curtains, terrified to step outside? Was withholding terrifying details about the level of Seth's obsession with me that much different? They've been trying to protect me, even if their methods left something to be desired.

I've spent so long thinking that reasoning with alphas was an exercise in futility. Any time I'd asked for some control, an alpha shut me down. Growing up, that had been my father, using my mother to impose his will on me. The things they taught me warped my view of the world so badly that Darren had no problem tricking me into believing he loved me and wanted to take care of me. But what Darren and I had wasn't love; it was toxic codependence. He needed me to feed his ego, someone he could tear down to make himself feel like a man. And I needed to please my parents, to gain their approval for once in my life that I willingly walked back into the arms of the alpha, who very well could have been my murderer.

But Pack St. Clair has never asked anything from me. They've offered me shelter, protection, a place inside their inner circle without ever expecting anything in return. Rhett has never asked for my body in exchange for his love. Mateo hasn't ever withheld his heart from me on the condition of my unquestioning loyalty. And Lex... she's never made me feel less than simply because of who I am.

Have I let my family ruin the one real chance I had for freedom?

"Is... is that what you want? For me to not come back?" I ask, trying not to let myself get washed away in the tide of my thoughts.

Lucas blinks slowly once before letting out an ironic bark of a laugh. "Fuck, no, that's not what I want. Watching you leave and not chasing after you was the hardest thing I've ever had to do. You've only been gone a few days, but it's felt like an eternity," he says, dropping to one knee in front of me, taking one of my hands in both of his as he looks up at me with wide, emotion-filled eyes. "I want you to be happy, and I know me and my pack can do that for you. But if that's not what you want, if we're not what you want, then..."

As his voice cracks and fails, his hands squeeze mine tight. Words fail me as I try to grapple with the weight of his words. Somewhere in the depths of my mind, on an instinctual level, I know that if I decided to get up and walk away right now, leaving this pack behind for good, Lucas would do everything in his power to make his alphas forget about me. He'd do whatever it took to stop Pack St. Clair from ever interfering in my life again.

But as I consider that option, of moving on with my life, the past several months becoming nothing more than a memory, I whimper at the pain in my chest. I could walk away, but I would never be free of them. They've done so much for me, changed me so fundamentally for the better that I don't know if I could ever exist without them. I try to look back and remember what my life was like a year ago, back before fate decided to intervene, and I can't picture it. How did I wake up in the morning and not share coffee with the most generous woman I've ever known? How did I get through a workday without the knowledge that the most amazing men would be waiting for me at the home we share? How did I sleep at night without their arms around me, their warmth keeping me safe from bad dreams?

How could I go on living without them beside me?

"I don't want that, Lucas," I whisper at last.

We look up and meet each other's gaze at the same time, and the hope staring back at me makes my eyes burn with unshed tears. He smiles at me, and my whole world seems to get a little brighter. When he leans in and brushes my lips with his, I can't help but smile.

"I... thank you, Lydi-bug," he breathes, resting his forehead on mine.

"What for?" I question, a little dreamily.

"For not giving up on us, even if we've given up on ourselves."

I kiss him again, intentionally pulling away before I can give in to the want starting to pool in my belly. Lucas steps back, letting go of my hand as he leans against the desk again.

"Do you want me to tell them?" he asks.

I shake my head. "I... I want to talk to them first. Mateo's already apologized, but I need to hear what Lex and Rhett have to say before..."

Lucas hums understandingly. "If nothing else, I'll make sure Rhett keeps kneepads at the ready, just so he can be prepared for when you do decide to come home."

We share a laugh, and I smile warmly. While I didn't understand it at first, I get why Caleb didn't let me talk to Rhett that first day. I would have forgiven him too easily, and he never would have had the time to miss me and learn. Now, after days of nothing but having to live with the consequences of his own actions, I think he's ready to listen and we can move forward together, better than we were before. Lex, on the other hand...

"I'll admit to not looking all that hard for Lex," Lucas says, reading my thoughts in my expression. "But I've got a fairly good guess as to where she could be hiding, if you were inclined to go seeking."

THIRTY-EIGHT

Alexandra

I'VE STARED AT THIS report for so long that the text on the screen no longer looks like real words. I toss it onto the table with a frustrated sigh, running my hand through my hair. It feels dirty, even though I washed it this morning. Every inch of me feels that way these days.

I look up and out of the window to my left, the branches of the lilac bush swaying in the wind. The leaves haven't started to turn yet, but it's coming. Soon all the greenery at Bright Hills will wither to brown husks, and we'll have to start bringing the potted plants out of the greenhouse. But it's all an illusion, meant to fool clients into believing the fantasy of southern pastoral timelessness. Nothing ever lasts, not even the things we need the most.

My cell phone pings next to my low-ball glass of neat whiskey I'd poured upon my arrival. I glance at the screen for just a moment, unable to stop the flare of futile hope in my chest that it might be her. But it's just my accountant, confirming the details of our meeting next week. I have half a mind to cancel. That project means nothing now that she's gone. But it'll be good for the Foundation, good for the...

The pack. Do I dare even call us that anymore? Once, before my ego ruined it all, we were. We moved together, always in sync as we rose like a rocket to power and status and wealth. There were no secrets, no days spent in stony silence, no resentments left too long to fester.

I reach out and take a large swallow of my drink, sitting with the burn for as long as I can before the inevitable numbness creeps in. I deserve the pain, deserve so much worse for what I've done to the people I love.

A soft knock on the open door frame on the other side of the room breaks the silence, but I don't look up.

"I'm fine for tonight, Jeanie," I drone, trying my best to keep the slur out of my words.

"You don't seem fine."

My head snaps up at the sound of her voice, and when I turn to look, I almost don't dare to believe what I'm seeing. Lydia is here, standing with her hands in the pockets of her sweatpants, leaning against the doorjamb like she hasn't just waltzed in and thrown my entire world out of balance again. Her hair is damp, like she showered not too long ago, face free of makeup. But she's so... perfect like this. Free from any pretense or barrier between her and the world. I'm suddenly aware of the messy bun I'd thrown my hair into, of the oversized and threadbare college sweatshirt, with a neck so stretched out, it falls off my shoulder. I wipe my hands on the thighs of my leggings, and I flush hot as I remember this is the second day in a row I've worn this outfit.

"H-how did you find me?" I ask, clearing my throat as I set my glass down. Anything to avoid looking into her eyes.

"Luc came to see me at Wickland House. Between the two of us, we put together a short list of your possible bolt holes," she explains, her inflection light, casual.

Nodding, I clear my throat again, shuffling papers around. My face feels hot, but it must just be the whiskey. Why else would my brain be so scrambled, so unsettled?

"Can I sit?" Lydia asks, closer than before.

I glance at the wingback chair on the opposite side of the small, round table from me and nod. It's not a perfect match to the chair I'm sitting in, the upholstery just the slightest bit pinker. Will Lydia notice? She perches cautiously on the antique, curling up like a cat in the block of sun still visible through the tall window. The beams are broken up by the lilac branches, and I get lost watching the light dance across the bridge of her perfectly upturned nose, cheekbones starting to show freckles from her time working out in the sun on State Street. I'm so absorbed that I don't notice her attention shifting from the table to my face until it's too late. Our eyes lock, and my heart breaks all over again.

"Lex, I—"

With a sharp inhale, I look away. Even hearing her say my name is too much. She shouldn't be here, shouldn't be looking at me with anything less than pure disgust in her eyes. But she's not. There's softness, and understanding, and I don't deserve that. Not from her.

"You should go, Lydia. Go find the boys and just..." I trail off, the catch in my throat making it hard to breathe.

"Not without some answers," she retorts without missing a beat.

I shake my head and look out of the window. I know that tone, because it's one I've used myself so many times. She's made up her mind, and there's nothing I can do to change it. Best just get this over with so she can move on.

"The tracker. What is that about?" she starts, full of determination.

Right for the jugular, then. I can appreciate that. "When the insurance adjuster looked at your car, they found a GPS device in one of the wheel wells. We couldn't prove anything, but I'd bet every penny in my trust fund Seth put it there, and that's how Davis knew where to find you."

She's quiet for a moment as she takes in my answer, and I catch her expression of wide-eyed shock out of the corner of my eye. She probably expected me to dance around, to play games and leave her in the dark. But if she's leaving, she at least deserves to know the whole truth. She'll be able to protect herself better this way.

"We learned recently that there may have been a connection between the man who hit you, and a private chat room Seth uses to communicate with his fans. They're still looking into the details, but my working theory is Seth found out you were going to join the pack from the public court records, and then groomed some desperate, naïve sycophant into doing his dirty work," I continue, not bothering to sugarcoat anything.

Lydia's soft gasp stabs me through the chest. It took her leaving for me to see how much I kept from her, from all of them. My secrets destroyed this family. I have to purge them in order for all of us to be able to move on, like drawing poison from a wound.

"Davis wasn't the only one following you, though he was the most dangerous. Seth's fans submitted dozens and dozens of candid photos of you to The Everton Review, most of you at work, but a few people got lucky and caught you running errands or on dates with the boys. Caleb's good with faces and has been keeping a running list of frequent flyers," I drone, still not looking away.

"He's known... all this time—"

"No one ever got close enough to be a true threat, at least not after that incident at the corporate mixer. Caleb wanted you to be at least aware of the situation, but I made the call not to tell you," I say, cutting her off.

Lydia's quiet for a long moment, and I settle more fully into my chair. The floodgates have blown wide, and I don't know if I could stop even if I wanted to.

"Jason's been emailing me just about every week since the article outing you was published. He's been trying to help, but the double agent role isn't easy. They're already less trusting of him, and ever since you've gone no contact, they've been even more guarded," I say, head warm as the whiskey starts to take hold.

"Who's 'they'?" Lydia asks.

"Darren. Your mother. Your brother, Adam, surprisingly. He showed up back at the Anderson compound, claiming medical discharge, but the records I found show a failed drug test, so who knows—"

"Adam's been kicked out of the Army?" Lydia interjects, more shocked than I would have thought she'd be.

I nod, giving her a sympathetic look for a moment before turning away. Her expression shows the reality sinking in, how much I know but have kept from her. Rhett and I talked the most about these things, making decisions on what was best for Lydia without ever asking what we'd done to deserve such a privilege.

"Wait, you said people were submitting photos to The Review. Why weren't they published?" she asks suddenly, words more clipped now.

"I told Tonya, the editor-in-chief, if she published anything about you again, I'd tell her husband how far she's willing to go to get the inside scoop," I drone, closing my eyes.

"What... what do you mean?" Lydia asks hesitantly, and rightly so.

"She was young and hungry once, and she wanted to get a statement on record about what sort of relationship Mateo, Rhett, and I had. So, I let her think she was one step ahead of me, but I knew what she wanted. She bought me a few drinks, got me talking, and talking led to a hotel room, and—"

"That's enough," Lydia whispers harshly.

"Sleeping with a journalist is hardly the worst thing I've done to protect this pack, Lydia," I scoff derisively.

If she knew how filthy my hands truly are, would she ever want me to touch her again?

"Why?" she breathes.

"Why, indeed," I say with an ironic chuckle. "Because those men have shown me more love and support than I've ever gotten from any of my blood relatives. Our motto, bonds stronger than blood, is why I protect them."

"No, that's not... why are you telling me all of this?" she demands, voice soft but not weak.

I pause and consider all the possible answers. Because I want her to have a complete list of my crimes, so she can know her hatred for me isn't misplaced. Because I can't stop myself from spilling all the things I've kept locked away for so long, even if it's only going to push her further away. Because...

"Because after being told my whole life that I couldn't rely on anyone but myself, I thought I'd found a group of people I could trust, that I found someone who loved me and truly had my back. But then he turned around and used me, just like I'd been warned would happen if I let myself be vulnerable. I sat here, in this exact spot, for weeks, putting my walls back piece by piece, the smell of the lilacs outside the window soothing in a way I didn't understand. Not until Rhett brought that first bouquet to my office... brought your scent into my life.

"I never want you to think I don't care about you, that I don't respect you, or think of you as anything less than miraculous. I've been looking for you long before I ever knew you existed. Why am I telling you all of this? Because

I'm in love with you, and I can't stand the thought of you walking away without knowing I tried my best to do right by you," I breathe out, letting the tears fall from beneath my lowered lashes.

The room is silent for three agonizing heartbeats, and I have to open my eyes to make sure she's still there. When I do, I suck in a sharp breath, heart throbbing at the tears streaming down her face, the way her lower lip trembles even as she tries to smile. And then she's out of her seat, her hand on my wrist yanking me to my feet and into her arms. She's all softness and warmth, her lilac scent filling my nose as I press my face into her hair. I extract my arms from her grip and wrap them around her shoulders. Without my usual heels, I'm only an inch or two taller, but she fits against me seamlessly.

Then my body relaxes, and my mind drifts into peaceful emptiness as a gentle purr fills the air. Everything is warm, my fingers tingling as they thread into her hair. Relief and contentment replace doubt and grief, my world coming back into alignment with its new axis clutching me tight around the ribs. How could I possibly think I could let her go? She's everything I want to be, kind, open, generous, honest, compassionate. And when she pulls back to look me in the eye, the comfort of her purr fading, I can only marvel.

"I'm not leaving, Lex," she whispers, reaching up and tucking a stray hair behind my ear.

I blink in confusion. "But we've—"

"Made mistakes. But we can learn from them, and do better going forward, right?" she interrupts gently, cupping the side of my face.

Her forgiveness, the kindness in her emerald eyes, breaks something in my chest, and I can only nod. She smiles and the world falls away. And then she's kissing me, her lips soft and sweet, and I'm lost. I will do whatever it takes to deserve the woman in my arms. When we break apart for air, I rest my forehead against hers for a moment, just letting myself enjoy her closeness.

"I've talked to Matty and Luc, but I still need to see Rhett. Is he..." She trails off, the end of her sentence more of a question.

I sigh and shake my head slightly. He's not okay, but I've been at a loss as to how to help him. But I know if anyone can do it, Lydia can.

"I'll stay here one more night, if that's okay? You have stuff to figure out and I don't... yeah," I finish lamely.

Lydia nods and gives me another soft kiss. "I'll see you for coffee tomorrow," she says before stepping back.

"Wouldn't miss it for the world, sweetness."

THIRTY-NINE

Rhett

As a Dom, I've made it a point to test all my toys and tools on myself before I ever use them with a partner. I know the sting of the cane, the deep ache of a paddle, even the burn of stretching implements. I've submitted myself to punishments, just so I know what I'm asking of my subs, including edging and overstimulation. Neither bothered me enough to consider not engaging in that sort of play.

But if this overwhelming ache in my chest, this painful longing that drags at my lungs, leaving me weak and shaking at the mere thought of her, is what Lydia or Lucas experience when I edge them, I will never do it again. This is cruel and unusual in the extreme, and surely must violate the Geneva Conventions.

I reach for the glass to my right, but frown when I find it and the bottle next to it empty. Weren't they both full just a few minutes ago? I look up through the wide front windows and blink. I'd dragged myself out of bed and down to the table just before sunrise, and now the sky is a smoky gray-blue, orange and pink clouds smeared across the vista. Twilight. But I've only made it through three folders.

Maybe if ya weren't drinkin' yer meals, ya'd git moar done, my mother admonishes in the back of my head.

I shake my head, my hair falling limply over my forehead. There's a dull pulse of pain on the top of my skull, but it's far from becoming a true hangover. And I could always fight it off with the hair of the dog that bit me.

Yer a sorry excuse, Rhett Cooper. No son of mine—

Yeah, yeah, Ma. I know.

And it isn't imagined disappointment anymore. I'd gotten the tongue lashing of a lifetime when Tessa called two days ago, asking about holiday plans, and if Lydia would be joining me for the Cooper-Nolan Christmas extravaganza. She'd caught me at the bottom of a bottle, so the whole sorry story came out. Before I knew how it'd happened, I was enduring my mother's Irish accented lecture about how badly I'd failed, and how she couldn't believe I'd forgotten so much of what she'd taught me. I've been dodging voicemails and texts from my sisters ever since, and just like the coward I am, I've deleted them without even reading their contents. There's nothing they could say to me that I haven't already thought about myself.

Pushing back from the table, I stumble to my feet before shuffling into the kitchen. There's a long-cold plate of food on the island, stir-fry. Lucas had been cooking that when I came home from meeting Lydia for the first time. I dump it untouched into the trash, putting the plate and my glass in the sink and turning on the tap. There's a coffee cup already in there, and I recognize it as one that Lydia brought with her when she moved in.

My chest tightens, and I suddenly can't breathe. Every trace of her brings me back to that night. She walked out and left me. I keep waiting for the call, to hear Lee's voice on the other line telling me our luck ran out at last. Anything could happen, and I can't leave this God damned house. After Caleb turned me away, this has been the only place that makes sense. She has to come home, right? So I'd wait. But the days keep passing, and she still hasn't even called. Did something happen, and I wasn't there to protect her?

I close my eyes and grip the edge of the sink until my knuckles ache. The pain is real. I focus on it, trying to push away the despair. She's fine, she has to be. She's smart, so smart and capable. She wouldn't take unnecessary risks. And she has Caleb. He wouldn't let anything happen to her. I can't lose her. The world would cease to exist if she left it. Her smile is as eternal as the sunrise, her soft skin like the tides, her lilac and honey scent, so engrained in me that I can smell it even now.

The water suddenly cuts out, pulling my eyes open. There's a hand on the tap, one I'd know anywhere. I follow the line of creamy flesh up her arm, to her shoulder, along the slope of her throat. And her face...

"Lydia," I breathe, gasping for air.

She looks up at me silently, brow furrowed and emerald irises clouded with concern. I turn to face her more fully, hands shaking at my sides. I want to reach out and touch her, but I'm too afraid it'll shatter the dream, leaving me alone again.

"What's wrong?" she mutters.

I can't respond, her voice ringing in my head like a crystal bell. My vision blurs and I sway on the spot, my chest not obeying my command to expand. And then her hand is on my arm, warm and soft and *real*, and I can't take it. My knees give out, and I fall sideways into the cabinet below the sink before sliding to the floor at her feet. My face is wet with tears I can't stop, and my lips move, but no words come out. She's here, and she's alive.

"Rhett, you have to breathe. Can you do that with me?" she asks, dropping to kneel in front of me.

I'd do anything she asked. Rob Fort Knox, walk through a forest fire, bring back the dinosaurs, anything. Her word is my sacred mission. So when she takes my hand and presses it to her sternum, counting her inhales and exhales, I follow blindly. Five seconds in, seven seconds out. The air is thick with florals, and it's easy to let myself fall into the emerald sea of her eyes. The world slowly comes into focus, and I'm more aware of the subtle vibration beneath my palm. She's... purring for me.

"When... how..." I whisper, throat raw.

Lydia chuckles under her breath. "I don't know. I'm just... doing what feels right," she replies.

I shift forward to kneel, adjusting my grip until her hand is in mine, and I bring it to my forehead as I bend low in supplication. She starts to protest, but I shake my head, holding tighter as she tries to pull away.

"Lydia, I'm so sorry. Please, my love, I can't—please forgive me. I've done everything wrong, treated you with such disrespect and disregard. I don't deserve you, but—"

"Rhett, no. That's not true. You do—"

"You don't understand," I growl through gritted teeth. It feels so important, more important than anything, that she knows this. "I have spent these last several weeks imagining every possible scenario where you could be hurt, or worse. I've thought about little else, and I've let my fear blind me to the truth. I let it convince me you are this fragile thing, something so delicate and weak that any slight hurt would shatter you. I told myself I was protecting you, but I wasn't. I was demeaning you, and you never knew. I convinced myself I was right, that what I was doing was necessary, but there's no reason for anyone to think the things I've thought, to do the things I've done."

"You're not making any sense," Lydia says, confused.

I swallow, trying to stop my arms from shaking. May God forgive me, even if she never will.

"I've hidden things from you, kept you ignorant of the dangers happening around you, because I decided you weren't strong enough to handle them and make smart decisions about your own safety. I took away your freedom to choose how you live your life, all in the name of keeping you safe and… there's a part of me that would do it all again."

She slides her hands from my grip, but I stay hunched over, head low between my shoulders. My tears have stopped, at least, but my head feels full all the same. I take a deep breath and brace for her anger. I could endure that much, at least. But what I'm not prepared for is her arms around me, pulling me to rest my head on her shoulder as her fingers comb through my hair.

"Lex told me everything," she says simply, kissing my temple.

My heart sinks, dread pooling in the place it vacated. Lex and I talked about many things regarding Lydia's safety, and the pile of secrets between us is not insignificant. Lydia is quiet for another moment or so, and I let myself enjoy this while it lasts.

"Let's get you cleaned up, yeah?" she prompts, pulling back to give me a heartbreakingly kind smile.

I furrow my brow in confusion, but don't object when she helps me to my feet and guides me up the stairs and into my room. She leaves me to stand in the middle of my disaster of a room, bustling off to the bathroom. A moment later, the shower starts running, and she reappears. I'm so out of my depth, bewildered and fascinated as I watch her dart around the room, gathering dirty laundry in her arms and dumping it in my hamper. She straightens the bedding, fluffs the pillows, and even picks up empty bottles I'd dropped off the side of the bed. She looks up as she goes to the trash and smiles.

"Go on and get yourself cleaned up. You smell like the floor of a dive bar," she says with a laugh.

"What are you doing? Why—"

"Shower first, then we'll talk."

"But—"

"Now."

I blink at the stern growl in her voice, openly gaping. I've never seen her like this, so... focused. The alpha part of my mind, usually so ready to meet a challenge, only cowers meekly. She's... she's an omega, caring for an alpha. But—

"I will not repeat myself. Go," she says, pointing to the bathroom door.

Too stunned to object, I follow her command. I don't linger, and I feel noticeably better once the layer of grime and grief on my skin slides down the drain. Once I'm done, I turn off the water and wrap a towel securely around my waist before padding back out into my room. She's been busy, straightening and cleaning my mess until everything is back where it belongs. Lydia found her blanket stash and has wrapped herself in the twin to her favorite emerald green one. She's sitting up, but has cocooned herself in the soft material, even pulling it over her head so only her face is visible.

"So, now can we talk?" I ask, crossing my arms over my chest.

"Are you going to get dressed first?" she asks back, her eyes drifting down my body before flicking back to my face.

I already feel more like myself, just by having her in the same room, so it's easy to fall back into our old habits. I smirk and settle my stance more fully. "No, I don't think I will," I say at last.

She presses her lips together, and I wait, half hoping she'll object. Lydia's stubbornness and will are two of the many things I love about her, and it's only now that I'm seeing them again that I realize how little she's displayed those traits these last few weeks. But instead, she settles more fully into her blanket, fixing her eyes on mine.

"You were having a panic attack," she states, leaving no room for denials.

I sigh and look away, face heating slightly. "I was. I've had a few this week," I admit.

"Because I've been gone?"

"Because I didn't know for sure you were safe," I correct.

She hums noncommittally, but doesn't answer. I let my arms down to hang at my sides, trying not to fidget too much. Being alone has given me the room to reflect, and my panic has always stemmed from my fear for Lydia's safety, and not being there to save her.

"I know it's in your nature to need to protect me, but there has to be a limit. I can't...*We* can't keep doing this over and over. It's not healthy," Lydia says, low and serious.

I swallow and start to turn away, but stop. No, I can't hide from this. Not if I want any chance of repairing the trust between us. So instead of walking away, I move toward the bed, sitting on the edge facing the door. I'm close enough to feel the edge of the blanket brushing my side when I move, but I don't close the distance. I lean forward to rest my elbows on my knees, looking down to where my hands dangle limply.

"Doing what?" I ask dully, almost afraid of the answer.

Lydia scoffs, but I don't turn. "We keep secrets, stop talking to each other. And then we fight when we should be talking. I fell in love with you because you listened to me, but now I'm not sure if I—"

When she stops short, I turn to face her, my brows drawing low. "I will always listen to you, Lydia," I declare emphatically.

Lydia's eyes are distant, looking at a patch of my duvet cover but not really seeing it. "But will you hear me, even when I say things you don't want to hear? Because from what

I've seen, you have a tendency to act first and ask questions later."

I sit with that for a moment, and let the words sink in. She's right, of course. Even now, my first impulse is to deny it, which only further proves her point. But as I consider, this feels too specific to not be based on something that's happened. And then I remember that morning in the kitchen, when she and Lucas shut me out for the first time.

"After the break-in, you—"

"I caught Davis's scent outside of my apartment," Lydia finishes, looking up at me with stony eyes.

I blink, my mouth opening and closing as I try to form words. "Why didn't you say anything?" I manage at last.

"You know why," she rasps, not looking away.

And damn it if she's not right again. If she'd so much as hinted at a potential suspect that day, I'd be in prison facing murder charges at this very moment. Nothing and no one could have gotten in my way, not with everything as fresh as it was back then. Even now, there's a part of me that knows I could get away with making Davis disappear, and the only thing stopping me is the knowledge that his testimony is going to put Seth behind bars for good.

But the fact I'm even entertaining these thoughts just emphasizes why she felt she couldn't trust me, why she feels that way even now. I look away in shame, swallowing hard.

"You're right. And I'm sorry," I mutter.

"But we're not here to talk about me," she says with a heavy sigh.

I shake my head and take a deep breath, trying to get my thoughts in order. There are so many things I want to say, so many things I need to ask. But where to begin? Do I even deserve answers at this point? I swallow again, one question floating forward and refusing to be pushed aside.

"The night of your accident, when you got Darren's text, why did you keep driving?" I ask, trying not to make the question sound like an accusation.

It's the one thing I've never been able to push aside. I could explain the need for her to sleep in her apartment that night, the route she took, the speed she drove at, but I never could figure out why she didn't pull over and call me. She knew I was still awake, because I always stayed awake until I got a text from her to confirm she made it home safely. I would have been at her side in minutes, could have brought her back to the pack house, or driven with her to her nest if that's what she wanted. And when that driver came along, she would have been in the passenger seat, and I—

"I don't know, Rhett, and even if I did, telling you wouldn't solve this," she says, cutting through my thoughts.

I whip around to face her, eyes wide in alarm. I open my mouth to speak, to try to refute her, but then she looks up at me with eyes bright and lined with moisture. Everything I'd been about to say lodges in my throat.

"I forgive you, Rhett Cooper. I forgive you for letting me go that night, and everything that's happened since."

I can only stare, absolutely flummoxed. She... forgives me?

"I know you think that you're to blame for my injuries, but there was a tracker on my car. If he hadn't gone after me that night, he would have done it another time. You never failed me, not as my partner or my alpha. I don't fully understand why, but you've treated me with kindness and invited me into your family. I can't punish you for this, not when your very nature calls you to protect. So instead, I forgive you, because that's what you need," Lydia explains, looking me dead in the eye as she speaks slowly and clearly.

"But if I hadn't—"

"We can't let ourselves get pulled backwards, Rhett. I left because I thought y'all would be better off without me. That if I disappeared from your life, all your problems would go with me. But look what's happened. This pack is on the verge of collapse. We have to stop blaming ourselves and each other for the things we can't do anything about," she says emphatically, the blanket rustling as she talks with her hands.

I turn around fully, kneeling in front of her, searching her face, waiting for the penny to drop. But she just keeps staring at me with bright, hopeful eyes, and I can barely stand it. I start to turn away, but she extracts a hand and catches my chin between her thumb and forefinger.

"I love you. I never stopped loving you, not once. But if you don't..." She trails off, silvery tears starting to form along the edges of her lashes. My heart lurches into my throat, and I lunge forward, gathering her into my arms in a tight embrace.

"I love you, too, Lydia Anderson. My heart is yours, now and always. I'm so sorry for what I've done, and I promise I'll never do that again. I promise," I say, trailing off into a whisper.

She pulls back and looks up at me, a smile pulling her perfect lips. The blanket has slipped down, her toffee-brown hair gleaming in the lights on my bedside tables. Her fingers brush against the light dusting of hair on my chest, and I shudder. I slowly lift a hand and trace her cheekbone, over to the shell of her ear, until my fingers thread into her hair. I start to lean down, drawn like gravity to her lips, but she presses a finger to my mouth before I can fully close the distance.

"Just one more promise," she whispers seriously.

I nod, already agreeing before she even asks.

"No more secrets."

"No more secrets," I repeat.

And then I seal my vow with a kiss.

FORTY

Lucas

WHEN I'D SAID GOODBYE to Lydia at Wickland House, I honestly had no clue if my plan had worked. I'd gone to her, knowing full well she could tell me to fuck off and slam the door in my face, but I had to do something. I'd tried everything I could think of to get through to my alphas, but to no avail. Rhett was too deep into his personal pity party to see reason. Mateo and Lex had run, and weren't coming back, at least not for me alone. So I'd called in the big guns.

And the relief that rushes through my chest as I pull my bike into the lower garage and find my car parked in its usual place nearly knocks me off my feet. She's back. She's home.

I have to force myself to move normally, to put my riding jacket on its peg and wash the dust from my hands and face in the sink. I don't know what I'm going to find upstairs, and if I rush in, I could ruin whatever work Lydia's been doing with Rhett. The quiet on the main living floor bodes well, though I don't see anyone right away as I cautiously exit the basement door. The plate I made for Rhett is empty, and in the sink, along with his usual whiskey tumbler. A quick peek into the formal dining room and I smile to myself when I find the table empty of its usual occupant.

Keeping my footfalls light, I ascend the stairs and make my way into my room to change out of my work clothes. I can detect traces of Lydia's lilacs on the air, and the sound of running water from the shower between my room and

Rhett's settles my stomach. I leave them be for a few minutes after the water shuts off, but it doesn't take long for my curiosity to overwhelm my common sense. Easing the door open, I poke my head into the bathroom, finding it empty and the door to Rhett's room open. I tip-toe across the tile floor, their conversation getting louder as I press my back to the wall next to the door, hopefully out of sight.

"...thought y'all would be better off without me. That if I disappeared from your life, all your problems would go with me. But look what's happened. This pack is on the verge of collapse. We have to stop blaming ourselves and each other for the things we can't do anything about," Lydia is saying, voice trembling slightly in her passion.

Her words are like a punch to the gut. I wish I could record them, so I could play that back whenever Lex and Mateo get in their own heads about Seth. I have half a mind to walk away when they start exchanging words of love and devotion, but a pulse of longing stills my feet. It's not jealousy, but I can't quite put my finger on the name. It's like I was invited on a trip but declined, only to have to hear about how amazing it was from the person who asked me to go in the first place.

"Just one more promise," Lydia whispers seriously.

There's a pause, and I hold my breath. What could she possibly ask of Rhett?

"No more secrets."

"No more secrets," he repeats without missing a beat.

No more secrets.

But here I am, hiding in a bathroom, secretly spying on my alpha and my omega. Hiding from my feelings. Hiding them from her.

So I step out, crossing the threshold into Rhett's room. But I stop short, looking around. It's... tidy again. Rhett and Lydia are kneeling on a made bed, her with a blanket around her shoulders, him in just a towel slung low over his hips. It does absolutely nothing to hide the evidence of his excitement to see Lydia again, and her flushed face as she pulls away and smiles at me only makes me laugh.

"Luc! I didn't hear you come home," she says breathlessly.

"Well, it appears you've been busy," I manage to get out through my giggles.

I meet Rhett's eyes, and my smile softens at the light that's returned to the crystal blue orbs. He's still holding Lydia close, but he nods for me to join them. Not needing to be asked twice, I strip off my t-shirt and jeans before jogging over to the bed and snuggling Lydia from behind. She hums in delight as I pepper kisses over her hair and the side of her face, not letting go as she squirms. Having her back in my arms, smelling that delicious floral and honey nectar already has me half hard, and the appreciative look in Rhett's eyes as he watches us makes my skin go hot.

"I missed you so much, sweetheart. Can I make it up to you? Please?" I breathe into her ear.

"What did you have in mind?" she replies a little breathlessly.

"I'm feeling a bit hungry, and I'm suddenly overcome with a very particular craving," I purr, letting my fingers trail down her side.

"Is that okay with you, sir? Can Lucas have a snack?" she asks, tilting her head up to look into his eyes.

I look up through my lashes and find Rhett looking back at me, icy eyes sparking with desire. His pupils nearly swallow the irises, and the air is suddenly heavy with the scent of vanilla and whiskey. There's a silent question in his eyes, and I nod eagerly in response.

It's been something we'd talked about, but haven't had a chance to bring up to Lydia. I'd fantasized about letting Lydia be the alpha sub, for Rhett to use me as a means to bring her pleasure. I'd never thought of myself as the serving type, but I could worship at Lydia's feet for days and still want more. Rhett, of course, will relish any chance he can get to not have to beat me into submission.

"Little one, we'd like to try something. We would both play with our pet, and he would be at our mercy. Is that something you'd be comfortable exploring?" he asks, tone light but firm.

Lydia looks at me, assessing. I give her a smile and a nod, showing her I want this.

"I don't know if I'll be good at it..." she says, trailing off and biting her lip.

"You can't do anything wrong, sweetheart," I reply gently.

"We have our safe words, and you can always tell me if you aren't comfortable, and I'll take the lead," Rhett adds reassuringly.

Lydia gives me one last look, and my heart does a double backflip as she nods.

"Safe words," Rhett prompts.

"Red to stop, yellow to slow down."

Lydia and I answer almost in perfect unison, making us both giggle. Rhett gives us both a proud little grin that makes my stomach clench.

"Then let's play."

Rhett leans down and kisses Lydia deeply, and the sight of them makes my heart melt. They are beautiful together, her skin only slightly darker than his, but a perfect compliment. The jewel tone of her eyes and the crystal of his, coming together like a clear sky over a verdant meadow. When they pull apart and look at each other, the electricity between them is enough to make goosebumps rise on my arms.

"Our sweet omega is a little overdressed, pet. Let's fix that," Rhett purrs.

"Yes, sir," I pant, skin flushing hot at the intent in his icy eyes.

My eyes go back to Lydia's, watching as the black of her pupils swallows the bottle-green irises. Rhett and I move in tandem to the end of the bed, positioning Lydia so she sits between Rhett's spread knees while I kneel on the floor at her feet. The towel falls away, revealing how much he wants this. My mouth waters at the sight of his cock, but I can wait for that treat. I have another meal in mind.

Keeping my eyes locked with hers, I slowly drag the material of her yoga pants down her legs. I toss the garment carelessly to the side, my hands returning to massage the muscles of her legs. Rhett slides her shirt up and over her head, and then deftly pops the clasp of her bra. The way her breasts drop makes my brain short circuit, and I can't help but stare as Rhett takes the globes in his hands and kneads, occasionally rolling her nipples between his finger and thumb. I'm so caught up in the sight that I jump when Rhett subtly clears his throat and I remember I can move.

My gaze roves to the apex of Lydia's thighs, the patch of curls just barely visible through the sheer black lace of her panties. I lean in, nuzzling my nose against her soft thigh as I breathe in the sweet scent of her arousal. She shifts and I move in, laying down long, broad sweeps of my tongue over the damp fabric covering her pussy. She tastes like sweetness and sunshine, and I moan low in my throat.

"Like ambrosia from heaven, isn't she, pet?" Rhett purrs.

I hum my affirmative response, helping Lydia lift one of her legs over my shoulder so I can access her core more fully. I continue my teasing licks, smirking to myself at the whimpering noises Lydia can't seem to hold back. Bringing up one of my fingers, I tease the edge of the lace, pushing it to the side just enough for me to press a finger into her tight heat. She bucks and I move with her, continuing to lick at her clit through the ruined fabric.

I lose myself in the taste of her, the steady flow of slick coating my face and hand. I could spend an eternity here and die a happy man. I need more of her, need to taste her fully. I let her leg fall just long enough to yank her panties off and throw them away, diving straight back into her delicious pussy.

She moans long and low at the first brush of my tongue against her swollen clit, and I reward her with more, swirling and flicking over it until she's breathing hard. I dip my tongue into her opening, moaning as more of her cream fills my mouth. I lap it up, drinking deep until she's squirming, her hand in my hair holding me in place. As if anything could make me leave my current state.

A second hand comes to the back of my head, pushing me deeper into Lydia's core. I close my lips around her clit, sucking and flicking the bud with all I have. I curl my finger deep and moan as someone pulls my hair taut.

"Come for us, little one."

Rhett's command is all it takes for Lydia to shatter, her legs shaking around my head as her pussy spasms and coats my face in a flood of cream. I drink it down eagerly, the honey and vanilla and earthy rain taste heavenly on my tongue. I work her through the waves of pleasure, slowing, but not letting up until she's utterly boneless and whimpering.

"Do you think Lucas deserves a reward for his performance, my love?" Rhett asks into the silence, bringing our focus back.

I look up at Lydia, who stretches one arm up luxuriously, hooking it around the back of Rhett's neck as she considers me. The sight of her, pale skin pink with the last traces of her climax, eyes hazy with desire, takes my breath away. She could ask me to walk across hot coals right now, and I wouldn't hesitate.

"I want to taste him," she practically moans, beautiful lips tilting up in a sensual smile.

I'm moving before my brain fully catches up, and I launch myself onto Rhett's bed, sitting up against the headboard with my legs spread. Rhett and Lydia both chuckle at my eagerness, but I don't care. She gives Rhett a lingering kiss before pulling herself away from his arms and prowling her way up to me. The sway of her hips has me hypnotized, my jaw going slack as she crawls up to settle between my legs. I can't take my eyes off her, enthralled as she wraps her slim fingers around the base of my cock, hardly able to encircle its girth completely. Her tongue darts out, and she gives the head a little kitten lick, gathering up the pre-cum gleaming there.

I hiss in a sharp inhale, my head dropping back as she teases me with her tongue. My eyes roll into the back of my head, and I fist my hands in the sheets as I struggle to keep still. When she finally takes me fully into the wet heat of her mouth, I can't help the groan that spills from my throat. Rhett had described being with Lydia as a nearly religious experience, and I can't deny the truth of his words as my soul leaves my body the first time the head of my cock slips down the back of her throat.

"If you come before she does, then you won't get to come again tonight, understood, pet?"

I look up as Rhett growls, finding him lining his cock up to take her from behind. She wiggles her ass delectably, and he gives it a playful swat, which makes her squeal around my cock. I moan at the sensation and Rhett chuckles.

"Yes, sir," I pant when I remember he asked a question.

Rhett moans as he slides forward, and I moan at the look of bliss that comes over his face. Lydia echoes the noise, and I buck involuntarily at the vibration. She chokes and backs off, and I look down in panic. I gently push her hair back so I can see her face, then immediately relax when I see how her eyes are scrunched closed, mouth open in pleasure.

"Tap my legs if you want me to stop, okay, sweetheart?" I whisper, leaning down to speak into her ear.

"Are you going to fuck my throat?" she whimpers, body shaking as Rhett thrusts into her with a hard but steady rhythm.

"If you want me to, I will."

She turns her head and captures my lips with hers, and I move with her as our tongues tangle. She pulls away when Rhett hits her sweet spot, cursing and moaning.

"Make me choke on your cock, Luc. Please," she begs, voice high and breathy.

I don't need telling twice. I shift so I'm sitting on my heels and gather a more solid handful of her hair in my fist. Rhett growls, but I don't pay him any mind, guiding Lydia's mouth back to my cock. She takes the tip eagerly, hollowing out her cheeks as I thrust up, letting her get used to my size. She moans and whimpers, saliva running down my cock as Rhett and I pick up speed. His thrusts drive her deeper down onto me, and she chokes a few times before she adjusts and lets me slide even deeper.

"Touch your clit for me, sweetheart," I pant, tugging her hair slightly to slow her down.

She obeys without thought, one of her hands slipping between her legs. Rhett moans and drives deep, grinding his hips against hers to work her into a frenzy. Lydia pulls her head up to suck in a deep breath.

"I'm gonna, I'm close—"

"Come on our sir's cock. Do it for me," I beg, pulling her up for another bruising kiss.

I swallow her scream as she shakes, and I let her lean into me as Rhett slows, drawing out her pleasure. He finally stills and presses close, sandwiching Lydia's body between us, as we kneel on his bed. When I pull up for air, Rhett threads his fingers in my hair, pulling me in for a soft kiss.

"Let's give her a minute to breathe while I get you ready for me, hmm?" Rhett suggests, playful and tender in equal measure.

"I thought you'd never ask," I tease with a chuckle.

Rhett pulls free, and we gently lay Lydia down on her side and I recline on my back next to her, spreading my legs automatically. My cock bobs against my stomach, and Rhett gives it a few appreciative strokes before gathering the bottle of lube from near the foot of the bed. Lydia snuggles closer, and I lift my arm to allow her to curl into my side.

The first brush of Rhett's fingers against my hole makes me gasp, and I let my eyes slide closed as I relax. Lydia traces my tattoos with light fingers, a countermelody to the delicious pressure of Rhett's finger breaching me for the first time. We both groan, and I force my body to relax, allowing him in farther. His second finger comes soon after, and he thrusts and twists them, spreading me open for his cock.

"Do they hurt?" Lydia whispers curiously.

I look down to find her stroking the swirling letters of my pack tattoo, following the cursive text with a light touch that makes me shiver.

"I'm not sure I'm the right person to answer that question, sweetheart," I reply with a breathless little chuckle.

She looks up at me with a confused expression until my meaning dawns on her. Because, yes, tattoos can hurt—some more than others—but I enjoy the pain. It's actually how I discovered pain is one of my kinks. I never squirmed or complained while in the chair; instead, I'd just bask in the endorphins and try my best not to make it weird for the artist.

"He's such a good little pain slut," Rhett comments offhandedly, twisting his wrist at the exact right time to brush my prostate and make me see stars.

Lydia moans from beside me, and I feel her arm move. As I glance over, her fingers circle her clit idly while she watches Rhett fuck me with his fingers.

"Has he played with your ass before, sweetheart? He's always so good." I groan the last word as Rhett adds a third finger.

"A little. Does it feel good when he fucks you?" Lydia asks, words almost shy.

"So good. You feel so full and—oh, FUCK!"

I buck as Rhett drags a finger across my prostate, and I glare at him as he smirks. I try to growl, but it only comes out as a needy whine. Thankfully, he takes pity on me, withdrawing his fingers only to press the head of his cock against my fluttering hole. We moan together as he thrusts forward, and I pant as he bottoms out and then withdraws in one fluid roll of his hips.

I turn my head to find Lydia watching the place where Rhett and I come together, her eyes wide and cheeks flushed.

"Ride his cock, love. Let's make him feel good," Rhett instructs, not slowing down as he sits back.

Lydia looks at me, and I nod. She smiles as she throws her legs over my hips, taking my cock and guiding it to her still slick entrance. As she sinks down, Rhett stills and I shout, unable to contain the noise at the dual sensation of Rhett in my ass and Lydia hot and tight around my cock. They move slowly at first, and it's all I can do not to come. They work together, slowly building to a steady rocking that has my mind going into overdrive.

"Sir, please. I want you to—"

Lydia's plea breaks off in a whine as she shifts to a different angle, her hips grinding as she works herself on me. I finally remember that I still have limbs, and I take her hips in my hands to help her move.

"You want my fingers in that tight ass of yours, little one? Want me to stretch you like I did Luc?" Rhett asks, somehow still steady despite absolutely rocking my world.

"Please, please stretch me, sir," Lydia begs mindlessly.

"With pleasure."Rhett slows his pace, and I take over the movement, fucking myself down on him and up into her in turns. There's a pop of a cap, and Lydia tenses for a moment.

"Relax and breathe for me, sweetheart. There we go," I soothe, slowing to a smooth roll of my hips.

I feel Rhett's finger as he pushes past the ring of muscle, gasping as he strokes the underside of my cock through the thin wall between us. Lydia whines and arches, face tense but not with discomfort. If anything, she rocks down and back harder, trying to take more of both of us.

"Slow down, or I'm not going to last," I pant, pushing some of her hair back so I can see her face.

"I want more. Please," she whimpers, going still and dropping her head to rest on my sternum.

Rhett and I look up at the same time, locking eyes. His blue irises flash for a moment, the dom sliding back to allow our partner to take the lead.

"Are you asking me to fuck your ass, Lydia?" he asks gently.

There's a tense moment where all of us go still and silent. I know Lydia has been through some stuff, and this step has been something she and Rhett have been working on together. I smooth a hand down her back, stroking lightly to reassure her. But at long last, she nods.

"I want you. I want you both to fuck me," she whispers.

Rhett exhales, and I swear I hear a prayer of thanks under his breath. I feel him slide free of my body, but with Lydia still impaled on my throbbing cock, the absence doesn't leave me hollow or wanting. I lift her chin and bring her lips to mine, kissing her slowly and thoroughly as Rhett shuffles about for a moment, presumably cleaning himself up a bit before returning to the bed.

"You let me know if it's too much, okay?" he prompts.

Lydia nods against my mouth, nibbling on my bottom lip and making me chuckle. I slide a hand between us, circling her clit slowly as I feel Rhett's weight behind us. She sighs and relaxes into me, but tenses a moment later when Rhett's fingers probe her tight entrance again. One finger slides in with ease, and I rock my hips slowly in time with Rhett's hand, building that pleasure to distract from any discomfort. When his second finger joins the first, I moan at the pressure, excited to feel how tight she's going to be with both of us filling her.

Rhett whispers words of praise, but doesn't slow his work, coaxing a third finger in. Lydia pulls away from our kiss with a gasp, head pulling back to expose her throat. I nip and lick at the newly exposed skin, feeling her shudder and gasp.

"You ready, love?" Rhett asks breathlessly.

When Lydia nods frantically, my heart skips a beat. There's a moment of emptiness when Rhett pulls his hand away, and Lydia sinks down onto my chest. I pull my hand from her clit, wrapping both of my arms around her back to hold her close.

"Bear down when he pushes in," I whisper in her ear.

She nods, and I feel the way she tenses as the tip of Rhett's cock presses against her tight entrance. I gasp as he slips past the resistance, stars bursting behind my eyes as I feel the slide of him along my cock, that thin muscle the only thing separating us. Rhett rocks slowly, backing off before driving forward again, over and over until at last his hips are flush with hers.

"You feel so good, so fucking tight. My good girl, my sweet, good girl."

Rhett babbles praise, and I can't help but smile, especially when Lydia tucks her chin to hide her face, and I feel her smile pressing into my pectoral.

I'm the first to move, making both of them moan at the drag of my cock. It's almost too good, but I press my face into Lydia's hair, determined to get her to her release before me. I want her to feel how good she makes us feel, how intense this moment is.

"I love being inside of you, Lydia. You feel so good squeezing me like that," I whisper, not even caring if Rhett can hear.

"So full, oh my God. It's so much," she moans, eyes dazed as she looks up to meet my eyes.

"You take it so good, sweetheart. Let us take care of that pretty pussy and tight ass," I purr, holding her face between my hands as I move faster and harder.

Rhett growls and matches my pace, and it's like something comes over all of us. We're a writhing mess of limbs, chasing the pleasure that only we can bring each other. I can't look away from Lydia's impossibly green eyes, even as tears of pleasure leak from the corners of them.

"I'm going to fill you up with my cum, sweetheart. Fill you till you're bursting with it," I pant, sweat beading on my forehead.

"I want it, please. Please give me your cum," she parrots, and I don't even know if she's aware of what she's saying as she fights to meet our thrusts.

"You have to come for us first, little one. Come all over our cocks, and then we'll fill you to the brim."

"Please, I need it. I can't—"

There's a crack of flesh on flesh and Lydia shrieks as the pain of Rhett's hand on her ass arcs through her over sensitive body. I groan as her pussy clenches, and I have to fight against the squeeze of her channel just to keep moving. Rhett's thrusting gets more frantic, the bed creaking as he slams into her over and over. I push Lydia's chest up, changing the angle of her body just enough so the head of my cock can brush along that perfect spot. I know I've found it when her eyes fly open, and she screams. I don't let up, gritting my teeth to hold back the tingling at the base of my spine.

Rhett's hand comes out of nowhere and closes around her throat, making both Lydia and me gasp.

"Come on your alpha's cock as he fucks your tight ass. Now."

The command is a low growl, not a true bark, but whatever it is, Lydia explodes. A flood of wetness coats my hips, and I feel her walls spasming over and over. I can't hold back as she rides me through her release. I throw my head back and shout a curse to the ceiling, my entire body tingling as I feel my cock pulse, shooting my load deep into her. Rhett groans, and I feel him throb, unable to hold back his own orgasm. He thrusts forward a few more times, drawing out the sensations for all of us.

When it's over, I can hardly feel my legs and my head spins. I try to swallow, but my mouth is dry. I take a deep breath and look up to find Rhett leaning over us, one arm braced on the bed, the other between me and Lydia, holding her close as he kisses her shoulder. I can't help the fond smile that pulls on my lips as I reach up and run my fingers through Rhett's golden hair. He looks up at me through his brows and I give him a smile.

"I love you," Lydia whispers.

"Love you, too," Rhett replies automatically.

I swallow, not sure what I'm supposed to do. But then Lydia looks down at me and brushes a finger along my cheekbone.

"I love you, Luc," she says serenely.

My heart jumps into my throat, and my face breaks out into a wide smile. "You do?"

She nods and I reach up to cup her face.

"I love you, too, Lydi-bug."

Her nose crinkles and I can't help but laugh. Rhett joins me a moment later and Lydia's giggles follow shortly after. My heart is full, and after we clean up and settle down into bed,

Lydia tucked between my body and Rhett's, I sleep deeper, knowing that our family is whole again.

FORTY-ONE

Lydia

THE MORNING OF OUR flight dawns wet and dreary. It's too early for any sane human to be awake, but I'm here anyway, making myself a cup of coffee. I haven't been up this early since before the fire, so my body is slow to respond to any of my commands to do stuff.

It's been a week since the pack and I made amends, and I can admit to myself that it's good to be back home. My bed, my nest, felt like heaven the first night I returned to it, especially when I had all three of my boys piled in it with me. Mateo returned home not long after Rhett, Lucas, and I... made up, and he's been attached to me like a growth ever since. He's slept with me every night, even the night I tried to sleep in Rhett's room. It took me physically locking my door and making threats to get him to go back to work. They were empty threats, but it still got the job done.

Caleb's been hanging out at the pack house, which has helped everyone's overall anxiety level. I'd probably be fine on my own, but I can admit to feeling better and safer when he's around. Our days are mostly spent watching trash reality television—we've both become way too invested in a certain British baking competition show—but I've found time to rediscover some hobbies like doodling and reading.

He's also been working with me and the pack to finalize the plan for the wedding. We'd gone over every detail of the venue, walked through a hundred possible scenarios, all until I could repeat the steps in my sleep. But I guess it's better to be over-prepared than unprepared.

The coffee maker finishes dispensing into my mug, and I stir in the heaping serving of sugar, the clink of the spoon against the ceramic the only sound. Until I catch a footstep and a creaky foyer floorboard. I turn and relax as Lex saunters through the door, dressed only in a short silk bathrobe. She gives me a radiant smile before closing the distance between us. She brushes a sweet kiss against my cheek as she leans around me to restart the coffee machine. Her open displays of affection never fail to make me blush, despite them becoming more frequent. She stays close, fingers brushing my arm almost subconsciously.

"I'm glad we've got time for one last coffee date before you leave," she says warmly.

I chuckle under my breath. "Rhett's dragging Lucas out of bed. We might have time for two."

She returns my laugh, picking up her steaming black coffee and taking a sip. "Let's go upstairs," she says with a nod toward the foyer.

My brows twitch down in confusion, but she just smiles and starts walking, leaving me no choice but to follow. She glides up the stairs, hips swaying enticingly, the hem of her robe coming up enough to reveal the bottom curve of her perfect ass. But I don't let myself get too distracted, because I'd hate to spill hot coffee on the cream carpet running up the center of the stairs. I nearly stumble as Lex leads us toward a set of double doors I've never been brave enough to approach, the doors to her room. She doesn't even look back as she opens one and slips inside, leaving it cracked for me to follow.

Swallowing my nerves, I carefully enter and nudge it closed behind me with a hip. My chest immediately grows warm as I look up. Her furniture is expensive looking, especially the massive four-poster bed in the center, but there's an air of age to every piece. The carpet is thick and soft, and it tickles the spaces between my toes as I take a few steps forward. My eyes linger on the walls, decorated with dozens of framed photos of the pack, laminated newspaper articles, and awards. But as I scan to my right, my mouth falls open at the beautiful baby grand piano set in front of a bay window.

"You play?" I ask breathlessly, looking around for Lex.

"From time to time. I've been so busy lately that I haven't had a chance to sit down and practice," she calls, voice carrying through an open arch on the wall to the right of the piano.

I follow the sound, finding myself in a comfortably appointed boudoir. Her clothes hang neatly along the back wall, wrapping around slightly into built-in shelving units. Lex has settled onto a plush couch, looking out of massive windows that provide a panoramic view of the yard, the Everton skyline just visible over the tops of the trees. I move to the adjacent armchair, and I can only sigh as I sink into its incredibly comfortable cushions.

We're quiet for a while, just watching the clouds drifting across the slowly lightening sky. The rain patters gently against the glass, and the whole scene is so comfortable that I have to fight off sleep. Lex sets her cup down on the low coffee table and lets out a long sigh.

"It's not too late to change your mind," she starts, barely above a whisper.

I frown into my coffee, but don't respond. Mateo said something similar last night, but I have to do this. If our plan works, Jason will be safe, my trust will be secured, and I'll never have to see my mother or Darren ever again.

"I know you won't, but I just felt obligated to say it," Lex adds with an ironic chuckle.

I exhale a laugh through my nose and finish off the last of my coffee before setting the cup down on the table as well. I lean back, but a twinge of pain in my left shoulder makes me wince and shift. Lex's eyes snap to me, making me flush.

"Do you need more numbing cream? I made sure Rhett packed the moisturizer, but if—"

"No, I'm okay. Just getting used to it," I say, brushing off her doting.

She looks at me critically before dropping it. It's been a few days, and it's still weird to think that I did it. Lex brought me to see her friend Tate at their studio downtown, and I sat for my first ever tattoo. And what a tattoo it is. I'd fallen in love with Tate's design from the first moment they showed it to me. The tattoo is just big enough to cover the scar on my left shoulder blade, the petals of a rain lily positioned perfectly to disguise the missing flesh from Darren's bite. The Latin words of the pack motto, 'Bonds stronger than blood,' surround the flower, the whole design elegant and understated but somehow incredibly detailed. It'd taken a few hours, but Lex was there the whole time, holding my hand and soothing me through the worst of the pain.

And the whole time, I'd told her my story. Every gory, messy detail of my abuse at Darren's hands. It felt right, to finally let myself relive the trauma while also reclaiming the part of my body he ruined. I'd come back for another tattoo to cover the bite mark on my stomach, but the scar on my shoulder has been remade into something beautiful, and *mine*.

"Let's go through it, one last time," Lex says, cutting through my thoughts.

I roll my eyes but settle in. Ever since we'd finalized the details, she's been quizzing me on the plan at random times. I indulge her, because I know it's going to be hard for her with three of us gone and her not able to do anything to personally keep us safe.

"Jason booked a special spa day for the women of the bridal party, making sure my mother won't be around today. My father and brothers will be working right up until it's time for the rehearsal in New Orleans, and Jason has planned a meeting with their bank representative, so he has a reason to be at the credit union," I start, still a little in awe of how much Lex and Jason were able to get accomplished without alerting my family.

"I called our contact at the bank, and they'll have all of your paperwork ready. They have all the new account information to start the transfers, so you won't have to remember any of that. It'll just be a few signatures, some obligatory disclosures they have to read to you, and then you're done. If you're in the bank for more than a half hour, I'll be surprised," Lex continues.

I nod, smiling a little. She's been a machine making sure that every detail has been accounted for, and anything that could be done remotely has been taken care of. Speaking with the police chief about my status as a missing person, the bank manager about unlocking the account, even setting up a pack-protected account for me, nothing has been overlooked.

"Rhett has the keys to my apartment, and you'll stay there tonight. It's not much, but it'll be safe. The security team has been notified, and they know who is allowed into the building and who isn't," she says, and I nod, having already heard this information before.

"What's going to happen at the wedding?" she prompts sternly.

I swallow and brace myself. This is where things could get tricky. "Rhett is my plus one, but Caleb is going to be with us as my bodyguard. Between the two of them, I'm never going to be left alone. I won't get within ten feet of Darren, or my mother if I can avoid it. I won't talk to them, and I definitely won't let them corner me. Even if I have to go to the bathroom, Rhett will go inside with me while Caleb stands outside and prevents anyone from going in," I say, ticking off the checklist in my head.

"And you're going to leave at the first possible opportunity. You'll stay through dinner, as not to draw suspicion, but as soon as it's polite, you leave and don't say goodbye," Lex adds emphatically.

"Then we go back to the apartment, wait for the all-clear from Jason that everyone's gone back to their hotel or home to Chauvert. We're flying out first thing Sunday," I finish.

Lex nods in satisfaction, and I relax. Somewhere in the house, I hear footsteps and grumbling, and I smirk. Lucas must have finally gotten out of bed, and he's making it everyone's problem. Lex and I move in sync, standing and heading to her bedroom door. But before I can open it, she stops me with a hand on my wrist. I turn around and look curiously, finding her hazel eyes conflicted.

"Keep yourself safe, as best as you can. Rhett and Caleb will do whatever they have to do to keep you safe, but... I need you all to come home to me," she says, speaking slowly and trailing off to a whisper.

I reach out and cup her cheek in my palm, smiling gently as she meets my gaze. I step in, pressing my lips to hers for a soft, lingering kiss that makes my lips tingle even after I pull away.

"I promise I'll get us out of there, Alexandra. We'll be back before you even get a chance to miss us." I try to lighten her mood as best as I can.

She smiles, but it's a sad sort of smile that I don't get to think on for long as she pulls me into a tight embrace. I breathe in her mulled wine and spices scent, letting it settle my nerves at least for the moment. Her arms are steady, solid, and grounding. She's the foundation we've built our family on, but it's a heavy burden. If I can do anything to make that a little easier, then I will.

A soft knock on the door draws our attention, and we break apart as she answers. Rhett is outside, dressed comfortably but professionally. Mateo's just over his shoulder, yawning and shifting restlessly.

"I told you that you didn't have to get up," I chide, stepping out into the hallway and into Mateo's arms.

He snorts but wraps me up in a tight embrace all the same. "And not say goodbye? Fat chance," he mutters into my hair.

I look up and smile a little, closing my eyes as he kisses me fiercely. I'm breathless when he pulls away, my smile a bit more dazed. His eyes are serious, darting across every inch of my face like he's trying to memorize it.

"I love you, Lydia," he declares.

"Love you, too, Matty. I'll miss you," I reply, hugging him again and burying my face in his chest.

We sway a little on the spot, his lips brushing kisses against my hair and temple. But we're interrupted as Rhett clears his throat behind us.

"You can wait your turn for goodbye kisses, Rhett," Mateo drawls.

I try to suppress my giggles, but Lex laughs outright. When I pull away and step back, I watch a look pass between the alphas that I don't quite understand. It's stern, a warning and a promise all in one. Rhett doesn't back down under Mateo and Lex's silent assessment, but only nods. Then Mateo reaches out and pulls Rhett into a brief but tight hug. Lex kisses Rhett's cheek after Mateo steps back, then whispers something I don't quite catch. I open my mouth to ask, but Lucas's shout from the bottom of the stairs interrupts.

"Caleb's here! Let's go!" he says.

I look at Mateo and Lex one last time, giving them a reassuring smile before I follow Rhett down the stairs. As Lucas, Rhett, and Caleb pack the pile of suitcases into the back of his SUV, I dash across the distance from the porch to the car, managing to only get a little wet from the rain. I look back at the front door as the trunk slams closed, finding Lex and Mateo standing on the covered porch. They watch as the boys pile into the car, waving as we pull away.

FORTY-TWO

Lydia

THE RHYTHMIC SOUND OF the wipers on Caleb's windshield breaks up the patter of rain, the streetlights coloring the drops that slide down my window orange. September still counts as summer in Georgia, so the air is warm and sticky. We pull up to the side gate of Everton Airport, Rhett speaking with the security guard in hushed tones through the rear window. We're waved through, following a security vehicle across the tarmac to a hangar.

Once we're parked, I slide out of the front passenger seat and round the hood to stare up at the plane. I've never flown private before, but I'd imagined cramming into one of those tiny, single engine tuna can planes. But the jet parked in front of me is huge, as big as any commercial plane I've ever seen. There's a short set of stairs leading inside, with two impeccably dressed flight attendants waiting at the top.

"Let's get settled. It's going to take a bit to get everything ready for takeoff," Rhett says warmly, coming up behind me and resting a hand on my lower back affectionately.

I turn and look up at him, returning his gentle smile with a nervous one of my own. I let him go up first, following closely. My jaw pops as it drops, eyes going wide as I take in the luxurious interior. Huge leather armchairs surround a table, with a couch along the opposite wall. At the end of the room, there are two doors on either side of a wall, where a television is mounted. Everything is clean and polished, but lacking any of the pungent smell of blocking agents.

"There's a bedroom in the back, if a mile high club membership is something you're interested in," Lucas mutters in my ear before he scoots around me to throw himself on the sofa.

My face flushes hot, and I shoot him a half-hearted glare. Following Rhett's lead, I move to an armchair at the table, sighing as I sink into the cloud-like cushions. I pass on refreshments when the flight attendant asks, but Lucas orders a double shot of espresso, his voice gravelly from sleep.

"This seems a little excessive," I mutter, even as I relax.

"What's the point of even owning a private plane if you don't use it to fly frivolously short distances?" Lucas retorts, words dripping with sarcasm.

Rhett and I chuckle, and we fall into comfortable silence. Caleb boards shortly after us, taking a seat a respectable distance away. As we wait for the cabin crew and pilots to go through their checks, I shift in my seat, trying to relieve the itch on my left shoulder blade that has been growing steadily more annoying.

"Stop that. It won't heal right if you itch it," Lucas drones, not even looking at me.

"So what am I supposed to do? It's really annoying," I snap, leaning forward to rest my arms on the table and my forehead on them.

"Do you need more A&D cream?" Rhett asks.

I grumble something non-committal, stress and discomfort making me grumpy.

Rhett's fingers on my back send a shiver up my spine. He rubs soothing little circles on my shoulder, and I sigh as it relieves the itch there. I can feel his touch even through the fabric of my shirt and the thin layer of plastic protecting my clothes from bleeding ink.

My mind drifts away from his touch and into speculation. Despite going over the plan with Lex, I can't help but pick it apart. We'd gone over every contingency, even down to if the building suddenly catches on fire, but it still feels like we've missed something. It's a simple plan: just get in, keep our heads down, and get out as fast as possible. But maybe it's too simple. Caleb said anything more complicated could lead to unpredictable outcomes, but we're relying on a lot of assumptions.

We're assuming that Jason is right about my parents being out of town. If they or someone they know sees us at the bank, it could raise suspicions, and possibly tip my mother off to our plan. If she thinks she's losing her meal ticket, there's no telling what she'll do. We're assuming that we're going to be able to avoid speaking to her at the wedding, but that's a big ask. How could she possibly explain away my sudden reappearance when she's been pretending I've been a missing person for four years? For all we know, she could be planning to make a big production of it, and who knows if we'll be able to avoid unwanted attention then. And, most critically, we're assuming everyone is going to believe our bluff.

Despite having the pack motto inked on my skin, I'm still not an official member of Pack St. Clair, at least not legally speaking. In all other ways, though, I am. My bank accounts are now protected under the pack name. I'm living with them. I have their mark, and the acceptance of the prime alpha. Given enough time, all of those factors would combine to make me a common law member regardless of a judge's signature, but we don't have six years to wait for that to happen. So we're bluffing. We're hoping that by the time anyone thinks to question my official standing, I'll be back in Georgia with my money and under pack protection again.

But if it doesn't work, and my father pulls rank, defying him will only bring more trouble. Lex and the pack could be charged with obstructing the rights of a prime alpha, or worse, kidnapping, and then I'd never see them again. The thought alone is enough to make my skin crawl.

"Seatbelt, love. It's almost time," Rhett says, pulling me from my thoughts.

I sigh and sit up, buckling the belt across my hips. The door is closed, the engines whirring to life outside. They aren't as loud as I expected, just a pleasant background hum. Lucas is sitting up, though by the look on his face, it's reluctant. I look past Rhett out of the small window as I feel the plane start to move, my lips pulling up into a little smile. Despite the fear and worry crowding my chest, there's still a little kernel of excitement under it all. I haven't seen Jason in person for over a year, and I can't wait to see how he's changed. We taxi along the runway, and then we're off, gaining speed and rising through the rainy sky.

I settle back into my seat once we level out, trying not to rub my shoulder against the cushion when it starts to itch again. The captain lets us know that we're at cruising altitude and can remove our seatbelts, which I do gladly.

"If it's bothering you that bad, I know something to keep you distracted," Lucas drawls suggestively.

Shooting him an unamused look, I cock one eyebrow. "It's a three-hour flight," I reply.

"What's your point?" he asks, slightly confused.

"What would we do for the other two hours and forty-eight minutes?" I tease, smirking slightly.

Rhett snorts, trying to cover it with a cough, but I'm too distracted by Lucas's growl. Moving faster than I've seen, he's up off the couch and in front of me, one hand clamping around my wrist. I shriek as he yanks me to my feet, hefting me over one shoulder in a fireman's lift and stalking away toward the back of the plane.

It doesn't take long before my itchy tattoo and the uncertainty about what's going to happen over the next few days are the last things on my mind.

Rhett, Lucas, and I are curled up together on the massive bed when the pilot announces we're preparing for landing. I'm facing Rhett, with Lucas curled around my back, one hand idly tracing my new ink, massaging the healing cream into my skin. Besides my shirt, we'd put ourselves back together a while ago, but chose to stay back here enjoying one last moment of peace before whatever craziness is likely to come over the next few days.

"No matter what might happen tomorrow, we're going to keep you safe," Rhett says softly into my hair.

I nod, my heart twisting only a little at the thought of the wedding. I know Rhett will be with me the entire time, and Caleb won't be far, either. He's going to be at the reception with us, on guard but never out of line of sight if he can manage it. Lucas will be meeting up with a friend, but will be ready to move out if anything bad should happen. There are a lot of unknowns, but there isn't anything to be gained by trying to plan for all of them.

"You aren't going to murder Darren on sight, are you?" I ask, looking up into Rhett's face.

He hums like he's actually considering it, but then grins down at me when I gape. "No, love. I'm not going to intentionally cause a scene at your brother's wedding."

I relax a little, shaking my head slightly. Lucas lifts his head and looks at Rhett over me. I can only see Rhett's reaction, and he just rolls his eyes.

"I said I wouldn't kill him on sight, and I won't. Though if he even so much as lays a finger on you, then I might be inclined to break a bone or two. Just for good measure," Rhett adds.

"Breaking bones is causing a scene, Rhett!" I cry, running a hand over my face in exasperation.

"Only if you do it on the dance floor. If you're in the kitchen or even out behind the building, then—"

"Lucas!"

He laughs and I turn my head to give him a chastising glare, but that only makes him laugh harder. Rhett uses a finger to bring my attention back to him, and I go still at the serious expression on his face.

"I'll do what I have to do to get you out of there safe. If that means breaking a few fingers or fracturing a kneecap, or cracking a skull—"

"Don't put too much thought into this," I grumble.

Rhett chuckles but continues. "There isn't anything I wouldn't do to protect you, Lydia."

I can't help but melt at the depth of emotion behind his eyes. And even though I probably shouldn't, knowing that Rhett isn't afraid to cause violence in my defense makes me love him that much more.

FORTY-THREE

Lydia

WHEN WE MAKE THE turn onto the main drag of Chauvert, Louisiana, my stomach lurches into my throat. It's like stepping four years back in time. Nothing has changed, not one business or bench. I know exactly how the inside of the ice cream shop smells, the sound of the bell on the front door of the pharmacy. And when we pull into a parking spot outside of the credit union and step out of the SUV, the air is thick with humidity, smelling slightly of decay as the breeze comes in off the bayou. The deep clanging of the church bell two blocks away marks the hour, and my head turns automatically in the direction of the steeple just visible over the top of the buildings.

"This is where you grew up?" Lucas asks, closing the back passenger door and looking around.

I nod, lost in memories. Jason and I riding our bikes the six miles from the house to spend our allowance on candy and comic books from the corner store, or to see whatever movie was playing at the single screen theater up the street. Going on my first date with my high school boyfriend at the family restaurant, being so embarrassed when I realized that Sam and Adam were watching us from a few tables away. Learning to drive and parallel park in my dad's pickup truck in the residential streets that branch out away from this central artery.

"Not much to do," Caleb mumbles, standing on the sidewalk in front of the car, looking up and down the street.

"Still plenty of ways to get into trouble," I reply with a distant chuckle.

Like when Sam crashed his first car while street racing outside of town. Or when Jason and his friends got caught tagging the side of a building. Or when Adam's friend broke his leg bridge jumping into the canal. And that's only the times I know about. I was never given the freedom to roam like they had once I came into my designation.

Lucas slides his arm around my waist as we move to stand beside Caleb, and I look up and down the street for any sign of my brother. Rhett checks his watch before shoving his hands into his pockets. His eyes are hard, his jaw clenched into a serious line as he scans our surroundings. Caleb moves to my other side, adjusting so casually that any uninformed observer wouldn't be able to recognize the flanking position.

"If y'all'd've told me that we'd be playing spies, we could have met in the park. There are some hungry ducks in need of attention."

I spin at the sound of the deep Southern drawl, my face splitting in a wide smile at the first sight of my brother. I detangle myself from Lucas's hold and run the few paces between us, launching myself at him, latching my arms around his neck in a tight embrace. Jason is tall like all of the men in my family, so when he straightens to his full height, he pulls me off my feet for a moment before setting me back down. The first inhale of his juniper and cucumber scent brings sudden moisture to my eyes, and I have to blink it away. That scent has been my safe place for so long, and I hadn't realized how much I'd missed it.

"I can't believe you're actually here, Lydi," he whispers in my ear.

"I missed you so much, Jace," I reply, voice cracking slightly.

"I missed you, too."

We break apart, and I look him over. He's still as bulky as I remember, broad shoulders and muscled arms. His platinum blond hair is longer than I'm used to seeing, but it suits him somehow. He's dressed in jeans and an open button-down, with a white t-shirt under it. I feel a little overdressed, with my black skater skirt and breezy white top, but I try to push the nervous feeling aside. Jason's green eyes, twin in color and shape to my own, scan me as I assess him, and he smiles a lopsided grin when he gets back to my face.

"You look great, Lydi. Georgia is good for you," he says fondly, a sly twinkle in his eye.

I roll my eyes at the subtle tease. I'm about to retort when I sense Rhett coming up beside me. Jason's attention moves to him, spine straightening to his full height. He's still a few inches shorter than Rhett, but his bulk makes up for the difference.

"You must be Jason. It's good to finally meet you in person," he says, holding out a hand to Jason to shake.

"You, too, man," Jason replies, taking the offered hand.

The handshake lasts a moment longer than it should, and I catch how their knuckles whiten slightly as they squeeze, trying to get the other to flinch. Rhett's pleasant smile never wavers and Jason's eyes flash when he finally lets go.

"I'm Lucas, Rhett and Lydia's other boyfriend."

I jump as Lucas comes up and throws his arm back around my shoulders, squeezing between Rhett and me to shake Jason's hand as well. If Jason is surprised by the bold introduction, he doesn't let it show in his face. He just smiles and shakes Lucas's hand, and I do notice the little quirk in Jason's eyebrows as he feels the thick calluses from all the time Lucas spends wielding knives.

"He part of your harem, too?" Jason asks, nodding over our shoulders to where Caleb is still standing, hanging back.

A muscle in Rhett's jaw twitches, but I merely roll my eyes. "Caleb's just my security detail. And I'm pretty sure his mate would claw my eyes out if I tried to move in on the father of her child," I say pointedly.

Jason laughs, but I notice the shift in his face, the slight relaxing around his eyes. After spending our whole lives together, I know that's respect in his eyes, the change in attitude as he realizes that this pack has actually kept their word to protect me. Rhett shifts on his feet, his hand coming to rest on my lower back.

"Let's get this over with. We have a lot to discuss," he says, tone never wavering from polite and pleasant.

Jason nods, then heads off toward the front door. Lucas kisses my cheek before leaning in my ear. "He's cute. Too bad," he whispers.

I elbow him hard in the gut, making him laugh before he wanders off to stand with Caleb. Rhett gives me a questioning look, but I just shake my head. We can deal with Lucas later.

By the time the last 'i' is dotted and 't' is crossed, my head is pounding. I'd expected there to be a not-insignificant amount of money in my trust, but I wasn't expecting it to be nearly eight figures. Jason teased me that I always was MawMaw's favorite, but I could tell he hadn't been expecting there to be that much in the account either. It's no wonder then that my mother was trying to get her hands on my money. But it's too late now. The transfer process has started and by the time she realizes what has happened, it will be irreversible.

We finish saying goodbye to the teller just as the church bells ring out the hour. My face hurts from all the forced smiling I've been doing, and I let it drop as soon as I turn my back on the short, balding beta.

"If I never have to hear the term 'investment opportunity' or 'compound interest,' it'll be too soon," I grumble when we're out of earshot.

"Aw, come on, Lydi. Accountants have to find the fun somewhere," Jason says lightly, shoving my shoulder with his own.

I'm about to shove him back when I hear a loud gasp. I look up and I feel the blood drain from my face as my feet come to a sudden stop.

"Oh, my goodness! Lydia Anderson, is that truly you?" a familiar voice crows.

Directly in front of us, and making a beeline in our direction, is a woman I never thought I'd see again: Andrea McLaughlin, Darren's mother.

She's hardly changed at all since the last time I saw her, face still smooth and tan in an unsettling, uncanny valley way, as a result of years of Botox and fillers. Her lips are painted a bright berry pink, an exact match to her outdated blazer and pencil skirt set. As she crushes me to her chest, I smell a heavy layer of hairspray and Chanel perfume that only lets a trickle of her pear and moss beta scent through.

"Mrs. McLaughlin. I wasn't–what a surprise!" I exclaim, pulling back as quick as I can to stop myself from coughing.

"It is! A pleasant one, of course. Though I'm sure your brothers told you we'd be in town," she says, waving a hand dismissively before clasping them tightly at her waist.

I can hardly look at her face, the muddy brown of her eyes almost an exact match to her son's. So I look to Jason, asking with my eyes for help. But he seems just as caught off-guard as I am.

"They did not. Does Pastor McLaughlin have an engagement?" I ask, trying to give Jason any excuse to jump in and help me.

Andrea laughs, an ear-piercing trill that brings back memories I thought I'd buried, of years spent in too-hot Sunday school rooms and the sting of a rubber band on my wrist when I'd stumble in my recitations. "You could say that. Samuel Jr. asked my dear husband to officiate the wedding tomorrow. Isn't that lovely?"

"What a treat. It's been a while since I've heard him do something like that," I reply, hardly aware of what my brain is sending out of my mouth as I fall back into old, people-pleasing habits.

"I'm sure it has been a while since you've heard a preacher, my dear. My son has told me about the trials and tribulations y'all have been going through. I've made sure to keep you in my prayers, to help guide you back to where you belong," she says, dropping her voice and stepping in closer to take my hand.

I want to flinch back, but I can't do anything except smile blandly and wait. My heart pounds as I try to come up with some sort of response that wouldn't offend, but nothing in my brain is working. Rhett's hand on my lower back flexes, his scent shifting to paper and leather.

"Mrs. McLaughlin? Why, you must be Darren's mother. I've heard so much about you," Rhett says, jumping in at last to catch her extended palm in a shake.

Andrea blinks, startled by Rhett's sudden and enthusiastic entrance into the conversation. "I am, but I'm terribly sorry. I don't believe we've been introduced."

"Rhett Cooper, ma'am, Lydia's new pack mate," Rhett informs her, and I can't help but notice how thick his accent has become all of a sudden.

"Pack mate? I... I'm afraid you must be mistaken. I haven't heard–"

"Well, it seems that news is falling through the cracks left, right, and center. Though I don't blame you. It did happen rather recently," Rhett says, laughing at his own joke.

There's a moment when I think Andrea might try to push, but as someone enters from behind her, the instinct to not cause a public scene that's bred into every Southern woman takes hold. Her lips tighten into a truly forced smile that looks more like a grimace, and she steps back, adjusting her handbag on her arm.

"Well, that's just the best news. We all want to belong somewhere, and the Lord guides his flock to where they are most needed."

Rhett tries to shake her hand again as we're making our goodbyes, but she skillfully dodges. She gives Jason a slight incline of her dyed-blonde head before moving in to kiss my cheek.

"I would like to take a moment, if you'd be so kind," she says, taking my hands in a firm grip.

As soon as she bows her head and closes her eyes, my stomach falls to somewhere around my knees. Deeply ingrained instinct takes over, and I drop my chin as Andrea starts speaking.

"Our heavenly Father, who looks down on us with mercy and grace, I come to you now in this moment to pray for your guidance. Our Lord and Savior, who never turns away the poor and meek, who heals all ills and brings everlasting life to your children, we ask that you shine your light down upon us and guide your lost lamb home. We pray in your name–"

"What the–"

Rhett starts and then Jason shushes him, and I catch him waving frantically, head bowed in prayer as well. My heart hammers and Andrea goes on, asking God over and over to help me find my way back to the light and be healed of sin, and I lose track of the thread after a while. I want to pull away, but her dry, weirdly cold hands have mine in a white-knuckled grip, so tight it almost hurts. Several people enter and exit the bank, but only spare us a glance before moving about their business.

"As you tell us in the book of John, Chapter 10, verse 1: "I tell you the truth, the man who does not enter the sheep pen by the gate, but climbs in by some other way, is a thief and a robber. The man who enters by the gate is the shepherd of his sheep." Our sheep, our poor lost lamb, has been stolen from us, Lord, and we come to you now, praying to help her find her way back into your loving embrace, and back to the flock. We ask all of this in your name. Amen."

"Amen," I echo automatically.

She finally lets me go, and I take a step back, fighting the urge to wipe my hands on my skirt. She gives me a meaningful look and a nod, adjusting her handbag one more time before moving off toward the tellers. Jason ushers us outside, Rhett moving in close.

"Are you okay, love?" he breathes.

I nod, flexing and releasing my hands to stop their shaking. This definitely rattled me, but it could have been worse. She might tell my mother about this encounter, but the odds favor her not having the opportunity to do so with all the chaos of the wedding. At least not until it's too late and we're already halfway back to Georgia.

"What the hell was that?" Rhett snaps, turning on Jason.

"Honestly? Shorter than I expected," Jason replies with a heavy sigh.

I nod in agreement, even as my stomach twists and churns. I can feel the cold sweat on my back, and I have to shake my head to clear it of the panic starting to form. It's been so long since someone felt the need to pray in public that I'd forgotten how awful it could be.

"So who was the Preacher's Wife Barbie?" Lucas asks when we're close enough.

"Darren's mom. Her and Pastor Joe are going to be there tomorrow. Which is information I would have liked to learn before this moment, Jason," I say pointedly, turning to snap at my brother.

"I didn't fucking know either," he returns, running a hand through his hair.

"Why is this important?" Caleb asks seriously, his brow furrowed in concentration mode.

I sigh harshly, rubbing my face. "Darren was always the worst when his parents were around. His father's pseudo-celebrity status among the fundamentalist crowd makes him think he's untouchable."

"Dad's also angling to lock down a huge contract for Pastor Joe's next megachurch project. Darren might try to use that as leverage against him," Jason adds.

I let out a colorful curse, pacing around slightly. This complicates things, but there isn't any way to back out now.

"Jason, I know we've put you in a tough spot these last few weeks, but I have to know. If shit hits the fan..."

"I'm with you, Lydi. Even if I still don't get why you're still going after everything. If you go to the wedding tomorrow and Dad tries to make you stay, or if Darren tries to pull some fucked up shit, I'm not going to let you get hurt again," he says, picking up as I trail off.

I sigh and nod, heart heavy. "Okay. Trust me, if I had another choice, then I wouldn't be going, but—"

"Who said you don't have a choice?" Jason cuts in, voice low with a growl.

I give him a long look, and he reads the answer in my eyes. Letting out a curse that would make a sailor blush, he walks four long paces away, hands on his hips.

"We've got this under control. As long as we don't have any more surprises, then we can get in, get out, and get gone before anything can happen," Rhett states calmly, taking a step toward Jason.

"How? I can't call you or text you, so it's not like I'm going to be much of help," Jason snaps, turning back to glare at him.

"Yeah, I guess you are a bit of a liability right now," Lucas drawls.

Rhett and I both turn to stare at the beta, my eyes wide with confusion, while Rhett's brows drop into a harsh glare. Lucas and Caleb share a look and a nod, and my heart flip-flops at the grim frown my bodyguard wears as he steps forward.

"What's going on?" I ask breathlessly, stepping between Caleb and Jason on instinct.

"I'm taking care of the problem," Caleb says simply.

And, to my absolute shock and horror, Caleb's hand starts reaching into his jacket. Everything seems to slow, and I gasp, throwing my hands up to try to stop Caleb from getting any closer. Rhett is furiously demanding someone tell him what's going on, but I'm focused on Caleb's hand. I know he's armed; he always is. Jason wasn't a liability, not enough to warrant any of this.

I blink, and the world seems to spin back up to speed as Caleb pulls a small, black rectangular shaped object from the inner pocket of his jacket. It's way too small to be a gun, and when Caleb flicks his thumb, the lid opens, revealing a screen and dial pad.

"What—a phone?" I stammer, rocking back onto my heels.

"In the industry, it's called a burner. We think someone cloned the SIM card of your cell phone, so this should fix that. Can't clone a SIM if there isn't one," Caleb explains simply, reaching around me to hand the device to Jason.

"I thought... I thought you were going to—"

"Shoot him? That's insane," Lucas snorts.

Rhett throws him a growl, not amused in the slightest at this practical joke. I look up into Caleb's face, and while he reads as stoic and emotionless, there's a spark of amusement in his gray eyes.

"Yes, insane. It would be too risky to shoot someone here. Too many witnesses," Caleb adds dryly.

Before I can stop myself, I pull my fist back and punch his bicep as hard as I can. To my eternal embarrassment, I only manage to make my hand ache, and Caleb laugh. I shake out the sting, joining in with the chuckle. Rhett and Jason share a commiserating glance, shaking their heads.

Forty-four

Lydia

I LOOK AT THE alarm clock on the bedside table again, twisting my fingers around themselves as I listen to the shower running from the next room. We're leaving for the wedding in less than two hours, and I can't keep still. I've showered and my hair is curled and pinned into place. My makeup is done, but I'm still waiting to put on my dress. I look at it where it hangs from the closet door. It's an absolutely stunning piece, purple so dark that it appears black in most lights, unless light hits it the right way. The silhouette is the vintage-inspired A-line cut I like best, with a plunging neckline covered by sheer black lace that comes up to the base of my throat and into little cap sleeves. There are tiny fabric button details from the waistline to my throat, and a small bow belt to highlight the dip of my waist. The back is covered in the same lace, which will leave my tattoo visible if someone looks close enough.

Rhett had surprised me with the dress and the matching kitten heels this morning, promising another surprise later.

I look up at the sound of a knock on the bedroom door, finding Lucas leaning against the frame. His hands are deep in the pockets of his jeans, and his face smooth, but concern swirls in his steel-blue eyes.

"While I don't mind, I think your family would be quite scandalized if you showed up in your underthings," he says after a moment.

I snort a laugh, shaking my head slightly. "I'd really be disowned then."

Lucas chuckles once and then pushes off the frame to come sit next to me on the bed. I lean my weight on his shoulder.

"You can do this, Lydi-bug. I know you can," he whispers.

I nod, still looking at my dress. "Help me get into it?"

Lucas nods and we both move at the same time. The water shuts off in the bathroom, and by the time Lucas is zipping me up, I turn just in time to see Rhett in the bathroom doorway, towel slung low around his hips.

"Absolutely stunning, love," he breathes, staring at me.

I blush hot, tucking my chin. Lucas slips his arms around my waist, resting his chin on my shoulder.

"He's a tall drink of water, isn't he, sweetheart?" he whispers in my ear, making me giggle.

Rhett cocks an eyebrow, but that only makes me giggle harder. I kiss Lucas's cheek and extricate myself from his grip, moving to finish my hair. I leave it mostly down, taming it into vintage waves with pieces pulled back away from my face.

By the time I come back out, I stop dead in my tracks, jaw falling open as I stare at Rhett. He's dressed in black on black, his pants, shoes, and shirt all matching, and his tie a shimmery midnight purple to match my dress. But what has me nearly drooling is his vest, if you could call it that. The front is a black and gray damask pattern, with silver clasps instead of buttons. And as he turns, I realize it laces up the back like a corset, cinching him in all the right places to accentuate the curve of his waist, the bulk of his chest, and somehow even his ass looks better. He turns around and smirks like the cat that got the cream as he sees my blatant ogling.

"He's far too good looking for his own good," Lucas comments from where he's lounging on the bed, hands folded behind his head, as he also openly admires Rhett from behind.

"It's not just aesthetic. It's carbon-fiber reinforced," Rhett says, and I swear there's a hint of color in his cheeks.

"That's the sexiest bulletproof vest I've ever seen," I say after clearing my throat.

Rhett chuckles and runs a hand through his hair. "Not quite that strong. A knife, sure, no problem. But I'm hoping we won't have to be dodging bullets at a wedding."

"This is the South. Anything's possible," Lucas snorts.

Rhett shakes his head and puts his hands in his pockets. I gasp as he withdraws them, a signature blue box with a white ribbon in his fingers. It's too big and flat to be a ring, but my brain still short-circuits.

"You fucking didn't!" I exclaim, not able to move as Rhett closes the distance between us.

"I've held off on spoiling you for as long as I can take, love. And I couldn't pass this up," Rhett says seriously, opening the box.

Tears burn the back of my eyes as I look down at the bracelet and matching earrings sitting in the white satin. The bracelet is a thin silver chain with five round emeralds set at regular intervals, surrounded by tiny diamonds. The stud earrings have the same round emerald and diamonds. The set is dainty and understated and beautiful, exactly the sort of thing I love. I look up to Rhett to find his eyes shining with joy, and seeing how much he loves this makes it easier to accept such an extravagant gift. He doesn't speak as he helps me put it on, and I turn to the mirror to slip the earrings into place.

Rhett comes up behind me and puts his hands on my shoulders. I suck in a breath at the sight of us, dressed to kill. I'd never really understood what Lucas meant when he said that we look good together, but seeing us done up to the nines, I can admit that we make quite the pair. And for the first time, I don't feel out of place at Rhett's side. I belong here, and that feeling helps to settle the last of my nerves for the moment.

There's a knock at the door, and Rhett and I turn to Caleb leaning his head into the open door. "Car's ready when you are," he says.

Lucas climbs off the bed and comes to stand by my side. He smooths down a flyaway before cupping the back of my neck. I look up into his uncharacteristically serious face and swallow hard.

"You are strong, and capable, and so fucking gorgeous. You are so much more than anything those people think of you. I love you, Lydi-bug," he says firmly.

Nodding, my heart swells under his praise. He leans down and kisses me softly, careful not to smudge my lipstick. When he breaks away, he keeps his hand on my neck but turns to face Rhett.

"Keep her safe, and don't do anything stupid, alright?" he says, a touch exasperated.

Rhett chuckles but nods. "We're only going to be gone for a couple of hours. How much trouble could I possibly get into?"

"A lot."

"Plenty."

Lucas and I speak at the same time, and all three of us share a laugh. Rhett leans in and gives Lucas a brief but intense kiss before stepping back to slide into his black suit jacket. He looks every inch the dark protector, and I can't help the little shiver that runs down my spine. I slip into my shoes, looking at Lucas one more time and mouthing 'I love you' before letting Rhett take my hand, looping it through his arm as he escorts me out of the apartment.

FORTY-FIVE

Lydia

As WE PULL UP to the venue, my stomach feels like it's folded itself into a dense knot and lodged itself behind my lungs. We're directed down a driveway that runs to a parking lot behind the venue proper, and I'm too nervous to even look out of the window. Rhett holds my hand tight, but I can feel the cold sweat forming on my palms. By the time we've parked and joined the flow of people heading along the path, I feel almost detached from my body. Rhett has my hand resting in the crook of his arm, and I can feel Caleb's body heat as he sticks close behind us.

There's a small queue of people, and I see someone with a clipboard near the gate, my heart sinking as dread creeps in.

"Names?" the security guard drawls as we reach the front.

"Lydia Anderson and guests," I reply, glad my voice is steadier than I feel.

The guard flips a page and I feel my face drain of blood as his brow furrows and he looks back up at us.

"I'm sorry, ma'am, but we've got you down for just one guest," he says, looking up with sympathy in his eyes.

I turn to look at Caleb, not sure how to even answer. But my bodyguard doesn't look fazed.

"Understandable. But she's my mark, if you know what I mean. My employer wouldn't be pleased if I can't do the job they're paying me to do," he says, dropping his voice so the people just joining behind us can't hear.

The security guard seems to realize what Caleb's getting at, and there's a moment of hesitation. But then he shakes his head.

"Listen, if you want to talk to my boss about your arrangement, I'm sure they'd be happy to have someone look after y'all. But I can't let you in as a guest, ya feel me?"

I turn to Rhett with wide eyes, trying to convey my fear silently. His eyes flick to me and then to Caleb.

"Should we abort?" Rhett hisses low enough for only me and Caleb to hear.

"We can't. Jason—"

"Going in by ourselves could be too risky," Rhett snaps over me, a flash of heat in his eyes before he catches himself.

"It's too suspicious to bail now. I'll see what I can do, and hopefully I can see y'all after the ceremony," Caleb says.

"Keep your phone on you, just in case," Rhett says with a nod.

My stomach drops to somewhere around my knees as Caleb steps out of the queue and starts walking back toward the parking lot. Rhett leads me past the guard, and we follow the signs toward the ceremony space.

"I don't like this," Rhett whispers, intentionally slowing our steps as if we're admiring the garden.

"Neither do I. But what other choice do we have? We need them to not suspect anything until we're safe back home," I hiss with a touch more exasperation than I intended.

"I know, love. But it doesn't mean I have to like it. Do you think your mother has something to do with this?" Rhett whispers back.

"Oh, most definitely," I snap under my breath.

Rhett takes a deep breath before settling his shoulders. He reaches into his jacket pocket and slips my phone out from within, casually sliding it into a hidden pocket in the side of my skirt.

"We'll stick close together as best as we can, but I'd rather you have that on you," he says with a small smile.

I nod and take a steadying breath. We continue walking down the path, and I have to admire the attention to detail the venue has put into their landscaping. Even the ceremony space is absolutely perfect, right down to the spacing of the folding chairs on either side of the stone and brick path. Rhett and I find seats near the back, on the outside edge opposite the aisle, and I take a moment to look around. They set the altar up on the front porch of the plantation style house, and there's a massive live oak tree to the left of the front garden. Everything is decorated in fairly standard wedding decor, white tulle and silver accents, the occasional splash of pale pink or beige breaking up the color palette. It's not the tackiest or most basic wedding I've ever seen, and it allows the natural beauty of the venue to shine through.

We intentionally arrived as close to the specified starting time to avoid having to mingle, and it seems like it worked. Most of the seats are full, with only a few stragglers making their way up the path from the parking lot. We only have to sit for a few minutes as the last of the guests find seats, and talking swells in anticipation. No one has noticed Rhett or me, though I catch a few strange looks from people I vaguely recognize. But thankfully, a string quartet begins to play, and attention collectively turns to face the end of the aisle.

My brother, Samuel Jr., walks down the aisle first, and I can't help but smile a little. We share the same toffee brown hair, but his skews more red than blond. He's dressed in a gray suit with a stunning boutonniere pinned to the lapel. He looks good, strong and healthy, if a little nervous. I try to catch his eye, but he's focused on the altar at the end of the aisle.

My father comes next, escorting a middle-aged woman I can only assume is Ally's mother. My father's eyes seem to find me like a heat-seeking missile, and my mouth goes dry as I try not to wither under his assessing stare. His green eyes, the gift he's given to all of his children, spark for a moment, but the look is gone before I can interpret it, and he's moved past my row. I feel Rhett's hand on my lower back, his thumb brushing soothingly.

For all of my nervousness at seeing my father again, I can't contain my shudder as my mother starts her slow jaunt toward the altar. She's thin, much thinner than I remember, and she's seemed to have aged like milk since the last time I saw her. Her hair, naturally a light auburn brown, has been dyed a truly awful chestnut color that only makes her skin look sickly. She's dolled up with a makeup look meant for someone ten years younger, and her mother of the bride dress is a champagne color that is so light it could almost be ivory, with enough beading to make me flinch away when the setting sun catches it. She's being escorted down the aisle by another familiar face, the second oldest of my siblings, Adam. He's still sporting that military haircut that makes his blond hair look like peach fuzz on the sides of his head, and his thin lips are pulled up in a smile that could be seen as genuine to anyone who doesn't know him.

Diane Anderson preens and flounces her way to the front, looking for all the world like this is her wedding. She's so lost in the attention that her eyes skate right over Rhett and me, which I'm grateful for. I'm sure we'll have to deal with her soon enough, but that's a problem for future me. For the moment, I hold my breath and look away from the back, knowing who will be coming up soon enough. I turn back to face the front, bringing my attention to stare at a spot just to the left of the officiant, away from where the groomsmen are standing. I see figures moving out of the corner of my eye, but I focus on watching Ally's two bridesmaids and maid of honor stepping into formation.

I can feel the heat of someone's stare on the side of my face, but I refuse to give in and look. The music changes and everyone gets to their feet, giving me a perfect excuse to put my back to the wedding party. I sigh with everyone else, watching as Ally and her father pull up to the gate in a horse-drawn carriage, exiting smoothly. Ally is beautiful, with dark brown hair and big blue eyes, and a smile that makes her entire face brighter. She looks every inch the fairytale princess, and I can't help the little smile as she starts her walk up the aisle.

Unable to put it off any longer once Ally reaches the stairs, my eyes flick along the line of groomsmen. Adam is standing next to Sam, acting as the best man. Jason comes next, and I can't deny how well he cleans up, his matching gray suit really bringing out the green of his eyes. And then my eyes slide one more place to the right, and I feel my heart stop.

Darren McLaughlin.

He hasn't changed a bit since the last time I saw him, when he was passed out in bed after violating me and ripping pieces of my skin out with his teeth. His rusty red hair is gelled into a trendy casual mop that only serves to remind me of Mateo, and how he always looks like he just rolled out of bed. On Mateo, it's sexy, unintentionally making people think about him in bed. But on Darren, it looks haphazard, almost like he's trying too hard to appear like he doesn't care. His cheekbones are sharp, almost too pronounced, which, combined with his harshly angled jaw, gives him almost a hawklike appearance. I don't know how I ever thought he was attractive.

But it's his eyes that I can't look away from. Muddy brown, but full of a fire that makes my fight-or-flight instinct kick into overdrive. I know I shouldn't be the first to back down, but the longer I stare back, the harder it gets to breathe. I can feel phantom pain in my shoulder and stomach, and my knees feel liable to give out.

"Focus on my voice, little one. We're sitting down. That's a good girl."

Rhett's whisper in my ear makes me jump, and I'm grateful I manage to contain my yelp and cover it with a cough. I let Rhett's hand on my lower back guide me into my seat, even as the world rocks a little under my feet as a sudden wave of dizziness comes over me.

"Here, take this and breathe," Rhett prompts.

I look down and watch him pull a purple handkerchief from inside of a small leather pouch, about the size of a pocket watch. I don't have it in me to question, so I follow his instructions. Pressing the silk cloth over my nose, I try to pass it off like I've started crying and take a deep inhale. My body instantly relaxes as the soothing scent of clean towels, lemonade, and mulled wine fills my nose.

"He's the redhead, then?" Rhett asks, leaning over to whisper in my ear as the officiant starts the ceremony proper.

I give him a slight dip of my chin, closing my eyes and breathing in the combined scents of my pack, Rhett's leather and whiskey joining the mix as he puts an arm around my shoulders and shifts in his seat until I can feel his hip against mine.

I don't look at anyone other than Sam and Ally for the rest of the ceremony, even as I feel Darren's stare on my face like a white-hot brand. Rhett stays close, whispering now and then to keep me grounded and in the present despite my mind wanting to slip into memories and fear. At long last, the officiant declares the couple to be man and wife, and I applaud with the other guests. I expect the wedding party to make a recessional down the aisle again, but instead, the parents of the bride and groom stand, and I watch as everyone shuffles into place before the officiant announces the guests should come forward and make their way inside for cocktails.

A receiving line.

Fuck.

FORTY-SIX

Lydia

RHETT AND I JOIN the mass of people moving toward the front of the building, shuffling inexorably forward to where the wedding party is greeting the guests.

"We can try to go around the side, bypass this all together," I suggest under my breath.

Rhett shakes his head, taking my hand to loop under his arm again. I move in as close as I can without physically climbing him, looking up in disbelief as we move within half a dozen people at the end of the receiving line.

"We get this over now, then they can't make a scene later when we're not expecting it. Plus, it would look more suspicious if we never spoke with your brother and his new wife on their wedding day," Rhett says smoothly, face free of any sort of tell to his anxiety.

I huff out a sigh, not liking it but knowing he's right. This would give us a perfect out if anyone accused us of avoiding speaking with my parents. And etiquette in a receiving line would prevent any sort of extended conversation.

"Miss Lydia! Is that really you?"

I turn at the sound of my name, my customer service smile sliding into place as I approach Mrs. Goodreaux, Ally's mother. I shake her hand and lean in to kiss her cheek as she does the same.

"Yes, ma'am. In the flesh," I say, internally cringing at how much fake cheer I'm adding to my voice.

"We'd heard that there's been a development in your case, but we never expected to see you here! Where have you been?" she goes on, her bright blue eyes genuinely happy.

"Not too far. I'm glad I could make it. Ally looks so gorgeous," I redirect skillfully.

She doesn't get to push as I'm moved along by the flow of the queue, passing up a few people I don't recognize, probably relations of the bride, until I'm forced to a stop in front of my parents.

"Oh, Lydia! I can't believe it!" my mother crows, throwing her arms around my shoulders and dragging me into a hug.

I don't bother untangling my arm from Rhett's escort, or containing my eye roll. "You can lay off the act, Diane."

"I can't believe you showed up dressed like this. It's a wedding, not a funeral," she hisses in my ear.

I don't cave to the bait, pulling back to look at my father. His brow is stern as he looks me over and I swallow.

"Hello, Daddy. It's good to see you," I say, standing on my tiptoes to press a quick peck to his cheek.

"Lydia. Not been causing any trouble, have you?" he grumbles, voice deep and gravelly.

"No, sir. I'd actually like to introduce you to my boyfriend, Rhett Cooper," I say, words coming out in a tumble.

"It's so good to meet you, Mr. Anderson, Mrs. Anderson. Lydia has told me all about you." Rhett offers his hand to shake.

My father, not one to pass up social niceties, shakes it once firmly, but drops Rhett's hand like it's on fire. Rhett offers his hand to my mother, and to my surprise, lifts it so he can kiss the back of her knuckles. There's a flash in his eyes, the one that he wears when he's spotted a challenge or a puzzle.

"Has she? Well, we haven't heard anything about you," Diane says, giving me a disdainful look before sniffing.

"Ah, well. Perhaps you've heard of my pack. Pack St. Clair?" he offers, conversationally.

There's a moment when my father blinks and his gaze flicks to me before going back to Rhett, the only sign of his surprise. "I have. What do you do specifically?"

"I'm a structural engineer and historian, sir. We specialize in restoration. I'm told you're a contractor," Rhett continues, deflecting masterfully.

It's easy to get my father talking about work, and my mother has too much fundamentalist in her to speak over her husband. A masterstroke that makes Rhett look good while taking the pressure off me to carry the conversation.

"We're holding up the line. We'll have to catch up later. Lovely to meet you," Rhett says in a pause in my father's monologue.

We move off before either of them can recover. Thankfully, one of their friends steps up and they're too busy to stop us. Despite one last nasty look from my mother, I can't say that went horribly. We move with the flow for a moment before I tense, realizing that the bridesmaids and groomsmen are next.

"Lydi, you look pale."

I jump at the sound of Jason's voice and whip around to him standing next to me. I gather him up in a tight hug, which he returns.

"Mom's going to want you for pictures," he whispers in my ear.

"Well, I want a lifetime supply of chocolate cake, but we don't always get what we want, now do we?" I return, more bite in my voice than I'd intended.

Jason still chuckles before releasing me. He nods at Rhett, and the two pretend to introduce themselves again. It's part of the act, planned in advance to throw off suspicion. I turn to continue down the line, but Rhett steps around me, shifting his escort to put himself between me and the receiving line.

"Have you seen the gardens, love? I can't get over the way they've landscaped this place. Do you think we should send some pictures back to Lex, so we can try doing something like this at Bright Hills?"

Rhett points at something off to my right, and I look with a confused frown pulling at my mouth. I try to find what he's talking about, inhaling sharply as he leans down so his mouth is next to my ear.

"Keep looking over there. Don't look behind us. Good girl," he purrs.

I can't help the way my stomach flips, even as I realize what Rhett is doing. My skin goes cold, but I keep up the inane conversation about gardening, following Rhett's lead as we slowly move forward. His steps falter for a moment, and I feel him shrug his shoulder back, but he doesn't comment on it.

"Little Lydia!"

"Adam," I say through a forced smile, turning at last to face him.

His square jaw is clean shaven, and his nose looks crooked, like it's been broken since the last time I saw him, but otherwise, the only thing that's changed about him is his muscle mass. I can feel the bulk of his arms as he leans down to hug me, even if it's a loose embrace. I take in his familiar smokey amber and mint scent, pulling away quickly.

"You look great," he comments, looking me up and down once before turning to Rhett.

"Thanks. This is my boyfriend, Rhett Cooper," I say, slipping my hand back into the bend of his elbow.

Rhett and Adam shake hands, but it's tense, the look in Adam's eyes reading as confusion. He glances down the line for a moment, but chooses not to comment. We exchange a few shallow pleasantries, but the conversation ends when someone in a venue uniform walks behind him with a tray of drinks. He gives me a terse smile before turning to snag one.

"Charming," Rhett mutters, and I have to hide my snort of laughter behind my hand.

"Oh em gee! Lydia, it's really you!"

I turn at the squeal of delight, letting out a little 'oof' as I'm dragged into a tight hug. I take in the crisp apple and soft bamboo scent, smiling as I hug Ally back.

"Congrats, girlie! Everything was beautiful," I gush, finally able to relax from my fake smile and forced cheer.

"Thank you so much! Where have you been? You just up and left, and your poor momma's been worried sick," Ally says, her twang deeper than the smooth Louisiana accent I'm used to from my family.

"I moved. But that's not important. I have to ask about your flowers. I'm a florist, and I cannot believe how amazing the arrangements were."

Ally goes on for a moment about the design of her bridal bouquet, and I try to keep an ear on the conversation, but a breeze from behind me sends a wave of scents from the crowd to my overly sensitive nose. I feel the sweat running down my back as a trace of tobacco hits me, but it's gone before I can fully panic.

"But listen to me rattlin' on. Who's this handsome man you've got dangling off your arm?" Ally asks, looking Rhett up and down.

Sam disengages from the conversation he'd been in a moment before, turning his attention to us. I make the introductions again, still pleasantly surprised at how nice it feels to call Rhett my boyfriend in public.

"Lydia, I know this is a lot, but Mom's going to kill me if I don't say anything. We're going to be getting some family pictures and it would mean a lot if you could—"

"Sam, I know. But I'm not really comfortable getting my picture taken right now," I say, giving him a significant look.

It's not lost on me that he knows Darren has seen covert photographs of me, and Sam has the decency to look a little bashful. Ally gives me an innocently confused look, taking my free hand.

"Is everything all right, hun? Sammy said something about you and—"

"Yeah, I'm good. I'm happy to support y'all, and if you want to get some candid photos later, I'd be more than happy. I'm just trying not to cause a fuss on your big day," I say, lowering my voice and squeezing her hand.

She brings me in for another hug, and I wrap both of my arms around her this time.

"He was trouble from the jump, and I'm glad you've got someone at your back. Don't worry about the pictures," she whispers in my hair.

I let out a grateful exhale. Ally really is too good to be true, and she's definitely too kind for someone as block-headed as my brother.

Sam gives me a pat on the shoulder. "I do appreciate you being here, Lydia. I know it's never been easy with you and..." He breaks off and gestures vaguely down the line. "But I'd like to talk more, after things settle down a little. I have a feeling that there's a side to everything I'm missing."

I can't help but sag in relief before lunging forward and hugging Sam around the neck. I'm careful to avoid his boutonniere, but I can't help it. Adam would never understand, but hearing my oldest brother say he's willing to hear my side of the story after years of believing the lie, it feels better than I could have ever dreamed.

Thankfully, Sam is at the end of the line, and the doors to the house stand open. I hook my arm around Rhett's again.

"Let's get something to drink," I say with an exhale.

He chuckles and leads me into the interior, following the flow toward the bar. The rest of the night will be relatively simple, just making sure we keep track of Darren and avoid being caught in a conversation with my mother. Liquid courage will go a long way to making the time fly by.

FORTY-SEVEN

Rhett

Lex: How's it going?
Me: Had to think fast to keep him away from her. Who does a receiving line in this day and age?
Lex: The old guard of Southern matrons. How's she doing?
Me: Fine for the moment. They stopped Caleb at the gate.
Lex: I know. He texted earlier. I tried contacting the venue, but no one is answering. Don't take risks, Rhett.
Me: Why does everyone assume I'm going to be the one to start something?
Lex: Because we know you. And we know how far you'll go to keep your loved ones safe.
Me: Point made and taken.

I SLIDE MY PHONE back into the inside pocket of my jacket, lifting my glass of bourbon to take a sip. My other hand tightens on Lydia's lower back, just reassuring myself she's still there. She slides a little closer around the back of the cocktail table we're standing at, keeping it between us and the rest of the room. I'd nabbed this spot so we could keep a distance from the crowd while still being able to keep an eye out for Darren.

Darren McLaughlin.

I'd never asked Lydia what he looked like, just out of respect. I was expecting someone a little more like Seth, not someone who I could probably bench press. He might be hiding muscle under his cheap suit, but he doesn't strike me as the type to go to the gym.

But there was something undeniably sinister about the way he looked at Lydia throughout the entire ceremony. While everyone else was focused on the bride and groom, Darren didn't look away from Lydia. She did a good job either ignoring him, or simply not noticing his leering, but I certainly did. There was nothing but cold possession and deep, calculating rage.

So when it came time to walk that God damn receiving line, I made sure that Lydia was nowhere near him. Even when he tried to grab my arm and pull us back, I kept moving. If we could get through this night without him even getting within arm's reach of her, then I'd consider it a success.

Lydia disengages from her latest conversation with a relative, artfully dodging personal questions about where she's been for the last almost five years. She's on her third drink, but I'm still nursing my first. I need to keep my head on straight, but I can understand why Lydia needs the alcohol. I also don't have the heart to tell her 'no' right now, not after everything we've been through. I've been introduced to more aunts, uncles, cousins, and in-laws than I could count, and I'm about ready to lose it.

"If everyone could please grab their last drink and then make their way to the ballroom. We're going to be closing the bar for a while for speeches and first dances. Dinner will be passed plates, so feel free to stop any of our staff to try a little of what they've got."

I hum thoughtfully after the announcement, looking down at Lydia. She throws back the rest of her cocktail before sighing. Her scent is still floral forward, with just a hint of burnt sugar, though I don't suspect anyone who doesn't know Lydia as well as I do would pick up on it.

"Let's go before the good spots are taken," she says, a definite drag to her words.

"We'll stay until the dancing starts and then we can go home," I remind her.

"Hopefully, the food is good. I've never heard of passed plates for dinner before," she says, accepting my arm as I offer it to her.

"Me either. If it works, we might be able to talk Lex into researching if it'll work for our venues," I reply, happy to talk about something other than the elephant dick in the room.

The conversation continues as we head into the ballroom, and I have to admit that I'm impressed. Instead of the large eight seat tables, there are small four-person tables scattered throughout the open, airy space. Lydia and I make a beeline to one of the half-booth tables in the corner, happy to stay out of the central room for the time being. The table next to us fills up with two younger couples that seem to know each other, though Lydia gives no sign of recognition.

The wait staff circulates, and the small-serving dishes all taste incredible. It's a mix of wedding staples like pasta and potatoes, along with Southern comfort food like jambalaya and seafood. The food stops for a moment as the wedding party makes their entrance, dispersing among the crowd rather than sitting at a designated table. Jason finds his way to us, giving the fourth chair to another table so no one else can join us. Lydia sits as close as she can to me without being in my lap, though I'm sorely tempted. I have to remind myself our mission is to keep Darren from starting a scene, not antagonize him.

The atmosphere is lively and relaxed, the bride and groom able to eat and make the rounds thanks to not needing to be tied down to a special table. If my plan for our next project works out, then this could be exactly what could set it apart. Lydia seems to be thinking the same, judging by the way she's observing everything with that excited twinkle in her eye that I adore so much.

By the time Sam and Ally cut the cake and the announcement is made that the best man and maid of honor will be making their speeches, I've watched Lydia down another gin and tonic, as well as a glass of champagne. Jason is watching her while I watch the room, but Darren is sitting with Adam and someone else that, judging by his build and features, looks to be a cousin. If I've counted correctly, he's had at least six beers, which is too many for my taste.

Lydia moves, but I whip my head around and catch her elbow before she fully slides out from the booth, giving her a questioning look.

"I have to use the ladies'. I'll be right back," she says softly, words muffled as applause breaks out when the maid of honor steps onto the dancefloor.

"I'll go with you," I blurt.

Lydia looks at me for a moment, and I think she's going to try to fight me. But then her eyes flick over my shoulder and she swallows, nodding. Jason gives us a nod as we both stand and head off through an open doorway off the ballroom and down a short hallway. She slips through the door to the ladies' room, and I stand off to the side, watching the end of the hall.

I'm not standing there for long when I feel my phone vibrate against my chest. When I pull it out and see Lex's name on the screen, I dismiss the call. Noise is picking up from the speeches and the music for Sam and Ally's first dance starts up, and I'll talk to Lex later when I can find a quiet moment. But even as I think that, Lex calls again. I don't want to leave Lydia, but as Lex calls a third time in a row, I sigh. Lex wouldn't be doing this unless it was important.

"What's going on?" I say as I answer, plugging my other ear as I walk half a dozen paces down the hall where it's quieter.

"Seth. We just got word from the court," she starts, the end of her sentence getting drowned out by a round of cheering when a popular song comes on.

"Say that again, Lex," I say, ducking into a side room.

"The judge signed a warrant for Seth's arrest," she repeats, speaking slowly and clearly.

I give myself a singular moment of celebration. It's taken far too long to get here, but I'm glad we've finally gotten what we've been after. If Seth is charged and found guilty, it's going to be that much easier for Lex and Mateo to get the court to agree to a forced termination of their bond.

"What charges?" I ask, smiling triumphantly.

"Conspiracy to commit arson, aggravated harassment, and vehicular manslaughter," Lex says, and even with all the noise on my end, I can still hear the gloating little bounce to her words.

"This is fucking fantastic! Have they brought him in yet? I can't wait to see his fucking mugshot," I ask excitedly.

"That's why I'm calling instead of texting. They went to go serve the warrant, but he's gone. Completely MIA," she says.

I whip around, feet freezing, as I slowly absorb her meaning. Shit. He could be anywhere.

"I've got to go. Can you get our flight plan moved up? I want—"

"One step ahead of you. Lucas is already packing at the apartment," she tells me calmly.

We hang up, and my mind is running into overdrive. We need to get home, and fast. There's no way of knowing where Seth could be, and we'll be safer together. As I reach the bathroom door, I shove my phone in my pocket, shifting nervously on my feet. But then suddenly, I hear a wordless scream of pain, and my heart stops.

Lydia.

FORTY-EIGHT

Lydia

I STEP UP TO the counter and turn on the tap to wash my hands, feeling the world sway slightly as the alcohol finally hits my system. It's amazing how you don't feel drunk when you're sitting down, but then you stand up and *bam*. I giggle under my breath at my own thoughts. Yeah, I definitely need to switch to water if we plan on staying for any longer. Though by the sounds coming from outside the door, if the dancing's started, then this might be the perfect opportunity to slip out unnoticed.

"Hello, petal."

I gasp and look up from the running water, my blood freezing solid as my eyes land on Darren McLaughlin in the mirror. I whip around, my still wet hands slipping slightly against the marble counter. Darren is between me and the door, cutting off my only means of escape. The three stalls to my left won't offer any sort of long-term shelter.

"Aw, come on now 'chere. Don't look too excited to see your alpha now," Darren slurs, his Cajun accent all the worse from intoxication.

"You're not my alpha," I reply, trying to sound calmer than I feel. Thankfully, my words are steady, even though my stomach quakes worse than a flag in a hurricane.

Darren sucks his teeth as he prowls forward, rubbing at the stubble on his jaw. His rusty red hair is even more disheveled than before, and his tie hangs loose around his neck. There's an unsteadiness to his gait that sends up warning bells loud and clear. He's drunk, too drunk. I try to step back as he closes in on my space, but my hips only dig into the hard edge of the counter.

"You know, petal, you always have been easy on the eyes, and when you clean up like this, it's enough to make anyone go crazy, alpha or nah," Darren purrs, reaching up to brush a knuckle along my hair.

I flinch back, bile rising in the back of my throat at the look of disappointment he levels at me.

"It doesn't have to be like this, ya know. We had good times, didn't we? Don't you miss that?" he whispers.

His tobacco and bitter almond scent fills my head, and I curse my heart for flipping at the almost gentle tone, the softness to his muddy brown eyes. But it only takes a glance at his other hand, and the scar along his middle finger to remember the bad times. He cut himself on glass as he was throwing a drink at me, then blamed me for the mess.

"No, I don't. And you can cut the crap," I snap, looking up to glare directly into his eyes.

The shift is subtle, but the way his eyes harden and his lopsided smile turns makes sweat break out across my palms.

"Do we want to start in so soon, my petal? We got so much catching up–"

"Stop calling me that. I'm not your anything anymore," I cut in, gritting the words out through my teeth. I ball my hands in my skirt, trying to stop their shaking by sheer force of will.

"'Cause you got all them queers up in Georgia now, right? Do they know how much of a little whore you are, running around behind your alpha's back?" he throws back at me.

The words land like a slap, but it's a pain I'm used to. "What did I just tell you? You're not my alpha. There's nothing between us. Or did I not make myself clear when I ran out the night you raped me?"

"See, I remember that night a little different. I asked you to be my wife, and you agreed. And there's the little detail about my marks," he says, almost casually.

Five years ago, I would have stopped and considered his words. I would have questioned my memories, my reality.

And if I'm too busy questioning myself, then I can't question him or his motives. But not anymore. I know this song and dance, but I refuse to allow him this power over me. Anger burns away my fear, and I can look up into his face with my head high.

"No, you don't get to rewrite what you did to me. You asked, and I said I wanted to wait. You didn't like that answer and raped me. Well, guess what, asshole? I never went into heat, so all you did was give me some scars," I retort, raising an angry finger into his face.

The crack of his hand against my cheek registers before the sting of the blow, and I gasp. I touch it gingerly, but a second blow across the other side of my face makes my head spin.

"That's a warning not to raise your hand against an alpha, Omega. Now you shut your worthless mouth and listen. You've got it in your stupid, pathetic brain that you're somehow the victim in all of this, like you didn't deserve everything you made me do." Darren lets out a dark, humorless chuckle that sends a shiver down my spine. "You should count your blessings that I'm willing to even consider keeping you after you've gone and spread your legs for who knows how many scumbags."

He steps forward, and I have to lean back, hands slipping on some stray water. Darren's hand darts out and closes around my jaw and throat, holding painfully as he looks down on me, disgust written in his features. And the primal part of my mind seems to writhe in pain. Because despite all the ways he's hurt me over the years, that part of me that's pure omega wants to please an alpha.

"You, me, and your daddy are going to have a long talk here about what to do with you. As your prime alpha, it'll be his call in the end, but I'm sure he'll let me handle your penance. After your prissy little rich boy goes back home to the fag and the bitch, we'll get you settled in nice and comfy for your heat," he goes on, clay-scented anger clogging my nose and throat.

I can hardly breathe around the fear now flaring inside me, every nerve in my body trying to fire at once to do something, anything, to escape from this alpha with murder in his eyes. His words shake something loose in my head, and I latch onto it. Prime alpha, my prime alpha.

With all my strength, I bring my forearm down onto his elbow, breaking his hold on my throat. I use my other hand to push his chest, trying to create just the smallest bit of room to move. He's surprised enough to stumble back a step and I push my advantage. He's never seen me fight back, so I try to capitalize on the element of surprise by stepping up into his space.

"You're too late, you abusive prick. I've joined another pack. My father has no authority over me, not anymore," I snarl, rising on to my full height.

Darren blinks and, for one heartbeat, I think that my chest-puffing and posturing worked. But then his eyes flick to the mirror, and his face morphs into something out of my nightmares. I scream as he grabs my upper arm and spins me, slamming me hard into the counter, my face pressed to the mirror by his arm.

"What the fuck is this?" he growls.

I struggle to throw him off, but he just uses his hips to pin me, hard. There's a metallic click, and I freeze at the first touch of cold steel against my back. My whole body shakes as I look up and see the rage growing on Darren's face with every cut he makes into the back of my dress. One of my hands comes up to keep the front of my dress in place, but my left shoulder blade is exposed to his stare.

"A tattoo? What sort of–"

"It's my pack motto," I snap, trying to shift and get him to let up as my neck aches from the way it's pressed against the glass.

"You put it over our bond mark," he replies, speaking almost to himself now instead of me.

"It never fucking took. It was just a scar, and this is my body. You have no claim over me," I say, nearly shouting.

Darren snarls, and his hand comes up, gripping my hair near the roots. I scream again as he cranks back, my hands scrabbling for balance.

"These sorts of marks are just skin deep. But don't worry. I can fix that," Darren says, a manic edge to his words.

I struggle more at the flash of his knife in the mirror, hands flailing as I try to scratch or punch or kick my way free.

"If ye want to keep yer fuckin' hand, you best drop that right now."

Darren and I both look in the direction of Rhett's voice, and I nearly sob in relief at the sight of him standing in the door, eyes blue pits of fiery rage trained on Darren.

FORTY-NINE

Rhett

AT THE SOUND OF my voice, Darren whips around, teeth bared in a snarl. But my eyes are on Lydia's face. There's a dark red spot suspiciously shaped like fingers on the cheek I can see, and my vision goes red. The only thing stopping me from flying into a full rage is years of training. There's a weapon in play, and going straight to fighting would be a mistake.

"This doesn't concern you," Darren snaps.

"When you've got your hands on my omega, it absolutely does concern me," I return, low and dangerous.

Darren's eyes flash, and I see my opening. I shift my weight as I step forward, planting my feet and setting my foundation. I'll try not to enjoy this too much.

"I was told you were an alpha. But all I see is a limp-dicked rapist coward," I sneer, smirking.

Just like I'd expected, he lets go of Lydia to face me. He doesn't move enough to give her room to escape yet, but at least she can breathe.

"What the fuck did you just say to me?" he growls, adjusting the knife in his hand.

I don't take my eyes off it for long, the situation too unpredictable. But I've been on the other side of this sort of goading enough times to know how to play the game.

"You fucking heard me, or are your ears as defective as the Tic Tac between your legs?" I reply, throwing in a scathing laugh for effect.

Lydia's looking at me like I've lost my mind, and maybe I have. All of my muscles are coiled tight, preparing for the fight. I try to tell Lydia with my eyes that she should make a break for the door as soon as it's clear, but I don't know how effective I am when I don't dare take my eyes off the volatile alpha with a knife in front of me.

Darren advances on me, trying to go nose to nose with me. My snort of amusement isn't for show as I realize the top of his head only comes up to my eye level. He tries to puff his chest and get in my face, but it's hard to find someone you literally look down on seriously.

"You have a lot of fucking nerve trying to lay claim on someone else's omega," he says, the low growl in his throat less threatening now.

"You talk a big game for someone who is only breathing right now because I value keeping my word over teaching you a lesson in manners. But keep pushing me. See how well that works out for you. I dare you," I say, leaning down to truly look him in the eye as I speak.

Out of the corner of my eye, Lydia shifts slightly, trying to edge toward the door. My eyes flick away for less than a heartbeat, but that's all it takes. Because we're so close, I don't have time to react as he lets out a roar. Almost in slow motion, his arm cranks back, and then there's a blinding flash of pain in my left leg. I look down to the knife buried several inches in my thigh. My adrenaline spikes as the pain takes hold, and I manage to contain my shout into a snarl. But the coward drops his shoulder and barrels us both backwards.

My spine screams as it comes in contact with the vertical support of the stall, and I fall sideways through the door. I manage to catch myself before I crash into the toilet, but my left leg protests as I try to put any weight on it.

"Run, Lydia! Get to Caleb!" I shout, words echoing off the tile walls.

Darren whips around as I hear movement, and I seize my opportunity. I get my right leg under me and use the momentum to drive my body forward, grabbing Darren's jacket lapel to bring him back around to face me and swinging my other fist in a hard cross. The crack of bone under my fist sings to the violent side of my soul, and I can't help the feral grin that creeps across my face as I move with Darren. I follow him back, landing blow after blow as I drive him out of the stalls and toward the sink. At the edge of my attention, I hear the brief rise in volume of the music as the door opens and closes.

Knowing Lydia is out of harm's way, I don't hold back, throwing punch after punch to Darren's face and torso. He tries to strike back, but even with an injured leg, I have years of training and instincts on my side, so I'm able to dodge his sloppy punches. He stumbles back, grunting as his side hits the marble of the sink. I try to advance, hissing as my left leg takes my weight. Darren tries to lunge, but I duck his wild haymaker, elbowing him in the gut again.

He slips on something on the floor—my blood, I realize—and goes down to one knee next to the sink. Then I advance again, only to lean back as he tries to swing a decorative vase at me. I knock it out of his grip with a strike to his elbow, finally getting into his guard. Wrapping his tie around my fist once, I drag him back to his feet.

"You aren't ever going to hurt my omega again, you understand me?" I growl, trying to push as much command as I can into my words. I wouldn't count on a bark working against another alpha, but it's worth a shot.

"She's not your—"

I don't let him finish before I slam the side of his head into the counter between the sinks, his shouted curse like music to my ears. I drag him back up to go nose to nose, not giving him a choice but to look directly into my eyes. I only have a few minutes to teach this bastard a lesson, so I don't bother beating around the bush.

"Forget Lydia Anderson ever existed. This is your last warning."

Darren looks like he's about to protest, but I just grin. I grab a handful of his burnt orange hair and haul him up with brute strength alone. With a growl of pure primal violence, I bring his jaw down onto the edge of the counter. There's a gut-churning crunch, and Darren slumps to the floor as I release him, out cold.

I step back and look down at my leg. I'd chosen to wear black for this exact reason. Something in me knew that I wouldn't be escaping this evening without some sort of altercation, and I was, unfortunately, correct. There's a bit of shine around the entry wound, but otherwise, no sign of blood. Gritting my teeth, I shrug out of my jacket, slipping my cell phone into my pocket before ripping one of the silk lining pieces away. I pull a few paper towels from the dispenser and lean against the wall, bracing myself.

If the knife hurt going in, that was nothing to the feeling of it coming out. It's a pretty standard pocketknife, and the small section of serrated teeth hurt the most as I drag them free. The world grays out for a moment, but I manage to keep myself conscious. Packing the area with the towels, I use the bit of silk to hold them in place. It won't hold for long, but it should hold until we can get to Lucas and possibly a first aid kit.

I push myself to my feet, knife in one hand, jacket in the other, then look to Darren's limp form on the pristine white tile. The weight of the knife sinks into my palm, and my heart pounds against my ribs. At this point, my blood is everywhere, and I have a wound to prove that this could have all been in self-defense. If he were permanently removed from the equation, then would that be such a bad thing? What's a little jail time compared to keeping Lydia safe?

But as soon as the thought fully sinks in, I reject it. I'm a lot of things, but a murderer isn't one of them. And anything that would separate me from my omega isn't worth it. I take a limping step forward and toss the knife on the floor next to him.

And just because I can, I kick his legs as I head out the door to find Lydia and get the hell out of here.

FIFTY

Lydia

"RUN, LYDIA! GET TO Caleb!"

Rhett's shout shocks me out of my frozen stupor, and I obey without a second thought. Darren and Rhett are locked in combat, fists flying and blood splattering. I stumble out into the hallway, running into the wall opposite as I try to gain my balance. I realize I'm hyperventilating as I continue to lurch toward the doorway to the ballroom. Everything is spinning, with the edges of my vision turning gray.

"Lydi, what the hell—what happened?"

The touch of Jason's hands on my arms, and the sound of his voice over the pounding music, makes me jump and yelp. I try to sort through my thoughts as I look up into his face, but they slide like sand through my fingers.

"R-Rhett... Darren... I need—I need Caleb. We need to get to Caleb," I say, starting off stumbling but finishing on the edge of hysteria.

"Okay, it's okay. Let's get some air, okay?" Jason says soothingly.

I nod and let him lead me out of the front door and onto the path that leads toward the parking lot. I pull out my phone, my fingers shaking so much that it takes twice as long for me to fire off an emergency text to Caleb. Jason stops us about halfway down the path. The music is muffled out here, the only lights coming from the solar powered path markers.

"So, what's happened with Rhett and Darren?" Jason asks, turning around to look back toward the entrance.

I gulp down air, leaning forward and putting my hands on my knees. "Darren–Darren followed me into the bathroom. There was a knife, and Rhett's hurt–"

"Jason? Lydia? What are you doing out here?"

Jason and I turn at the sound of a voice, and my eyebrows shoot up as Sam and Adam step into the light from behind a row of bushes. As they get closer, I wrinkle my nose at the pungent smell coming from them, straightening to stand again. Adam's gaze is unfocused as he looks at us, but Sam looks much more alert. His eyes catch on my torn dress and come up to my face.

"Are you okay?" he asks, concern pulling his brow down low.

I open my mouth to deny it, but I settle on a shrug and a shake of my head. Because my face throbs and my heart still pounds like a war drum in my chest.

"You look... rough, Lydia. You sneak off into a corner with your boy toy?" Adam snorts, words slurring together. He breaks off, laughing at his own joke, but none of us join him.

I narrow my eyes at him. "Are you fucking *high*, Adam?"

"How else am I supposed to get through this? No offense, Sammy, but–"

"Yeah, yeah, fuck off. But seriously, are you hurt?" Sam asks, turning back to me.

"Darren cornered me," I say simply, not sure I could even adequately describe what just happened.

"Here we go again. This is getting old, you know. Darren is a nice guy," Adam says dramatically.

"Are you seriously defending him? After all the shit he's done, you're seriously taking his side?" Jason growls, stepping up to stand between me and them.

I look back at the front door, heart throbbing anxiously, my fingers twitching to do something. Where is Rhett? He should have been right behind me.

"All we have to go on is his word and hers. And he's done nothing but help our pack and work hard over the last few years. What has Lydia done?" he says, pointing an accusatory finger at me.

"Wow, that's quite a magic trick. I see your lips moving, but all I can hear coming out of your mouth is Mom's voice," I retort sarcastically, not even bothering to turn around and acknowledge him, my eyes still locked on the door.

"What the fuck is that supposed to mean?" he asks harshly, a low growl in the back of his throat.

I whip back to face my brother so fast my hair fans out and hits Jason's shoulder. "Darren fucking *raped* me, you obnoxious, self-absorbed dickwad. He's been having me followed and stalked, and you think because he's spent the last four years kissing Mom and Dad's asses that he's this innocent little angel?" I shoot back, voice rising to nearly a shout.

"It's always got to be so dramatic with you. Have you ever thought that maybe if you—"

"You think that I want any of this? I ran away to get away from Mom and Darren and all of their manipulation and abuse. God, you're as bad as them," I shout, throwing my shaking hands up.

I put my back to my brothers again, shifting my weight. This is taking too long. Should I go back and find him? And where is Caleb?

"Lydia, that's enough. We all need to take a breath," Sam says calmly, stepping between us with his hands up.

"Don't act like you're innocent in all of this, Sam. I know Darren told you what he was doing to me. Jason heard you two talking. Even after that, you still think I'm making this shit up?" I ask, voice cracking as tears rise in my throat.

"What were you doing, spying—"

"Is that what you're taking from that, Adam? All that dope must have killed the last functioning brain cell you had," Jason says, sarcasm cutting deep.

I look over my shoulder at Sam and watch his throat bob as he swallows. "I... I don't know. Yeah, Darren said some fucked up shit, but... it's just talk, right? Like, I've said I want to kill someone, but I'd never actually—"

I shake my head, cutting him off. There's a shift in his eyes as he looks down at me, and I'm not sure what he sees, but I watch his eyes go wide with realization. He opens his mouth, but a new voice echoes through the garden, turning my blood to ice.

"Samuel? Adam? Where are you? It's almost time for the garter and bouquet toss," Diane Anderson calls.

All of us whip around to see her coming down the stairs, and we don't have time to hide before she spots us and makes a beeline in our direction. On instinct, I take a step back and to the side, shifting to partially hide behind Jason. I don't miss how Sam subtly shifts his stance, also moving to stand in front of me.

"What are y'all doing out here? The party is inside," Diane says brightly as she reaches us.

"Just wanted to get some air. We'll be right in," Jason says smoothly.

For a brief heartbeat, it seems like she's going to take that at face value, but Adam takes that moment to shove past me, his shoulder knocking hard into my back and sending me stumbling into Jason. He turns and catches me before I can fall all the way to the ground, but my mother notices me at last.

"What is–Lydia, you look–this is a wedding, your brother's wedding, and you can't keep yourself presentable for three hours?" she hisses, hand clamping down on my arm and dragging me to my feet.

I wince as her nails dig into my skin, and I try to pull away. Her eyes roam over me, her mouth twisted in a disgusted sneer. I have no idea how I look, but with my hair messed up and my dress cut to shreds on one side, I'm sure it's not the greatest. But the judgement in her expression is too much for my fragile nerves. My head wants to run for the parking lot, and my heart wants to go back into the building, but my mother's hand on my arm keeps me from doing either. I can feel my brothers' eyes on me, and it's enough to cut the last thread holding my patience and common sense in check.

"Darren hit me, Mom. Again. And he threatened to cut my tattoo from my skin," I snap, watching her carefully for her reaction.

I want to be disappointed when there's no change to her expression, but at this point, I almost expected it.

"You got a tattoo? The Bible–"

"Fuck the Bible, Mom! I just told you that someone assaulted me, and all you hear is that? Are you serious?" I shout, finally tearing my arm free of her grip.

Diane inhales sharply, and I have to look away before I lose it. Of course, she's clutching her pearls over my blasphemy. Because she doesn't care about Darren hitting me. She never has.

"I can't with this right now. As soon as Rhett gets out here, we're leaving–"

"You will do no such thing, young lady," my mother snaps with an honest to God stomp of her foot.

"Why? Afraid that you'll lose your last chance to steal my trust fund? Because you're already too late for that," I snap, mouth working before my brain.

Her jaw drops, and she leans back, hand to her chest. It's such a perfect picture of shock and disbelief that I can't help but laugh outright. Sam and Adam look between us, confusion clear on their faces.

"Oh, that's rich. Too fucking bad that I know all of the crap you and Darren have been doing over the last couple of months. Did he show you the pictures that the stalker he hired took of me? The ones when I was just trying to eat lunch? Or go for a walk? Or how about the ones when I was fucking my boyfriend in my nest?" I throw at her, anger long suppressed, boiling hot in my chest.

"Lydia, that's quite enough. I can't believe you'd use such lewd language in front of your own mother," Diane blusters. But she's not looking at me, and she certainly isn't denying it.

"Maybe you'd like to explain how you kept getting my phone number, even though I changed it three times in as many months?" I ask, taking a step in her direction.

"Are you trying to say that our mother was hacking your phone from four states away?" Adam asks incredulously.

"No, I'm saying that I think she hacked mine and was reading all my messages," Jason snarls, so low I almost don't hear him.

We all look at our mother, waiting for the denial, but the longer she stays silent, the harder my heart beats.

"Sam, did she tell you that I wasn't going to come tonight? I didn't want to take the risk of ruining this day for you with all this bullshit," I start, looking to my eldest brother. He blinks, the only sign of his surprise. So she didn't tell him.

"You know, you never told me why you changed your mind," Jason says, genuine curiosity coming forward.

I look at my mother's face for a long moment, and her mouth is pressed into a tight line. Her eyes are hard, flashing a silent warning. But I'm past caring. If I'm cutting ties, I might as well do a thorough job of it.

"She told me that if I didn't come, she'd tell Dad that you've been disloyal to the pack and have you disowned, kicked out, and cut off," I say, speaking slowly and clearly so they all hear every damning word.

Jason turns his head slowly, jaw tight and eyes narrow in a harsh glare. "Is that true, Mom?" he asks, no emotion in his voice.

She scoffs and shifts backward, taking a little step away from him. "Well, can you blame me? You've been going behind our backs for years, keeping Lydia away from me, from us."

Wrong answer. Jason growls and looks away, fists shaking at his sides. I start to reach up to put a hand to his shoulder, but he steps away, not looking at any of us.

"Lydia!"

The shout from the front door draws everyone's attention and I nearly sag in relief as Rhett comes limping down the stairs, a sob breaking free from my throat. I shove through my family to meet him a little ways up the path, letting him sling one arm around my shoulders so I can support his weight. He's heavy, but I don't care. He's alive, and that's all that matters.

"Where's Caleb? We're leaving," he says lowly, speaking through gritted teeth.

"I don't know. I texted him—"

As if on cue, pounding footsteps sound on the path leading toward the parking lot. Caleb comes into view a moment later, hardly winded at all, even as he skids to a stop. Sam and Adam are shouting questions, but I ignore them as I help Rhett move toward my bodyguard. Even in the low light, Rhett looks exceptionally pale. He needs a doctor or something. He's fashioned a makeshift bandage, but it won't last for long.

"Where do you think you're going?" my mother shrieks from behind us.

"Away from you," I reply shortly, relieved when Caleb takes over Rhett's weight.

"Your father–"

"Omega, you will freeze this instant!"

My entire body locks up, the air in my lungs whooshing out of my chest as I flush ice cold, crashing hard to the ground, not even able to cry out as the skin of my knees splits at the impact. I look up to three, possibly four, figures moving toward us down the path. At the head of the group, I see the gleam of platinum blond hair.

Speak of the devil, and he shall appear.

FIFTY-ONE

Lydia

I BARELY HAVE THE strength to lift my head and watch as Samuel Anderson Sr. stalks forward, followed closely by Pastor Joe and Andrea, supporting a bloody and barely conscious Darren between them. Rhett tries to step in front of me, but only gasps in pain as it puts weight on his injured leg.

"You will tell me the truth of what happened tonight, Omega," Samuel growls, the command sliding down my spine and making me shiver uncontrollably.

"You will do no such thing, Omega. Get behind me," Rhett commands.

The dual sensations of my father's bark and Rhett's bark is unlike anything I've ever experienced in my life. The icy grip around my muscles seems to lessen, and I sag as I take gasping breaths. Warmth fills my chest, and with a shake of my head, I'm able to throw off the last of Samuel's command to be still and speak. His eyes, so like mine, are wide as I scramble backwards and to my feet, tucking myself behind Rhett and Caleb.

"Just who the hell do you think you are, speaking over a prime alpha's command of one of his pack?" Pastor Joe shouts, momentarily dropping his support of Darren's arm to step forward and thrust an accusatory finger in Rhett's direction.

"She's not yours to command. Not anymore," Rhett says, not looking away from Samuel.

"She's my omega," Samuel responds calmly, as if they are just discussing the weather.

"She's your fucking daughter," Rhett retorts hotly.

"Samuel, we have a deal. If you can't bring her to heel–"

"I'm not a dog," I snap, glaring around Rhett at Pastor Joe.

"You will speak when spoken to, Omega," he spits, not even sparing me a glance.

"You watch your tone with my pack mate," Rhett growls, turning his gaze to glare at Pastor Joe.

"Pack mate?" Samuel asks, true confusion coming through.

"This is absurd. Sam–"

"Silence, Diane," my father snaps as my mother tries to interrupt, and like the obedient wife, she listens and backs off.

"The Lord has spoken, and He has shown us the way. Lydia is to belong to our son, as–"

"God doesn't get to decide that, and neither do you nor my father!" I shout, cutting across Pastor Joe. I take Rhett's hand tight in my own, stomach twisting as I feel how sticky it is with blood. "I decide that. And I've made my choice."

There's a low moan that draws all of our attention, and I suck in a sharp breath through my nose. Darren is getting to his feet, though very shakily. He can barely hold his head up, and the lower half of his face is swollen almost beyond recognition. He staggers forward a step, standing level with my father and within arm's reach of me and Rhett.

"Omega whore," he says, words garbled as he barely manages to open his mouth to speak.

I hold my breath, watching as the barest hint of a smirk crosses his face. Then, before I can react, he hocks and spits a glob of red in my face. My gag reflex is instant, and I double over retching as I try to wipe the spit and blood away. Rhett's hand comes free from mine, and I look up just in time to him kicking out with his bad leg at Darren's knee. There's a crack like a baseball bat connecting with a ball, and Darren crumples. There's shouting, a woman's scream, but no one is fast enough to stop Rhett's fist from connecting with Darren's jaw once, twice, and then he goes down, unconscious again.

I straighten as my stomach settles, though I still feel the burn of bile in the back of my throat. Sam and Jason are holding Adam, who is swearing to make Rhett pay and half a dozen other things. My eyes connect with theirs, and Sam gives me a sad, resigned look while Jason looks determined. But even through those emotions, I can sense their silent plea for me to leave. Pastor Joe is on the ground, fanning his wife, who has appeared to have fainted. Rhett and Samuel are chest-to-chest, eyes level with each other.

"Pack St. Clair claims Lydia Anderson. Come near her, and we'll make sure it's the last thing you ever do," Rhett growls.

"Is that a threat?" Samuel responds, sounding almost amused.

"I don't make threats," Rhett responds.

"Lydia, are you going to let your father be disrespected like this?" Diane screams, motioning wildly.

I look at her, really look at her for the first time. She's an aging beauty, past her prime. Her dress and makeup overpower whatever charm could be lying beneath the surface. She looks on the edge of tears, desperation twisting her face into something ugly.

"Let's go home, Rhett," I say softly, taking his hand again.

Rhett turns when I tug lightly, and I let him lean on me as we turn our backs on my family for the last time. Caleb watches for a long moment, following after us, but keeping his body angled to keep watching behind us.

"You don't get to walk away, you ungrateful little bitch! I raised you, and you—"

"Do not take another step closer, or I will be forced to take appropriate countermeasures," Caleb growls.

Rhett and I whip around and Caleb's facing away from us, gun drawn but down at his side.

Completely undeterred, Diane takes another step forward and glares at me. "You walk away, and I will make you regret ever daring to defy me. You think you've known suffering? I will teach you—"

"Are you making threats against the life of my charge? Because if that's the case..."

Caleb's soft, Eastern-European accented voice still manages to cut through my mother's tantrum. Even the insects seem to go still as the gentle 'click' of the hammer being cocked fills the gulf between us.

"Diane, enough. Let them go," Samuel orders, but not in a true bark.

I wonder for a moment if she's going to take the risk, to call the bluff. But she backs down, taking a step back, though her glare never wavers.

"*Voyin,* the car is at the end of the path. Go," Caleb instructs, not taking his eyes off them.

I nod, trying to contain my trembling long enough to get Rhett and myself into the backseat of the SUV. Moments later, Caleb is in the front, and in a spray of gravel, we're off into the night.

FIFTY-TWO

Lydia

I LOOK UP INTO Caleb's eyes as we make our way through the nearly deserted New Orleans streets toward the CBD. He's focused entirely on the road, but his eyes flick back to meet mine for a heartbeat. I nod my thanks, not trusting my voice right now. He blinks in acknowledgement before going back to watching the road.

"That yours or his?" Caleb asks into the silence.

I look down at Rhett's leg, my stomach turning as the orange glow of a passing streetlight reveals a strip of black silk tied around his thigh, the surrounding fabric of his pants soaked and sticking to his skin.

"Mine. Fucker stabbed me," Rhett replies, shifting slightly and gasping as he tries to straighten his leg.

"We need to get you to a doctor," I say, looking around for anything to add to the makeshift bandage and stop the bleeding.

"No time. We need to get back home," Rhett grits out, handing me his jacket.

I rip at the already partially damaged lining, packing the area around the wound as gently as I can. Rhett puts up a solid front, but even in the dark, the pain in his pale face stands out. Only instincts to protect and soothe and heal my alpha keep me from dissolving in a sobbing mess. I can freak out later, when we're not running seemingly for our lives.

"We'll need to get you knife-proof pants for the next wedding," I try to joke, my laugh coming out weak and watery.

Rhett grabs my hand before I put pressure on his leg, gripping it tight. I look up into his eyes, swallowing hard at the hazy, unfocused glaze taking over.

"Did he hurt you?" he asks seriously.

I let out an involuntary cough of a laugh, shaking my head slightly in disbelief. "You've been stabbed, and you're worried about me?"

"I'll always be worried about you, love," Rhett replies simply.

Shaking my head, I pull my hand away to press lightly against his leg. "I'll be fine. We need to take care of you first," I say, looking down as I feel warm wetness seep up between my fingers.

"You're going to have to use more pressure than that, *voyin*. And more cloth," Caleb instructs as he turns the corner.

I look up to Rhett again, and he nods, bracing himself. I steel myself as I press, hard, heart twisting at the grunt of pain Rhett releases.

"Once we get on the plane, I can put in some temporary stitches, but you'll have to get looked at by a professional as soon as we land in Georgia," Caleb tells us sternly.

"Good enough. We can let Lex know what's going on then. We just need to get wheels up as soon as possible," Rhett says, breathing heavily.

"What's going on? Why are we running?" I ask, unable to stand it a moment longer.

Rhett swallows and wipes his forehead. I can make out the smear of dark blood in the light of another streetlight.

"There's a warrant out for Seth's arrest. I don't know all the details, but I know that when they went to arrest him, he was gone. And no one knows where he went," Rhett explains.

My stomach drops and I feel sick again. He could be anywhere, doing anything. And he's proven that he doesn't need to be physically present to make my life a living hell.

"Once we're all together again, we can figure out what our next move is going to be," Rhett finishes, dropping his head back to rest against the seat.

I nod, turning my attention back to keeping pressure on his wound.

A few minutes later, Caleb comes to a smooth stop on the curb outside of the apartment building. Lucas stands on the sidewalk, all of our bags around him. Caleb gets out to help load the trunk, and I turn to look back to Rhett. He's been quiet, eyes closed. I only know he's still alive by the steady rise and fall of his chest. I want to wake him, to make sure he's still with us, but I can't bring myself to lift my trembling hands from his thigh.

Caleb and Lucas slam their doors as they slide into the front seats, and Lucas turns around to look at me. I'm not sure what exactly he's able to see in the low light, but it can't be good. I haven't felt any fresh bleeding in a minute or two, but I don't dare lift my hands. Lucas swallows, eyes wide.

"I'm alive, Luc. I'll be okay."

We both whip our heads around at the sound of Rhett's voice. He hasn't lifted his head or opened his eyes, but knowing he's awake helps to settle my roiling stomach a fraction.

"If you'd let some dickless alpha take you out, I'd have to bring you back so I could kill you myself," Lucas replies, his words teasing but his tone falling flat.

Rhett still chuckles softly, and I can't help but smile a little. Caleb throws the car into gear and speeds off toward the airport. The ride there, getting through the gate and into the hangar, all passes in a blur. I'm too focused on keeping pressure on Rhett's leg and watching his chest rise and fall. Once we come to a stop, Lucas jumps out with Caleb, and the back doors open, Caleb and Lucas in front of me with the door behind open wide.

"This is going to suck, but hopefully not for long," Caleb says, reaching in and grabbing Rhett's arm.

"Just do it," Rhett says, already gritting his teeth.

"Lydia, on my count, let go and get on the plane. I need you to find as many towels as you can and get them laid out over the couch. Can you do that?" Caleb instructs.

My heart settles under his calm, careful guidance and I nod, shifting my feet out from under me in preparation. Caleb counts down from three, and in the same moment I lift my hands, Caleb yanks Rhett toward him and Lucas, catching his nearly limp body. I don't stick around to see much more, sprinting across the short distance between the backseat and the plane's staircase. The flight attendants are already there, handing me towels and sheets. There's a commotion from behind me, but I focus on covering as much of the white leather couch with towels as possible.

I turn as footsteps sound behind me, Caleb and Lucas supporting Rhett between them. The strength goes out from my knees as I see Rhett in full light for the first time since this all started. His face is pale, almost grayish. The fabric of his left pant leg clings to his thigh, and I can see droplets falling from his shoe as they drag across the pristine floor. I stumble backwards, landing in an armchair as Caleb and Lucas get Rhett onto the couch.

"First aid kit, here," one of the flight attendants says, coming up with a large white box and a red duffle bag.

"We need to clean this. Water, hot water," Caleb says, voice clipped in a way I've never heard before.

Lucas steps back as Caleb starts ripping at Rhett's pant leg, exposing the wound more fully. I look up at the beta, and he's pale, almost a little green. I whimper and reach out to him, realizing with a bolt of horror that my hands are covered in blood, Rhett's blood.

"Come on, sweetheart. Let's get you changed and cleaned up," he says, moving to my side.

I look back to Rhett, limp on the couch, and Caleb kneeling at his side, taking a bucket of hot water and a rag from the flight attendant.

"I can't leave him," I whisper, lower lip trembling.

Lucas looks back to our alpha, and he nods, sinking down to sit on the floor in front of my knees, facing Rhett. The next few minutes are silent and tense, both of us too scared to breathe too loudly as Caleb works. He washes a river of blood away from Rhett's leg, revealing a thin cut, maybe an inch long. But it's deep, and Caleb mutters under his breath in his native tongue the whole time he stitches. After what feels like hours, he eventually sits back, exhaling heavily.

"It's not pretty, but it'll last the few hours between here and Everton. He's lost a decent amount of blood, so we just need–"

Suddenly, the still air of the hangar splits wide with the sound of sirens, a dozen or more of them. My head whips around to see a small army of police squad cars screeching to a halt around the entrance to the plane, and even more outside of the hangar door. I look at Lucas, eyes wide and mouth agape.

"Rhett Cooper! This is the Jefferson Parish Police Department! You are under arrest. Come out with your hands up!"

Fifty-Three

Lydia

The words echo in the cavernous space, amplified by a bullhorn. But they seem to linger in my bones even after the sound dies away. My eyes burn, tears clogging my throat and making it hard to breathe. I thought we'd made it; thought we'd moved fast enough to get away before the last few hours could come back to haunt us. But we were wrong.

"What do we do?" Lucas asks, voice a hoarse whisper.

I look up from my seat across from Rhett, finding Lucas's beautiful face pale and drawn as he looks out of the window behind me. His stormy blue-gray eyes are wide, and I watch his throat bob as he swallows hard.

"I'm going to talk to them," Caleb says solemnly, shifting to get to his feet.

Sucking in a sharp breath, I reach out and grab his wrist with both of my hands. He looks down at me, square jaw set, but his eyes are soft and understanding. As a private security officer, he has experience with law enforcement, but my mind is screaming for him to stay in my line of sight. I need his strength, his unshaking calm right now. He seems to read the desperation in my face, and his thin lips pull up at the corners in a tiny smile.

"I will be right back. I need you to get Rhett out of his vest while I'm gone. Can you do that, *voyin*?"

His words rumble with a soft alpha purr, his scent of cedar and sage and snickerdoodles pushing past the metallic tang of blood in the air to calm my roiling gut for a moment. Even though I don't understand why, I nod and release his wrist. Caleb looks at Lucas, then claps a hand on his shoulder, whispering something in his ear as he passes. Lucas swallows again and nods, finally turning his stare away from the window. Caleb moves off and I shift from my seat to kneel down next to Rhett's head. His golden hair, so perfectly styled only hours ago, falls over his forehead and brow. I reach up with trembling fingers and brush some strands away, flinching at the blood that's still staining my hands. Lucas gets down next to me, and stops, inspecting Rhett's face.

I jump and stifle a yelp as Rhett groans, his eyes squeezing shut before cracking open slightly. The crystal blue of his irises is clouded with pain, and it takes him a moment to focus on our faces.

"What's going on?" he rasps, looking between us.

"The police... they're outside," Lucas starts, breaking off as his voice cracks.

"They say you're under arrest. But I don't know how they could have gotten here so fast," I continue, trying to keep my voice down.

Rhett's face hardens as he listens, his jaw tightening under his well-groomed beard. His eyes dart to look behind us, and I turn for the first time and look out of the window. My view is limited, but there seems to be over a dozen squad cars, all with their lights flashing. I can't see or hear Caleb, but the hangar distorts even the low conversation between the officers, making it impossible to discern any specific thread of conversation.

"Caleb's out talking with them. What are we going to do?" I ask, turning back to Rhett.

He sits for a moment, eyes distant in thought. I can feel panic at the edges of my mind, buzzing like a swarm of angry hornets. Finally, with some effort, Rhett pushes himself up into a sitting position and reaches behind him for something.

"What–"

"When I go out there, I can't make it look like I was expecting a fight at the wedding. Help me unlace this, Luc, please," Rhett says quickly and quietly.

I stare open-mouthed as Lucas jumps into action, unlacing the black, carbon-fiber reinforced corset vest Rhett had worn to the wedding. It was supposed to be knife-proof, to protect his vital organs. Not that it helped when Darren went for the leg.

"You can't be–Rhett, if you go out there–"

Rhett and Lucas slide the vest off, and Rhett turns to me, placing a hand on my cheek. The tender touch breaks the crumbling dam that's been holding back my tears, and they spill hot down my cheeks. Rhett looks at me, eyes scanning each part of my face as if he were trying to memorize it. My heart throbs in my chest, and I clutch his wrist.

"You can't leave me," I whimper, lower lip trembling as I teeter on the edge of sobs.

"I'll do anything to protect you, my love. And if that means going to jail so you and Luc can get home, then so be it," Rhett says solemnly.

"Rhett, let's think this through. There has to be another way," Lucas nearly begs.

Rhett reaches out his other hand, pulling both of us to his chest in a tight embrace. I wrap my arms around his chest, taking deep, gulping inhales of his whiskey and leather and dark chocolate scent. The scent that has become my shelter from the storm, my safety, my home.

"I need you both to be safe. Please," Rhett whispers, just loud enough for us both to hear.

"You can't give in to this bullshit. I won't let you," Lucas growls, the heat diminished by the shaking of his shoulders.

"You can and you will," Rhett replies, as stern as ever.

"We'll go back to the apartment, then. We're not leaving you in this city alone," Lucas counters, pulling away.

I draw back and look between them as they face off. Rhett's brow is pulled low, his eyes not angry, but almost proud. Lucas's face is wet with tears, drops running pink where they meet the blood on his cheeks. Rhett's thumb tenderly wipes one away before pulling our beta lover in for a searing kiss. My heart aches in my chest, but there's a small flip of wonder in my stomach at the sight of them, the love I can feel rolling off of them in waves. The kiss is short, and when Rhett breaks it, he rests his forehead against Lucas's.

"Lex is going to need you, Luc. Please, I need to know you're safe. I couldn't bear it if something happened to you on my account. Please," Rhett begs.

Looking away, heat rises in my cheeks. This feels more intimate than anything I've ever witnessed between them, and it almost feels like I'm invading. Lucas growls low, then releases a sigh. But before I can look back, footsteps on the entry stairs draw my attention. Caleb climbs back through the door, making quick strides in our direction.

"I managed to talk them out of storming the plane, but they aren't giving us more time. I told them you need an ambulance, but they say it'll be faster just to take you to a hospital in the squad car," he says, words tumbling out in a rush.

I whip back around to look at Rhett, all heat draining from my body. Rhett merely nods and begins getting to his feet. I can't move, all control of my limbs fleeing at the knowledge that, once Rhett walks out of this plane, he'll be lost to me for who knows how long. My whole body shakes, and the sobs I've been holding back bubble to the surface. With a groan of pain, Lucas and Caleb haul Rhett upright, and start walking him toward the door.

"No! No, you can't–Rhett, please–I need you," I yell, scrambling on hands and knees until I've caught hold of Rhett's good leg.

A gentle hand under my arm pulls me off the floor, but I only collapse forward into Rhett's chest. I wrap my arms around him, hardly able to breathe around the panic and loss in my chest. His hands stroke my hair, tilting my chin up to look at him.

"I love you so much, Lydia. So much," Rhett whispers, voice breaking for the first time.

"Don't talk like that. I'm going–I'll go with you, explain everything. They can't–"

"No," Rhett growls, and the heat in his voice stops me short. His face tightens, but then softens into something kinder.

"No, my love. You need to get home to Mateo and Lex, and we'll figure out a plan once you're safe. I need you to do this for me," Rhett says, ever so gently.

I want to disagree, to fight more, but the pain clouding his features only seems to be growing. Every second he's here is another second spent away from a doctor who could properly treat his injury.

"Stay safe. I'll be home before you know it," Rhett says, and the smile he tries to give me is sad and bittersweet.

I lift myself onto the tips of my toes and throw my arms around his neck, pulling his mouth down to meet mine. Rhett's hands tighten on the sides of my head, and his lips move with mine. He tastes like whiskey and salt and smoke, but I don't care. It feels like no time at all when Caleb clears his throat, and we have to break apart.

"I love you, Rhett Cooper," I whisper, touching his face one last time.

"I love you, too, Lydia. Now and always."

And as Rhett is pulled from my arms and disappears out of the door, I collapse back to my knees, not even feeling the sting of the impact. My heart beats hard against my ribs, as if trying to break free and follow him into the back of the squad car and away from me.

Thank you for reading

ENJOYED THE STORY?

Please consider writing a review

Amazon

Goodreads

Bookbub

Want to review on social media? Tag Thora so she can see it!

Instagram: @thora_woods_author

Twitter: @_thora_woods

TikTok: @thora_wood_sauthor

The story continues...

Experience the conclusion of Pack Saint Clair's incredible journey in...

Laurels and Liquor: Pack Saint Clair Book 3

Coming Fall 2022

Acknowledgments

We did it! It may have felt like no time at all, or a thousand years, but we made it here. And if you're reading this, then I just want to take a moment to say thank you. Each and every one of my you reading this have changed my life in ways you can't even imagine. You've made my dreams come true, and then some. But I wouldn't have gotten here without the help of a few people in particular.

First, I need to give a special thank you to my beta reader, website designer, cover artist, and friend Sandra. You've been an invaluable part of this process since the beginning. Your feedback has pushed me to try things I'd never consider otherwise, and you always know how to make me laugh.

I also need to take a few moments to thank my best friend, book wife, partner in crime, and platonic soulmate, Merri Bright. We've been on this road together from the start, and I don't know if I could have ever done as much without your support. Your work ethic is unparalleled and you make my world so much brighter (pun absolutely intended).

I couldn't put together a list of 'thank you's without including my PA, Halla Lester. We haven't been together very long, but you have done so much that it would be impractical to list all of the ways you've helped me in the last few months. To put it simply, I literally wouldn't be able to do this without you.

My editor Mackenzie from Nice Girl, Naughty Edits deserves her own special moment in the sun. We've worked

ACKNOWLEDGMENTS   415

together for months, and I've never enjoyed the editing process more. I can't wait to do it all again.

And last, I need to thank my husband. He still doesn't quite understand everything in the omegaverse, but that hasn't stopped him from telling anyone who'll listen that he's the trophy husband to a best selling smut author. So to my biggest cheerleader, my shoulder to cry on, my violence consultant, and the man who keeps me humble, thank you for everything.

About Author

Thora Woods is a lifelong writer, reader, and creator. Born in New Orleans, LA, she began her writing journey in her pre-teens, growing her skills at SUNY Fredonia in their Creative Writing program. Thora lives in Western New York with her two dogs, Fritter and Pepper, two cats, Impala and Hoagie, and her husband.